The Great Martian War

The Gathering Storm

By Scott Washburn

The Great Martian War: The Gathering Storm
By Scott Washburn
Cover by Michael Nigro
Zmok Books an imprint of
Pike & Powder Publishing Group, LLC, 1525 Hulse Road, Unit 1, Point Pleasant, NJ 08742

This edition published in 2020 Copyright ©Winged Hussar Publishing, LLC

ISBN 978-1-94543-059-6 Paperback
ISBN 978-1-950423-33-0 Ebook
Library of Congress No. 2020935721
Bibliographical references and index
1.Science Fiction 2. Alternative History 3. Action & Adventure

Winged Hussar Publishing, LLC & Pike & Powder Publishing Group, LLC
All rights reserved

For more information on Winged Hussar Publishing, LLC, visit us at:
https://www.WingedHussarPublishing.com
Twitter: WingHusPubLLC
Facebook: Winged Hussar Publishing LLC

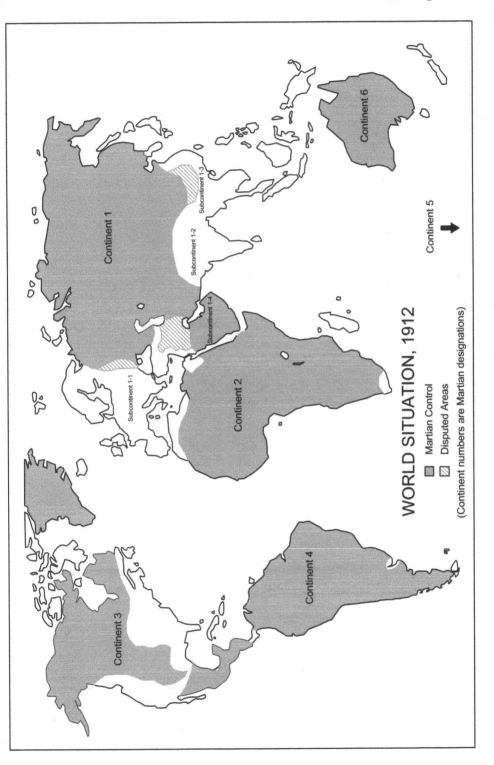

WORLD SITUATION, 1912

- ▨ Martian Control
- ▨ Disputed Areas

(Continent numbers are Martian designations)

Prologue

Excerpt from "The First Interplanetary War, Volume 1", by Winston Spencer Churchill, 1929. Reprinted with permission.

Although few outside of Great Britain today remember, the First Interplanetary War can properly be thought to have begun in the spring of the year 1900. Although most people at that time considered 1900 to be the first year of the new century, it was, in fact, the last year of the old. And along with it, were swept out all of our preconceived and haughty notions of Man's place in this universe. In that fateful season, the first cylinders from the Red Planet fell upon England's peaceful countryside as unexpectedly as a lightning bolt out of a clear blue sky.

In fairness, it should be stated that there were a handful of scientists around the globe who were not taken completely by surprise by the arrival of the Martians. Astronomers had observed strange and unprecedented gas eruptions upon the surface of Mars in the months preceding the arrival of the cylinders. While they had no way of knowing what those events heralded, these men instantly realized the truth when news of the cylinders reached them.

The invaders, who we now know were a mere scouting expedition, first landed near the town of Woking about 20 miles southwest of London. Over the course of the next few days, nine more of their cylinders fell in the southern parts of England. The peace-loving English people, having no inkling of the hostile and indeed murderous intent of the invaders, were slow to respond, thus giving the Martians time to debark and assemble their formidable war machines. Further time was squandered in well-intended, but ultimately fatal attempts to communicate with the Martians.

By the time the authorities became fully aware of the danger, the Martians were ready for battle. Sadly, with the bulk of the regular British Army dealing with the Boers in South Africa, where I, myself, was also involved, the only forces available to confront the Martians were the Territorial troops. These men, although of undoubted bravery, were poorly equipped and not at all trained to deal with the crisis now at hand.

The initial battles went badly, and the defenders of London suffered very heavy losses and were scattered by the Martian heat rays and their vile black dust weapons. It should be noted, however, that these brave men did destroy one of the enemy machines with conventional artillery. This accomplishment is often overlooked, but it was of great importance for it proved that the enemy was not invulnerable. Indeed, several more of their machines were later destroyed both by the Army and the Royal Navy before the Martians succumbed to the microbes which proved deadly to them.

In the immediate aftermath, many people felt that the demise of the Martians was an act of divine intervention and that our salvation or destruction was strictly in the hands of God. Even at the time I felt this overly simplistic and indeed an insult to the courage, skill, and tenacity of the British people. Since it had been proved that we could destroy the Martians, it was simply a matter of time before sufficient force was brought to bear to allow us to do so. Consultations with many military men of great experience has confirmed that they are of the same opinion. It was only the completely unforeseeable nature of the attack which made it so deadly.

There is no denying, of course, how deadly the attack was. Even with the short duration it lasted, dozens of towns and villages and large sections of London were laid waste. Over one hundred thousands of our citizens lost their lives either as a direct result of the Martian attack, or as a secondary effect of the panicked flight before them. Even the Royal Family was forced to evacuate, and many are of the opinion that it was this extreme stress which brought about the passing of Queen Victoria just a few months later.

As tragic as was the loss of life and the damage to property, which was later tallied at over one hundred million pounds sterling, perhaps the greatest blow was to the psyche of the English people. For it had been nearly a hundred years since the last serious threat of invasion, and close to a thousand since any invader had in fact set foot upon the soil of our island nation. For centuries we had lived in safety and security behind the impenetrable shield of the Royal Navy.

But despite the Navy's one hundred battleships and hundreds of cruisers and lesser vessels, the invaders had landed unopposed. Men, women, and children had been roused from their beds and forced to flee for their lives with no warning, no notice. Their world, which had seemed secure and predictable, was suddenly proved to be neither. The dead could be buried, the rubble cleared away, and the buildings rebuilt, but nothing could ever give back that same sense of security.

For although we had been spared once, be it by an act of God, a force of natural science, or the belated might of the Army and Navy, there was nothing to prevent it from happening again. Mars was still there in its unalterable orbit, which every twenty-six months would bring it in close proximity to Earth. And even though we knew where the enemy lay, we could not blockade his harbours or strangle his trade or intercept his invasion armadas as we had done to keep us safe in centuries past. They had come once and could come again if they so close.

With eyes cast fearfully skyward, the people demanded that measures be taken. The members of Parliament, the Ministers in their councils, and indeed, our new sovereign, Edward VII, could do naught but agree. The army in South Africa was withdrawn, the Boers given the independence they demanded (little good that it did them a few years hence), and our strength brought home to defend the island against the possibility of another invasion.

I came with them, arriving in Southampton in June of 1900. Although the bodies had been buried by that time, the work of reconstruction had barely begun. By a happy chance, my ship arrived the same day as the famous aid ship from America, organized and accompanied by Theodore Roosevelt. Roosevelt was then the governor of the state of New York and that very month would be nominated for the vice presidency in the election to be held that November. But his great sense of compassion - and it must be said, outrage - had caused him to organize an outpouring of aid from the citizens of his state for their cousins across the sea. Through certain family connections, I was invited to dine with Roosevelt, and I found the man to be a veritable dynamo of energy. I have no notion of what he thought of me, and as a very young man with only a few notable accomplishments to my name, he can be forgiven for paying small note of me. Little did either of us realize at the time how our destinies would become entwined in the future.

The next day I walked through the devastated streets of London with Roosevelt and we were as thoroughly thunderstruck as every other returning soldier, and vowed, as many of them did, to see that this could never happen again. Entire neighborhoods had been reduced to ashes, just a few blackened piles of bricks marking where homes had once stood. I was especially stricken to see that even Nelson's Column had not been spared; the noble statue had been melted into an unrecognizable lump and the column itself toppled.

Roosevelt, and indeed, I, too, were dumfounded when we discovered that we were not to be permitted to examine the Martian war machines close up. The spots where the machines had halted when their operators were struck down had been cordoned off and no one, not even an important dignitary like Roosevelt, was allowed through. We could see the tripod machines from several hundred yards away, but no closer. The Ministry of War had ordered this. The reason given was that there were fears of the deadly Martian black dust weapon being present and as this was not an unreasonable concern, Roosevelt made no protest, though his disappointment was profound.

Tragically, this turned out not to be some temporary expedient for safety reasons, but a long-term policy to deny access to the Martians' wondrous machines to everyone except ourselves. While there was some small justification in the reasoning that since the British paid the price in acquiring the equipment, the British should reap the benefits, the inevitable long-term effects were so severe and so detrimental to our relations with the rest of the world that this foolish policy should never have been adopted.

The European Powers, especially our closest neighbor, France, became convinced that we intended to use the Martian science against them in a bid for world domination. I'm embarrassed to have to admit that there was more than a little justification to their fears. High-ranking members in the government and the military did indeed have visions of an invincible military imposing a Pax Britannica on the world. And even if this did not prove possible, it was deemed that the technical knowledge needed to be kept out of potentially hostile hands at all costs. Prime Minister Lord Robert Cecil, was convinced of the necessity of this policy by his cabinet, even though it eventually led to the downfall of the Conservative Party.

I was elected to Parliament from Oldham that fall and joined the Conservatives as was expected of me, being my father's son. The primary issue facing Parliament, indeed the whole nation, was what preparations needed to be taken to meet another invasion. For most of us were unwilling to stake the fate of our nation and our people on the totally unsubstantiated notion that the Martians, having been defeated once, would not try again. There is no doubt that many in England and around the world believed that very thing, but this was wishful thinking at its very worst.

The challenge was to decide what sort of preparations were needed. Throughout England's history a serious external threat had almost always involved some rival navy and the countermeasures were obvious: strengthen the Fleet. But this time, the threat did not have to fight its way past the Royal Navy. Our battleships and cruisers could not intercept the enemy troop transports before they reached shore. If the invaders strayed too close to the coastline they might be brought under fire by the guns of the Fleet, but if they stayed inland, only the Army could engage them.

And so the Army had to be strengthened. New regiments had to be raised, new artillery batteries created and equipped, new fortified posts constructed, new warning systems devised and of utmost importance, new and better weapons invented. And it was not just the home islands which were at risk. Even though that was where the enemy had first struck, if they came again, they could land anywhere. India, Canada, South Africa, Egypt, Australia, all were at risk and all had to be defended. The cost of this was, of course, enormous. There was no lack of eager recruits to fill the ranks of these new formation, but the facilities and equipment all needed to be constructed and paid for.

The government's plan to raise the money involved significant duties on all foreign imports. This was an issue which had been a much-debated topic even before the first invasion. Many in industry and business favored such a move since it would help them against growing competition from Germany and the United States. Others in the government felt that since it would also protect the Commonwealth's economy, it would help to bind the Empire into a more solid whole.

I immediately saw the folly of the idea. Combined with the strict secrecy over the Martian technology, this action could only serve to further alienate the Empire from the other great powers, and so it proved. By 1903 the structure of the European alliances had been profoundly altered. Each nation, now fearing and resenting Britain more than their traditional foes, changed their plans and policies to meet the new situation. The Triple Alliance of Germany, Austria-Hungary, and Italy softened its stance toward Russia and her ally, France. Russia reciprocated by making certain compromises over its policies in the Balkans, and France turned away from its obsession with avenging the insults of 1870 and recovering the lost provinces of Alsace and Lorraine - something which would have been unthinkable only a few years earlier.

Great Britain thus found itself with few friends in the world. Even the United States, though now led by Roosevelt, regarded us coldly. Of all the powers, only Japan looked upon us kindly, and this was primarily due to our sympathy toward them in the war that broke out between them and Russia in 1904.

Still the Conservative government, now led by Arthur Balfour, would not relent in its policies. I spoke out against them strongly, making many enemies, and eventually decided I could no longer support them. I crossed the aisle to join the Liberal Party in 1904. While I cannot take much credit for it, the Balfour government fell the next year and Sir Henry Campbell-Bannerman became prime minister.

The new government attempted to rectify the mistakes of the old, but with only limited success. The tariffs were done away with and new taxes levied to make up the shortfall. But the policy of secrecy involving the Martian technology could not so easily be reversed. The hostility of the other Great Powers was now well established, and it was feared that if the secrets of the Martians - the few we had unraveled so far - might now be used against us. A few concessions were made, but in general the policy of the previous government was continued - out of necessity now rather than stupidity.

I found myself appointed as Undersecretary of State for the Colonies in that same year. Lord Elgin was secretary, a man of considerable experience, having served as Viceroy of India and who also had headed a commission investigating the performance of the army both in South Africa and during the Martian invasion at home. Our primary task at this point was to evaluate the defense needs for the colonies, working in conjunction with the War Office. It was a task which I relished, and I threw myself into it with great enthusiasm.

The latter half of 1905 and well into 1906 saw me travelling all around the world to the far reaches of the Empire. It was my task to meet with the colonial governments to determine what they would need to defend themselves from a second Martian invasion. A group of men from the Army and the War Office accompanied me. What we saw was daunting indeed.

Maps cannot convey the vastness of the British Empire at that time. The maps that every schoolboy sees in his books and hanging on classroom walls, maps with large areas of red upon them, denoting the boundaries of our vast realm, might instill pride, but they cannot truly teach the reality of it. I had done a fair bit of travelling in my youth, India, the Sudan, South Africa, but even I was taken aback by how much there was—how much that might need to be defended.

It quickly became apparent that there *was* no hope in trying to defend every square mile. Such a policy was being followed at home, but with the huge, but nearly unpeopled regions of central Australia, northern Canada, southern Egypt and Africa such a thing was simply impossible. The strategy which had been devised for the defense of the home islands was to have forces standing in readiness to swoop down on the Martian landing sites and wipe them out before they could assemble their war machines. It was a sound plan, which if it had been available in 1900 might have saved us so much woe but could only work if the areas involved were small and with a good transportation network in place. Similar strategies were being evolved by the other Great Powers in Europe, Japan, and in America. But there was no hope to do so in our colonies, except for India.

The most we could hope to do was to fortify the cities and larger towns and pray that they could resist the initial assaults until help could arrive from England. It was assumed that once the attacks at home were defeated, powerful forces could then be dispatched to aid the colonies.

I met with many men in many places during my journeys. Some were doubters, men who believed that the Martians would never return or, if they did, that they would not land in their part of the world. Others acknowledged the threat but did not want to expend the effort or the money needed to see to their defenses. Most, however, were sensible men and were willing to do what they could.

A few were even men of vision who made contributions not just to their local defense, but to the defense of the whole world. One such was an Australian civil engineer with the wonderful name of Lancelot de Mole. Perhaps inspired by the knightly armour of his namesake, he presented me with a detailed set of plans for a remarkable device when I met him at a conference in Sydney in December 1905. Mr. de Mole had observed that during the first invasion, conventional field artillery had proved capable of destroying the enemy tripod machines, but was in turn, extremely vulnerable to the Martian heat rays and poisonous black dust weapon. His invention took a field gun, encased it in metal armour, and mounted it all on a steam tractor to give it mobility. I immediately saw the genius of his conception and passed it along to the War Office with my strongest possible endorsement.

Of all my actions during that period, this one perhaps paid the highest rewards. This invention - unfairly, but irrevocably, dubbed a 'tank' by some unknown wag - became the mainstay of nearly every modern army in the coming conflict. It, or variations on it - armored, self-propelled artillery - proved to be our most effective weapon against the invaders. Sadly, there were far too few of them ready for action when the Martians returned.

And, of course, this was the great unknown: when were the invaders going to return? How long did we have to prepare? Five years? Ten? Twenty? If only we had been given twenty years, how much suffering might have been averted! Or perhaps not. Twenty years might have been too long a time to maintain the sense of urgency among the people. Ah, but what I would have paid to be given even ten!

As it happened, we were given eight years and a few months. In November of 1907 the same type of foreboding gas eruptions were sighted on Mars which had preceded the first invasion. The Red Planet had been kept under constant observation with some of our most sophisticated telescopes and the eruptions were spotted immediately. But unlike the first invasion where a mere ten cylinders were launched, this time the eruptions went on and on until nearly two hundred were sighted or presumed. The word went out: the Martians were coming again - and in much greater force.

Chapter One

May 1911, Sydney, New South Wales, Australia

"Harry, come on! We've got to go! We've got to go *right now!*"

Lieutenant Harry Calloway gave one more futile tug on the body, lying half-buried in the rubble, and conceded that the man was dead. The face was smeared with blood and soot and in the gray light before dawn he couldn't tell who it was. One of his men, almost certainly, someone from his platoon. His responsibility, but there was nothing more he could do for him.

A loud, shrill whistle filled the air and he instinctively crouched low as an artillery shell passed overhead and exploded only a hundred yards away. It had been a large shell - navy for sure. The covering barrage was getting close; yes, definitely time to go. They had to get back to the ships and get out of here.

He peered around the pile of rubble and looked west, where the Martians would be coming from and didn't see anything but clouds of smoke, dark and ominous, not yet touched by the coming dawn. Looking back east, he saw Burford Sampson, the lieutenant commanding 11 Platoon, still waving to him from behind a building at the end of the block. They were in Camperdown, a suburb on Sydney's outskirts. It had once been a fashionable place to live, but an earlier Martian attack had broken through almost to here before being thrown back and it wasn't nearly so fashionable anymore. Crouching low, Harry ran along the sidewalk, past rows of shops, their shattered window glass making the footing treacherous, until he reached Sampson. The man looked angry.

"Dammit, boy! What the bloody 'ell you think yer doin'?"

"Don't call me boy," he said automatically. Gasping for breath, he waved his arm back toward where he'd been. "One of my men, there. He's dead, but I had to check. Not leavin' anyone behind."

Sampson's expression softened until he merely looked annoyed. "Right, right, no one gets left behind—including you! Now come on, the rest of the company is already three blocks away and... *oh, shit!*"

Only one thing could have pull that from Sampson's mouth. Harry twisted around and looked down the street. Emerging from the smoke was a large gray shape. Four stories tall, a bulbous head the size of an elephant with a glowing red eye in the center of it was perched atop a cylinder which sprouted arms and tentacles. The whole mass sat atop three long, thin legs which moved with a gait unlike that of any earthly creature.

It was a Martian tripod, an alien war machine which was the primary weapon the invaders from the Red Planet had used to conquer huge swaths of the Earth. And which they were using now to conquer the last bit of Australia still in human hands. Harry clenched his fists at that thought. Sydney was going to fall; his home was going to fall.

"Come on," hissed Sampson, as if the Martians might overhear. He grabbed Harry by the arm and shoved him toward an alley which would take them east, toward the harbor. A loud shriek, like a buzz saw cutting wood, sounded behind him, but he didn't look back. He was all too familiar with the sound. The Martians were firing their heat rays, beams of pure energy which could turn a man to ashes in an eye-blink. They were burning all the buildings, every man-made object, as they advanced. Harry didn't know if that was to be sure they'd driven out any humans who might be hiding in the buildings, out of some alien hate, or just to create smoke to conceal them from artillery spotters. Perhaps some of each.

Harry and Sampson sprinted down the alley to the next street, passed across it and continued on until they caught up with some of their men. Twenty or thirty men of C Company, 15th New Castle Battalion, were waiting there, part of the rear guard. But there were also... who were those...?

"Oh bloody hell!" swore Sampson. "Where in Bleedin' Christ did you find those?!"

Civilians. A dozen civilians; women, kids, a couple of old men. All of the civilians were supposed to have been evacuated by now. That's what the troops had been holding the line for during the last two weeks. That was what a quarter of the battalion had died for yesterday. They should have all been gone by midnight the night before.

Sampson's question had been directed at a sergeant, Dawkins, he thought it was, from 9 Platoon, the whole company was all jumbled together now. Harry didn't see anyone from his own 12 Platoon, but they were around here somewhere, he was sure. He hoped.

Dawkins shrugged. "Came outta that shop as we was fallin' back, sir. Says they was lookin' for something to eat."

"We 'aven't had any food for two days!" said one of the women angrily.

"Well, if you don't get the hell to the ships, you won't ever need food again, you damn fools!" snarled Sampson.

"Are... are those devils coming?" asked one of the old men.

"Coming? They're bloody well here! Not two blocks away. Now let's move!"

One of the other women gasped, several of the children screamed in terror. As if in answer, one of the heat rays shrieked, from much too nearby. The tops of a block of buildings a hundred yards off burst into flames.

"Go! Go! Move!"

They pushed and shoved the civilians into motion. Harry glanced at the street sign, *Grose Lane*, he knew where he was now. Several of the soldiers scooped up the kids and carried them. They hurried down another street. Port Jackson, as Sydney's harbor was called, was still nearly two miles away, but they had to get there. The last of the transport ships were waiting to take off the rear guard, but they couldn't wait there forever. As they moved, another salvo of artillery roared overhear to explode behind them. Hopefully among the Martians. Even if none of the bastards was hit, it might slow them down; they were afraid of the navy's big guns. An eighteen-pound field gun might hurt a tripod with a lucky hit, and the twenty-five pounders mounted on the steam tanks had an even better chance, but a six or seven-point-five-inch shell from a cruiser would tear them apart. The Martians had learned to avoid the navy.

But they couldn't avoid them today, not if they wanted Sydney—and they wanted Sydney. Apparently, they wanted the whole world.

They had first come to take it in 1900. Harry had only been a kid then, but he remembered all the fuss, all the stories in the newspapers, his father and mother so upset. But the invasion had been far away in England and the Martians had all died in a very short time. Most people in Australia quickly forgot about it. There had been some preparations, Harry's father, a prominent lawyer in Sydney, had helped raise a volunteer battalion, accepting a captain's commission in the process, but most people felt the danger had passed. Then, in September of 1908, the cylinders had rained down again, all over the world—including Australia.

The noise of the heat rays was fainter now. Harry helped one of the old men to move faster, but they were both gasping for breath when they reached a large open space that surrounded the university, his alma mater—almost. It had once been a green park but had become one of many tent cities during the worst of the refugee crisis and was now just a dreary patch of bare dirt, every tree cut down for firewood. There were many more troops gathered there and several of the precious steam tanks, but to his dismay, there were also more civilians, a hundred of them at least. He stopped, letting the old man slump to his knees, and saw Captain Berwick, the commander of C Company, jogging toward them.

"Well there you are!" he cried. "I was afraid I'd lost the lot of you."

"What's happening, sir?" asked Sampson. "Who are all they?" He gestured to the civilians.

Berwick shook his head. "Damn bunch of fools, is who. Idiots who refused to go when we announced the final evacuation."

"Maybe… Maybe they didn't get the word," said Harry.

"Not bloody likely!" snapped Sampson. "We've been shouting it from the roof tops for the last week. Probably a bunch of damn looters if you ask me. Waitin' 'til near everyone's gone and then go looking for valuables left behind."

Berwick frowned. "I'm afraid you're probably right, Burford, quite a few have turned up with bags full of stuff that I rather doubt belongs to them."

"And now that we've come to the last throw, they expect us to save their skins."

"Yes, and we have no choice but to do it. The ones you see here are only a fraction of what are showing up, and a lot of them are women and kids. The colonel has ordered us to form a line and hold here long enough to get them all out."

Sampson growled out an amazing obscenity, but immediately started rounding up his platoon. Harry left the old man and did the same. He was heartened by how many he found. B Company had been all but wiped out yesterday, but C Company was still nearly intact. Harry sighed in relief; C Company was really the only family he had left. His father had been its first captain but died of a heart seizure the year before the Martians returned, and the men had elected Harry to be a lieutenant, even though he had been only nineteen years old. He'd still been in school and had only attended the drills when he could, but it had still been quite an honor, even though it felt more like a game than something real. His mother and two sisters had been proud of him.

Then the astronomers had seen the gas eruptions on Mars again, and it wasn't a game anymore. The battalion had been mobilized and Harry, like many of the students, had gotten a leave of absence from school, confident he would soon be back there again once the alarm was over. That was two and a half years ago and he had not been back to his school in all that time—until now, and he wouldn't be staying long.

Instead of studying law, he had studied tactics manuals, or more frequently, engineering manuals. There had been a frantic race to fortify Sydney before the Martians arrived. All the stories about what had happened to London were on everyone's mind. They needed to be ready to defend the city against an attack. Fortunately, Sydney was built on a peninsula between Botany Bay on the south and a complex of smaller bays linked to the ocean on the north. The main defense line, between Botany Bay and Iron Cove, was only a little more than five miles long. A few defenses were built along the other shore lines, but those approaches were mostly left to the navy to defend.

The new volunteer battalions did most of the digging. Other troops, the better trained and equipped Territorials and a few regulars, made ready to swoop down on the enemy landing sites in hopes of wiping them out before they could assemble their fearsome war machines.

But the Martians refused to cooperate.

Instead of landing close to the large cities – and the waiting troops – they had landed far away, in Australia's huge outback. The vast, nearly unpeopled, center of the country had provided the Martians with landing sites beyond quick reach of the defending forces. They came down in four groups and had their war machines unloaded and assembled before anyone could come to stop them. By the time the landing sites had been located and troops gathered, the enemy was too strong for any mobile force to overcome. Cavalry and infantry alone had no chance against the Martian machines. Artillery and tanks were needed, and they were in short supply. Until recently, heavy equipment had to come all the way from England, a two-month sea voyage, and the home country had been very stingy with such things, which they felt were needed for their own defense. The new Sydney arsenal was the only one in Australia which could produce the steel and the guns and the components for tanks. It worked around the clock for months to produce what was needed, but there simply hadn't been enough time.

"Come on you buggers, get ready!" shouted Sergeant Milroy, Harry's platoon sergeant. The battalion was taking up positions beyond the northwestern edge of the park. C Company was responsible for holding a city block and Harry's platoon occupied several of the buildings on the north side, along Parramatta Road. This deep in the city, the damage to the buildings had been minimal, but his soldiers quickly began smashing out the windows to clear their fields of fire.

Not that their Short Magazine Lee-Enfield rifles could do much of anything against a Martian tripod. Harry had heard it said that a damaged tripod, one which had had some of its armor stripped away by something heavier, could be brought down by massed rifle fire. But he'd never seen it happen, nor met anyone who had.

They set up their sole remaining Maxim gun on one of the upper floors. He had seen a machine gun hurt a tripod once. Not destroy it but do enough damage to drive it off. But in truth, the best hope of the infantry to hurt the tripods was with their bombs. They had been equipped with explosive bombs, first made from dynamite and later using gelignite. They were very easy to use; first ignite the fuse with a simple friction primer, and then attach the bomb to the tripod.

It was that second part that was so tricky.

It took a very brave or very lucky man to manage, but there were a lot of very brave men defending Sydney. A few lucky ones, too. The brave ones sometimes destroyed a tripod. The lucky ones destroyed them and lived to talk about it.

Harry checked on his men and made sure they were in the best positions possible. That meant a way to shoot at the Martians or throw bombs, but also a quick way to get out a back door or window, before the aliens turned the place into an inferno with their heat rays. Everything seemed to be in order. His men knew what they were doing. Once they had been green volunteers, now they were veterans.

After their landing, the Martians had lain quiescent for months, bothering no one except kangaroos and aborigines and the occasional rancher or prospector. Hope had grown among the Australians that they would be given the time they needed to prepare. Men had flocked to the new units being raised. They had been issued rifles, but they looked to the new arsenal to give them the weapons they had really need to fight.

They had also looked to England.

The home islands had not been invaded like last time. Not a single cylinder had fallen in England's green valleys. Surely the new armies which had been massed there, surely at least some of them would be sent to Australia. Some help *had* come, a few brigades of infantry, a few battalions of tanks and artillery, but not enough, not nearly enough. The Empire had other responsibilities, they were told. Canada and South Africa, Egypt with the vital canal at Suez, and above all India had to be defended. The men and guns and tanks had flowed out of England, shepherded by the Royal Navy, but too few of the ships had come to Australia. Even months after the landing, Harry's men still had only rifles, but they spent more time with shovels, digging trenches and building bunkers to protect Sydney.

They had dug some very impressive trenches and right now Harry wished that they were still defending them rather than trying to defend this makeshift position. The Martians had given them enough time to make the trenches truly formidable. Deep and secure with concealed firing positions, reinforced bunkers for the machine guns and revetments for artillery and steam tanks. And pit traps, lots and lots of pit traps. The Martians tripods walked about on long, spindly legs. The pointed feet would punch right through the covers of concealed pits and with luck immobilize the machine, leaving it an easy target for artillery—or brave infantry with their bombs. They'd dug thousands, tens of thousands of them all along Sydney's defense line. Harry looked out on the street and wished they had time to dig a few of them here.

Prowling through the house, clearly the home of whoever owned the shop down on the first floor, Harry discovered the way up on to the flat roof of the building. Some of his men were already up there, checking the fuses on their bombs. He could see some men from A Company on the roofs of the buildings across the street.

"Hey, sir," called one of them, Private Haskins, "From up here we can drop these right down on the bastards! Could never do that in the trenches!"

Harry smiled and nodded, but privately wondered if the Martians would be so obliging as to walk right past and let them do it. More likely they'd set the buildings afire before they got that close. "Good idea," he said aloud. "But be ready to get out."

"Oh, we will sir, you can be sure o' that!" They laughed, but there was a strained tone to it. They all knew how slim their chances were.

He walked over to the parapet that ringed the edge of the roof and rested his hands on it and looked west. There was a nearly solid wall of smoke in that direction, changing color from gray to pink as the beams of the rising sun touched them. From time to time there would be a bright red glow through the clouds; Martian heat rays, but they were still a way off; the enemy wasn't advancing very fast. *They've got all the time in the world.*

The flash of exploding artillery lit up the clouds, too. Nearly all the heavy guns had already been evacuated, but the navy was still off shore, still firing. The wind was blowing from the southwest so most of the smoke was drifting more to the north rather than right toward him, but the smell of burning was strong in the air. Sydney was burning. His home was burning. The house he grew up in was about a mile to the northwest, in Balmain, behind those clouds. Was it still there?

Somehow he never thought it would really come to this. They'd read about the fighting in Africa and India, Asia and the Americas, but as the months passed, hope began to grow that somehow Australia might be spared. The hope died in June of '09 when the Martians had come boiling out of the outback. A hundred or more of their tripod machines had struck Darwin on the north coast. The city's defenses had been overrun in hours and most of the people and the defenders had been slaughtered. From there, the Martians had split into two groups sweeping down the coasts in both directions, smashing each city in turn. Cairns, Broome, Townsville, Brisbane, one after the other they'd fallen, the defender's scatters or killed, the cities burned to ashes, the people... there were terrible stories about what was happening to the people who couldn't get away. Survivors had fled, by boat, by train, on horseback, or on foot, desperately trying to stay ahead of the invaders.

In September the situation was deemed hopeless and the order had come from the government: evacuate. The people would gather in Sydney, Melbourne and Perth. Ships would carry them to New Zealand, Tasmania, and India. But Australia had four million people, evacuating all would be a colossal task. Ships were summoned or hired or hijacked from all over the Pacific, but the only way an evacuation could succeed was if the troops could hold off the Martians long enough. The defenders of Sydney had been told that they had to hold as long as necessary—no matter what.

All through the summer and fall a seemingly endless stream of people had flowed into the city; people fleeing from the Martians. Thousands, tens of thousands, ultimately hundreds of thousands of people. The ships could not begin to carry them away as quickly as they arrived and huge camps had sprung up inside the defense lines. Every building and home in the city took people in. At one point, Harry's mother and sisters had twenty-five people sharing the house. It had been a bad time. Sanitation was inadequate and food was short, despite the herds of cattle also driven into the city. A lot of people got sick and far too many of them died. Some people couldn't stand it and fled further south along the coast, perhaps in hope they could find a ship at some smaller harbor.

But the Martians took their time and only advanced slowly along the coasts, harried every mile by the Royal Navy. It was November before they neared Sydney. The stream of refugees swelled to a flood—and then tailed off to nothing.

"Harry, you all right, boy?"

He looked around and saw that Sampson was on another roof just across an alley. He had an expression of concern on his face. Burford was an older man; he was from Tasmania and had fought the Boers in South Africa before the first invasion. He was a rough-spoken and sometimes downright callous fellow, but he'd seemed to take a liking to Harry and looked out for him and helped him learn how to command an infantry platoon—even though he kept calling him 'boy'.

"I'm fine. Well, as fine as anyone can be, I guess. This is it, isn't it?"

"What? Our last stand? Don't you start thinking like that Mister Calloway! We're going to hold here a while and then we are going to stroll down to the harbor and get aboard a big fat transport and sail away."

Harry snorted. "As easy as that, is it? Well, why was I even worried?"

"Because you think too much. Stop it and do your job." He stiffened and pointed. "Looks like they are coming. Get ready."

Harry looked down the street and saw the dark shapes emerging from the smoke, about three blocks away. Heat rays stabbed out and buildings on either side of the street erupted in flames. He could see that there were other groups of the enemy advancing down parallel streets, all heading for the center of the city and the vital harbor. A shudder ran through him, but he forced his fear into a dark recess in his mind and took a deep breath. *You've fought them before. You've fought them before and won.*

They had fought them, and they had won—at least for a while. The Martians had first hit Sydney in late November 1909. They'd hit it—and been driven back. It had been a near run thing for sure, but Sydney's defenses held. Harry and his men weren't really in the thick of it, but they were on the edge of the fighting and fired some shots and lost some men. Burford Sampson had proved to be one of those lucky ones who killed a tripod with a bomb and lived to talk about it. There'd been some talk about a medal for him, no one was bothering much with medals these days.

The Martians had hit them twice on two consecutive nights, but then seemed to give up. They'd retreated back into the interior and weren't seen again for a long while. Meanwhile, the ships were evacuating the civilians. It was thirteen hundred miles to New Zealand, a ten-day round trip for a typical steamer. They left, packed with humanity and enough food and water to reach their destination, but not much more. There was no room for more than a person could carry, and mountains of abandoned belongings piled up near the docks. After the first repulse of the Martians some said the evacuations should be halted, but Harry, suspecting that things were going to get much worse, insisted that his mother and two sisters should not wait. He practically had to drag them to a ship, but in the end they had gone.

He was surely glad of that now.

Granted it was over a year since the first attack, but the enemy had put the time to better use than the defenders. More cylinders had come from Mars and the Martians already here had built factories in their remote fortresses to create more tripods. When they were ready, they attacked again. A few months ago, they had concentrated and hit Perth with overwhelming numbers and annihilated the defenders. Their tripod machines gave them a mobility unprecedented in warfare. Scouts and the few aircraft available had reported that the enemy host was crossing the outback heading east, heading for Sydney.

And here they were.

"Get ready, men!" he shouted. "Keep your heads down and let them get close." His men obeyed, crouching below the parapet. He wasn't sure how much protection the brick would provide, but it was better than nothing.

Harry popped up for a look and he saw two tripods nearing the end of the next block. They were burning each building as they came to it, their heat rays stabbing out relentlessly. Flames gushed out of windows and roared up through the roofs. *This isn't going to work, we'll be burned to a crisp before they get close enough for us to hurt them!* He looked around frantically. Should he order his men out now, while there was still a chance to get away?

17

A roar and high-pitched squeals from behind made him pop up again and look back toward the park. There in the street were a pair of the steam tanks, black smoke puffing out of their stacks, their caterpillar tracks making the squeal he'd heard. One was the standard brown-tan color, but the other was just rusty, bare metal; so fresh from the factory that it hadn't even been painted.

The tanks halted and the twenty-five pounder guns mounted in their prows roared out almost in unison, filling the street with smoke. Whipping his head around, Harry saw the leading tripod stagger as the shells burst against its armor. For a moment it looked like some punch-drunk boxer who had just taken a strong blow to the head. It shifted sideways and bumped into a building and stopped, some smoke was drifting out of what might be a hole in its body. Another tripod moved forward past it and fired its heat ray.

The beam speared out to touch one of the tanks. Harry could feel the heat of it even though it passed a dozen yards away and wasn't aimed at him. But the tanks were already in motion, backing up as quickly as they could. Their armor glowed red but held long enough for them to haul themselves back around the corner at the end of the block and reach safety. The ray switched off and the tripod came forward. The three-legged gait of the tripods looked awkward and ungainly, but the things could move with surprising speed when they wanted to. Now the Martian sprang forward in pursuit of the tanks which had dared to hurt its comrade.

"Yes!" cried Harry. "They suckered him in! Get ready!"

The tripod was coming down the street, intent on the retreating tanks, and not bothering to set the buildings on fire. The troops in those buildings clutched their weapons and readied their bombs.

Fifty yards, thirty yards, the enemy got closer and closer. Some rifle fire rattled out, but the Martian did not pause. It was almost here…

"Now! Give it to him!"

The Maxim gun opened fire and bombs started flying out from windows and rooftops. The tripod was coming abreast of Harry, the top of its metal head almost level with him, when the bombs started exploding. He was crouching below the parapet, but the concussion still blew his helmet off. One man, a few yards from him, was still standing and tumbled backwards to sprawl on the rooftop, clutching his face which was red with blood. He hoped his men on the lower floors had found cover.

A cloud of smoke boiled up out of the street and onto the roof, he couldn't see a thing and coughed as he tried to clear his lungs. Two more explosions shook the building. He felt around and found his helmet and put it back on his head. Men were shouting, but to his stunned ears they sounded faint and far away. He crawled back to the parapet and pulled himself up to peer over.

The freshening breeze pulled the smoke away and Harry shouted in joy at the sight which met his eyes. The tripod was collapsed in the street, a leg blown completely off. One of its arms was scrabbling at the pavement, trying to push itself up enough that it could bring the heat ray on its other arm to bear. But as he watched, a man dashed out of a building and looped a bomb around that arm with a rope, ignited the fuse, and ran for shelter. Harry ducked back an instant before the explosion, and when he looked again, the tripod's arm with the heat ray was gone and the whole machine lay still. He could hear cheers and whoops from all around.

The cheers were suddenly cut off by the noise of a heat ray. Harry had one instant to see that the second damaged tripod had recovered and was sweeping its ray across the tops of the buildings. He stood there, frozen as the beam swept his way, and then someone tackled him and dragged him down, behind the parapet.

The bricks shattered and popped like kernels of corn, showering him with hot fragments, but the ray swept by so quickly it couldn't complete the destruction of the parapet, nor turn Harry to ash. Still, it felt like he was about to burst into flames from the heat for a moment. Then it was passed, and cooler air touched his face. But he had no doubt the ray would be back; they needed to get out of there before it did. He disentangled himself from the man who had saved him, Private Halloran, he saw it was, and struggled to his feet. They probably only had seconds to get away...

A pair of loud concussions nearly knocked him down again. Cannons firing, from close by. The tanks! The pair which had suckered in the tripod were back, clanking around the corner again and firing at the damaged tripod down the street.

He looked toward the Martian and saw it staggered again, smoke drifting away from where it was hit. It tried to fire back at the tanks, but it was clearly hurt and only blasted a glowing trench in the street before the guns roared out again. The enemy machine stumbled backward and then fell to the ground, black smoke spewing out of a hole in its head.

Gasping for breath, Harry looked for more enemies. There were none to be seen on the street passing his building, although he could not see more than a few blocks to the west because of the smoke. He saw the top of one tripod the next block over, but it seemed to be retreating. There were a few more, much farther away, which could be glimpsed through the flames and smoke, but they were no immediate threat. He was suddenly very tired. Tired and thirsty.

Harry reached for his canteen and noticed that he had dozens of tiny holes in his tunic where the red-hot brick fragments had burned through. He took a gulp of tepid water and then looked to his men. Only one man on the rooftop was down, Corporal Kelly, who had been wounded by his own bomb. He had a bad cut on his forehead, but his mates were binding it up.

"Lieutenant? Lieutenant Calloway?" He turned and saw a man he didn't recognize, although he had the 15th New Castle patch on the shoulder of his tunic.

"Yes, what is it?"

"Orders from the Colonel, sir. You're to pull out immediately. Head for the harbor, sir!"

"Very well, thank..." but before he could even finish his reply, the man was gone. Harry blinked and turned back to his men. "All right, we're leaving. Gather your stuff and let's go. Spread the word."

They quickly went down the stairs, collecting the men on the lower floors as they went. The platoon assembled at the end of the block, at the edge of the park; the other platoons of C Company collected nearby. The whole battalion was assembling and there was Colonel Anderson giving direction. Harry saw Burford Sampson with his own men a few yards away. The man always seemed energized by combat and right now his eyes were blazing.

They had a moment while they were reorganizing and Harry went over to one of the tanks. The crewmen were hanging out of the hatches trying to cool off. Those poor blighters had to contend with the heat of their own boiler as well as enemy rays. "I wanted thank you fellows," he said, almost shouting due to his still stunned ears and the noise from the tank. "We would have been cooked but for you."

One of the tankers glanced at him, not looking happy, and growled, "Glad to do it. Hadn't you better be on your way... sir?"

"We'll be moving in a minute. You, too, surely...?"

"We've been ordered to stay until you blokes are all clear."

"Crikey," breathed Harry. "Well, God bless you — and good luck. I just hope..."

Suddenly there was loud whistling, and everyone froze. Artillery coming in but...

"It's a short!" shouted someone. "Down! Get down!"

Harry threw himself down on the hard pavement and then the world blew up around him. Not just one short round but a whole salvo, at least a half-dozen all exploding so close together to almost seem like one long blast. Smoke engulfed him and stones pelted him. A moment later there was another explosion; close by, but sounding different from the others.

He lay there tensing for more, but that was all for the moment. He slowly climbed to his feet, a pain in his left shoulder where something heavy had hit him. There were a lot of people shouting now and a few cries of pain. The smoke dispersed and Harry could see again.

Several of the buildings on the edge of the square—buildings until moments ago occupied by the 15th New Castle—had partially collapsed, there were a couple of large craters in the street, and the second tank—the unpainted one—was burning fiercely. The man he'd been talking to in the first tank was cursing just as fiercely. "Damn them! Damn the bloody navy!"

Harry had no inclination to remind the tanker how often navy guns had saved them during the long siege. Instead he went back to where his platoon was rising to its feet. None of them had been hurt, fortunately, but the tiny remnants of the hard-luck B Company had been reduced by half by one of the errant shells. Men clustered around the dead and wounded.

"Come on move!" shouted Colonel Anderson, "Let's get out of here before we get hit again!"

No one was inclined to argue and in moments the battalion was heading across the park and toward the harbor, carrying their weapons and kits and their wounded. The lonely steam tank remained behind, guarding the rear.

They made it across the park and onto a street heading the right direction. This part of town hadn't been damaged at all, but it had a sad and shabby look to it. The streets hadn't been swept in months and all manner of things had been abandoned along it; pieces of furniture, clothing, luggage, books, papers, a baby's pram...

More artillery fire screamed by overhead, but it all passed well to the west before exploding. Harry hoped none of it landed on the poor crew of that tank. How long would those men hold their position? Would they even have a chance to run? Would he ever know what happened to them? *Sampson's right, I think too much. Stop it.*

As they neared the harbor, they encountered more troops falling back. The rear guard was composed of several brigades and they were all converging on the only way out. To Harry's dismay, some of them seemed to be in a state of complete disorder and off to the north he could hear the sound of heat rays. A few of these other men were shouting something about being flanked, cut off from the harbor. Some alarming new clouds of black smoke were rising up in that direction, and the sound of heavy guns was growing in intensity.

They instinctively picked up their pace, but the other units started crowding into them, intermingling, and order was being lost. There was a growing tingle of panic among the troops. Harry could almost see a ripple of fear passing through the ranks of the 15th New Castle. What if they couldn't reach the ships in time? "Steady lads!" he called. His voice sounded shrill in his ears and he forced himself to sound calm. "Keep together!"

It wasn't quite a mob which emerged from the streets at the waterfront, but it didn't look much like a military organization, either. Sydney's harbor was built around a small bay that extended southwards from the larger bay to the north which connected to the sea. Most of the docks and wharfs were on the eastern shore, although there were a few on the western side as well.

The ones on the west were in flames and Martian tripods walked among them.

"Oh, bloody hell!" snarled Burford Sampson. "The bastards must have waded across Iron Cove when the navy pulled back!" Warships had been holding that flank of the defense line all through the siege, but they must have left too soon, leaving the way open for the Martians.

The harbor was in bedlam. There had been four large transport ships waiting to take off the rear guard, but Harry only saw one tied to a pier. Another was just turning out into the main channel to the sea and a third was on fire from stem to stern, drifting a few hundred yards from shore. A navy warship, a light cruiser it looked like, was at the head of the bay slugging it out with a dozen tripods at point blank range.

As the stunned soldiers watched, the cruiser's guns blew a tripod to bits. But this was not the sort of fight the navy wanted. Their guns had a vastly longer range than the Martians' heat rays and they liked to engage from a safe distance. This was definitely not a safe distance.

The Martians were all firing back, and the heat rays were burning through the ship's thin armor with ease. Fires were breaking out all over and there some explosions as the secondary armament's ready-use ammunition was ignited.

"Get out of there, you idiots!" cried Sampson. "You can't win this fight!"

But it was too late. The warship destroyed another tripod, but then a ray found its way through to a magazine and the cruiser blew up in a fiery explosion which leapt hundreds of feet into the air. The concussion smote Harry's ears even from a half mile away. The ship broke in two and settled quickly, its bow and stern sticking up almost vertically. The wreck blocked the harbor exit so that the last transport couldn't get out even it could run the gauntlet of the enemy rays.

"So now what?" cried someone. Every man there was wondering the same thing. More tripods were emerging from the smoke on the west side of the harbor. Sampson was right, they must have gotten across Iron Cove and made their way here through... Balmain. The neighborhood where his house was. *It's probably not there anymore.* A feeling of profound sadness passed through him, despite his peril. But what to do? As he stood there, people started pouring down the gangways of the ship tied to the dock. They knew they weren't getting out that way.

"South! Head south!" shouted someone. An officer was forcing his way through the mob, shouting and pointing. "Head for Botany Bay! The navy will pick us up there!"

The soldiers seemed to sway like a forest before a strong wind and then turned almost as one and surged southward, even the ones who could not possibly have heard the officer's shouts. Later, Harry would be appalled at how quickly disciplined fighting men, men who not long before had been fighting Martians from close enough to spit at, could disintegrate into a frenzied mob.

But a mob they had become and there wasn't a thing he could do about it except be swept along with all the rest. He made one futile attempt to keep his own platoon in a group around him, but it was hopeless; within moments everyone around him was a stranger.

So south he went. Botany Bay was a good five miles from where they were, but the street grid of the city provided a half dozen wide boulevards heading that direction and the crush of the mob soon lessened as men turned down side streets to find less crowded paths. Some men were running flat out, but most, like Harry, moved at a sort of jog, all casting fearful glances to the west. The main Martian attack force was still coming from that way. Would it be able to cut off their retreat? Catch them before they made it to the water? The smoke was thickening in that direction and while the sound of heat rays to the north was fading, he thought he could hear some to the west.

While looking west, he bumped right into a man, who wasn't moving. He started to go around when he realized the man was wounded. He had bandages covering his face and his eyes, but the top of his head was exposed and badly burned, not a trace of hair on the purplish, blistered flesh.

Harry grimaced. He'd seen this sort of wound all too often. Some poor sod who had ducked a heat ray quick enough to avoid being vaporized, but not quite quick enough to escape entirely. The bandages had been hastily applied, the wound was fresh. Why was he here alone? Had his mates lost him? Abandoned him?

"Keep moving, boy!"

The familiar voice startled him. There was Burford Sampson grabbing him by the arm, trying to pull him along.

"We can't leave this man!"

Sampson stopped, looked at the man, cursed, and shook his head, but he then went to the other side of him, grabbed one arm, while Harry

23

took the other. "Come along, mate," he said as calmly as if inviting the fellow for a stroll, "we need to get moving."

The man didn't say anything Harry could hear through the slit in the bandages where his mouth was, but he did move. They hustled him down the street as quickly as they could, but not nearly as fast as Harry would have liked. The noises to the west were getting louder. One block, two blocks, three blocks, they hurried along. The street was littered with discarded gear; helmets, backpacks, a machine gun and ammo boxes.

When they reached the end of the fourth block, Harry gasped when he spotted a tripod down the street to the west. It was still a few blocks away, but much too close. Many of the men, seeing it, too, immediately turned east and ran down the street directly away from the threat. Few of them seemed to even have a rifle anymore.

Sampson dragged them across to the next block and kept going. Harry was getting very tired and was stumbling almost as much as the blind man. At the next street there were no Martians in sight, but they had to keep going. There were fewer men around them now, they were being left behind, due to their slower pace.

Two more blocks, three, and the buildings were getting lower and more spread out as they left the center of Sydney behind. Harry thought he could see the sparkle of sunlight on water in the distance. Maybe they'd make it...

"Bloody hell! Look out!"

A tripod emerged from the next intersection ahead. Right in front of them. It wasn't fifty yards away, towering over them, its gray, metallic skin glistening like it was wet. Before they could even move, it fired its heat ray—but not at them. It was shooting at something farther south. It hadn't seen them yet. Burford dragged them up against the wall of a building. "We've got to get around it!" he hissed.

They slid backwards along the wall until they came to a narrow alley between buildings. Pushing and pulling the wounded man, who still had not made a sound, they made their way around to the rear of the building and then through a small back yard with a weed-filled garden and an empty clothesline that swayed forlornly in the breeze. More heat rays could be heard to the west and smoke was swirling around them now. They were running out of time.

Passing through several other yards they finally made it to the next street—the one the Martian had come down. Peering out, they could see that the tripod had continued moving and was half a block away with its back to them. Nothing but smoke could be seen to the west. "All right," said Sampson, "Across we go."

Gathering themselves, they sprinted through the open space, half-carrying the man until they reached an alley on the other side. They all stumbled to their knees, gasping for breath. "Got to keep going, Harry. They won't keep those boats for us."

"If there are any boats."

"Yeah, well let's go see if there are." He pulled them up and they stumbled on.

At the end of the next block some of the buildings were on fire—and a tripod was there burning them. They looked this way and that, but there was no way to get through. And how long before the building they were sheltering behind had a heat ray turned against it?

"Maybe we can..." began Sampson.

He was cut off by the howl of incoming shells. The navy guns had almost stopped since they fled from the harbor, but now they started again. A salvo exploded the next block over, shaking the ground.

"Damn, that's the big stuff," said Sampson. "A battleship maybe."

More howls, louder than before...

An enormous roar, the air was pulled from his lungs, and Harry was knocked flat. A sharp pain stung his arm and debris came raining down on him; for a moment he couldn't see a thing but smoke.

He tried to get up, but there was stuff pinning him down. "Harry! Harry! You all right?" Then Sampson was there, pulling him free from the wreckage.

"I'm... I'm okay, I think. Hurt my arm..." The smoke wafted away, and he could see again. The building they'd been next to had partially collapsed. There was a big crater out in the street—and a wrecked tripod right next to it.

Sampson grabbed his arm and peered at it. "You'll live," he declared. "Unlike our poor friend here."

For a moment Harry thought he was talking about the Martian, but then he realized it was the wounded man he was talking about. He wasn't wounded anymore, he was dead. A large splinter of wood was protruding from his chest.

"Damn... didn't even know his name..."

"No time to worry about it, boy. We gotta move."

"Don't call me boy."

"Shut up and run."

They couldn't run, but they could trot. Without the wounded man to slow them, they could trot. Harry cast a glance backwards, but he could not spot him among the debris.

They went down the street toward the bay, many of the buildings were on fire, and they had to stay in the middle of the street, perfect targets. But they didn't meet any more tripods. Shells were falling, seemingly at random, but the tripods appeared to be drawing off to the north. Maybe they didn't think killing a mob of fleeing soldiers was worth the risk of getting hit by the navy's big guns. He hoped so.

After what seemed like hours, they came out of the smoke and past the last of the closely set buildings and there was Botany Bay in front of them.

There were a few small docks sticking out into the water, but it was mostly just open beach. The initial settlers had not bothered to develop it once they found the vastly superior harbor just a few miles north. Now that beach was filled with men wading out to small boats which bobbed in the gentle surf. Ships waited out in the bay. Harry sighed in relief.

They had made, but just barely. As they stumbled across the sand, the last of the men climbed into the boats and they began to shove off. Someone shouted to them and he and Sampson stumbled a little faster. Water splashed around his feet, up to his knees, and then strong hand grabbed him and pulled him aboard.

"Yer a pair o' lucky blokes!" said someone. "Ye nearly got left behind!"

Chapter Two

June 1911, North of Devonport, Tasmania

The coast of Tasmania was just a dark streak fading on the southern horizon as Harry leaned against the rail of the SS *Hartlepool*. Burford Sampson was a few yards away staring in the same direction, a strange look on his face.

"Sorry we couldn't stay longer, Burf," he said. "A shame you couldn't get to visit your home."

Sampson shrugged and seemed to shake himself. "No matter. I hadn't really thought of it as home for years. And now I doubt it would..." he trailed off.

Harry nodded. He'd never been to Tasmania before, but he could guess what Sampson meant. The island off the south coast of Australia was the closest substantial landmass and it had been the destination for a huge number of refugees. Devonport had been a town of fewer than ten thousand before the invasion. When they'd stopped there a few days ago, there were vast tent cities all around it which must have held a hundred thousand at least.

A hundred thousand with more coming every day. The task force carrying the troops had needed to thread its way through an armada of tramp steamers, ferries, sailboats, rowboats, and rafts bringing people to Tasmania. Vessels crammed to the rails with desperate people – or empty ones heading back for more across the hundred and forty mile wide Bass Strait which separated Tasmania from Australia proper.

Australia might be officially evacuated now, but no one could guess how many people were still there, trying to avoid the Martians, trying to get away. There weren't actually that many Martians and there was so much land to hid in, Harry guessed that more people would be showing up here for years to come.

The flotilla of small vessels at Devonport had reminded him of the mob of boats which had taken them off the beach in Botany Bay. That had been one of the most harrowing moments of his life. Somehow, bobbing there, completely exposed had been more frightening than dodging tripods in the streets of Sydney. If a tripod had caught them like that there would have been nowhere to hide and as exhausted as he was, he would have gone straight to the bottom if he'd jumped into the water. Burn or drown? Which would be worse?

But he hadn't had to do either. The navy's guns had kept the Martians at bay and the boats had made it back to the ships and he'd managed to climb aboard. Someone had thrown a blanket over his shoulders and handed him a mug of hot tea as the ships pulled away.

And now the ships were taking them... where?

They ought to be taking us back to Australia, dammit!

When they realized that the ships were taking them from Sydney to Tasmania rather than to New Zealand, there had been hope that it would be to a base which was preparing for a counterattack. A base to stage the liberation of their homes.

But they'd only stayed long enough to get food for the men and coal for the ships and to redistribute the troops. They'd gotten all mixed up during the mad scramble to get away, but now the companies and battalions were all back together again, and the 15th New Castle Battalion was aboard the *Hartlepool*.

No one, of course, had bothered to tell them where they were going.

Rumors were rife, but real information was scarce. They were heading west, so that indicated South Africa, India, or Egypt, but it could have been any of them, or somewhere else entirely. All they really knew was that it wasn't home.

"Why the hell do we got to sail halfway round the bleedin' world to fight Martians?" demanded one of the men when the company had assembled. "We've got Martians right *here*!" Several others had agreed and a sort of growl ran through the whole body of men.

"Because we can't *beat* them here, you silly sod!" Burford Sampson had said, standing in front of them, fists planted on his hips. "We found that out at Perth and a dozen other places. So they are sending us someplace where we *can* beat the bastards. When we've done that there, we can come back here and finish the job!"

That seemed to satisfy most of the men, although there was still some grumbling. Captain Berwick had nodded gratefully at Sampson and then dismissed the company.

The ship wasn't large and with the whole battalion and a few support units aboard it was badly overcrowded. Even the senior officers were jammed in two or three to a cabin. Junior officers, like Harry and Sampson were given quarters little better than the enlisted men, although they did have actual bunks rather than hammocks. And a porthole; the small round window was a godsend. Even though it was fall in this part of the world, the heat below decks was stifling. Harry pitied his troops who had no such luxury.

There really wasn't room for everyone up on deck at once, and as soon as the coast had dropped out of sight, the colonel ordered a system to rotate the men up there two companies at a time. Officers, of course, could go up there whenever they wanted, and Harry took advantage of that.

There were five officers in C Company, Captain Berwick, Lieutenant MacDonald, Lieutenant Miller, Burford Sampson, and himself. They'd gotten to know each other very well during the long siege of Sydney and they tended to go around together. Proper *British* officers would each have their own batman or dog-robber, as they were sometimes called, but In C Company only the Captain had his own, and the lieutenants all shared one, splitting the costs. Their man was Lance Corporal Ralph Scoggins, a bandy-legged ape of a fellow, who claimed that he'd been a dockyard worker before the war. Harry suspected that his 'work' at the dockyards had not been of any strictly legal sort, but he was a good soldier and a great scrounger, and he was willing to forgive him his past sins.

So it seemed almost normal when Scoggins, bearing a tray with a tall pot and mugs, found the five of them slouching on the ship's fo'c'sle watching the sun sliding down the sky in the west.

"No proper tea service to be found on this here ship, sirs," he apologized. "'Less you want me to borrow the captain's, o' course."

They all chuckled and took a mug. "This will do fine, Ralph," said Berwick. "Have you seen Cartwright about?" Cartwright was his own batman.

"I saw him tidying up your bunk a while ago, sir. Forlorn hope that is. Not proper a t'all."

"We'll make do," said Sampson. "And what about you? Found a spot for yourself?"

"Oh, yes, sir. The main berthing areas were a tad crowded, an' more than a tad smelly—honest to God I don't think they've mucked the place out since before the evacuation began—so I looked around a bit. Knowin' ships and knowin' sailors as I do, I had a little chat with one o' the stewards and worked out an arrangement. Got a fine little cubby just aft of the galley, sir."

Harry snorted and wondered what, exactly Scoggins had traded to get his fine little cubby. And just how nice it really was. Wouldn't surprise him if it was nicer than the place he and the other officers shared. The man had a talent for certain. He slurped his tea and winced. No sugar.

"And in your scouting, did you happen to see what sort of provisions they were able to bring aboard at Devonport?" asked MacDonald. "Can we expect eggs and bacon for breakfast, or just ship's biscuits like before?"

Scoggins frowned. "Eggs might be a problem, sir. An' it might be salt pork rather than bacon. Things were damn tight what with all those poor refugees to feed. But I'll do me best."

"We know you will," said Sampson. "Well, carry on."

"Right, sir." The man moved away, stared at—sometimes glared at—by other officers whose men hadn't even managed the tea for them.

They sat, looked forward, and watched the sun touch the ocean. The western sky was a fiery red. As the night quickly deepened around them, they drifted off to their bunks.

A week later, beyond the western edge of Australia, the ships turned northwest. That ruled out South Africa as a destination, but left India, Persia, or Egypt as a possibility. Sampson said they weren't missing anything in South Africa.

Two more weeks and the amateur navigators aboard were sure it was Egypt. Or at the very least, the Suez Canal; who knew where they might be headed after that? "Can't be Canada," said some. "They would have sent us across the Pacific instead of the long way 'round!" "Don't be so sure!' laughed others. "The navy may be giving us the scenic tour!"

But wherever they were headed, the men were becoming edgy to get there. The fresh meat and greens they'd gotten in Tasmania were all eaten up, leaving just the salt pork and biscuits, and the water was tasting mighty stale. The limited space aboard restricted the drill which could be done and Harry and the other officer wracked their brains to find things to keep the men busy. The Indian Ocean seemed empty of shipping and their convoy was all alone in the vast reaches.

But finally, in the fourth week, the cry of 'land ho!' came from the lookout and a hazy bump was seen on the horizon ahead. One of the ship's crew told them it was Socotra Island at the mouth of the Gulf of Aden. It was a barren and desolate pile of rock, but there were a dozen ships at anchor, despite the lack of a good harbor. When the Martians had overrun the Arabian Peninsula, the British government in Aden had relocated here.

The convoy paused briefly to receive communications. Harry took the opportunity to mail several letters he'd written to his mother. He had no idea if the letters would ever reach them. There was probably a better chance that letters from his mother might eventually catch up with him, but that would only happen once he stayed in one spot long enough.

When the ships moved on again, orders appeared from General Legge, the commander of the entire force, to be ready for hostile action. The ships were indeed headed for the Suez Canal, and to reach it they had to pass through the narrow Strait of Bab al-Mandab between Arabia and the African mainland. Martian war machines were often seen in the area on both shores and ships making the passage had to stay on the alert.

The men were pressed into service to strip the upper works of anything which might catch fire under a Martian heat ray. Flammable items which couldn't be moved was protected with metal sheets or anything else they could find aboard which wouldn't burn. The captain frowned at the mess they'd made of his ship.

As they neared the strait, they could hear intermittent gunfire rumbling across the waters. It wasn't the steady roar like they'd heard during the attacks on Sydney, just a thud or a boom now and then, growing louder as they got closer.

The men were turned out in full kit and lined the barricaded rails, rifles ready. The battalion's four Maxim machine guns were set up in positions with good fields of fire. Harry stood behind the men of his platoon and thought how ridiculously flimsy the barricades were. A heat ray at close range would burn through them in seconds.

When the strait became visible he, and everyone else breathed a sigh of relief. Bab al-Mandab might have been small for a sea passage, but it was still miles wide at its narrowest point.

A small island named Perim was close to the Arabian side of the strait, only a mile or so offshore and that was where the gunfire had been coming from. Several navy warships, including an old battleship, guarded the strait, but there appeared to be a garrison on the island with some heavy guns, too. These were slowly firing at something off to the east. Harry took out his field glasses and looking in that direction but could not see anything except drifting clouds of smoke and dust.

"Must be what? Twelve miles from the African shore to that island?" said Sampson. "With their heat rays only dangerous to an exposed man for two miles or so, we should be fine if we stay in the middle."

"That water on the left looks pretty shallow from the color of it," said Harry. "I wonder how far out a tripod could wade? Close enough to take a shot at us?"

Sampson frowned and shook his head. "They'd have to walk four or five miles and they'd be sitting ducks for the navy guns the whole way. There don't seem to be any of the blighters around today, anyhow."

No, that was true; the African shore was deserted in both directions and for miles inland. Still, the convoy commander was taking no chances. The three columns of transports merged into a single long line to thread some imaginary needle in the center of the straight. An hour later they were in the Red Sea, which did not look particularly red to Harry.

They stood down and relaxed but were told to leave their makeshift defenses in place. It was still another four days travel to reach the canal, and as the sea broadened out again beyond the strait, the shore on both sides was lost to sight and it was like being out on the open ocean again. Still, the prospect of reaching some destination brightened the spirits of the men. They were tired of the ship and the drab rations and wanted to get off and kill some Martians.

Before noon on the third day after the strait, they saw a line of fortifications on the western shore. They started at the water's edge near the little port town of Qoseir and stretched out of sight into the desert. From what Harry had heard, they went all the way to the Nile and then took up again on the other side and went on to meet the Mediterranean a hundred miles further on. As they drew closer, they could see that they were far more massive than what they'd been able to build around Sydney. Thick, high walls of stone or concrete were studded with heavy guns. A deep moat had been dug in front of the walls. More guns were in emplacements behind the walls and there were vehicle parks filled with tanks and armored cars.

As impressive as it was, the Australians just shook their heads or cursed. If a fraction of this had been given to them, maybe they wouldn't be refugees from their homes now! The Empire had so much strength; why couldn't more of it been spared for Australia?

By the start of the fourth day, they had entered the much narrower Gulf of Suez and could see both shores again. There were more military camps but all on the western side. Harry turned away and went over to the other side of the ship. After a while he noticed that Burford Sampson had joined him.

"No defenses on the eastern side there," he said pointing. "They're all on the other side of Sinai. They have a line of forts running from Aqaba to Jerusalem and then on to the Med farther north."

A few hours later they reached the canal, which was just a big ditch cut through the sands. Somehow, Harry was expecting something more, and he realized that greater effort had probably gone into the fortification line they'd seen earlier. They had to reduce speed to prevent the wakes of the ships from eroding the sides of the canal, so it was well after dark by the time they reached Port Said at the other end. The night was clear, and the waters of the Mediterranean glittered in the moonlight. Sampson muttered something about 'wine dark seas'.

Noon of the next day saw them in Alexandria. The legendary port was busy, although not as busy as modest Devonport had been. There were swarms of fishing boats, but they were just fishing, not carrying refugees. Still, *Hartlepool* had to wait until nearly nightfall before it got its turn at one of the piers.

The 15th New Castle Battalion marched stiffly down the gangways onto solid ground for the first time in over a month. There was an officer waiting to greet them.

"Gentlemen," he said, "welcome to Egypt."

Chapter Three

September, 1911, Kena, Egypt

"**A**ll right, lads, these little blighters are a bit tricky to use, so pay close attention."

Harry and the men of his platoon closed in around the British ordnance officer and peered at the object he held in his hand. It looked like a black grapefruit on a stick. Looking closer, he saw that the 'grapefruit' was actually a metal sphere and the stick was a metal rod attached to the sphere. It was called a 'Mills Bomb' after the fellow who had invented it.

They were on the outskirts of the town of Kena, which was where the defense line running from the Red Sea met the Nile River. The 15th New Castle Battalion, after a week at Alexandria, had been shipped out with most of the other Australian troops to help man the line. It was a hot, dry, dusty place, but the line had been established and held for over a year, so it had far more amenities than Harry had been expecting. They lived in tidy tent cities. Field kitchens supplied hot meals and there was even enough water piped in from the river to allow for bathing facilities. A narrow-gauge railway had been constructed behind the line to carry supplies and move troops around.

All of this was possible because the Martians were leaving them alone. They had attacked the defenses here about nine months earlier, been repulsed, and then retreated back into the desert. They had not come back — at least not to this part of the line. Apparently the high command thought that this was a good spot to allow the Aussies to get acclimated to their new location. And also to be given some new equipment.

"The first step is to release the top half of the sphere," continued the officer, a captain named Smyth. "The two halves are held together and sealed by this tin strap, which goes all the way round. You peel up the end of it here, like this, and then just pull the whole thing loose and the top comes right off." He followed his own instructions and a moment later the top was off. The contents of the sphere were them exposed. It just looked like a whitish lump of clay.

"What you see is a coating of untreated rubber, mixed with a few other things. It's sticky as hell, so don't take the cover off until you plan to use it. Underneath that is about a pound of gelignite, which I'm sure most of you know is a powerful explosive. There is a detonator at the bottom of this sphere and the fuse is ignited by pulling a pin inside the handle here.

34

There's a cap over it to prevent accidents. Just unscrew the cap to get at the pin." The cap he spoke of was at the end of the metal rod. He unscrewed it and there was, indeed, a small ring, attached to a cord inside.

Smyth held it up, ran his gaze over the men, and pointed to the ring. "Pull this and you've got ten seconds until it explodes. There is no way to stop it once the fuse is ignited. So don't pull the bloody ring until you are ready to use it. Got that?"

"Yes, sir!" said all the assembled men.

"Now the idea, of course, is to use the sticky part of the bomb to attach it to the Martian tripod. Up until now, we've had a dozen different variations on bundles of Dynamite or other explosives, attached to ropes that the men try to somehow tie to a tripod or throw up on to one and hope it gets tangled. Works about one time in ten. But I'm told you lads are combat veterans so I don't need to tell you that."

"Damn bleedin' right, mate!" said someone in the group, getting a laugh. Even Smyth smiled. Harry suspected it was Private Killian, the platoon's wiseacre.

"All right, let me show you what this can do. Please take cover behind the sand bags."

They were on a firing range which had been built near Kena, which was about twenty miles west of their camps. There were targets for rifle fire and also other weapons, but today they were here for something different. About twenty paces from the sandbag barrier there was a row of wooden logs sticking up from the ground; they may have once been telegraph poles. Some of the poles had already been broken off, apparently by earlier demonstrations. When everyone was behind cover, peering over the tops of the sandbags, Smyth walked out toward the poles.

"Let's pretend that this is the leg of one of the tripods. Don't pull the cord for the primer until you are ready to attach the bomb," he called back to them. "Damned embarrassing to pull it early and then have the bugger walk off before you can attach it and leave you there holding the bag, so to speak. I image you fellows have seen the real thing close up before."

"Too damned often, mate! 'Ave you?" Yes, it was definitely Killian.

Smyth tried to smile again, although it looked more like a grimace. "All right, here we go." He tugged at the ring and pulled the cord out of the tube attached to the bomb and then using the tube like the hilt of a knife, stabbed the bomb at the pole, as high up as he could easily reach. Just as he'd promised, the thing stuck fast. "Now you run like hell!"

He sprinted back towards them, waving his arms. "Down! Get down!" Harry obediently ducked behind the sandbags, making sure all his men did as well. A moment later Smyth tore around the end of the sandbag wall and skidded to a halt. "Stay down!"

After a few heartbeats, there was a sizeable bang and a small concussion. Smythe stood up and then said: "All good, you can get up now." Harry stood up and saw a cloud of smoke rolling away from him, borne by the steady desert breeze. The pole had been blown in two, the bottom still standing upright, but ending in a blossom of splinters about four feet above the ground. The top part was lying a dozen feet away. "Come take a look, gentlemen," said Smyth.

Harry and his men gathered around the pole. The bomb had blown through it with apparent ease. But it was only a piece of wood...

"Captain," he said, "has this been tested on actual Martian equipment? We've found them to be a bit tougher than... wood."

"They have," replied the ordnance officer. "We've used them on the legs of enemy tripods we've salvaged, and the Mills Bomb is capable of blasting through their metal skins. It won't always blow a leg clean off, mind you, but it will do significant damage."

"And what's the danger radius from the blast? To the men using it, I mean. You had us back off a good ways, and we won't always have a convenient sand bag wall to hide behind."

Smyth nodded. "The metal casing for the bomb does throw off shrapnel for some distance. We're looking at using a different material which will be safer, but this is what we have for now. We believe this to be a significant improvement over the bombs you have been using."

"Well, that's God's truth, sir," said Sergeant Milroy, the platoon sergeant. "And if we need t'tackle one of these bastards close up, we're going t'lose some lads no matter what we do." The men nodded. They all had learned that there was no easy way for infantry to kill a tripod.

"Sir?" Private Greene raised his hand. "Can you throw the bomb? I mean throw it up at the main body of the tripod. Will it still stick?"

The captain made a sour face and shook his head slightly. "Well, if you made a perfect throw, then maybe. Much more likely is that it will bounce off. And once it's fallen down and gotten dirt and sand on its sticky part, then it won't stick at all. So I'm afraid you are going to need to walk right up to the tripod to slap one of these on. And while I can see you Australian fellows are tall blokes, you'll still only be able to reach the lower legs. You'll need to blow off a leg or two to bring them down to size. We're working on a better way to deliver the bombs to the target, but for right now, this is what we have."

"Have they tried magnets, sir?" asked Harry.

Smyth shook his head. "Won't work. The Martian metal doesn't have a lot of iron in it, so magnets won't stick to it."

"Maybe we could tie one to a long pole, or something," said someone in the group. Other suggestions were forthcoming, which quickly became ridiculous and even rude, until Harry stopped them.

Captain Smyth smiled and said, "Nothing to stop you from using your ingenuity, lads. But if you do come up with something that works better, be sure you let the Ordnance Department know, right?"

"Yes, sir," said Harry. "When will we be issued these things, sir?"

"They are being shipped here, to Egypt, right now. But they've only just started being produced in mass and are still in short supply. I'm sorry I can't let you all try one out today, but I'm sure you will get the hang of them with no problem. We've made them about as fool proof as can be."

"Dunno, sir," said Sergeant Milroy, "we've got an amazing batch of fools here." That got a laugh from everyone.

Smyth nodded to Harry. "Carry on Lieutenant."

Harry saluted and told Milroy to stand the men to. They fell into ranks and he marched them off to where the rest of the company was waiting. They passed another platoon marching up to the firing range. The whole battalion had been brought up for instructions and each platoon would have its turn.

He had the men stack their arms and then allowed them to break ranks and rest. There was no shade and it was damned hot. It was always damned hot during the day. Dry as dust, of course; in the month they'd been out on the line, it had not rained once. One of the British officers he'd spoken to said that he'd been here nearly a year and he'd only seen it rain twice in all that time, and even then only a few drops. Australia was hot in the summer, but it did rain from time to time. Harry had never seen anything like this. Of course, it was a desert...

"How'd it go?' asked Burford Sampson, walking up to him, Ian MacDonald and Paul Miller, the other platoon commanders in C Company followed along. They had all already had the instruction. "Nobody blow himself up?"

"No, but Captain Smyth murdered another telegraph pole. What do you think of those things, those Mills Bombs?"

Samson shrugged. "Probably better'n the dynamite bombs we were using back home. At least they are trying to give us better stuff."

"There has to be a better way to get the bomb to the Martian," said MacDonald.

"Almost anything would be better than having to get within spitting distance," added Miller

"Well, if you figure something out, be sure to tell Smyth."

"Yeah, right."

They sat in silence for a while and Harry observed his men. They had been in hearteningly good humor during the demonstration, but now, just killing time in the heat, they mostly lapsed into silence; smoking cigarettes, or pouring sand out of their boots.

"Burf…?"

Sampson turned to look at him, a half smile on his face. "What is it *Harry*? You only call me *Burf* when you want something."

Harry didn't smile back. "I'm worried about the men. They're not happy being here…"

"None of us are," said MacDonald.

"They're not happy and discipline is getting worse. It wasn't like this back home, not even after holding the line at Sydney for a year or more. I… I don't know what to do about it."

Sampson shrugged. "At Sydney they were defending their own homes. They could look over their shoulders and *see 'em*. When we got time off, we could *go* home. Or at least you fellows could. Everyone could see the need. But here…" He waved his hand around to take in the vast expanse of sand and scrub brush. "…here, what are we defending?"

"A patch o' desert and a bunch o' bloody wogs!" said MacDonald

Harry frowned. "I don't like that word," he said quietly.

"Neither do the wogs," replied MacDonald, totally unabashed. "But the boys just see the millions of 'em that have come crowdin' in behind the defense lines and wonder why they can't take over the job here and let us go back and retake our own homes."

"There *are* a lot of native troops helping out…" said Harry.

"Not as many as there *should* be. It's their homes under attack, their holy places that have been desecrated. Why'n hell don't more of 'em join the ranks and fight?" MacDonald spat in the dust.

"A lot of them did fight in the beginning, when the Martians overran Mecca and all," said Sampson. "They got slaughtered. Hard to fight tripods with nothing but muskets and a few rifles."

"We haven't got much more than rifles — and Mills Bombs," replied MacDonald.

"We've got a lot more," insisted Sampson. "Machine guns, artillery, tanks, and navy warships. Maybe not right in our battalion, but close by."

"Not enough, though," said Miller. "Never enough."

"Yeah, but how long could we have held Sydney if we didn't have any at all? And if millions of our mates had gotten killed tryin' to fight like that, how eager would the rest of us be to get stuck in again?"

No one had an answer to that.

"Maybe," said Harry after a while, "maybe they can start equipping the natives with better weapons…"

"Can hardly do that while *we* are still waiting for better weapons," snorted Sampson. "How would the boys feel if they knew that the natives were being given tanks and guns and Mills Bombs while we were still waiting for them?"

"Now *that's* God's truth!" said Miller. "We'd have a bloody riot on our hands!"

With that, silence fell over the little group, interrupted from time to time by an exploding bomb down at the range. The last platoon of D Company was down there now. When they were finished, the battalion could go back to camp. Back to their tents, where they would spend another amazingly chilly night, followed by another scorching day. The battalion had its own small section of the defense lines about twenty miles east of the Nile, but with the Martians well off to the south in their fortress, there was no need to keep it fully manned all the time. Usually just one company would take a day-long turn standing watch, while the other three... sweated.

They had only been there a month but the days were already blending into a blur, like some shimmering desert mirage. Everyone was wondering how long they would be stuck there. Months? Years? The defenses, which protected the lower Nile, Cairo, Alexandria, and the Suez Canal were truly formidable. Tall concrete walls, with ditches in front. Heavy artillery mounted on the walls and in positions behind it. Tank battalions sitting in reserve to deal with any possible breakthrough. And navy warships on the Nile and the Red Sea ready to throw in their help if needed — although their guns could not reach the center areas of the line. It seemed to Harry that the Martians would be fools to attack.

And if they didn't, what was the point of the 15th New Castle Battalion being here?

Someone had to do it, of course, but why them? That was the question on the mind of every man.

The last of D Company returned and the Colonel stood them to and marched them off to the railroad depot where a train took them back to their own part of the line. Some of the men looked longingly back at the town of Kena; they had been hoping that perhaps after their instruction, they'd be granted some time off in the town. It was the only place that offered any real chance of recreation in the vicinity. On weekends men could get passes to visit, but none were forthcoming now. There was another town, Qoseir, at the east end of the line on the Red Sea that was rumored to have even better facilities, but they had not been permitted to visit there yet. Supposedly, after they had been here longer, there would even be opportunities to go back to Cairo.

The train ride took about an hour and the wind generated by their speed was hugely welcome. Since the train was moving, not the air, there wasn't even any dust or sand being blown into their faces like when the true winds came off the desert, as they often did. They passed numerous camps on their way, many of them occupied by other Australian troops. This led to a great deal of shouting, waving, and mock insults being thrown back and forth, as men spotted people they knew. The Australian battalions had been spread out among the other troops, supposedly to allow them to learn the ropes from their more experienced neighbors. The grumblers said it was to keep the Aussies from becoming a unified force. Harry wondered if that was true.

By the end of the long defense of Sydney, the troops had grown to the equivalent of about three or four divisions in size. Their upper level organization was a bit sketchy by British standards, but it had worked well enough for a static situation like that. The battalions had been formed into brigades and the brigades had been grouped together into what could have been called divisions — with division commanders — and the whole lot had been dubbed the Sydney Defense Force under the command of General Legge. But since arriving in Egypt, all trace of that earlier organization had vanished. They'd heard nothing from Legge, and even the old brigade commanders seemed to have dropped off the face of the earth. There were whispers that the Australians would just be used as replacements for the British units and would ultimately vanish as distinct formations. If that was really true it was going to lead to trouble — bad trouble.

They stopped at a little siding next to their camp and debarked. There was the usual crowd of native children clustered about, begging for food or money or anything else they could get. They were a mix of Egyptian, Sudanese, and Ethiopians, ranging in color from little darker than the suntanned Aussies, to the deep, deep brown of the Sub-Saharan Africans.

Just like back home, the Martians had landed in the central, inaccessible regions of the continent and then, when they were ready, surged outward, smashing everything in their path. Anyone who was able had fled, some to the coasts where a few of the colonial powers had set up fortified enclaves. Some had made it to French-controlled Madagascar, which the Martians had not invaded. Others had braved the Sahara and gone north into Morocco, Algeria, Tunisia, and Libya, where the French and Italians had set up defenses.

And then there those who lived in British-controlled Sudan and Egypt.

As the Martians swept north, those who could fled before them along the only practicable route — the Nile. The initial attacks had come along the west side of the great river. They destroyed Khartoum and then moved north along the winding river and pushed to within fifty miles of Cairo, before being stopped by a hastily dispatched British army and by a fleet of gunboats on the river.

After being repulsed, the enemy had fallen back into the desert. A year later a new advance on the east side of the river had also been stopped.

Things had been relatively stable since then. The defense lines were strong now and the route to Cairo, Alexandria and the Canal were safe.

But millions of refugees were now crowded into the space north of the defenses and they all needed to be fed, housed and cared for. Theoretically this was the responsibility of the Egyptian government, but it had proved a task far beyond their capabilities. Makeshift camps had been set up and some food was shipped in, but from what Harry had heard, the conditions there were grim. Sentries guarded the camps twenty-four hours a day, not to warn of a Martian attack, but to keep the refugees from stealing anything not nailed down. The men all pitied the emaciated children, but they were on strict orders not to share any food with them. Rations, even for the troops, were in short supply, but few men could not help but break the orders from time to time. On this day, Harry didn't give in to temptation. A few of his men did, but he made a point not to notice.

The battalion's camp was on a flat piece of desert a quarter-mile square. Each company had a 'street' with a row of the conical 'bell' tents lining it on either side. Each twelve-man squad had a tent, four squads made a platoon and four platoons made the company, so there were eight tents on each side of the street. At the head of the street, separated from the others by about twenty yards, there was a tent for the platoon officers and another for the captain. At the foot of the street there was a tent for the senior NCOs and another that was the company cook tent. The four companies each had their own street, which were treated like sovereign nations—no outsiders allowed without permission.

Beyond the heads of the company streets there was a short row of tents for the battalion officers and staff, the colonel rating a larger marquee-style tent. Beyond the foot of the streets was the battalion color line where they would fall into ranks. Beyond that—well beyond—were the loos. The camp was all laid out in strict accordance with regulations. Identical camps, like clumps of mushrooms, sprouted all along the rail line as far as the eye could see.

The battalion marched down to the color line and was then dismissed—all except an unlucky platoon from B Company who had guard duty. They relieved the platoon from the neighboring 4th Sheffield Battalion which had been covering for them while they were off learning about the Mills Bombs.

Harry and the other officers trudged up the dusty street to their tent and stripped off their gear. Scoggins was there in an amazingly short time with a pot of tea. He poured out cups and then gathered up their kits to clean. Harry was sure that he'd been with them for the demonstration and only just got back, too. "How does he manage to do this?" he muttered.

"He nipped off as soon as the train stopped," said Paul Miller. "Didn't go down to the color line with the rest of us."

"Man's worth his weight in gold," said MacDonald ."How much are we paying him?"

"Not enough," said Miller. "What with the situation around here I'm amazed he's keeping us this well supplied with edible food."

"You can be sure he's doing just fine," said Sampson. "With the money, I mean."

Harry frowned. As junior, he had the job of keeping the account books. "He's not cheating us," he protested. "I've checked."

"Never said that he was," replied Sampson. "But he's a wheeler-dealer. I'm sure that when he finds a bargain on eggs, he buys more than we need—using our money—and then sells the excess at a profit. He pays us back so our account squares, but he still makes money."

"Huh,' said Harry in surprise. "Is that... is that *proper*? Should we try to stop him?"

"Are you bloody crazy?" laughed MacDonald. "Kill the goose who lays golden eggs? I think not!"

"Not hurting anyone," said Sampson. "Leave well enough alone, Harry."

"All right, if you say so." He threw himself down on his cot and closed his eyes. They were gritty with the ever-present dust and he gently scrubbed at them to get it out. Maybe he would take a bath tonight. The piped in water from the Nile was a godsend—although every mile of it had to be guarded to keep the natives from breaking it open. Sometimes it seemed that the biggest threat came from the rear.

As he lay there waiting for Scoggins to arrive with dinner, he heard a rising and falling voice in the distance. Their *other* neighbor was an Egyptian regiment. All of them were Muslims, of course, and the voice was calling them to their sunset prayer. Five times a day that call was sounded. Some of the men were irritated by it—especially the night prayer—but Harry found it rather soothing. He had nearly dozed off when Scoggins brought the food.

They ate mostly in silence, having exhausted all their ready store of conversation during the waits for the Mills Bomb demonstrations. Harry regarded his fellow officers. They were all good men, and while they treated him like a kid brother, he liked them and trusted them. He'd served with them for a long time and he knew he was lucky that none of them had gotten killed during the siege. Some other companies and battalions had been decimated by Martian attacks, their officers wiped out completely. He wasn't sure what he'd do if they weren't around to help him out.

After dinner Harry decided he was too tired for the bath and he returned to his cot. Sampson and Miller set up a chess game and MacDonald disappeared somewhere. A few hours later he was suddenly awakened by a very excited MacDonald bursting into the tent.

"Hey! Hey!" he nearly shouted. "We're gonna be moving out!"

"When?" demanded Sampson.

"Where to?" asked Harry.

"How do you know?" said Miller.

"I was hanging around the battalion headquarters tent. The colonel was talking with some bloke from brigade. He said we needed to be ready to move the day after tomorrow!"

"Where are they sending us?" asked Harry again.

"I didn't hear. I don't think even the colonel knows."

"How typical," said Sampson. "Presumably someone does."

"But as usual they aren't telling us!" said Miller disgustedly. "You'd think that they're afraid we'll run off and tell the Martians."

"Military habits," said Sampson.

"Military stupidity!" said MacDonald. "To those bastards in London we're just a pin stuck in a map. They pluck it out and stick it in again somewhere else. No need to tell us!"

"I just hope whoever is doing the plucking and sticking knows what they're doing."

"When did anyone in London ever know what they're doing?" said MacDonald.

Harry looked on as the other officers talked. He really wouldn't mind moving again, just so long as it was to somewhere that mattered. But he wondered if MacDonald was right; did anyone in London really know what they were doing?

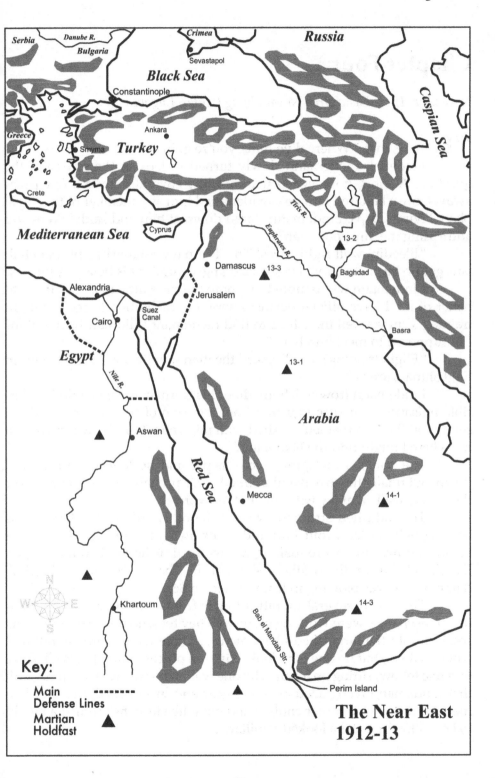

The Near East 1912-13

Key:

Main Defense Lines ---------

Martian Holdfast ▲

Chapter Four

November, 1911, Eastchurch Naval Flying Center, England

"**E**y there, mate! Where d'ye think you're goin'?"

Frederick Lindemann slowly turned to look at the source of the question. A short, bow-legged man in filthy coveralls stood a few paces away. Only a battered fatigue cap identified him as a member of the Royal Navy Flying Corps. Lindemann stared down at him and said: "Were you addressing me, my good man?"

"Bleedin' well right I was! This is a navy establishment and civilians got no business 'ere!" He scowled angrily under his bushy eyebrows.

Lindemann was tempted to ignore the rude little man, but thought better of it. "I have official business here. I'm scheduled to receive flight training. Can you tell me where to find Lieutenant Wildman-Lushington? I'm supposed to meet him here."

"Flight training? You?" asked the man skeptically. "Y'ain't even an Englishman, are ye?"

Lindemann frowned. Sometimes his German accent could be a terrible nuisance. "I assure you that I am a citizen of the Empire. And the sentries at the gate seemed satisfied with my credentials. Now can you tell me where I might find the lieutenant?"

The man's scowl grew even deeper and he looked him up and down, but finally he turned and pointed. "'E's probably in that 'angar over there." He walked away without another word.

The indicated structure was on the other side of the large grass landing field, at least four hundred yards away. It had rained the night before and his shoes were soaking wet by the time he reached the hangar. Eastchurch was on the southern shore of the Thames estuary and a chill, damp breeze was blowing in from the North Sea.

There were several aircraft sitting in front of the hangar and a number of mechanics were working on them. They took no notice of him, so he went on into the large shed-like structure. There were more aircraft and workers there, but no one who looked like an officer, or a pilot. Well, there was one fellow, sitting on a bench by one wall, who was wearing a coverall that Lindemann recognized as flying gear and he clutched a leather helmet. But despite his rather chubby and baby-like face, he seemed a bit old to be a pilot. In fact, he looked familiar...

"Excuse me, I'm looking for Lieutenant Wildman-Lushington," said Lindemann. "Is he about?"

"Oh, he was here a moment ago," replied the man. "I imagine he'll be back shortly. He's giving me some flying instructions in a little while."

"Really? I was supposed to meet him here for that very purpose, as well." He pulled out his pocket watch and checked the time. "In just a few minutes, in fact."

"Ah, well, I'm afraid I may have jumped the queue, here. I was forced to change my schedule and the lieutenant was kind enough to fit me in."

Lindemann frowned. This had all been arranged. How dare this fellow push in front of him? "And you are…?" he said coldly.

"Churchill, Winston Churchill. And you?"

Lindemann blinked. "Churchill? You - you're the First Lord of the Admiralty… sir?" In an instant he realized why the man looked familiar.

"For the moment. And you?"

"Lindemann, Professor Frederick Lindemann. I… I uh work at the National Physical Laboratory. I'm on the Advisory Committee for Aeronautics."

"Really? Why that's splendid. I know some of the men in charge over there. And a professor? You look so young, you must be very good at whatever you do. A professor of what, may I ask?"

"Physics, from the University of Berlin." He didn't add that he'd graduated the previous spring—nor that he was only twenty-five. "I'm attempting to apply experimental physics to aeronautics. As I'm sure you know, the engineering aspects of flight have far outstripped our understanding of the physics behind it all."

"If you say so," said Churchill, smiling. "Never had a head for numbers, I'm afraid. I would not have even passed the examination for Sandhurst without help from Mr. Mayo, one of the masters at Harrow. He convinced me that mathematics was not a hopeless bog of nonsense, and that there were meanings and rhythms behind all of the hieroglyphics. He taught me enough to pass the examination, but that was in 1894 and I'm afraid I've forgotten it all since then." He looked more closely at him. "But you, you understand all of that stuff. And now you are learning to fly…?"

"It seemed the logical thing to do. There are problems which need to be solved and I've always believed in direct experimentation. How can I do that if I don't fly? But you, sir, with all your immense responsibilities, why would you be taking flying lessons?" Churchill, also quite young compared to your typical government ministers, held one of the most important posts in the Empire. He was responsible for the entire vast machine that was the Royal Navy. Surely, he had better things to do.

"It seemed the logical thing to do—although my wife surely disagrees!" He grinned, and in spite of himself Lindemann grinned back. He found himself liking Churchill. "But seriously, I'm very keen on aircraft. It seems to be the one field in which we have actually outdone the Martians. It would be madness not to exploit the advantage as much as we can. I got so sick of the Cabinet dragging its feet on the issue that I decided if they wouldn't take the lead, then the navy would. And since I happen to be in charge of the navy, I was able to make it happen. But just reading reports about progress wasn't enough. I want to see it firsthand."

"I see, sir, very wise. Is… is this going to be your first lesson?"

"Oh no, not at all. I've doing this on and off since last spring. I've been up dozens of times."

"You must be nearly ready to solo then."

"Ha! I was ready a month ago! But the instructors won't let me. I think they are so worried about letting a lord of the admiralty kill himself in one of their machines that they are making excuses to prevent me. Damned unfair of them, if you ask me."

Lindemann found that his sympathies lay with the instructors rather than Churchill. They and their commanders must have been gnawing their fingernails down to the nub every time he went up. Aloud he said: "I'm sure they will let you soon, sir."

"Perhaps. But physics, is it? Then you must have some understanding of the Martian science, too, don't you?"

"I'm trying to acquire some. Because… of my mixed parentage—my father is German—I was denied access to such knowledge when I applied to university here. So I ended up in Berlin. I know those restrictions were lifted a few years ago, but I was already so far along in my studies there, I stayed and finished my degree. But now I'm home and I hope to fill in the gaps in my education." There, he'd said it. How would Churchill react? He was half American himself, perhaps he would understand.

"Those damnable laws were foolish from the start," he said, scowling and waving his hand. "Argued against them in the Commons until I was blue in the face. Didn't help. But tell me: do you know anything about these blasted coil guns?"

"Sir? Yes, sir, a bit. They use an electromagnetic field to accelerate a projectile to high speed. They have range and striking power far in excess of conventional artillery."

"Yes, that part's been explained to me. It's the detailed working of the things which elude me. As I'm sure you know, we've been putting the things into some of our warships, but there are always these technical issues. How can I make decisions about things I don't understand? Jacky Fisher, the First Sea Lord, is always so keen about new things, but

48

sometimes his enthusiasm outweighs his good sense. But it's hard for me to keep him in check about things when I can't argue from a position of knowledge."

"I can see how that would be difficult, sir. I'm not an expert on the coil guns, you understand, but perhaps I could help you."

"That would be splendid! I've had scientists and engineers come talk to me, of course, but they are all these old, scratchy fellows who talk in that strange language of theirs. Perhaps a younger man, such as yourself could do a better job."

"I'd be happy to try, sir."

"Excellent! I'll have someone get in touch with you and we'll arrange a meeting. Oh, here comes the lieutenant, I must be off. A pleasure meeting you, Professor." Churchill got up from his bench and went off with Wildman-Lushington. Lindemann watched them get into one of the aircraft and after a short delay, take off.

Normally, Lindemann would have been badly put out to be forced to wait like this, but meeting Churchill made it well worthwhile. Careers were often dependent upon who you knew and at the moment there were few people more worth knowing than Winston Churchill.

* * * * *

Lindemann came back for lessons for a few more weeks before the weather turned too bad, but he did not encounter Churchill again, which was disappointing. Perhaps the First Lord had finally soloed. His own lessons were proceeding well. He had a natural feel for flying and his instructor was full of compliments for him. Working with the Advisory Committee for Aeronautics, he had developed a theory on the causes and remedies for an aircraft caught in a spin and he wanted to test it out. Wildman-Lushington and every other pilot he talked to seemed to feel that a spin was an almost certain death sentence, but he felt otherwise. Still, he needed to become much better at flying before he could try anything so daring.

His normal activities with the Advisory Committee were mostly routine; reading papers and reports from other researchers and distilling them down to summaries which Lord Rayleigh, the president of the committee, and the other ranking members could understand and present to their own boss — who happened to be Prime Minister Asquith.

But he only worked for the Committee part time. His actual employer was the National Physical Laboratory. It had been conceived originally as a way to bring scientific knowledge to bear practically upon everyday industrial and commercial life. But the first Martian invasion had seen it converted almost instantly into the government's official program to unlock the secrets of the captured Martian technology. It was an effort with the highest possible priority and it drew on all the best minds of the Empire.

As a teenager, he'd dreamed of joining the Laboratory and he'd devoted all his energies to mastering the sciences he'd need to qualify. His German heritage and the strict government policies of the time had barred him from the most direct path there, but a long detour through Berlin had finally led him back to his dream.

It had not turned out quite as he'd hoped.

He told himself that he was doing important work, but it really did not seem that way most of the time. He had a small office in Bushy House, the former abode of William IV, in Teddington, in the western part of London. He, with several assistants, had nearly unlimited access to pieces of Martian equipment. All the treasures he had dreamed about were his to tinker with. It should have been perfect...

He'd had visions of working alongside the giants in British physics, like Rutherford and Crookes, and helping them make the great breakthroughs which would allow them to understand the Martian machines. In his own daydreams, of course, he saw himself as the one to make the breakthroughs. Rutherford and the others would hail him as their worthy successor as Britain's top physicist, and the rewards and acclaim would follow. A Nobel Prize, a knighthood, perhaps an earldom down the line. Oh yes, a pleasant dream to be sure.

So far, unfortunately, none of it had come true. He hadn't even met Rutherford face to face and his immediate boss was a man named William Eccles who was only a few years older than himself. Eccles was a pleasant enough fellow, but wasn't especially well known and didn't have the influence to have his team assigned to the really interesting projects — the ones which were leading to new devices and weapons which could be actually built and employed.

As a result, Lindemann had been given puzzles to solve which had already passed through the hands of the 'great men' — who had failed to solve them. For that was the sad fact: even after more than ten years, the vast majority of the Martian technology was still as much of a mystery as it had been on the very first day. Their captured machines had been disassembled, every piece photographed, weighed, measured, converted to mechanical drawings, and cataloged. And while it had been possible to deduce *what* many of the devices did, it had rarely proved possible to discover *how* they did it. In most cases it had proved impossible to get the devices to work at all.

There had been a few exceptions, the most notable being the Martians' primary weapon, the heat ray. Supplied with sufficient power, it was possible to get them to fire. It had proved a simple puzzle — even the Americans had figured it out—but as for how the device worked... no one knew. It had also proved impossible to duplicate the ray weapons. Certain vital components had been created using methods unknown to human science and while it was possible to discern what they were made of, the process by which the alloys were forged continued to defy analysis.

This was also true of the Martians' marvelous electrical wire. It had the property of conducting current with no resistance whatsoever. This was a remarkable capability with a multitude of applications, but no one had any idea how it was done. Just recently a Dutch physicist had proved that even ordinary materials, like copper, could be made to behave in this fashion, but only at extremely low temperatures. The Martian wire did it at room temperatures. Even though the chemical composition of the wire could be determined, the method of its creation was unknown and all attempts to duplicate it had failed.

So, the British had been reduced to using what devices they had captured intact. Twenty of the original heat rays were now emplaced as part of the defenses of London, although trying to power them all at once would have required nearly the total electrical generating capacity of the entire city. Four more had been mounted on navy warships which had steam turbines large enough to provide the needed power. The rest had been sacrificed to the analysis teams. Tens of thousands of miles of the precious wire had been salvaged, too. The Martians' power storage devices each held huge quantities of it. The wire had been used on the military's coil guns and also on miniature radio transmitters, but until the second invasion, there had been no way to acquire more.

That was changing now. Even though the Martians had overrun half the world, they had been beaten now and again and more of their wrecked machines were falling into human hands all the time. There were several facilities in the south of England working full time to process the salvaged equipment.

What this meant for Lindemann was that instead of working with other great physicists and making grand discoveries, he was sitting in his office, or the workshop, day after day trying to make sense of things which made no sense to anyone.

Two months after his meeting with Churchill, shortly after New Years, he started another day as he started almost every other: with a visit to the workshop in hopes of finding inspiration. It was a cold, blustery day and he clutched his work coat around him as he hurried down the gravel path to the large brick structure. He let himself inside and walked down to the particular section where his project was situated, rubbing his hands together to warm them up. The building was heated, but not nearly well enough.

His area had a wood and wire fence around it and inside, an entire Martian tripod machine, rising forty feet high, almost to the building's rafters. It ought to have been the best prize in the entire world to work on, but after months, Lindemenn was growing to hate it. The thing towered there, mocking him and his inability to unlock its secrets. The machine was almost completely enclosed with scaffolding and many of its exterior plates had been removed, but it was still imposing.

He was surprised to find the gate in the enclosure unlocked and standing open. Two people were inside. He knew they wasn't his assistants as he'd left them back at the main building so who...?

"Ah, there you are Freddy," said one of them, spying him.

It was Eccles, of course, no one else around here dared to call him 'Freddy'.

"Good morning, *Bill*," he replied. "You're up bright and early. What brings you here?"

"I've got someone I'd like you to meet," he said, gesturing to the other person there with him. He was a young man with a long nose, a large forehead and a shock of very dark hair which was already receding. "This is Jimmy Chadwick. He just graduated from Victoria University of Manchester. He's going to be working with you for a while."

"Really?" said Lindemann.

"Yes, he's just started here and I thought you could show him the ropes and get him up to speed."

"I see. And he'll be working... with me?" *Not for me?* He wasn't sure he liked the sound of that.

"Yes, Rutherford isn't sure exactly where Jimmy will best fit in, so we intend to rotate him around a bit. We'll start him with you and see what happens. All right?"

"Certainly."

"Good, good. Well, carry on." Eccles nodded to both of them and then left.

Lindemann stared at Chadwick and Chadwick stared back. Eventually Chadwick spoke: "I look forward to working with you, Professor."

"Victoria University, eh?" replied Lindemann.

"Yes, sir. I did my final work under Rutherford, we were developing a means of quantifying the radiation given off from different samples of Radium. The paper is going to be published next year."

Lindemann flinched. This young pup had worked directly with Rutherford? Lindemann still hadn't even met the man yet! But that explained what Chadwick was doing here. Some pet of Rutherford's; he'd have to treat him with kid gloves.

"It's really something, isn't it, sir?" said Chadwick leaning back and looking up at the Martian machine.

"Yes, yes it is."

"Mr. Eccles said that you were working on the control system. Can you tell me about that, sir?"

"Uh, well, yes, I suppose I can. We may as well go up to the cockpit. Follow me — and be careful where you step."

The cockpit, or control cabin as some called it, was in the machine's head, all the way at the top. He led Chadwick up a series of ladders from level to level of the scaffolding. "I understand that the Martians don't use wheels or gears or even fixed pivots at the joints, is that right?" Chadwick asked, pointing to the curious 'hip' joint of one of the legs. All the cover panels there had been removed, revealing the mechanism beneath.

"Yes, that's true, but then that's true for most living creatures here on earth. The joints are an amazingly intricate series of small metal plates which can slide over each other in different directions, all contained in a sort of elastic sheath. The actual motion is provided by bundles of fibers which can contract just like a muscle when a current is passed through them. Here, watch." He climbed around onto a different platform to where one of the machine's arms had been partially disassembled and some power leads had been attached. He flipped a few switches and then slowly tuned the knob on a rheostat. The arm twitched and then gradually rose. He reduced the current and it lowered back down to where it was before. Chadwick was gaping.

"That's amazing, sir!"

"Just a parlor trick, Mr. Chadwick. No more amazing than using an electric current to make a severed frog's leg move — and just about as useful."

"But you can control their machine, sir. From what Mr. Eccles was saying it sounded like you couldn't, but you can."

"No, Mr. Chadwick, I *cannot* control their machines."

"But..."

"Follow me," said Lindemann, climbing higher. Up another ladder and then onto the platform surrounding the machine's head. Here a large section of the machine's skin had been removed allowing easy access to the control cabin.

"Watch your head," he cautioned. "The Martians are a lot shorter than we are." Indeed, the only way to access the control station was to wriggle forward on their bellies. Lindemann sometimes thought that perhaps the reason the senior researchers had given up on this was because it was so uncomfortable. He didn't have any trouble with it and Chadwick eagerly squirmed in beside him. "Here we are," he said.

Chadwick looked around, his face growing more puzzled by the second. "But... but where are the controls?"

Lindemann gestured to two small rods extending up from a console in front of them. The rods were about six inches long and an inch thick. They were made of some black substance, but they were covered with hundreds of small gold metal dots. "There they are."

Chadwick tentatively reached out to touch them. Lightly at first, but then he took a firmer grip and tried to move them. They wouldn't. "They don't move?"

"No. They are fixed in place. They aren't like the wheel of a ship or an automobile, or the control yoke of an aircraft. Controlling the machine doesn't depend on some physical manipulation of the rods."

"I... I was expecting switches and levers and dials and gauges and such."

"Well, there aren't any. If there were, that would make our job so much simpler. Actually, I take that back, there are some switches down inside the machine, but they are main cut-off switches for the power supply. Probably for maintenance or emergency shut-downs."

"So how does it work?"

"That is the grand question. Those little gold pads on the rods are made of their resistance-free metal. The standing theory is that somehow the Martian is able to transmit its orders to the machine in a fashion similar to how an animal's nervous system would function. We have found dead Martians in wrecked machines with their tendrils still wrapped around the rods. We think the pads in the rods functioned like neurons and transmit impulses from the Martian to the machine. Dissection of Martian corpses by some of the top biological scientists has determined that there is a high concentration of what appeared to be neurons in their tentacles. The conclusion is that the machines acted like an extension of the Martians' own bodies."

"That's amazing!" said Chadwick.

"Yes, but also damn frustrating for us. If there were switches and levers and such, we could just try them and see what happens. But here, we don't even know where to start. We've tried sending weak electrical pulses into the pads of the rods, but with no effect. The problem seems more like a biological one than mechanical. How do we simulate Martian brain impulses when we know neither the code nor the language? I've tried to familiarize myself with the subject of brain structure and nervous systems, reading the works of the experts, men like Muller, von Helmoltz, and Ramon y Cajal, but I've not come up with anything useful." He didn't add that Eccles was gently hinting that perhaps it was time to submit a final report and move on to something else. Lindemann would be happy to see the last of this puzzle, but he hated to have to report a failure.

"Yes, yes, I can see how frustrating this must be," said Chadwick. "Even if you could figure out how to send signals through the control rods, it would probably all be gibberish to the machines at the other end. It would be like an English ship captain shouting commands down the voice pipe to an engine room crewed entirely by Chinese. Even if they could hear him, they wouldn't know what he wanted."

"Yes, exactly. Good analogy, that."

"But if we cannot use their control system, might it be possible to substitute one of our own?"

"We've done that with their heat rays, and you saw what I could do with this machine's arm. But simply switching something on isn't the same as controlling it."

"No, that's true, but what if we..."

Chadwick then spent a half hour suggesting things which had already been tried before. Lindemann explained why his ideas wouldn't work as patiently as he could, but he was getting rather tired of it when a sudden shout from down below caught their attention

"Professor Lindemann, are you up there?"

Lindemann, happy for the interruption, wormed his way back out of the cockpit and saw that one of his assistants was on the floor below him. "Yes, what is it?"

"Special delivery for you, Professor. Came by motorcycle courier." The man hesitated. "Uh, he said he would wait for a reply."

"All right, I'll come down." He made his way down the ladders and took an envelope the man held out.

Lindemann's eyebrows went up when he spotted the seal of the Admiralty on the envelope. Churchill? Who else did he know there? Who else there knew of him? He quickly opened the envelope and pulled out the contents. It was a single sheet, from the office of the First Lord, inviting him to attend a staff meeting at Admiralty House at two o'clock, two days hence. It was signed by an Edward Marsh, 'at the direction of' Churchill. He read it twice, in hopes of squeezing any additional information from the stubborn paper, but that was all there was. He snatched a blank sheet from a workbench and hastily penned a note acknowledging receipt of the message and assuring his eager attendance. He folded it, put it in another envelope, addressed it to the First Lord and gave it to his assistant to run it back to the waiting courier.

Lindemann went to the door of the workshop and watched the man scurry down the path. In the distance there was a motorcycle and rider waiting there. As he looked, his assistant handed the envelope to the rider, who placed it in a satchel and motored off.

"Something interesting, sir?" asked Chadwick, who had come up behind him.

"I hope so, Mr. Chadwick, I surely hope so."

For the next two days, Lindemann found it very difficult to concentrate on his work. Instead of staring at the Martian control mechanisms, he prowled Bushy House, digging up everything he could on the subject of coil guns, convinced that Churchill would want to talk about them. Chadwick was a bit of nuisance, but he found odd jobs to keep him busy. Fortunately, Eccles gave him no difficulty about leaving work early to attend the meeting.

In fact, he barely came to work at all that day. After only an hour or so at his desk, he slipped off and returned to his apartment in Brentford to bathe and dress. The generous allowance his father granted, along with his salary from the Laboratory, allowed him to dress like a proper gentleman, even though he did not employ an actual valet. He vacillated a bit over exactly which suit to wear, but eventually decided on sober gray trousers and vest with a vertical pinstripe, white shirt, black cravat, a slightly darker gray jacket, and a light gray top hat with black band. He recalled that in photos he'd seen of Churchill, he rarely wore spats, so Lindemann dispensed with those. A gold watch and chain completed the ensemble. He hesitated a moment on whether to carry a walking stick, but finally decided against it. A young, healthy man carrying a stick seemed like an affectation—and if he didn't carry one, he wouldn't have to figure out what to do with it once he got there.

He hired a cab to make the trip to Admiralty House, which was about six miles from Brentford. The early January weather was brisk, but warmer than normal for that time of year, so he dispensed with an overcoat. The streets were moderately crowded, but mostly with civilians. During the periods of alert when Mars came into opposition with Earth and a new wave of cylinders could be expected, there would be soldiers everywhere, but in the intervals—like now—the army was less numerous.

Admiralty House was a four-story structure of yellow brick built in the Georgian style. Its three broad bays faced Whitehall and its entrance was on the corner of Ripley Courtyard. The rear of the large structure was on the Horse Guards Parade, beyond which was Downing Street where the Prime Minister's home was situated. That side of the building had been heavily damaged during the first invasion and had been largely rebuilt. The workmen had done a fine job, but you could see where the new met the old.

Lindemann, in fear of being late, had arrived very early and spent the next hour strolling about the neighborhood, dodging snow flurries and taking care not to get any dirt on his fine suit. This wasn't easy because with London's thousands of factories working around the clock, everything had a fine layer of coal soot on it. The air was thick with the stuff, making him cough. He pondered whether the humans were unwittingly creating their own version of the Martians' poisonous black dust weapon and using it on themselves.

Finally, it was time and he presented himself to the Royal Marine sentry at the doors of Admiralty House, showed him his letter of invitation, and was ushered inside. He had mentally prepared himself to have to ask someone where he should go in the large building since the invitation had not given any details, so he was much surprised to find Churchill right there in the foyer.

He was engaged in an animated discussion with another man, shorter and stouter than himself, and considerably older. But despite his age, the other man was waving his arms around and speaking loudly and forcefully. "Winston, it doesn't matter a damn what *kind* of guns we have! The only thing which matters is hitting the damn target! Gunnery! Gunnery! Gunnery! Hit them before that can hit us!"

Churchill appeared to be mustering a response when he glanced up and saw Lindemann. He smiled and took the other man by the arm and turned him around. "Ah, Jacky, here's the fellow I was telling you about. Professor Lindemann, so good of you to join us." He stepped forward and extended his hand. Lindemann had never liked the unsanitary custom, but there was no choice here. He grasped Churchill's hand and shook it.

"Honored to be here, sir."

"Jacky, this is Professor Lindemann of the National Physical Laboratory. Professor, I imagine you recognize our First Sea Lord?"

Now Lindemann did recognize the man, but he had to force himself not to flinch away. Admiral Sir John Arbuthnot Fisher, Baron Fisher, GBC, OM, GCVO, the First Sea Lord, was a legend, perhaps the second most famous admiral in British history, behind only Nelson, himself. Despite the fact that he had never commanded a fleet in combat, he had left his mark on the navy and generations of sailors, like no one before him. Now seventy, he was still in the thick of things, helping direct the navy's actions against the Martians.

Photographs of Fisher that Lindemann had seen had always seemed a bit... off. There was something very odd about the man's eyes. But now, seeing him in the flesh; flesh that had a decidedly yellowish tinge, along with those Mongoloid eyes, why the man looked like a bloody Chinaman! Lindemann had always been uncomfortable around other races and he tried to avoid them whenever possible. But there was no avoiding Lord Fisher.

"Uh, very pleased to meet, you, sir."

Fisher frowned. "So you're the scientist fellow Winston's been going on about? Hope you can add something useful to the circus today." He did not offer his hand and Lindemann was grateful.

"I'm sure he will, Jacky," said Churchill. "But look at the time, we'd better be along." He steered them toward the grand staircase at the far end of the foyer and they went up, only slowing their pace slightly to match the elderly Fisher. On the second floor they went into a large meeting room which had tall windows looking out on to the Horse Guards Parade, although today there were drapes nearly covering them. The room was sumptuously appointed and there was a huge octagonal table in the center of it. A map of the world nearly covered the wall opposite the windows. It had hundreds of pins stuck in it, each with a small colored label.

There were a dozen other men in the room, about half in uniform and the rest in civilian clothing. Churchill did not attempt to introduce them all, but did present Lindemann to the assembly, calling him 'my new science advisor'. Lindemann nodded to the men, but his attention was focused on the First Lord. *My Science Advisor!* Did he really mean that

Churchill called the meeting to order and they all took seats. Lindemann noted with interest that the higher-ranking men had a whole side of the octagon to themselves, while the lower ranking ones had to double up. He found himself sitting next to the Third Sea Lord, Rear Admiral Charles Briggs. A half-dozen junior officers stood around the periphery ready to supply their seniors whatever they needed, be it refreshments or information.

The meeting began and Lindemann quickly became totally lost in the technical navy reports which followed. Reports on new ships under construction, ships in repair yards, ships taking on supplies, men training to man the new ships, officers being promoted or transferred to command those ships; the amount of information flowing across the table was enormous. The Royal Navy was a vast organization, but he had never appreciated just how vast until now. Hundreds of ships and thousands upon thousands of men scattered across the globe and they were all directed from this room. A thrill passed through him at the thought that he had been invited here. But to do what?

After an hour or so there was a short break and Lindemann accepted a cup of tea and then had to awkwardly ask one of the junior officers where the facilities were located. But they were soon back at the table again and Churchill said: "Now gentlemen, I want to get your opinion on the matter of these coil guns." Lindemann immediately came to attention. "As you know, after we figured out the properties of the Martian wire, we realized we could build coil guns with it. So, we built some. A few hundred smaller ones for the army and a few dozen larger ones for the navy. But we only had a limited amount of the stuff and no way to make any more.

"But now, thanks to successes in India and Egypt, we have access to a new supply. Teams of brave men are salvaging the wrecks of the Martian machines wherever they can get to them and sending the useful materials back home. We can now build coil guns again, although we are also finding new uses for the wire, too, so the supply is limited and somewhat dependent on the fortunes of war. The question is now who gets the wire? Naturally, we would like the navy to get its fair share, but K of K is demanding virtually all of it for the army."

There was a rumble around the table. Lindemann blinked in confusion for a second, and then realized that 'K of K' was Lord Kitchener. 'Kitchener of Khartoum', Field Marshal and Secretary of State for War, a general every bit as legendary as Admiral Fisher was with the navy; the most famous and admired military commander since Wellington.

The rumble grew to a shout when Fisher rose to his feet and flung his arms in the air. "All? All for the army? Is he mad? He cannot be allowed to get away with this! Winston, we must stop the bounder!"

"I know, Jacky, I know," said Churchill, making calming motions with his hands. "The Prime Minister has promised we will get a fair share. But we need to give him an honest appraisal of just what our fair share should be..."

"Half! At least half! The honor of the Fleet is at stake!"

"I know how you feel, but we have to be realistic here. The army is facing the Martians on a dozen fronts every day. The navy is helping them wherever we can, but only when the Martians get close enough to the water to come within range."

"If we had the wire to make bigger coil guns, we could hit them a hundred miles from the sea! Farther!" Lord Fisher's face was turning red and Lindemann was afraid the old man was going to have a stroke. But no one else in the room seemed concerned. Indeed, a few were rolling their eyes. Did he do this at every meeting?

"Well, that's something we need to talk about and one of the reasons I've asked Professor Lindemann to join us. Kitchener has argued that scoring hits at such ranges is next to impossible and that it makes far more sense to make a larger number of smaller guns which the army can bring into effective range. Can we produce a counter-argument in favor of more and larger naval coil guns? Professor, do you have any thoughts?"

All eyes turned to Lindemann and he felt like he was sitting in the sights of a coil gun right at that moment. What to say? It was clear what Churchill and Fisher, and probably all the others at the table, wanted, but could he give it to them? Field Marshal Kitchener's argument was a strong one. The Martians fought on land and sea power could only be brought to bear if they got too near the ocean. The army, on the other hand, could go where the Martians were. It probably made sense to give the army the lion's share of the wire. But if he said that, it would disappoint Churchill and probably enrage Fisher and it would be highly unlikely that he'd ever be invited to another meeting.

And he very much wanted to be invited to more meetings. Despite his lack of understanding of naval matters, this was a place where *things happened.* This was one of the primary centers of power in the Empire and he desperately wanted to be a part of it, have a voice in it, contribute to it. So, naval coil guns… He'd looked over the technical specifications carefully, but he had not given much thought to the tactics of using them. What advantages did they have over army coil guns? He thought furiously.

"Professor?" prompted the First Lord.

"Uh, yes. Well, there are a number of factors concerning the coil guns which need to be considered. First is the, uh, unprecedented velocity of the projectiles. A standard chemically propelled projectile might have an initial velocity of from two thousand to as much as two thousand-five hundred feet per second. Coil guns can accelerate the projectile to much higher velocities; six, seven, even eight thousand feet per second. You must understand that I am no expert on gunnery, but one of the main factors in hitting a moving target is the time it takes the projectile to travel from the gun to the target. The longer the time, the less chance of a hit you will have. Conversely, the shorter the time, the greater the chance. With a coil gun, that time is going to be from one half, to as little as one third the time as a conventional projectile. It would seem to me then, that this would significantly increase the range of the weapon. Ships equipped with coil guns could hit targets at much greater ranges but with the same accuracy of conventional guns at shorter ranges."

"Yes!" cried Fisher, on his feet again. "Exactly what I've been saying! Exactly what I've been saying! This young man is a genius! Listen to him!" The First Sea Lord smiled at him and Lindemann found himself smiling back.

"But Admiral," said another officer, the second sea lord, Lindemann thought. "That fact holds true whether the gun is mounted on a ship or on the ground. Lord Kitchener can make the same argument in favor of giving him more coil guns. Fisher sputtered and looked back at Lindemann.

In the crosshairs again, he frantically tried to assemble an argument in seconds which he normally would have spent days perfecting. "Uh, well, another factor we need to consider is the size of the projectile, sir. The standard coil guns currently in use by the army fire a very small projectile weighing only two pounds. It is so small it carries no bursting charge at all. It relies on the enormous kinetic energy its velocity gives it to smash through the Martian armor and destroy their machines through impact alone. While it has proved effective, it must score a direct hit to have any effect. The coil guns built so far by the navy are somewhat larger, firing a twelve pound projectile, I believe, and do carry a small bursting charge, but still so small as to not be of much effect unless it too, scores a direct hit." He swallowed, resisted the urge to wipe the beads of sweat on his brow, the room suddenly seemed very hot, and continued.

"But there is no theoretical upper limit to the size of a coil gun projectile, any more than there is with conventional artillery. We could, in theory, build coil guns which would have the same sort of bursting charge as current large naval guns, but keeping the unprecedented range of the coil gun. Such projectiles have proven capable of doing heavy damage to Martian machines with even a near miss."

Fisher slammed his fist down on the table. "Yes!"

"And... uh, and such large coil guns would have a size and weight — and most importantly — power demands which would make them impractical to mount on anything other than a naval vessel." He finished the last sentence in a rush and then gasped for breath.

"There! There!" said Fisher in triumph. "Let K of K put that in his pipe and smoke it!"

Churchill was nodding and seemed satisfied. "Very good, thank you, Professor, you've been invaluable today. I will prepare a report for the Prime Minister presenting these very compelling arguments for our case."

"And don't forget to demand a decision on my new battlecruiser design," said Fisher. "And warn him about the bloody Germans, too! They're building dreadnoughts at a furious rate!"

"I will, Jacky, I will." Churchill stood up. "I think that wraps things up for the moment. I will see you all again next week." The others in the room, got up and moved away. Fisher strode off, head down, hands clasped behind his back, but Churchill lingered a bit and came over to Lindemann.

"That was extremely useful, Professor, you have my thanks."

"I was glad to be of service, sir. And I'm at your service any time you might need me."

"Good, good, I was hoping that would be the case. Please come to our next meeting. Oh, and are you free for dinner next Tuesday? I was hoping we could have a bit of a chat."

"Sir? Yes, certainly, sir. I'd be honored." Honored and eager. This was exactly what he'd been hoping for.

"Excellent. I have a few ideas I'd like to run by you."

"I, uh, on any particular topic, sir? I can... I can be of more help if I have the time to prepare."

"Of course, of course. Preparation is the key, always. As for my idea, well, despite your excellent reasoning today, the fact remains that we can only get at the bloody Martians when they venture too near the coast. And truthfully, it isn't going to matter much if 'too near' is twenty miles or fifty, we still can't reach inland far enough. We need a way to project our power farther ashore."

"I can see that, sir."

"Ah, but can you see how? I've gotten word that the Americans have started work on some sort of giant land-ship. A battleship on wheels or something like that. I've talked to a few men and they think the idea is ridiculous, but I'm not so sure. By God, they thought the idea for the tanks was ridiculous when I brought it back from Australia and look where we are now: tanks are our most effective land weapon! So I want to pursue this and I'd be grateful if you can help me with the technical details."

"I'd be happy to, sir," replied Lindemann, his mind already working on the problem.

"Good, good! See you on Tuesday."

"Yes, sir. Oh, can we get more information on what the Americans are doing? Do we have any observers over there?"

"Observers? God in Heaven, yes, we have observers. Everyone has observers. Us, the French, the Germans, the Russians, Italians, Japanese, you name it. Observers watching everything — including the other observers. But we do have some people over there in America. I'll see what they can do."

Chapter Five

Washington, DC, May, 1912

"**A**h, Major Bridges, good to see you. You come highly recommended to us."

Major George Tom Molesworth Bridges stood at attention before the desk of Colonel Lloyd Ellington, His Majesty's Military Attaché to the United States. "Thank you, sir," he replied. "Most kind of you to say so."

"Not at all, not at all; stand easy, Major." Ellington glanced down at a dossier on his desk and paged through it. "Let's see... Newton Abbot College, Royal Military Academy at Woolwhich... Royal Artillery... saw action in South Africa against the Boers... Instructor at the Cavalry School, transfers to 4th Hussars... action in Afghanistan against the Martians... wounded. Lucky man, not many wounded against the Martians."

"Yes, sir." Bridges grimaced at the memory. Technically, he had not been *wounded* by the Martians, he'd broken his damn arm flinging himself into a ditch to avoid being *killed* by the Martians.

"Returns to England for convalescence..." continued Ellington. "Military attaché to the Low Countries and Scandinavia... requests transfer... comes to the United States... my predecessor attaches you to the American 1st Cavalry Division... and now you are here. I read your report, by the by. First rate stuff there."

"Thank you, sir. The Americans are doing some interesting things with their cavalry and with using aircraft in conjunction. We can learn some things from them."

"Yes, the War Secretary agrees. In fact, that's why I've called for you. We want you to learn some more."

Bridges stiffened. "I... had been promised some leave at home, sir."

Ellington frowned. "Needs of the service come first, I shouldn't have to tell you that."

"Of course not, sir. Where am I going now?"

"South. Not exactly sure where. The Yanks have built some sort of gigantic war machines. Land ironclads they are calling them."

"I think I saw something in a newspaper about them," said Bridges.

"Yes, there was quite a to-do about them when the first six left Philadelphia last month, headed for the Mississippi. That seemed to wake up the people back home and now they want you to join up with them. We've gotten permission from the Americans. Last word was they would be stopping in Charleston to refuel. Perhaps you can take a train and catch them there. If you miss them, try one of the Gulf ports. Shouldn't be too hard to find the great things. Find 'em, get aboard, look and learn. Clear?"

"Yes, sir. Uh, for how long?"

"Until you don't think you can learn anything more, or until you are recalled." He rummaged through some papers on his desk. "I'll be expecting regular reports."

"Yes, sir, I understand."

"Good, that's all, carry on." Bridges saluted and took his leave.

The British legation in Washington was a rambling collection of buildings built on Connecticut Avenue in the 1870s in the Second Empire style. It had been perfectly adequate in those quiet times, but these days, with the whole world at war, it was far, far too small. There had been talk of constructing a new and larger compound, but with every construction firm on the continent tied up with essential military work, it had proved impossible.

There were people working at desks in the hallways and tucked into corners and alcoves. Nearly every person, except for the ambassador himself, was forced to find living space outside of the legation, and with the situation being similar in most of the other legations, housing anywhere near Embassy Row could not be had for love or money. Bridges was staying in a rather run-down inn eight blocks away.

Washington was a pleasant enough city, but not in late May. The heat and humidity was already stifling. Bridges was no stranger to such conditions; it had been even worse in India, but he was still sweating beneath his uniform and was fairly soaked by the time he reached his room. He quickly changed out of the uniform into much more comfortable civilian clothes.

He opened up his luggage and spread his belonging out on the bed and looked them over. If he was going to be on the move again, he was going to have to pare things down a bit. He missed Eames, his old batman, but he'd been killed in the same fight where Bridges had broken his arm. Afterwards, he'd been on the observer missions and had not gotten another man to look after his kit. He'd shared a man with an American officer while he was with their cavalry. He wasn't sure what opportunities for a servant this new assignment would provide.

By the time the landlady rang the dinner bell, he had compressed his possessions down to a couple of valises which he could carry himself. The rest he'd package up and the embassy could ship them home. He went downstairs to join the other guests in the dining room. Many of them were from embassies in the city and the polyglot uproar made him think of Babel. The woman, a formidable matron named Mertz, took it all in stride while she and several serving girls set out the meal.

When they were all seated, Mrs. Mertz apologized for the quality of the food, complaining about the shortages and high prices due to the war. Bridges felt there was no reason to apologize. Food rationing had been in effect in England for several years now, with the main suppliers in America and Canada no longer able to meet their own needs, let alone export anything. The Martians had invaded in spots well away from the big cities and that meant an awful lot of agricultural land was now occupied by the invaders. England was squeezing by somehow, but in many places, packed with refugees, there was serious want and sometimes outright famine. In that light Washington wasn't doing badly at all.

After the meal he sought out the landlady. "Mrs. Mertz, would you happen to have a train schedule about?"

"Why certainly, Major," she replied. "With all the people coming and going I always make sure I have an up to date one on hand." She went over to the mantelpiece and pulled out a folded paper from behind the clock. "Here it is. Oh, I hope you aren't leaving already?"

"I'm afraid so. A day or two and I'll be on my way."

"Back to England?"

"No, south. Charleston."

"Oh, I hear that's a lovely city. But whatever will you be doing there?

"Just a rendezvous. I expect I'll be heading out west, to the Mississippi Line. Tennessee, maybe."

"I hear there's fighting out there!"

"Well, there is no fighting in Tennessee, the last I heard, but close by."

"Oh, do be careful!"

"I intend to be, madam, I intend to be."

* * * * *

June 1912, Somewhere above Thrace

Captain Erich Serno stared down from an observation window in the LZ-15 as it cruised over the rugged Greek countryside. Or at least he assumed it was Greece. Surely the route from Vienna to Constantinople must pass over Greece somewhere along the way?

Or maybe not. Considering the ungodly mess in the Balkans these days, who could tell what anything was anymore? He noticed a black cloud in the distance and knew that it was probably another burning village. He'd seen a lot of those today. But it wasn't Martians who were doing the burning. No, it was other humans. Serno shook his head in disgust.

The Earth had been invaded. Alien monsters had overrun half the planet, slaughtered millions, devastated cities, and were bent on turning humanity into food animals, but some people could not put old hatreds and old ambitions aside.

The Ottoman Empire, already falling to pieces even before the Martians arrived, was in more dire straits now. It's holdings in North Africa were entirely gone, either overrun by the Martians, or seized by European powers. Arabia was almost completely under the invaders' control and they were pushing northward into Iraq, Syria and Turkey.

So now, when every human should be rallying to the common defense, the Serbs, Greeks, and Bulgarians, ancient enemies and subjects of the Turks, decided it was the perfect opportunity to throw the Mohammedans out of Europe! Instead of sending their forces to help hold back the aliens, they stabbed their neighbor in the back. Did the fools think that if the Martians crushed the Turks, they would stop at the Bosporus? Serno didn't know what they thought—or if they thought at all.

Of course, this nonsense had been going on for a long time—decades before the Martians arrived. The Serbs had won their independence in the 1860s but had not been satisfied with the territory they were given. They dreamed of a 'Greater Serbia'. But Serbia could only become greater at the expense of its neighbors and this meant either the Ottomans, or the Austro-Hungarians. Austria, allies of Germany, did not want to see a strong Serbia due to the large number of ethnic Serbs inside their borders. But they couldn't subjugate the Serbs because Russia sympathized with its Slavic brethren—and they had their own ambitions in the area. The other European powers did not want to see the Russians expanding into Ottoman territory and hoped to preserve the status quo. Throw in Albanians, Montenegrins, Greeks, Macedonians, and God knew who else, all wanting their freedom and a slice of the pie and you had a pressure cooker waiting to explode.

It *had* exploded from time to time, but somehow, each time, outside parties had been able to use threats, promises, and treaties to stuff it all back in the pot again.

But this most recent explosion was different. The Serbs and Bulgarians either didn't realize or didn't care that their great protector, Russia, was itself in deadly peril and in no shape to threaten to send aid to their Slavic friends in the Balkan. Austria had had enough, and the Kaiser had had enough, too. An Austrian army, aided by a German corps, had taken Belgrade and was moving south, crushing everything in its path. The railroad to Constantinople would be re-opened and kept open so that aid could reach there.

What form that aid would take was still being debated, Serno, knew. Sending whole armies into Asia Minor to aid the Turks would be an enormous and logistically difficult operation. Risky, too, since with Russia teetering on the brink of collapse, Germany and Austria needed to protect their eastern borders. So the aid might be limited to equipment and the advisors to show the Turks how to use it.

That part of the program was already under way and that was why Erich Serno was travelling to Constantinople. He was a pilot, a member of Aircraft Company 2, and he was being sent to help the Turks create their own air force. He pulled the orders out of his tunic pocket and read them for the hundredth time.

Imperial General Staff Headquarters
Berlin

April 18th, 1912

Upon receipt of these orders Leutnant Erich Serno shall travel to Constantinople by the fastest means possible. Upon arrival he will report to General Liman von Sanders and provide all assistance possible in the development of a Turkish force of military aircraft. Lieutenant Serno is promoted to the rank of captain, effective immediately.

It was signed by some staff officer Serno had never heard of, but all the authorizations were in place and there was nothing to be done but go. The promotion was welcome, but he had no idea what he would face once he was there. He'd heard that some aircraft, along with ground crews and support equipment had been shipped to Turkey, but he didn't know exactly where they were. He'd also heard frightening things about the chaos in the Turkish military. Add in the fact that he didn't speak a word of the language and he wondered what sort of a nightmare he was walking into.

Aside from what a failure might do to his career, he did not want to waste time—or his life—in some futile effort. He wanted to fight Martians. Any man with a shred of honor should be fighting the Martians these days. He was more than a little ashamed that of all the great powers, Germany had, perhaps, made the least contribution in this great war. Oh yes, the Kaiser had sent several small expeditions to South America, mostly to create safe havens for the large numbers of German citizens there. But they were strictly defensive measures and employed a miniscule number of soldiers. Germany's huge and powerful military was mostly standing idle at home.

Granted that it wasn't easy for that army to get at the Martians. Currently there wasn't a single Martian within a thousand kilometers of Berlin. The closest ones were rampaging around the Ukraine and slowly moving west as the Russian army collapsed. It seemed to Serno that that was the most logical place to commit Germany's might. True, the Russian rail system would be hard pressed to transport and supply German armies that far east, but wouldn't it be better to fight the Martians on Russian ground than wait until they reached Germany's borders? His own home and family were in Darmstadt, even further from the danger, but unless the aliens were defeated even they might be threatened someday.

Tired of sitting, Serno got up and stretched and walked up and down the aisle in the zeppelin's passenger compartment. The LZ-15 was a military airship, but it could transport a few dozen passengers in addition to its normal crew. Most of the other seats were occupied, some by men in uniform and some by people in civilian dress; diplomats, he supposed. His cousin was in the diplomatic corps and he'd told him that this was some sort of golden age for German diplomacy. With its vast, mostly unemployed army, and powerful industrial base, Germany had much it could offer—or withhold—and this gave it a lot of leverage. It was a role that England had once held, but the English were heavily engaged on many fronts in their far-flung empire. They had far less to offer prospective allies these days and Germany had moved into the vacuum. Serno wondered just what Germany was getting out of this deal to help the Ottomans? The Kaiser was a great man, but there was no doubt he was hugely ambitious, he would not be giving this aid for nothing.

At the rear of the compartment he encountered an ensign, one of the airship's crew, passing through. "About three more hours, sir," he said. "We should be in Constantinople by four o'clock." Serno nodded, turned so the man could squeeze past, and then after a few more minutes, returned to his seat and watched the troubled land below.

As promised, a few hours later, the mountainous terrain started leveling out. But the airship, if anything, was gaining altitude. Shortly afterward, Serno saw why. They were passing over the front lines between the Turkish and Serbo-Bulgarian armies. He'd been told that the fighting there had nearly stopped, with the Serbs and Bulgars pulled away to face the Austro-German forces rolling down from the north. But obviously the zeppelin's captain was taking no chances that some angry Serb might take a shot at the passing airship. Serno looked down and could see the trenches, gun emplacements, and supply dumps, but there did not appear to be any fighting going on here. At a hundred kilometers an hour, the area was quickly left behind.

In a surprisingly short time one of the other passengers called out that he could see Constantinople ahead. Serno stuck his head out the window and, squinting against the wind, looked forward. Sure enough, he could see the city in the distance. From looking at maps he knew that the Serbs and Bulgarians had driven close to the city, but it had not really registered just how close. Were it not for the Austro-German intervention, they might well have taken the city.

Now over friendly territory (at least he hoped it was friendly) the airship began to descend. The city was located on a peninsula of land. To the south was the Sea of Marmora, to the northeast was the so-called Golden Horn, a body of water which met the sea where it joined with the narrow Bosporus coming down from the Black Sea. Protected on three sides by water and on the fourth by massive walls, the city had been the capital of the Byzantine Empire for a thousand years until the Mohammedans had finally taken it in the 1400's.

Serno could see some of the remains of those walls, although they were surrounded with more modern structures as the city grew in the only direction it could grow. The place wasn't as large as Berlin or Vienna, but he could feel the age of it, even from a thousand meters. Most of the streets looked narrow with the buildings crammed close together, but there were a few more open spaces where there were palaces or mosques, their needle-like minarets pointing skyward. He spotted what he though was the famous Hagia Sofia with its domed roof, although there was actually a similar structure not far from it, and he wasn't sure which one was the mosque.

The zeppelin swept over the city and kept going. The aerodrome was actually on the Asian side of the Bosporus near the city of Skutari which hugged the coastline opposite Constantinople. The waters around the city were filled with ships and boats of all kinds, including some warships of substantial size. The Turks didn't have much of a navy, so these clearly must belong to someone else. He wondered who; with the world situation they could easily be British or French or Italian, or even German. Or Russian. The Russians had lost control of all their major ports on the Black Sea, except for in the Crimea, which was still holding out. Some Russian ships were probably finding refuge here. Or perhaps they were here taking on supplies to ship to the men defending in Crimea. He looked to the left, out the windows on the other side of the cabin and thought he could see the Black Sea through the haze.

Skutari wasn't nearly as large or grand as Constantinople, with no great walls, glittering palaces, or soaring mosques. It was low, drab, and as they got lower, he could see it was rather squalid. The outskirts appeared to be filled with tents and shacks and Serno suddenly realized that they were refugee camps. The Ottoman Empire was being squeezed between the Martians driving north and west and the Serbs and Bulgarians driving south and east. The people were fleeing the only place left to go: northern Turkey.

Crowds of those people were coming out of their tents to gawk at the airship. Many stood and pointed, but others seemed terrified and ran for cover. Well, with airship service to Constantinople a new thing, most had probably never even heard about the huge flying vehicles. They probably thought it was some sort of Martian machine.

Spreading panic in its wake, the LZ-15 approached the aerodrome. It was a flat field east of the city. A few hangars, sheds, and other buildings lined the edges of it and Serno spotted some aircraft parked near them. He recognized them as German models, so perhaps he had found his command.

There was a tall metal tower at the far end of the field and the zeppelin was lining itself up on it and dropping down to just a few dozen meters above the ground. A crowd of men was waiting to receive the lines which were lowered to them from the airship. They grabbed them and slowly pulled the LZ-15 to the tower. After a few minutes there was a bump and a loud clang indicating that the nose had been clamped to the tower and they were now securely moored.

One of the airship's officers announced that they would be ready to debark shortly, and everyone should get ready. Serno grabbed his leather briefcase from under his seat. He had several larger pieces of luggage which he hoped were still in the cargo hold. After a few minutes, a gangway was let down from the passenger compartment and they were allowed off. Serno had not been on the ground since the brief stop-over in Vienna, almost sixteen hours earlier and he was glad to be able to stretch his legs.

Several of the other passengers had been high-ranking officers and there were staff automobiles waiting for them and they quickly departed. The civilian diplomats also had waiting transport. Serno looked around in vain for anyone who might have been waiting for him. His orders said to report to General von Sanders, but where in all creation was, he supposed to find him?

Perhaps there would be someone he could ask over where he saw the aircraft parked. At the very least they must be connected to his command here. He went over to where men were unloading the baggage and found his two bags. Tucking his briefcase under his arm, he grabbed the bags and turned toward the hangars.

He had barely started walking when a motorcycle, roaring and backfiring loudly, appeared and came straight toward him. He stopped and the vehicle rolled to a halt a few meters away. It had a sidecar and was driven by a young man in a lieutenant's uniform. He had a leather flying cap and a pair of goggles. He jumped off the 'cycle and said: "Captain Serno?"

"Yes, that's me. Who are you?"

"Leutnant Wulzinger, sir, Carl Wulzinger. Sorry I'm late. Your airship arrived earlier than we'd expected."

"We had a nice tailwind most of the way. You're here to pick me up?"

"Yes, sir, I'm to take you to General von Sanders."

"I see," he said, relieved. "You're one of his aides?"

"I was, sir. Now I'm yours."

"What?"

"I've been assigned as your aide. Here, let me take those." He came forward and took Serno's luggage. "I think we can strap these on the back, sir." The two of them, working with a piece of rope, managed to get the bags tied to the rear of the sidecar. Wulzinger handed him a pair of goggles and invited him to take a seat.

"Where are we going?" asked Serno.

"The General's headquarters is in an old villa about fifteen kilometers north of here, sir. It used to be in the city, but I gather the general wanted to get away from all the politics there. Poisonous stuff, from what I've heard." Wulzinger stamped on the starter bar and the motorcycle roared to life.

With the noise, it was hard to hear and the pair found themselves shouting at each other. "How much flying experience do you have, Leutnant?"

"What? Oh, the helmet! No sir, I'm not a pilot. I just got one of these for driving the motorcycle. My hat kept coming off."

Serno could understand that; he had to use one hand to keep his own from flying away. "So you don't know anything about aircraft or training pilots?"

"I'm afraid not, sir. But I do speak the language here. The general thought you might find that useful."

"I surely will!" cried Serno sincerely. "I wondered how I was going to manage training the Turks."

"A few of their officers do speak German, and quite a few more know French. But the bulk of them only speak Turkish."

"And how did you come to learn that?"

"I seem to have a knack for languages, sir. But I was a university student before the war. Archeology. I've wanted to come to this part of the world since I was kid. Learning the language seemed a good idea."

"Well, it will certainly be helpful now. I'm going to have to rely on you, Leutnant."

"I'll do my best, sir."

They rode for a while without speaking as Wulzinger threaded his way through the narrow streets of Skutari. There were plenty of civilians, but many men in uniform as well. The look of the Turkish troops did not impress Serno. He couldn't imagine how they hoped to stand up to the Martians.

After a while, they left the built-up areas behind and went north along a dirt road that paralleled the Bosporus which was off to their left. Ships were making their way along the narrow waterway in both directions. Wulzinger may not have been a pilot, but he seemed to know how make a motorcycle nearly get off the ground. He opened up the throttle and they fairly flew along the bumpy and rutted road.

At that speed they reached their destination in just a few minutes. On a rise of ground overlooking the Bosporus there was a walled compound with a group of buildings inside. The largest one was not quite what Serno would have called a palace, but almost. It had once been a grand place with an elegant colonnaded front, tall narrow windows and even a small attached mosque with gilded dome. But it had clearly seen better days and was now sad and shabby with peeling paint and cracked or missing window glass. Nearly all of the gilding on the dome was peeled away.

But it surely was not abandoned. There were sentries at the gates, Turks, but they carried themselves like Germans and demanded Serno's papers before they would let him in. Wulzinger they seemed to know. There were men scurrying around the courtyard, parked staff cars, and tethered horses waiting for couriers. "Looks busy," commented Serno.

"Oh yes, sir, at all hours. The general always has a full head of steam. He takes his post here very seriously and is determined to whip the Turks into shape."

"Is he having much success?"

Wulzinger suppressed a smile and shrugged as he parked the motorcycle and swung himself off. "You'll have to ask the general that, sir." He stuck out his hand and helped Serno pull himself out of the cramped sidecar. "I'll have someone take your gear to your room. But I'm sure the general will want to see you right away, so if you'll follow me."

Serno brushed at his now dust-covered uniform and followed the leutnant into the building. The inside seemed in better shape than the outside and they walked past a beautiful pool with a small fountain, and up a grand staircase with mosaic walls. "Quite a place," he observed. "What was it originally?"

"The Sultan Selim III had it built back in the late Eighteenth Century. Like General von Sanders, he wanted a place away from the capital. Didn't save him, though, he was assassinated in 1807."

"You *are* the scholar."

"Was. Just a hobby now, I'm afraid."

The inside was as busy as the outside, although most of the men he saw now were in German uniforms. Glancing through open doors, he saw desks stacked with paper and people working at them.

"When I was first posted here," said Wulzinger, quietly, "I assumed we were here to teach the Turks *how to* fight. But it turns out what they really need to know is staff-work. When it comes to that, they have no clue."

"I see. How long have you been here?"

"Since last November, sir." He paused for a moment and then looked at Serno. "I sure wouldn't mind getting some leave at home."

"Maybe once the railroad is reopened, you'll be able to get some."

"That would be nice. Here we are, sir." They had reached a set of double doors which were also standing open. Inside, there was a large outer office with several desks, chairs, and numerous filing cabinets. Tall windows on the side walls let in the last of the afternoon light. An ornate circular candelabra hung down from the high ceiling. Its candles were unlit—missing in fact—but modern electric lights had been nailed up in various spots, unmindful of the damage done to the antique wood paneling. An elaborate archway at the rear led into another room.

A colonel was sitting at one of the desks, but Serno's eyes were drawn to the tall man leaning over him as they engaged in an animated discussion. He looked to be in his late 50s, trim and fit, although his cheeks and chin seemed strangely rounded and chubby above his tight, high collar. He had a thin, closely cropped moustache, gone mostly gray like the thinning hair on his head. When he turned at their entry, he fixed sharp, deep-set eyes on them. He wore the uniform of a general. Serno could only assume it was von Sanders.

"You Serno?" he snapped without any preamble.

"Uh, yes, sir." He came to attention and saluted.

"About time," replied the general, not bothering to return the salute. "Come with me." He turned and marched through the archway, leaving the colonel frozen at his desk in mid-sentence. Serno glanced at Wulzinger, who merely made a go-on gesture with his head. Serno hurried after the general, with Wulzinger close behind.

Through the archway was another office. It was as elaborately decorated as the rest of the place with a thick carpet on the floor and thin lace draperies on the windows. One entire wall was covered with a huge map of the Ottoman Empire, stretching from the Balkans in the north all the way down through Turkey and the Levant to the Arabian Peninsula in the south. Pins of many colors were stuck all over it. Serno couldn't help but notice the large number of red pins which occupied nearly all of Arabia and much of the Levant. The general went right to the map.

"Captain, we've got a hell of mess here. The Martians came down in the deserts of Arabia three years ago and the Turks had nothing close by to engage them. Same story as everywhere else in the world: they hit us where we weren't. But unlike most other areas, the Turks didn't even attempt to assemble a force to deal with them. They were all tied up with trouble in the Balkans and with Italy invading their holdings in North Africa. So they just ignored the Martians in Arabia and hoped they would go away. Obviously they didn't.

"In the spring of 1909 they came charging out of the deep desert and swept away all resistance. They quickly overran the whole peninsula from Kuwait to the Gulf of Aqaba and into parts of Palestine and Syria. All of the major cities and towns were destroyed and much of their population slaughtered. Medina, Yembo, Riyedh, and of course, Mecca. That drove the Mohammedans all over the region mad. For the next year, ragtag armies of religious zealots poured into Arabia to liberate their holy places. The fools had little better than muskets and swords. They were massacred, of course. The Ottoman government tried to rein them in, but it was hopeless."

Serno nodded his head. He'd read stories in the newspapers about this.

"It was shameful waste of manpower," continued the general. "Properly trained and armed, those men could have been the core of a useful army. Instead, most of their bravest men were killed to no purpose. When the initial hysteria died down, the Ottomans were able to recruit the survivors and some of them are doing good work now — or as good as their current system can allow.

"Since then the Martians have been quiet, we assume they are consolidating their conquests and building more of their fortresses. That's what they have done in the other regions they control. The pause has been a Godsend to us, but it can't possibly last. They are bound to attack again."

The general paused, sighed and shook his head. Serno was nearly certain that this must be von Sanders, but he wished someone had properly introduced them so he could be sure.

"It is our job, Captain, to try and whip the Ottoman Army into a shape which can resist them."

"I understand, sir."

"Do you? I doubt it," said the general with a snort. "I certainly didn't when I was first assigned here. Did you understand, Leutnant

Wulzinger?"

"Sir? No, sir. But I've been learning."

"Yes, that's all we can do: learn and do what we can." He turned and fixed his gaze on Serno. "You, Captain, are here to help the Turks create an air force, isn't that right?"

"Yes, sir."

"And what function do think that air force will be expected to serve?"

"Sir? Well, other militaries have developed aircraft and techniques for bombing the Martian fortresses, and for attacking their tripod machines on the battlefield in support of ground troops, but probably the main function for a Turkish air force—at least at first—would be..."

"Scouting!" snapped the general.

"Uh, yes, sir, reconnaissance."

"Exactly. Right now our biggest lack—aside from artillery, tanks, and machine guns—is knowledge about what the hell the Martians are doing out there. We do send out scouts, parties of Bedouins or other locals, slipping through the desert or landed on the coasts by ship, but many never return and even those that do can take weeks and months. If a major attack was brewing, we'd never know until it hit us. We need a better system than that. That is your mission, Captain, establish scouting squadrons and get them up and running as quickly as you can."

"Yes, sir, I'll do my best."

"See that you do." The general turned back to the map and tapped his finger on it near the little red flags. "We need to know what those devils are up to."

Chapter Six

Holdfast 14-3, Cycle 597,845.2

Kandanginar of Clan Patralvus hauled itself out of its travel chair and slumped down in front of the communication panel. An important conference would soon begin and as the third-most senior member of the clan on the target world and as the subcommander in charge of Holdfast 14-3 it would be included in the meeting.

It shifted itself into position with some difficulty. Despite being in its third body since reaching the target world, it still found the heavy gravity irksome and oppressive. There was no doubt that each succeeding body was adapting to the new environment, but it wondered if it would ever grow strong enough so this world's gravity felt normal. The buds, those born on the target world, seemed to be adapting much faster. Kandanginar was curious as to why that should be and would have liked to investigate the phenomenon. At its core, Kandanginar was a scientist. Unfortunately, with the needs of the continuing conflict with the prey-creatures, little scientific research could be devoted to such questions. All effort had to be directed to developing new weapons, mechanisms, and techniques to bring about final victory.

Victory still seemed a long way off.

It remembered the planning sessions prior to launching the great expedition to conquer this world. All were confident that a quick victory would be achieved over the primitive creatures who inhabited it. The first small expedition had been destroyed by the world's micro-organisms, but with proper precautions that danger could be overcome, and the larger organisms could be quickly subdued. A few cycles might be needed to establish control over so large a planet—even with three quarters of its surface covered by seas, there was still as much land area as on the entire Homeworld—but no one doubted that it would happen. A colony would be established, and the others could leave the dying Homeworld and come here. The superiority of the Race was unquestioned.

At first, it seemed as though the initial confidence was fully justified. The landings took place almost without incident. The transports were unloaded, the machines assembled, and when the time was right, the attacks were launched. On every front the resistance offered by the prey-creatures was weak and disorganized. Their armies, though large in number, carried weapons which were almost totally ineffective against the

Race's fighting machines. They did have some larger weapons capable of throwing explosive projectiles long distances which proved dangerous, but they were clumsy to move and could be easily destroyed. The Race's heat rays incinerated the prey-creatures wherever they were encountered.

Within a quarter cycle vast areas of the planet had been overrun. The central region of the largest land mass, Continent 1, was secured, all of Continent 2 except for the northern coast and a few coastal pockets and an area in the south, and all of Continent 4, except, again, a few isolated areas bordering the sea. The smallest continent, number 6, was the same. The southernmost continent, ice-covered number 5, had proven devoid of the intelligent prey-creatures and was taken with no resistance.

Only on Continent 3 had there been any significant resistance in the early stages. Clan Bajantus had suffered a humiliating defeat and was nearly wiped out by the prey creatures. Only help from a neighboring clan had allowed them to survive. At the time, few had placed any significance on the event and had dismissed it as an aberration.

Despite the enormous and unprecedented effort put into launching the invasion, only six hundred members of the Race had arrived on the target world in the first wave and so few could not hope to control, or even patrol, such enormous regions. A pause in the expansion was called for. New holdfasts were constructed, new buds were created, and new war machines built for them to use. This also allowed time for the next wave of transport vehicles to arrive. Reinforcements from the Homeworld would be launched each cycle as the planets came into opposition. Unfortunately, the prey-creatures had also made good use of the time given to them.

When the next stage of expansion began, unexpected resistance was encountered again and again. Not only had the prey-creatures gathered their huge numbers, but they had developed new weapons to equip them with. Self-propelled and armored vehicles now gave the clumsy projectile throwers mobility and some protection from the heat rays. Flying machines, something the Race had never employed on the Homeworld, gave the prey-creatures the ability to spy out the Race's movement, and even attack them at times. The formerly helpless individual warriors had been given explosives to use against the war machines, which made them far more dangerous. Strong fortresses had been constructed to impede movement and protect strategic points. Fleets of very powerful water-vessels made any operation near the coastlines dangerous. While many successes were accomplished, a shocking number of reverses and a few outright defeats had occurred. The expansion had slowed nearly to a halt.

The ability of the prey-creatures to adapt and innovate so quickly had come as an unpleasant surprise. The Race's knowledge was vast and its intellect unmatched, but change was... difficult. New ideas were slow to be accepted. They had to be evaluated, discussed, pondered… at length. That took time.

Time the colony did not have.

Kandanginar grasped the control rods with its manipulating tendrils and activated the communications screen. The image of Jakruvnar, the leader of Clan Patralvus on the target world appeared. It was in Hold-fast 14-1 and had ordered a conference of the senior clan members. Within moments all were linked in and Jakruvnar began.

"As you know, yesterday I attended a meeting of the Colonial Conclave and received orders for our clan in upcoming operations. I will now pass on those orders and entertain any discussion or suggestions. The Race will be launching a number of offensives on this planet soon, but the part to be undertaken by Clan Patralvus is straightforward.

"The goal for the upcoming cycles is to link the separate areas the Race controls into larger groups. Right now, we hold large areas, but they are isolated from each other which makes the transfer of resources and the coordination of military efforts difficult or impossible. We must remedy this. Our immediate task is to establish a direct link with the groups on Continent 2. Once that is complete, our combined forces will drive north to link up with the groups on the main part of Continent 1."

Kandanginar absorbed this and saw the wisdom in it. The great area of Continent 1 had been, for convenience, divided in a number of sub-continents. Subcontinent 1-1 was the westernmost regions where the population of the prey-creatures and their industry was very dense. So far, none of the Race's forces had reached that area—aside from the first, failed, expedition to a far western island off the coast of the mainland. Subcontinent 1-2 was a large peninsula jutting off the southern coast, shielded by an immense mountain range. It too, had not been subjugated, although there had been several failed attempts to penetrate the mountain barrier. Subcontinent 1-3 was the southeastern part of the continent. This area was densely populated, but also overgrown with thick vegetation which was difficult to penetrate. Finally, there was Subcontinent 1-4, another large peninsula extending from the southwestern part of the continent and in close proximity to Continent 2. It was a dry, desert land, which resembled the Homeworld in many ways, except for the very high temperatures, of course. Clan Patralvus' territory lay in this region, which put it closest to Continent 2, clearly they would play a major role in the upcoming operations.

The clan on the target world had been designated 'Group 14'. The invasion groups sometimes included members from more than one clan and were thus numbered rather than named. Group 14, consisting only of Clan Patralvus, held the southern region of Subcontinent 1-4, while Group

13, a combination of two clans, held the northern. The area assigned to Group 14 was a good one. Water could be found underground, or if necessary purified from the seas which bordered the area on three sides. The lack of precipitation was a good thing; reports from outer groups often mentioned the problems created by an overabundance of water, which seeped into holdfasts and made movement on the surface difficult, or sometimes impossible. No such problems had bothered Clan Patralvus.

Early surveys had also discovered an abundance of mineral resources, including the vital power metals, elements 90 and 92. Mining operations had commenced and a sufficient supply of raw materials for construction seemed assured.

The only resource which might grow scarce was food. While the target world teemed with life, the warm-blooded animals upon which the Race depended were much fewer in the arid regions of Group 14 than in other locations on the planet. At the time of the initial landing there had been more than enough, but as time passed, the intelligent prey-creatures had fled the region, often taking the non-intelligent ones with them. So far, attempts to raise non-intelligent animals in the holdfasts had not been successful and the gatherer groups had to range farther and farther to secure prey. It was not a crisis yet but might become one over time. Continent 2, to the southwest, had food animals in abundance, however, so establishing a direct connection would be an excellent thing.

"The only direct land connection between the continents lie to the northwest," continued Jakruvnar. We shall mount an offensive toward that junction along with Group 13. The groups on Continent 2 will attack toward that same area from their side. We shall crush the defenders between us and open up the connection."

"Commander," said Xlatanginoor, the commander of Holdfast 14-2, "the prey creatures have heavily fortified that region facing both us and the groups on Continent 2. We can expect serious losses if we launch a frontal attack."

"Yes, that is true, but there is no alternative route. We must coordinate our attack with the one from Continent 2 so the enemy cannot concentrate their reserves against either attack. It is true we can expect heavy losses, but so be it. We have our orders and they must be obeyed."

That was certainly true. Obedience was an integral part of the Race. Reproduction was accomplished by a budding process and the new individual had an instinctive and irresistible obedience to its progenitor and all related ancestors and offshoots in the clan. Orders from senior members had to be obeyed.

Normally.

A disturbing phenomena had been observed among the new members of the Race which had been budded on the target world. While they retained the absolute obedience to their progenitors and their seniors who were on this world at the time of their budding, they had no such obedience to those on the Homeworld. Even when those who normally would have commanded their obedience arrived later from the Homeworld, the link of obedience was not found. As long as their progenitors were present this did not pose a serious threat to the stability of the clan, but if those progenitors should be slain in battle, there was a danger of no longer being able to control whole groups. Still, there was no problem at the moment.

The discussion was proceeding and the battle force was being organized and points of attack discussed. The last wave of reinforcements from the Homeworld had also brought an artificial satellite which was now in orbit and able to transmit detailed images of the planet's surface. This was enormously useful, but the images which they had received of the intended target area were alarming. The fortified lines the enemy had built to protect the connection between the continents were truly formidable. There were tall walls with ditches in front of them which could prove impassible to the fighting machines. They were mostly constructed of a cast stone material which was highly resistant to the heat rays. Hundreds of the large projectile throwers had been mounted on the walls or behind them, and great numbers of the self-propelled armored gun vehicles were in reserve. Wherever the defenses were close to the sea, there were clusters of the dangerous water vessels. Attacking such defenses could prove extremely costly, perhaps more costly than the clan could afford.

Clan Paltravus on the target world had grown considerably from when it first arrived with a mere fifteen members. There were now nearly seven hundred, and when the next generation of buds matured, that number would grow to over a thousand. Unlike the primitive prey creatures, buds were born with a full set of basic abilities and could mature to a productive member in less than half a cycle. While not every member could be spared for battle, it would still be possible to field a very powerful force for the upcoming attack.

Still, the potential for serious loss was very high. And once the connection was opened, the combined groups were expected to quickly launch another attack far to the north. Would they have the strength left to undertake such a thing? Was there any alternative? Kandanginar's attention was drawn to the narrow bit of water which separated Subcontinent 1-4 from Continent 2 at its southwest tip. The two landmasses were only about ten *telequel* apart at that point and the prey creature defenses were not especially strong.

"Commander?"

"Yes, Kandanginar?" answered Jakruvnar. "You wish to comment?"

"Our orders were to open up a route of connection with the groups on Continent 2, correct? There was no specific order about what route we should take?"

"That is correct. No such specification was made since there is only one possible route."

"I submit that there is an alternate route which we should consider." It brought up the satellite map and put it on the display and indicated the region it meant. There was a lengthy silence from all the participants.

"There is no land connection," pointed out Xlatanginoor. "While the water there is not deep, many have often come to grief attempting to wade across substantial bodies of water. It would be a dangerous and unreliable connection."

"The prey creature water vessels also frequent the area," added Latabashti, a subordinate of Jakruvnar. "The connection there would be under constant threat of attack."

"I realize that," said Kandanginar, "but these difficulties can be overcome."

"How?" asked Xlatanginoor. "You are not suggesting we construct some sort of bridge across the water. That would be exceedingly vulnerable to enemy attack."

"No, I am not suggesting a route through or over the water, but rather under the water."

"A tunnel?" asked Jakruvnar.

"Yes, commander. Our excavation machines, the ones we use to build our holdfasts, are quite capable of cutting a tunnel of the size and distance required. If the groups in Continent 2 were to tunnel from their side and meet us in the middle, I estimate the tunnel could be completed in less than a hundred rotations of this planet."

"The ends of the tunnel could still be vulnerable," said Latabashti. "And if the prey creatures discovered the tunnel, they might even attempt to collapse it by exploding a very large device on the sea floor."

"This is true," said Kandanginar. "We would need to heavily fortify the terminuses of the tunnel. And I have another proposal as well. The prey creatures depend heavily on water transport. This narrow water passage sees a large amount of traffic. If we were to mount weapons on the shores and also on the island which sits in the passage, we might be able to deny them the use of it. This would not only safeguard the tunnel, but strike a blow against the enemy at the same time."

Jakruvnar waved several of its tendrils in interest. "This is a very clever proposal, Kandanginar. If we could bring about a junction of the continents without fighting a possibly ruinous battle it should certainly be considered. You are all aware of the very serious reverses recently suffered on Continent 3. Two powerful clans nearly wiped themselves out in a frontal attack against enemy fortifications. We want to suffer no such reverse here."

"You are gracious, commander," said Kandanginar. "Shall I draw up a detailed proposal?"

"Yes, do so at once. I will communicate with the groups on Continent 2 and see what their reaction is."

"As you command."

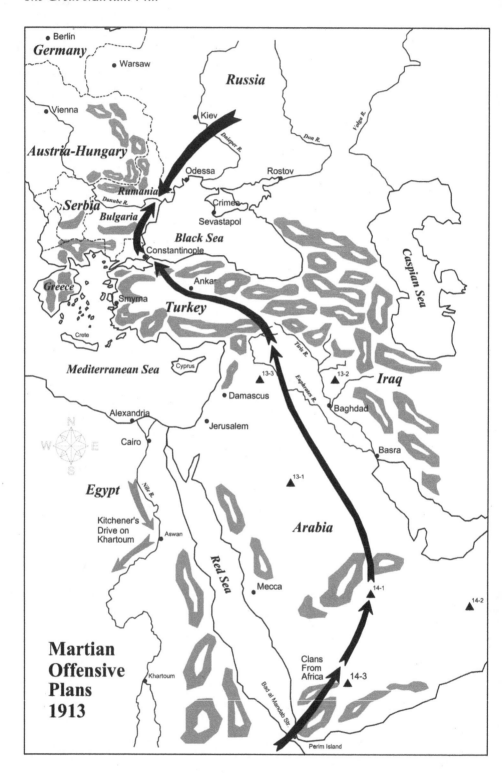

Martian Offensive Plans 1913

Chapter Seven

Aswan, Egypt, June, 1912

Harry Calloway gave a whoop and flung himself into the lake. It was shallow and he bounced off the silty bottom and sprang to his feet in the waist-deep water. The other officers of his company were close by. He'd deliberately splashed them and they responded with laughs and water splashed back at him.

They were in the lake behind the dam at Aswan. It was the largest masonry dam in the world and had been considered an engineering marvel when it had been completed in 1902. Apparently, it hadn't been marvelous enough though, because they had started work to make it even higher in 1907, but the work had not gotten far before the arrival of the Martians had put a stop to it. A lot of abandoned construction equipment was still in evidence. Harry was a bit surprised that the invaders had not destroyed the thing when they swept over the area. Perhaps they didn't know what it was.

It was back in human hands now.

The long campaign up the Nile had reached its first objective. The plan, which Ian McDonald had overheard back in November, had turned out to be a grand scheme by Field Marshal Kitchener to recapture the city of Khartoum in Sudan and liberate the fertile Nile valley. Some said it was just Kitchener trying to relive his great triumph against the Mahdists back in 1898, while others said it was a wise plan to drive back the Martians and incidentally help solve the great shortage of food in the region, by putting farmland along the river back into production. Harry didn't particularly care what the real reason was as long as they were hitting back against the invader instead of sitting on their arses back near Cairo.

Not that there had been much hitting back so far. The Martians did not occupy territory like human armies. They built fortresses in various locations and then maintained patrols around them with their war machines. They would attack anyone who got too close and they also scooped up people or other large animal which they apparently used as food. But they did not seem to pay much attention to intruders who kept their distance.

During their initial advances through Africa the Martians had destroyed cities and towns wherever they found them, but they had not built any fortresses very close to the Nile. So when Kitchener's offensive began they did not contest it. Even so, the advance had been very slow and methodical. Every twenty miles or so the army would stop and build a strong fortress to protect the line of communications and also to protect the swarms of people who hoped to resettle the Nile valley. It was only about 200 miles as the Nile flowed from their starting point to Aswan, but it had taken half a year to get there. Considering it was another thousand miles to Khartoum, Harry didn't like to think about how long he might spend on this odyssey.

"Well, this is certainly a treat," said Lieutenant Miller. "I didn't think I'd ever get all the dust off of me."

"Miss that piped-in water we had back on the line, Paul?" asked Captain Berwick.

"Not really, sir. I'd rather we were doing something, despite the hardship." That got a mutter of approval from all of them.

"I just wish that the doing involved killing more Martians," said MacDonald. "Hardly seen hide nor hair of the bastards this whole trip."

"Well, the mere fact that we haven't says a lot," said Burford Sampson.

"Like what?"

"Well, you remember what it was like back home. We huddled in our fortifications and didn't dare venture out with more than cavalry patrols. When we were on the line back near Cairo it seemed like more of the same. But here we are, away from our forts and the Martians haven't attacked us. Why not?"

"What do you think, Burf?" asked Harry. "You must have an opinion, or you wouldn't have said anything."

Sampson shrugged. "If I had to guess I'd say it was because we are a powerful enough force the blighters don't want to tangle with us. That's a damn comforting thought if you ask me."

"I suppose," admitted Miller. "But we do have a lot of the gunboats and monitors with us here on the river. The Martians don't like those. I'm not sure I'd feel so confident if we had to leave them behind."

"Fortunately, there is a ship lock for the dam, so they can follow us all the way to the second cataract," said Berwick.

"Is that where we're headed next, sir?" asked Harry.

"I haven't been told, but I imagine we'll be stopping here for a while so they can fortify the place. I saw barges full of construction supplies on the river yesterday."

"That seems to be the strategy, now, isn't it?" said Sampson. "Grab some territory and fortify the hell out of it and then move on and grab some more. Damn slow way to fight a war."

"Not much choice, Burf," replied the captain. "Their bloody machines give the Martians so much mobility, they can dash through any gap we leave in our lines and raise holy hell with our rear. They don't seem to depend on supply lines, but we do. If they can cut them, they can do to us what they did to the Americans back in 1910 and what they're doing to the Russians right now."

"So we sit here for a while."

"I imagine so."

They sat for a week, watching the engineers laying out the lines for the new fortress and the native laborers unloading the boats and barges carrying the materials for it. But then they had a surprise when several of those boats unloaded a batch of replacements. There were nearly a thousand of them and a hundred were for the 15th New Castle Battalion. It was an even greater surprise when all of them turned out to be Australians.

The battalion had been understrength when they escaped from Sydney, B Company in particular, was only about the size of a platoon. They'd gotten a few men when the remains of the shattered 11th Battalion had been broken up and distributed among the other units. But even sitting on the defense line had seen a small but steady trickle of losses as men got sick or injured. Harry's own platoon was down eight men. There had been a lot of speculation about what might happen in the long run. Would they get replacements who weren't Australians? If they did, how long before the battalion was Australian in name only? If they didn't get replacements, would they start combining battalions to keep them up to strength? If that happened how long before there was nothing left of the original units? It was an unsettling thought. Harry knew that every man in the battalion—all the battalions—was hoping that someday they would liberate their homeland. But what if there was no Australian army left? Would anyone still care enough to bother? Now it seemed like there might.

"Yes, they are all Aussies, like us," explained Captain Berwick when he gave them the news. "Most of 'em are damned young. They're recruiting them from the folks that got evacuated to New Zealand or Tasmania. When the boys come of age they're all mad to enlist. Seems like we'll have a steady flow of 'em now that they've got a system organized."

"Do they have any training, sir?" asked Sampson.

"I'm told they have set up training camps to give the lads the fundamentals. So, they'll know how to salute and march and shoot a rifle, but as for how to really fight the Martians, that will be up to us to teach them."

"We'll do our best, sir," said Harry.

When the men arrived, Harry had to agree that they did look awfully young. He might have only been twenty-four himself, but these boys were all still in their teens. Excited, eager, they were itching to fight Martians. They were disappointed when they heard that there had been no fighting so far on this campaign.

The men welcomed them warmly; there were few of the taunts or harassment that veterans sometimes inflicted on new men. For one thing, everyone was eager for news about the conditions in New Zealand and Tasmania. Most of them had family in those places and the mail service was still pretty sporadic. The reports they got from the replacements weren't terribly reassuring.

"It's pretty rough," said one boy named Kinney. "Most folks are still livin' in tents or lean-tos. They're buildin' dormitories usin' all the wood from the trees they're clearin' to make new farmland. But the lack of food is the worst thing. Never get enough to eat. Glad for these army rations, I can tell you!" Harry frowned when he heard that. The letters he'd gotten from his mother had been encouraging, but short on details about the day to day lives of her and his sisters.

"Everybody works," added Kinney. "Sunup to sundown and sometimes afterwards. The army is easy compared to that."

Five of the new men were assigned to his platoon and Harry made sure that the sergeants and corporals took good care of them and taught them the things they'd need to know if they did end up fighting Martians.

Two weeks later they were surprised to learn that they would be part of a large reconnaissance being sent out into the desert to the west. They were even more surprised when they learned they wouldn't have to march. "We'll ride like proper gentlemen," said Captain Berwick with a smile. "The ships have brought a few dozen of those new Raglan motorized carriers we've been hearing about. Enough for our battalion and several others. Get your men ready, we leave before dawn tomorrow."

After the months of dull routine, the men were eager to go, and they had no trouble getting them up and going in the chilly dark before dawn. Harry was still amazed at how cold it got at night. Or how clear; the stars were incredibly bright in the black sky. He could see the Milky Way with no trouble all, along some of the more familiar stars and constellations. He thought he could spot Mars. It seemed strange to be able to actually see the enemy's home, the place where all their woes were coming from. It was up there, in plain sight, but totally beyond reach. *Someday we'll have to find a way to get there. A way to hit them where they live.*

The men were all up, dressed, and equipped when the quiet was ripped away by the roar of engines approaching. Unlike the tanks Harry had fought alongside in Sydney, the Raglans, along with most of the other vehicles he'd seen in Egypt, were not powered by steam. They had petrol engines, which seemed a lot noisier. A British officer had explained that while steam had a few advantages, a steam engine used two pounds of water for every pound of fuel it consumed. In the desert, that just wasn't practical.

The carriers, about forty of them, rolled up to their camp and halted. They had caterpillar tracks, like the tanks, but no big guns. There was a compartment in the front for the driver and a machine gunner, but behind that was just a big armored box with seats and storage room. The roof of the box was in sections and had hinges so it could be folded back to give the men air. A light framework above held a canvas canopy to keep out the sun. Each vehicle could hold about a squad, so Harry's platoon boarded four of them. He and his platoon sergeant squeezed in with second squad which was still several men short.

When the battalion was loaded, the Raglans lurched into motion and headed west. The sun was just cracking the horizon behind them when they left the green strip bordering the river and entered the true desert. The temperature quickly rose, making Harry wonder if he'd just imagined the chill of the night. But the canopy kept the sun off of him and the breeze from their motion made the heat tolerable.

In the growing light, they saw they weren't alone. A second group of Raglans, presumably carrying another battalion, was angling in from the right to join them. Out in front was a screen of the outlandish 'unitanks' the British had developed. They looked like two huge pie plates that had been joined together at their rims. A flexible drive track went all the way around their edges and allowed them to zip along at a remarkable speed like a motorcycle wheel all on its own. Somehow the inside of the thing, where the two-man crew were, didn't spin, just the edge of it. There were two smaller wheels on struts sticking out of the sides and angled rearward to keep the things from falling over when they were moving slowly. Apparently, some sort of gyroscopic force kept them upright while moving fast—and they could move quite fast. A small automatic cannon was mounted on each side of the contraptions. They were fascinating to watch, but Harry had to wonder how practical they really were. The fact that the army seemed to be replacing them with more conventional armored cars indicated that he wasn't the only one.

Looking behind, he saw more vehicles following them. With all the dust being thrown up he couldn't see them too clearly. They might be tanks, or maybe some sort of vehicle-mounted artillery, he couldn't tell.

The Raglans could move at a pretty good clip, maybe fifteen or even twenty miles an hour. But they were noisy as hell and conversations could only be carried on by shouting, so Harry and his men were content to ride and watch.

After about an hour, Sergeant Milroy leaned over to him and shouted, "Any idea where we're going, sir?"

Harry shook his head. "Just a recon of some sort. I understand there is a Martian fortress about a hundred miles west of the river. Maybe we're

91

gonna pay them a visit."

"I've heard they can be mighty rude to visitors, sir. Hope the generals know what they're about."

"Yeah, me, too. Oh, look, we've got some air support." A flicker of motion had caught Harry's eye. There was a flight of four or five aeroplanes a few miles to their left. They were coming up from behind and slowly passing them.

Milroy frowned. "If they just want to take a look at the blighters, those planes can surely do it quicker 'n easier than us. Why're they sending this circus along?"

"Maybe we're supposed to do more than just look."

They rode on for several more hours, going deeper and deeper into the vast Sahara. After a while, Harry got out his field glasses and scanned the horizon, looking for... well, looking for anything. He saw dunes and he saw patches of scrub brush and from time to time he saw flights of aircraft. But no Martians. Well, that was a good thing, he supposed. He wasn't thrilled with the idea of fighting them out in the open like this. The armor on the Raglans wasn't thick enough to stop a heat ray for long. He surely hoped the generals weren't thinking they could roll right up to a tripod, casually dismount and then attack it.

As they drove on, he saw more and more patches of that damned red weed. It was a lichen-like growth that the Martians had brought with them. Whether accidentally or on purpose was a matter of debate, but the stuff started growing anywhere the Martians established a base. Left unchecked, it would grow and grow, choking out the native plants. By the time Harry and the others had been driven out of Australia, scouts were reporting that huge swaths of the interior had been covered by it. If they ever did manage to retake their homeland it might take generations to clean it all out and make it livable again.

He swept his glasses across the other batch of Raglans and paused. He focused on them as well as the lurching motion of his own carrier would allow and looked closer.

"See something, sir? asked Milroy.

"No... well, no. That's odd."

"What?"

"It doesn't look like there's anyone in that other batch of carriers."

"Maybe all the blokes are just sitting down. Ya wouldn't be able to see 'em then."

"All of them? Look at our boys; half of them hanging out, trying to catch the breeze, or just looking around. Why would all of them be out of sight?"

Milroy shrugged. "Dunno, sir."

Harry kept his eyes on the other carriers after that, but mile after mile he saw no one, except occasionally the gunners popping their heads out of their hatch.

Around mid-day, the vehicles altered course slightly and Harry thought he could see something in the distance. He got out his glasses again. "It looks like some aircraft are landed up ahead."

"Just one?" asked Milroy.

"No, there are a bunch. Three... four... eight... a dozen, at least."

"Wonder what that's all about."

"Yeah, me, too. Well, we're headed right for them, so I guess we'll find out."

They were further away than he'd realized, so it took another twenty minutes to get there, but as they closed, Harry could see that there were crewmen sitting in the shade under the wings of the craft and a few more were up and waving.. The unitanks got there well ahead of everyone else and they rolled to a stop near the planes and their own crews debarked. The rest of the force followed and parked themselves in a circle around the aircraft. The engines switched off and the silence that followed left Harry's ears ringing.

The word came that they could dismount and stretch their legs and eat their rations, but they were strictly warned not to light any fires. A few men grumbled about making tea, but then the Raglan crews opened up the engine compartments of their vehicles and showed the men how they could heat their water on the tops of the engines, which were hot as stoves by this time. Some of the airmen were hauling cans of petrol out of the unoccupied carriers and filling the fuel tanks of their machines, which appeared to be two-seater de Havillands.

Then Harry saw that the other vehicles which had been following them were motorized artillery. *Longbows* they were called, and they had a twenty-five-pounder gun mounted on a chassis very similar to the Raglans. There were eight of them.

He made sure his men were taking care of themselves and then drifted over to where the other company officers were gathered. He sidled up to Sampson. "So, what's going on, Burf?"

"Cattle rustling, from what I hear."

"Beg your pardon?"

"The colonel's gonna brief us all in a few minutes, look, here he comes." Indeed, Colonel Anderson and most of the other officers in the battalion were approaching. He had them all gather round, while he climbed up on the lower deck of one of the Raglans.

"Morning, gentlemen," he said. "Although it's nearly afternoon now, isn't it? We've got an interesting job today. Another sixty or seventy miles in that direction," he pointed to the west, "there's a Martian fortress. Now, we aren't going to try and tangle with that today, so don't worry. But about thirty miles closer, there is a bit of an oasis. Air reconnaissance, and some close in scouting work has told us that the bloody Martians are running what amounts to a cattle ranch at this place." The colonel's expression, which was usually light-hearted, darkened. "They are raising camels, sheep, goats — and people for their dinner tables there."

As the meaning of the colonel's words sank in there was some murmuring and cursing among the officers. There was no longer any doubt that the invaders ate people and would send their tripods out to scoop up any unlucky souls they could find. But a ranch?

"There are at least a few hundred people at this place. It is usually guarded by a half-dozen tripods or so, but being pretty close to their fortress, there are probably others which could show up quickly if there was trouble. We are also advised that the entire area is surrounded by a sort of fence. We've heard about these before, but this will be the first time we've encountered them ourselves. It's not like a usual fence. There is just a large fence post every hundred yards or so. Anything that tries to pass between them gets shot by a small heat ray. It's deadly to an unprotected person, but our vehicles should be able to smash down the fence posts and break open the barrier with no problem.

"Our job is to destroy or drive off the guarding tripods and then rescue the people there and scatter the other animals. You may have noticed those empty Raglans that came with us. They'll carry the freed prisoners. Obviously, we need to be quick. Get in, do the job, and then get out before more of those blighters can show up to ruin our party. Clear?"

"Yes, sir," answered some of the officers.

"We are hoping that the armored vehicles and aircraft will handle most of the sentries. Our primary task will be to round up the prisoners and get them loaded. But be prepared to fight, if you have to. There's no telling what condition these people are in or how they'll react to our arrival. Naturally, we can't expect any of them to speak the King's English. If they'll come on their own, fine, but if they're afraid of us or our vehicles or are confused, don't waste time trying to persuade them. Just grab 'em and go. Once we start loading we'll need people in each of the Raglans to keep order, so I'm afraid your squads are going to be split up."

"Sir?" said Burford Sampson. "Thirty miles ain't very far for those buggers. If they sent reinforcements from their fortress as soon as we attack, they could be on us in less than an hour."

"That's true and there's one more piece to this operation I haven't told you about yet," said Anderson. "Recently, the army activated a new force called the Deep Desert Group, the DDG. They're a band of specially trained chaps equipped with fast vehicles and heavy weapons. Their task is to go places where regular forces can't and raise hell wherever they can. I understand it was some of them who discovered the true nature of this 'ranch' we'll be raiding. About a hundred of them are going to raise some hell on the opposite side of the Martian fortress before we go into action. Hopefully that will draw off any forces the Martian have which could bother us. Understand?"

"Yes, sir," said Sampson. "Sounds like this has been thought out."

"Well, we can hope so," said Anderson, some of his usual good humor showing through. He pulled out his watch and checked it. "And those DDG chaps will be making their move very shortly. All right, gentlemen, stand your men to, let them know what we're about, and get them loaded up. We'll be moving out, shortly."

Harry assembled his platoon and gave them the news. Some seemed skeptical, but most appeared excited about actually hitting the Martians rather than waiting to be hit by them. Only a few minutes later they heard a whistle blowing and the engines on the vehicles started up. The aircraft crewmen sprang to their machines and prepared them for take off.

There was a short delay when one of the Raglans refused to start. Rather than try to fix it, it was abandoned, and its crew and passengers transferred to one of the spares. Then the whole task force set out, angling a bit to the southwest. Harry kept looking back and was eventually rewarded to see the flying machines lift into the air one by one. He expected them to fly in the same direction as the ground forces, but instead they just circled until they were lost to sight.

After looking ahead with his glasses and seeing nothing, he finally sat down and looked over the squad in his carrier. The men seemed eager and excited, although several — including one of the replacements — looked more nervous than excited. All of them were checking and rechecking their weapons; rifle, ammunition, and their Mills bombs. But one of them...

"What the devil do you have there?" shouted Harry. The man had a contraption which looked for all the world like some medieval crossbow.

The man looked up at him and then grinned sheepishly. He said something in reply, but Harry couldn't hear him above the engine noise. "What?"

"Oh, don't mind him, sir," said the squad corporal. "Greene, there is our mad inventor. Buildin' secret weapons to win the war."

Intrigued, Harry got up and moved over next to the man. "What's it supposed to do, private?"

"Uh, it's supposed to shoot one of the Mills bombs, sir. Get it to stick from a distance so we don't hafta walk right up to those buggers. Built it meself, sir. I made the bow part outta a leaf spring from a wrecked lorry.

The stock is a bit o' pipe I got when they were repairin' the pipeline that carried water to the camps. The rest I just sort of found." The man seemed delighted with the contraption.

"Does it work?"

The man's face fell. "Well, not yet, sir. Oh, it'll toss the bomb a good ways, seventy or eighty yards at least. But the bomb tumbles. Doesn't go rightway forward, so it won't stick when it hits. Still working on it, sir."

"You aren't using up bombs testing this thing, are you?" demanded Harry, aghast. The Mills bombs were still in short supply.

"Oh, no sir! Wouldn't do that. The blokes at the supply depot had a few with just the casings and no explosives inside. Not sure what they were for, but I got a few of them, and just filled 'em with sand to get the weight right. But don't worry, sir, I'll get this thing working yet."

Harry picked it up and saw that it weighed as much as a rifle. If it worked it might be useful, he supposed. "When you do, make sure you show me, eh?"

"Yes, sir!"

He went back to his seat. Sergeant Milroy leaned over and said, "We've got some crazy blokes in this outfit, don't we, sir?"

"Yeah, good men, though. I wouldn't trade 'em for the world."

"God's truth, sir."

It was the truth. Harry had never had any really close friends while growing up and his family was an impossible distance away, but after living and fighting alongside these men for years, they were as close as any friend or family he could imagine. When they got hurt, or died, it hurt him just as it had when his father died. Maybe more.

So far he'd been lucky and the deaths had come in ones or twos and separated by a bit of time. But he knew that it could get so much worse. Look at B Company, nearly wiped out in the fighting around Sydney. He couldn't imagine what it must be like for the survivors. Sampson and Miller and MacDonald were like big brothers to him. One bad day and he could lose all of them. The thought chilled him, despite the blazing heat inside the Raglan.

After a while longer, the little hatch between the passenger compartment and the place the driver and gunner sat slid open. The gunner shouted through: "We're getting close! Time to button up!"

"What?"

"The canopy! Take it down and get the roof closed up! Can't go into a fight like you are now!"

"Oh! All right." He turned to his men. "Take down that canopy."

The troops went to work and after a bit of puzzling managed to figure out how to take the canopy down. A whoop of laughter made Harry look out just in time to see the canopy on one of the other Raglans go flying as the passengers lost their grip on it in the wind. His men avoided that calamity and got the thing folded up and stowed. The metal doors covering the top were in multiple section but were still very heavy. One by one they clanged into place. Harry had them hold off on the one closest to the front so he could look out again. There were a number of small firing slits along the sides of the vehicle, but they were so narrow nothing much could be seen through them.

In the distance he thought he could glimpse something green. The oasis? The dust being kicked up by the unitanks made it hard to see, but after a while he was certain he could spot some palm trees. But were there any Martians? Their tripods were tall enough that he should be able to see them from quite a distance. At the moment he couldn't see any.

They rumbled closer and began to pass some patches of dry grass and clumps of thorny bushes. A series of sharp cracks came to his ears above the noise of the vehicles. After a moment he realized that must be the small cannons on the unitanks. In the distance he could see some flashes of red light through the dust. Still no sign of tripods, though. Could that be the fencing the colonel had spoken of?

Closer and closer and the firing was getting louder, but still no tripods. What were they shooting at? Finally, the wind dispersed enough of the dust that he could see. The unitanks were circling around and shooting at what must be the posts for the fence. They looked to be ten or twelve feet high and maybe two feet thick; ridiculously difficult targets for the speeding unitanks. As he watched, one of the leading Raglans passed between two of the posts, and a narrow heat ray shot out from one of them, the beam barely visible in the bright sunshine, splashed off the armored side of the vehicle with no noticeable effect. Another Raglan altered its course and drove straight at the nearest post. When it was a dozen yards away, another ray shot out of it, right at the oncoming carrier, but it didn't falter and a moment later, crashed right into the post, snapping it off, and crushing it under its tracks.

"Ha!" shouted Harry. "Nothing to it!" The fence was enough to stop unarmed people, but clearly wasn't designed to deal with armored vehicles.

The other drivers must have seen it, because immediately the other Raglans started veering around and aiming themselves at the nearest fence posts. The driver of Harry's vehicle changed directions several times, but every time they were lined up on one, another carrier beat them to it. Within minutes, all the posts they could see were down and the task force moved on into the oasis.

They soon began seeing animals wandering around, grazing on vegetation, seemingly oblivious to the noise. Harry tried to spot people, but didn't see any. Were they hiding? After another few minutes, they went down a slope and in front of them were a few pools of open water and groves of date palms, and what looked to be cultivated gardens. Some rough huts and lean-tos were also in evidence. The Raglans rolled to a halt.

"All right, lads! Up and at 'em!" ordered Harry. The top panels were slammed open and the men scrambled over the sides.

"Where are the bloody Martians?" asked Sergeant Milroy, cradling his Lee-Enfield.

"Maybe the diversionary attack drew them all off. But let's not wait around for them to come back. Check those huts, there are supposed to be people here."

The battalion quickly dismounted and spread out. The unitanks sped off, scouting for the enemy. The battery of Longbows rolled up and took up firing positions. Looking back to the east, Harry saw that the aircraft were finally approaching.

The men fanned out in skirmish order and quickly began finding people. Some were in the huts, while others were hiding in the bushes or crouching in gullies. They were mostly dark-skinned Africans, but there were some Sudanese and Egyptians, too, from the looks of them. Men, women, and children; they were dressed in ragged clothing, or in the case of many of the children, nothing at all. They were clearly frightened by the Australians and their noisy machines.

But the men had their orders and they began herding the people toward the waiting Raglans. Some came along without a fuss, but others tried to hold back. A few children broke free and ran and the soldiers pelted after them, shouting. Those who did reach the carriers were very reluctant to enter them. The vehicles were open on top, but also had a small, and totally inadequate hatch at the rear. To the natives it must have looked like a dark mouth. When the men tried to drag them inside, some began to scream.

"I imagine after what they've been through, they're a bit leery about being stuffed into metal machines," said Burford Sampson, coming up alongside Harry.

"Yeah, you're right." Harry stepped forward and shouted to his men. "Load them in the top! Some of you get inside and help them up. Let them know there's nothing to fear!"

That worked a bit better, but some people continued to resist and more attempted to break free. "Like herding cats," said Sampson. Harry anxiously looked off to the west. He could hear some firing and explosions in that direction, how long did they have before the Martian showed up?

"Sir? Sir!" One of Harry's men, Corporal Higgins, approached, dragging one of the natives. "One of these here wogs can speak some English."

"What? Bring him here!"

The native was a tall, skinny fellow with a scraggly beard and a tattered robe. He looked elderly to Harry, with wrinkled skin like old leather. He came up and made an awkward bow.

"Lord, lord, your men say you are here to save us from the monsters, is this true?" His voice was heavily accented, but Harry could understand him.

"Yes! Yes, we are here to take you to safety. Can you..."

"Where? Where is safety?"

"Uh, off to the north, near Cairo."

"Cairo still stands?" asked the man, his face lighting up with hope.

"Uh sure, it's well defended..."

"Allah be praised! The monsters destroy everything. Some say nothing is left anywhere."

"That's not true. We've stopped the blighters cold and..."

"Harry, we don't have time for this," said Sampson. He took the man by the arm. "Look, we need to get you folks loaded up and out of here. Can you tell your friends they can trust us? Get them into the carriers?"

The man nodded. "Surely! Surely!" He began shouting in a language Harry didn't recognize. The other natives stopped their struggling and listened for a few moments. Then they began shouting and scrambling to get into the Raglans.

Sampson grinned. "Just need to know how to talk to the buggers."

Captain Berwick hurried up to them. "Where'd you dig him up?" indicating the native.

"He found us, sir," said Harry.

"Well get him in a carrier and take him around the oasis and see if he can call more people out of hiding. There are still dozens of them out there and we can't catch them one by one. You go with him, Harry."

"Yes, sir!" He took hold of the man. "Can you help get the others to come with us? We have to hurry."

The man nodded and Harry hustled him to a Raglan. He told the driver what he wanted and then loaded the man and himself aboard. Rather than get down inside the passenger compartment, they perched up on top the driver's cabin. "Hang on!"

The carrier lurched into motion and Harry had to grab the native to keep him from tumbling off. The driver went a few hundred yards and then halted. The man stood up and shouted out his message. A few people popped out of hiding and shouted back. The man said some more and pointed back to there the carriers were waiting. The people whooped and hurried off. The driver drove another hundred yards and the exercise was repeated.

A few people tried to drag along camels or goats, but Harry told the man to tell them to let them go. When some seemed reluctant, Harry said: "Tell them they will be given, food, clothing, a place to live, and new animals where we are going." He had no idea if any of that was true, but there was no time to argue. It seemed to do the trick and the people abandoned their livestock and hurried off.

The oasis was larger than he'd realized, and they kept finding more and more areas where there were huts or livestock and at each place more people would emerge from hiding. Some were very cleverly hidden, too. Had they invented ways to avoid being 'harvested' when the Martians came around? But this was all taking too long. Harry kept nervously scanning the horizon for tripods.

They finally found one.

Skirting around the edge of a grove of date palms, they met a trio of the unitanks going the opposite direction at top speed. Harry heard the familiar shriek of a heat ray and the last tank exploded in flames. "Turn around!" shouted Harry to the driver, but he needn't have bothered because the man was already doing it. The Raglan spun in place, the tracks moving in opposite directions. Harry dragged the native back into the dubious protection of the passenger compartment.

Looking back, he saw a single tripod emerge from behind the trees. It was a few hundred yards off, but that was much too close. It fired a shot at the two remaining unitanks, but they vanished into a gully before it could hit them. The Raglan wasn't nearly so speedy, but the driver curved his path around the edge of the palm grove and put the trees between them and the Martian.

"Head back to the others!" Harry cried through the open hatch.

"Where the bleedin' 'ell do you think I'm going?" the man shouted back.

The carrier bounced along as fast as it could go, but they were running out of cover and Harry groaned when he saw the tripod in pursuit. It had a clear shot at them and the thin armor on the Raglan wouldn't protect them for long. A moment later, the heat ray stabbed out, slicing off some of the trees and swinging toward them.

But then several small explosions blossomed on the face of the enemy machine and Harry heard the bark of the cannons mounted by the unitanks. He twisted his head around and saw that the two who had fled earlier were back to avenge their fallen comrade. The absurd things emerged from the gully, their weapons popping away.

The tripod turned its weapon toward them, but they zipped right past before it could be brought to bear, one daring madman actually passing between its legs. The Martian turned to follow them, and Harry's heart started beating again. The Raglan maneuvered around another palm grove the enemy was lost to sight.

Just then, several aircraft roared past at low altitude, heading toward the enemy. A few moments later he heard several loud explosions and then the whole world turned a bright, eye-searing blue. An enormous roar shook the Raglan and seconds later, bits of metal, branches, and entire tree trunks came raining down all around them.

They got it!

Sometimes, when a tripod was destroyed, the device which stored its power would blow up in a huge explosion. Harry had only seen it happen once, back at Sydney, but that must have been what happened here. He found himself grinning. Rescuing people was fine, but nothing was better than killing Martians! Only belatedly did he wonder if the aircraft or the unitanks had been caught in the explosion.

The carrier bounced along for a few hundred yards and then, with no warning, one of the deHavilands screamed past overhead. It was trailing smoke and its wings were in tatters. It clipped one of the date palms and cartwheeled along the ground, shattering into a thousand pieces.

Harry stared in horror but then shouted to the driver: "Stop! Stop!"

"What the 'ell for?" he shouted back.

"The pilots! The pilots might be alive!"

"Are you daft? Nobody could have survived that!"

"They probably saved our lives and I won't leave them behind if they're alive. Now stop, damn you!" He pulled out his Webley and stuck it through the little hatch and waved next to the man's head.

The driver swore an oath, but the Raglan creaked to a halt and Harry jumped out. To his surprise the native followed him. At first, he was afraid the driver was right. The remains of the aircraft were strewn for a hundred yards and there were hardly any pieces larger than a knapsack.

"I see any more of those blighters and I'm leavin' without you, lieutenant!" cried the driver.

After a minute he found one of the pilots, but he was dead. Very dead. He was about to turn back to the carrier when the native cried out. "Here, lord! This one is alive!" Harry hurried over to where the man was standing. A man in flying gear was lying there. He had blood on his face and his right arm was twisted at a bizarre angle and was clearly broken, but he was moving and groaning.

Harry waved his hand. "Bring the carrier over here! Hurry!" The Raglan's engine roared. He knelt down next to the flier and tried to see if anything else was obviously hurt. The legs and the other arm didn't look too bad. No way to tell if anything was broken inside him. The carrier rolled to a stop a few yards away and the gunner popped out to help.

"Jennings..." moaned the flier. '... my gunner..." he waved his good hand toward the scattered wreckage.

"Sorry, I'm afraid he's dead. Look, we need to get you out of here."

The three of them managed to pull the man inside through the rear hatch and lay him out on the floor. The Raglan surged into motion again and a few minutes later they were back where the others were waiting. Harry looked out trying to spot a medic.

"Well there you are," said Burford Sampson trotting over. "We heard the shooting and I was afraid we'd lost you."

"You almost did! Is there a medic about? We've got an injured flier in here."

"The surgeon is over there, looking over some of the natives." Sampson spun about and started shouting. After a minute Harry saw the battalion surgeon, Doc Webster as he was called by everyone, hastening over, carrying his kit.

"What have you got, Harry?" Doc was on a first name basis with everyone.

Harry opened his mouth to answer, but his words were drowned out by a roar as the Longbows fired off a salvo. He looked around trying to see what they were shooting at, but he couldn't see anything. Almost immediately, some of the higher-ranking officer began blowing whistles and waving their arms.

"Looks like we're pulling out, Harry, said Sampson. "See you later." He sprinted off toward his own carrier. Harry glanced around, trying to locate his own platoon, but vehicles were already moving away. He'd just have to stay here.

Harry explained about the injured flier to Doc Webster. The Raglan lurched into motion and joined the others, some of which were literally covered with rescued natives. They turned east, heading out into the desert, some of the unitanks driving livestock before them, through the gaps in the fence. The aircraft, which were wheeling overhead like vultures, straightened out and also flew east.

The surgeon called to him for help in getting the flier out of his gear so he could examine him. Due to the broken arm taking off the leather jacket all the pilots seemed to wear no matter the weather proved impossible without cutting it to shreds. The man feebly protested but didn't resist. His tunic went the same way, Harry noting the lieutenant's insignia on it as he sliced it off.

"What's your name, son?" asked Doc Webster.

"Dalton... David Dalton."

"Well, Dave, your arm is rather badly broken in at least two places. Does anything else hurt?"

"Bloody near everything…"

"Yes, I imagine, so, falling out of the sky and all. Can't see how you chaps bring yourselves to do it. I get giddy just standing on a chair. Now you lie still while I poke around a bit."

Dalton didn't appear to be in any immediate danger and Doc Webster had the situation in hand, so Harry stood up and looked out. The swarms of Raglans were driving toward the Nile at top speed, kicking up clouds of dust. He could see the Longbows on the move, too. The unitanks were zipping around trying to herd the livestock, but it looked like a lot of them were slipping away and heading back toward the oasis where they knew there was food and water. Speaking of which, he suddenly realized he was very thirsty.

He pulled out his canteen and sat down. Taking a long drink of the tepid water, be noticed the native looking at him. Or looking at the canteen. After a moment's hesitation Harry held it out to him. "Here, thanks for your help back there."

The man took it, drank, and then gave it back. "Thank you, and thanks to Allah, you came to set us free."

"What's your name? How long were you in that place?"

I am Abdo Makur. I was there for… thirteen months."

"Where are you from? Originally, I mean? How did you end up there?"

"I am from Sakali a little village in Darfur. When the monsters came, they did not attack my village, it was too small, perhaps, but they destroyed Nyala, which was a much larger town not too far away. We stayed in our home for a while, but the monsters kept coming nearer and nearer and a few people were taken by them if they strayed too close. Finally, the elders said we should leave. Go north, maybe to Cairo. We hope the British can protect us.

"We travel far, very far. See monsters in many places, but always hide from them. Then, are careless and they see us. We all try to run, but they use their burning rays to herd us like cattle. My son… my son tried to escape, and he died. Others die, too." The man's face crumpled, and he looked away.

"I'm sorry," said Harry.

Abdo nodded and got control of himself. "The monsters scoop us up and carry us in metal baskets. They put us in the place where you found us. Other people already there. The monsters want us to raise the cattle and other animals. For them to eat, the others say. Every half-month they come and take some. Sometimes they take people, too. One time they take my wife and daughter."

"I'm sorry," Harry said again. What more was there to say?

"You come from England to drive away the monsters?"

"Well, I'm from Australia, but yes, our aim is to drive away the monsters."

"I like to help. They have already taken everything from me. Will I be allowed to help?"

Harry shrugged. There were huge numbers of natives helping the army in all sorts of ways. "I imagine we can find something for you to do."

"Good, good. Thank you. And thanks be to Allah."

"Right. Well, you can start helping right now," said Harry, squinting at the blazing sun overhead. It was a long way back to the Nile. "Let's get the canopy on this thing set up."

Chapter Eight

Aswan, Egypt, July, 1912

Harry made his way through the maze of tents, Abdo following close behind. The native had somehow attached himself to Harry as a sort of personal servant. The other officers in the company were tolerating it, since Abdo was perfectly happy to do work for them, too—and they weren't paying him anything beyond a food ration. Even Corporal Scoggins was accepting it, since that made him the *senior* dogrobber and could order Abdo about. The fact that he spoke the local dialects made him all the more useful. The native didn't seem to mind having multiple masters at all.

"So many," said Abdo in awe as he looked at the camp. "I never knew there were so many people in all the world."

"You should see the camps around Cairo. This is nothing compared to those. Ah, here we are." He pointed to a better organized set of tents, some of them flying large hospital flags.

He was coming to visit the pilot, David Dalton, who they'd rescued at the oasis. Harry felt that he owed the man a bit of a debt for destroying the tripod which had been chasing them. He'd managed to scrounge—well, actually it had been Scoggins—a couple of oranges as a gift.

The main administration tent was plainly marked and Harry walked in the entrance, Abdo, remaining outside. He asked a clerk where to find Dalton and after a bit of rummaging through papers, he was told where to go. The hospital was well organized; each tent had a number and there were wooden signs all over which gave directions, With only a few wrong turns, be managed to find the right tent. It was one of the big ones, which could hold several dozen patients. Harry stuck his head inside. There were two rows of cots along either side, but only a few of them were occupied. With no major fighting going on, the only patients would be men who got sick or injured accidentally—or a few men like Dalton. Stepping inside, he tried to spot the man he wanted.

"Can I help you, Lieutenant?"

The strong, feminine voice startled him and he spun around to see a woman dressed in the uniform of the Voluntary Aid Division. She was of average height, with a pleasant face and a cute nose. Light brown hair peeked out around the edges of her nurse's cap. Harry had heard that a number of women from the VAD were with the army, but this was the first time he'd seen one. He suddenly found himself tongue-tied.

"I... um, I was..."

"Are you here looking for someone, Lieutenant...?"

"Uh, Calloway, Harry Calloway."

"I'm sorry, I don't have anyone here by that name, Lieutenant. Perhaps in one of the other wards."

"What? Oh! No, *I'm* Harry Calloway; I'm looking for Lieutenant David Dalton."

"Oh, I see. Lieutenant Dalton is over there, but I'm afraid he's asleep. He just underwent surgery to mend his arm and they've given him something for the pain. I can't allow you to wake him just now. Perhaps if you came back tomorrow."

"Oh," said Harry, disappointed. "I... I brought him a few oranges. Could I leave them with you, miss...?"

"Brittain, Vera Brittain."

"Pleased to meet you, Miss Brittain."

"Charmed, I'm sure. I suppose I could keep your gift for Lieutenant Dalton. Here, let me lock them in the desk. Things like that do have a way of disappearing, I'm afraid." She led the way to a desk at the end of the tent.

"Yes, I can understand that. We have to keep a constant guard on our things." She sat down on the chair by the desk and held out her hand, Harry gave her the bag of oranges.

"Would you like to leave some message? Are you a friend of Lieutenant Dalton?"

"Well, not really a friend. His aircraft crashed the other day and me and a few others pulled him out of the wreck and brought him back. He crashed helping save us from a Martian tripod and I just wanted to thank him for that."

"That's very good of you, Lieutenant Calloway. So you were involved in that action which rescued all those prisoners?" The woman seemed much more interested now.

"Uh, yes. You've heard about that?"

"It's the talk of the camp." She pulled out a piece of paper and took up a pen. "Shall I just write: *From Lieutenant Calloway, with thanks?*"

"Uh, well, if you could say *Lieutenant Calloway and the 15th New Castle Battalion*, that might be better. Uh, we're Australian."

"I could tell. Very well." She began writing. She had very nice handwriting.

He looked over her shoulder and then noticed another piece of paper on the desk in that same lovely hand. A personal letter? No, it was... what? Poetry? His eyes automatically began reading...

107

Perhaps some day the sun will shine again,
And I shall see that still the skies are blue,
And feel once more I do not live in vain,
Although bereft of You...

"There." She finished the note, folded it, and put it in the bag with the oranges. She took out her keys, unlocked a drawer in the desk, and put the bag inside and relocked it. "Can I do anything else for you, Lieutenant?"

"Un, no, I guess that's all. Uh, did you write that?" He pointed to the poem. "It's really very good."

She frowned and turned the paper over. "Thank you. Is there anything else, Lieutenant?"

"Uh..." He tried to think of an excuse to stay longer, but came up blank. "I guess not. Do you think I could come back tomorrow? To see Dalton, I mean."

"If you like."

"Thank you, Miss Brittain. Thanks very much. Good day."

"Good day to you, Lieutenant." She turned back to the desk.

Harry slipped out of the tent, only looking back twice.

* * * * *

Near Little Rock, Arkansas, USA, August 1912

Major Tom Bridges leaned against a railing on the American land ironclad *Albuquerque* and surveyed the ruins of the Martian fortress. He had to admit that he was impressed, very impressed. The great earth and rock berm which made up the outer wall of the fortress had been breached in an amazingly short time by the American engineers and then the land ironclads had led the way through the gap. The Martians had thrown every tripod they had left, seemingly, and all three of the huge American machines had suffered serious damage.

But they had dished out some serious damage in return and they had so distracted the enemy that the following steam tanks had made it inside almost untouched and overwhelmed the defenders. Infantry had gotten down inside the underground passages and the word was that the place was now secure.

"Did you enjoy the show, Major?"

He turned and saw Commander Drew Harding coming up next to him. The American navy officer was an observer here like himself. He'd

The Gathering Storm

lost his ship in the fighting around Memphis a few weeks earlier and his arm was still in a sling.

"Oh, yes indeed!" he replied. "Probably the best show I've ever seen. And a real privilege, too. One doesn't often get the chance to see history being made."

"No, I suppose not."

"And that's what this is, Commander. You realize that, don't you? This is the first time, the very first time since the bloody Martians arrived four years ago, that we've actually taken back territory from them."

"I thought you Brits were driving up the Nile..."

"Against no opposition. Yes, we can occupy territory the Martians don't contest. But this is different. This time we've taken away something they obviously wanted to keep. This is the first hard proof that we can actually beat these blighters."

"I suppose you're right."

Bridges eyed the man, surprised by his lack of jubilation. All around them the American troops were cheering and tossing their helmets in the air. But these navy men, they were so attached to their bloody ships; British, American it seemed the same. Harding was clearly in mourning for his lost ship. And perhaps the crew, as well. From what he'd heard, Harding was the only survivor. *That* must be gnawing on him, too. Well, Bridges was sure he'd get over it.

"What are your plans now, Commander?"

Harding shrugged, and winced slightly, his arm apparently still troubling him. "Back to Washington, I suppose. There will have to be a hearing about what happened to... what happened to *Santa Fe*. Then I'll be looking for a new assignment—assuming anyone will give me one. You?"

"Washington as well. My immediate superior is there at the embassy. But I imagine I'll be sent on to London quick enough. A lot of important people are going to want a first-hand account of what you chaps have accomplished here!"

* * * * *

Skutari Airfield, August 1912

"Tell the mechanic that the switch is on," said Captain Erich Serno.

"Oh! Ah, yes, sir," replied Lieutenant Yusef Kenan in heavily accented German. The Turk straightened up in the forward cockpit of the Rumpler B.1 biplane and shouted: "Switch is on!" to the mechanic standing by the propeller.

The mechanic, also a Turk, spoke almost no German, but he, along with most of the men, could recognize certain standard phrases. He grabbed the propeller, gave it a pull, and jumped backward. The motor coughed, sputtered… and died. Serno said patiently: "Don't worry. Tell him to do it again."

Kenan shouted something in Turkish and the mechanic gingerly stepped forward and gave the propeller a stronger pull. This time the engine roared to life and kept going. The Rumpler shuddered and started to move forward. "Throttle back!" shouted Serno.

Kenan did so, but almost stalled the motor before finding the right setting. He finally did and the aircraft sat there vibrating. Then he waved to the other members of the ground crew and they took hold of the wings and tail and turned the Rumpler so it was pointed out across the large, flat, dusty plain which was the runway. Kenan twisted around to look at Serno, who nodded and made a *go on* gesture with his hand.

The Turk adjusted his goggles and pushed the throttle forward. The engine roared louder and the aircraft started forward, gaining speed every moment. Serno set his own goggles in place and sat ready to take the controls away from his student if it became necessary. The Rumpler went faster and faster, bouncing along the none-too smooth ground. Then the bouncing stopped and they were airborne.

The Earth fell away and Kenan put the craft into a gentle turn toward the southeast. His student had a good feel for flying once he was in the air. Serno had found that was common enough among new pilots. He had been that way himself when he first learned. Getting up, and even more so getting down again, were the tricky things. Once aloft, it seemed easy.

They slowly climbed to about a thousand meters and then levelled off. The Rumpler could cruise at about a hundred and twenty kilometers per hour and the breeze this created felt good after the sweltering heat at the airfield. The Sea of Marmara was off to the right, the blue waters glittering in the morning sunshine. They soon reached the eastern end of the sea and Lieutenant Kenan turned to shout at him.

"We still go to Eskisehir?" The man looked worried.

"Yes we do," he shouted back. "You did the navigation last night and you know the course. Now we do it."

Kenan, nodded, not looking much more confident. But he looked back to his controls and the plane banked slightly to the right and then settled down on a course of one hundred and twenty-six degrees.

Today's exercise was not so much one in flying, but in navigation. Serno's task of helping the Ottomans create an air force was coming along as well as could be expected considering the problems he faced. But bit by bit he was making progress. He had a few dozen pilot-recruits and a few hundred ground crew and now that the railroad to Europe had been re-opened, he had aircraft and spare parts and supplies coming in reasonable amounts.

A few of the pilots were showing real promise and he hoped that soon some of them, like Kenan, would be able to start teaching the new recruits he had been promised were coming. With any luck, he might have a dozen squadrons in operation by the end of the year.

But flying was more than just flying. There were a lot of other things these pilots were going to need to know. Navigation, for one. Most of the training was done within sight of the airfield. When the pilot was finished, his landing place was right there. Real missions, however, would take the pilot long distances from his starting point. He had to know how to get to where the mission was and then get back home afterward.

It was a lot harder than it sounded.

Landmarks on the ground could be difficult to spot and cloud cover could obscure even the easy ones. Maps in this part of the world were rarely accurate, and even compasses could trick you sometimes. In Europe navigation was relatively simple. You could always follow the railroads if you had to. Many towns had painted their name on the roof of the railway stations to help out fliers. But in this part of the world, railroads — and even paved roads — were a rarity. You had to trust your maps and your instruments — and your instincts.

Kenan stayed on the proper course while Serno kept an eye on the fuel gauges. The town of Eskisehir was nearly at the limit for the Rumpler. If they hadn't found it by the time they were nearing the half-full mark, they would have to turn back.

The land below was steadily rising and becoming rougher as they left the lowlands around the sea behind and flew toward the Anatolian highlands which made up the central part of the country. He could make out the peaks of the Pontic Mountains off to the east. The lieutenant put the plane into a gentle climb to keep his altitude above ground level constant.

After an hour or so, Kenan waggled the wings and pointed. Serno craned his neck and looked ahead. There was indeed a town there. It looked to be the proper size and in about the proper place. But was it Eskisehir? Well if it wasn't, they didn't have the fuel to look for the right town. This would have to do. Kenan looked back at him hopefully and Serno nodded and made a gesture with his hand inviting him to head for home. The man's expression became a mixture of elation and relief. He banked the aircraft and headed north.

A few hours later, Serno was on the ground, out of his flying gear, and sitting in a conference room in General von Sanders' headquarters.

Many of his staff were there and they all outranked Serno — most by quite a lot. He'd been at a number of these meeting since he arrived, but he rarely said anything unless asked a question.

"Well, gentlemen," said Sanders, "we finally have some good news. With the railroad re-opened, we can expect some serious help from home."

"Like what, sir?" asked Colonel von Kress. "Artillery? Tanks? Or just more rifles?"

Von Sanders gave the colonel a smug look. "Yes, yes, and yes. Artillery and tanks and yes, more rifles. Machine guns and aircraft, too, as you'll be happy to hear, Captain Serno." He glanced in his direction.

"That's excellent news, sir," said Colonel von Falkenberg. "When can we expect it, and how much?"

"I'm told it's already on the way, so the first of it in a few weeks, perhaps. As for how much, well, as you might expect, we are not getting the newest equipment in the arsenal. The most modern weapons and equipment are going to our own troops, as is only proper. But as those units get the new equipment their old stuff will be refurbished and sent here. So it will be an on-going process."

Everyone around the table nodded in understanding. And no one was disappointed; even the Imperial Army's cast-offs, would be far better than what most of the Ottoman Army possessed. Still…

"What about support services and spare parts, sir?" Serno asked. "Those old tanks are going to need a lot of loving care to keep running. And as I'm finding out with my aircraft, not many of the Turks are mechanically minded."

Von Sanders nodded. "Yes, that's going to be a real challenge. Keeping the equipment in service has proved a problem even for our own troops. There will be some technicians coming with the equipment, but we are going to have to set up training schools for mechanics, more training schools, I should say, since we do have a few already."

"Which Turkish units are going to be re-equipped first, sir? asked Colonel Bronsart. "Every general is going to be demanding the stuff and you know how touchy they are about their damned honor."

"Yes, that's true, too," said von Sanders. "I'll be consulting with the war minister about that. Logic would dictate that the units closest to the front lines with the Martians would get priority, but… logic may be in short supply, I'm afraid."

"Can we expect anything for my ships, general?" asked Admiral von Usedom, commander of the German naval squadron based in Constantinople. "Right now everything has to be brought in by sea, all the way from the Baltic ports."

"For now you'll have to keep doing that, Admiral. Although I'm told we can expect to have the Danube opened for traffic in the near future."

Von Sanders looked around the table, but there were no more immediate questions. The general's eyes stopped on Serno. "Captain."

"Sir?"

"What progress are you making on giving me the reconnaissance capabilities I asked you for?"

Serno winced and sat up straighter in his chair. "We have made a great deal of progress, sir. I have several dozen competent pilots and the training program is accelerating as the older pilots can start training the new ones. We are making similar progress with the ground crews. We have about thirty operational aircraft and we are hoping for more now that the railway is open and..."

"Are you conducting any reconnaissance flights against the enemy, captain?"

"Uh, no sir."

"And why not?" The general's voice was deceptively mild. Serno had seen him verbally tear the skin off subordinates when he got angry.

"As you know, sir, the range of the aircraft we have is very limited. Three hundred kilometers is as far as we can get from our base. To actually reach Martian territory we are going to need forward air bases, and even then our planes will only be able to reach a small portion of the occupied zone."

"So what do you need to provide me with accurate and timely information on enemy activities, captain?"

"Well, sir, in addition to the forward bases, longer ranged aircraft. If we could get a few of the new Gotha bombers, we could add extra fuel tanks to increase their operating radius. Of course none of our pilots—including me—has flown a large, multi-engined aircraft, so that would require additional training. But honestly, sir, what we really need are..."

"What?"

"Zeppelins, sir. They have almost unlimited range compared with other aircraft. They could reach the farthest reaches of the area we are concerned with."

"Zeppelins are filled with hydrogen, are they not, captain?" asked Colonel von Kress. "That's highly flammable. A bit dangerous when the enemy is using heat rays, isn't it?"

"Wood and canvas aircraft aren't any less vulnerable. We have to stay out of range if we want to survive. The zeppelins can fly at an altitude beyond the range of the Martian heat rays, sir."

"Really? Has it been tried?"

"Uh, not against the Martians, no, sir. But tests have been made on the effective range of captured heat rays, the Americans and British have done some good work on that. If the underside of the zeppelins were covered with aluminum paint it is estimated they could survive."

"I don't think I'd want to bet my life on such estimates."

Colonel von Falkenberg laughed. "Haven't you noticed that all fliers are a bit crazy, Freiherr? Risks like that don't bother them a bit."

"Is that true, Captain?" asked von Sanders. "You'd be willing to take the risk?"

"Any sort of flying has some risk, sir. But yes, I'd be willing to chance it."

Von Sanders smiled. "Then I have some good news for you... Major."

* * * * *

Advanced Base 14-3-1, Cycle 597,845.3

Kandanginar of Clan Patralvus watched the huge container emerge from the tunnel mouth and move smoothly away on the transport track toward the dispersal area. As soon as the way was clear, an empty container slid into place and began the descent to where the drill machine was working.

"This is most impressive," said Lutnapnitav from its travel chair. "How far is the excavation proceeding each day?"

Kandanginar glanced at Lutnapnitav, its eldest bud on the target world. "We are averaging slightly less than a *telequel* per day. The drill machines have proven quite capable of cutting through the rock in this area. Group 18 reports slower progress, though still satisfactory."

"But they have less far to dig, is that not so?"

"Yes, they had a better starting site than we did. It is vital that the prey creatures not realize what we are doing, so the tunnel entrances had to be well away from any observation point. Not just the entrances, but the locations where we dispose of the spoil. Unfortunately, due to the local topography we had to start a considerable distance from our objective."

"I understand this," said Lutnapnitav. "The distance will also make it difficult for the prey creatures to fire upon the entrances with their large projectile throwers. Once the tunnel is complete it should be possible to transfer material and personnel across the strait without interference. But I am curious about the second part of the plan, to close the straight to the prey creature water vessels. How is that to be done? Our heat rays, even if placed on the island in the strait do not have the range to interdict the passage."

Kandanginar waved its tendrils in a calming motion. "Yes, you have not been informed of the latest transmissions from the Homeworld. They have sent us the designs for several new weapons, one of which will be most useful in the coming endeavor."

"New weapons, Progenitor?"

"Yes. Almost from the moment we landed on the target world we had to face the unexpected situation that the prey creatures possessed weapons which could fire farther than our heat rays. Their large projectile throwers, while crude and inaccurate, could send explosive shells many times the distance at which our heat rays were effective. This allowed them to bombard our holdfasts or engage our fighting machines at distances where we could not reply."

"I am aware of this."

"Also, since these weapons throw their projectiles in a parabolic trajectory, they could fire at us from behind intervening terrain features such as hills or these dense growths of vegetation which cover large stretches of the wetter regions of the planet. Our weapons, dependent on a clear line of sight, were at a disadvantage.

"Once these facts became apparent, the scientist and engineers on the Homeworld began working on countermeasures. They have sent us construction templates for two of them. One is a weapon which will allow us to bombard the enemy when they are out of line of sight. It uses a magnetic accelerator to throw an explosive projectile, long distances in a parabolic trajectory."

"A chemical explosive, such as the prey creatures, use?" asked Lutnaptinvav.

"No, it proved simpler to use what amounts to a small power cell, deliberately designed to fail catastrophically at the proper moment. One of these accelerators and a supply of the power cells will be mounted on a large drone device which can accompany our fighting machines in the field, or be added to the defense of our holdfasts."

"What range does it have?"

"About ten *telequel*, although that will be affected by air pressure and wind conditions — something which would not be of great significance on the Homeworld. I'm told that if trials here are successful, larger versions with longer ranges may be designed."

"I see. And the other weapon?"

"That is the one which will allow us to seal off the waterway. It is a much larger version of our heat ray projector. It should be effective at five or six times the range of our standard heat rays and at closer ranges able to quickly burn through the armor of even the enemy's largest war vessels. This new projector is far too large and demands too much power to mount on our fighting machines, but if put in well protected casemates, connected to a power reactor, should be able to successfully engage the enemy water vessels if they should attempt to move through the strait."

"That sounds excellent, Progenitor. And it also explains the branch tunnels which are being dug. Those will lead to the casemates you describe?"

"Yes, we have chosen a number of locations where we will mount the projectors. The tunnels will be dug almost to those locations and then completed as soon as our operation goes into action. Group 18 is doing the same on its side of the strait. The power runs will be laid in advance and we will then only need to mount the projectors and finish the casemates. We will mount additional projectors on the island in the strait once we have captured it."

"And the reactor to power them?"

"Is being fabricated now. Fortunately, this region is rich in the power metals, Elements 90 and 92, so there will be no lack of fuel."

"That is indeed fortunate," said Lutnaptinav. "I have heard that some groups landed in regions with little or none."

"Yes, that is true. They are facing serious difficulties. All the more reason to carry out the Colonial Conclave's directive to link our territories. It will allow trading resources as well as coordinating military operations."

"Reserves of the power metals on the Homeworld are also running low, is that not true? Is that why they have directed us to build enormous launching guns to send resources there?"

Kandanginar moved its tendrils in a non-committal fashion. This was a very sensitive subject. The original plan, debated and agreed to by the Council of Three Hundred on the Homeworld, was to send the expedition to conquer the target world and then slowly relocate the entire Race as the Homeworld slowly died. The plan was proceeding, although at a slower rate than had been hoped, and everyone on the target world had expected that it would continue.

But then, a quarter cycle ago, a new directive had been received. There would be no relocation. Instead, those who were on the target world would construct launching guns, like those used to send the expedition here, but vastly larger due to the greater gravity, and use them to send vital resources back to the Homeworld.

Many privately questioned the wisdom of this decision, but none dared to openly challenge it. Or at least almost no one. Kandanginar had heard rumors that there were some among the new buds who dared. That was a shocking thing, but as long as it was no more than talk, it would have to be tolerated. There was no time or effort to be spared on internal conflict.

"One of several reasons," said Kandanginar finally. "But that need not concern us. There are no suitable locations for launching guns in our territory so we would only be expected to give aid to the groups who do have those locations. And in any case, our first goal is to complete the conquest of this world. Let us direct our full attention to this coming operation."

"As you command, Progenitor."

Chapter Nine

Admiralty House, London, September, 1912

Frederick Lindemann looked up from his soup as a particularly strong gust of wind drove the rain against the windows of Admiralty House. The first days of fall were bringing the marvelous summer weather to an end. The rain was falling so heavily he could barely see St. James Park beyond the Horse Guards Parade.

"Is the soup to your liking, Professor?"

He turned his head away from the window and down the table, past the half-dozen other dinner guests, to find Clementine Churchill, the first lord's wife looking at him. She was a lovely woman who Lindemann had grown quite fond of in the short time he'd known her. She was a trifle outspoken for his usual tastes, but she had a good brain for a woman and she played a very nice game of tennis. Lindemann liked the sport himself and learning this, she had invited him to several games with her friends. Her husband did not play, indeed Mr. Churchill did not appear to indulge in any physical activities beyond walking.

"Oh, yes indeed, ma'am, exquisite. Your cook is very talented." The half-dozen other dinner guests made noises of agreement.

"Simmons? Yes, he's splendid. And so adaptable. Winston always drags him along when he makes an inspection tour on the *Enchantress*. He's able to make wonderful meals ashore or afloat."

"Really?" said Lindemann. The *Enchantress* was the yacht that was for the first lord's use. "Do you take many trips, sir?" He directed the question at Churchill who had finished his soup and was sipping from his glass of champagne.

"Not as many as I used to. Not as many as I would like, certainly. Nothing gets results like an on site appearance, I've found. Send them a dispatch and they might get around to reading it, or obeying it. But show up in their headquarters or on the bridge of their ship and they can't ignore you."

"I wouldn't think so."

"But these days there is so much work to do, and the fleet is so scattered, it's hard to find the time to get around to them all anymore."

Lindemann glanced at the huge map on the wall of the dining room. Churchill had similar maps all through the Admiralty, which was connected to Admiralty House. Many of them seemed identical, with hundreds of little labelled pins marking the positions of navy vessels and constantly updated by swarms of clerks. The first lord wanted critical information close at hand no matter where he went. This map was of the whole world, and there were red pins in every ocean and most of the seas.

"Yes, the fleet does seem to be all over the place, doesn't it? Although there still seem to be quite a lot of them in home waters, sir." he gestured to the cluster of pins around the British Isles.

"Many of those are ships undergoing repairs or refits, Professor," said Churchill, nodding to a steward to remove the soup dishes and serve the next course—and refill his champagne glass. This was the third meal Lindemann had shared with Churchill and the man seemed to have a remarkable capacity for alcohol. "The ones with the white tags are new ships under construction. And..." he hesitated, looking closely at Lindemann.

"And?"

"Well, to be frank, despite the world situation, we can't leave the home islands undefended."

"Of course not, sir. The Martians can land anywhere they choose, and even though they've left Europe alone so far we can't..."

"Winston wasn't referring to the Martians, Professor," said David Lloyd George, the Chancellor of the Exchequer from across the table.

"Oh..." *Oh!* Lindemann realized that the First Lord was talking about the potential threat from other *human powers*. "I see..."

"Yes, dear old Willie continues to build dreadnoughts despite the growing threat to his east," said Churchill. "He keeps the bulk of them in the Baltic and perforce we need to keep a matching force in the North Sea."

"I know the Kaiser is ambitious, sir, but do you really think he would... at a time like this?"

"Probably not. He's ambitious, but he's not a fool. But I can't afford to be a fool, either, and to make a mistake about something like this could be fatal."

"Sometimes the Germans do seem terribly barbaric," said Margaret Lloyd George, the chancellor's wife. A moment after speaking she suddenly blanched and put her hand to her mouth. Lindemann was about to tell her she need not apologize to him, but instead she turned to the man to her left. "Oh, do forgive me Prince Battenberg! I... I didn't mean you!"

Vice Admiral Prince Louis of Battenberg returned her a thin smile. "No offense taken, madam," he said. "Actually, I was born in Austria. And I became a naturalized British citizen and a midshipman in the Royal Navy over a year before the German Empire even existed. And I agree that the Kaiser's behavior can often be... inexcusable."

Lindemann blinked. He had quite forgotten about the second sea lord's German parentage. Battenberg seemed to handle it very well; perhaps he should study the man.

Churchill cleared his throat. "As I was saying, the number of pins in the map in home waters is a bit deceiving. In addition to the others I mentioned, a large number of them are being assembled for the India Convoy. They'll be on their way very soon."

"So they are really going through with this?" asked Colonel Francis De La Mere from the far end of the table. "Seems like madness to me. Give the bloody wogs steel mills and the ability to make their own artillery and tanks and it's a recipe for rebellion."

An embarrassed silence filled the room for a few moments at the colonel's words. It was indeed a touchy subject. Lindemann did not follow the doings in Parliament closely—or he hadn't until he entered Churchill's inner circle—but no one could fail to know that there had been a huge row for months on the subject. The question was whether to provide the Indians with the infrastructure to build their own heavy weapons. At present they were dependent upon shipments from Great Britain for such things. From a strictly military viewpoint it did make sense to create industries close to where the output was needed, but there were other issues involved. Lindemann seriously doubted that the Indians were capable of governing themselves. Oh, a few were educated, and took on European airs, but the great masses were simple primitives. Without British guidance he was sure they'd quickly return to savagery.

"It's true there is a danger," said Churchill, "but we must hope that the Indian leaders will have the good sense to do no such thing while the Martians remain a threat. But it is also true that this will almost inevitably lead to some sort of home rule for them. I've opposed that idea for years, but we need to be realistic. The Martians are the real enemy and we need to deal with them."

"That's certainly true, sir, but once the Martians are defeated…"

"That's not likely to happen any time soon, Colonel, I'm afraid, so you need not worry about an immediate Indian revolt," said Lloyd George. "Don't you agree, Winston?"

Churchill took a bite of the poached salmon, chewed, frowned, and then replied. "I'm afraid that I do, David. We seem to be holding the bounders off on most fronts, and even making some headway against them like in Sudan or America, but they hold over half the world right now and it's going to take a great deal of time to root them all out. And we will be fighting on many very distant fronts. The navy and merchant fleets are stretched near to the breaking point keeping all our forces supplied. If we can relieve some of that pressure by setting up factories in other places in the Empire then that's what we must do. I've gotten word that if this venture in India works out we shall try to do the same in South Africa."

Lindemann glanced at the map again. It did not have colors denoting enemy held territory, but most thinking people knew where that was by heart these days. Northern Asia from Kamchatka to Ukraine, Australia, Arabia, Africa south of the Sahara, except for the extreme south; most of Canada, and nearly all of Central and South America. Far more than half the world was in the hands of the invader. Taking it all back, especially the areas far from cities or rail lines, could be the work of decades; generations. It was a daunting prospect, but this war might last the rest of their lifetimes.

"Must we kill every last one of them?" asked Mrs. Lloyd George. "Can't we try to communicate with them? Isn't there any way we can force them to pack up and go back to their homes?"

Colonel De La Mare snorted and her husband tried and failed to keep from smiling. Churchill drained his champagne glass, which was quickly refilled, and then said: "There have been numerous attempts to communicate with the Martians, all to no effect, Margaret. But that is still an interesting question. If—when—we clearly gain the upper hand, does the enemy have any means to leave? Could they flee even if they wanted to? What do you think, Professor?"

Lindemann was growing used to fielding unexpected questions like this from Churchill. He'd been to a number of Admiralty meetings and some dinners or luncheons like this one. So many, in fact that he wasn't spending much time at his real job anymore. Young Chadwick was filling in for him so far, but he wondered how long Eccles was going to put up with his frequent absences—and what he would do if Eccles made trouble?

"Excellent question, sir. We know that the Martians launch their cylinders with huge guns of some sort. So huge that the discharges can be seen from Earth with large telescopes. Theoretically, it may be possible to reverse the procedure, but the difficulties would be considerable. Due to Earth's much stronger gravity, and the fact that they would be trying to move outward from the sun to reach Mars—going 'uphill' as it were—the launching guns would have to be vastly larger than the ones they built on Mars. Either that, or the cylinders would have to be much smaller so the same size gun could accelerate it to a higher velocity."

"Of course, if they were simply interested in fleeing, they could leave all their equipment behind and just make the cylinders big enough to carry themselves," said Churchill. "They wouldn't have to take along their war machines and all the other things we know they brought to stage their invasion."

"Good point, sir. But the construction of the guns must take years. They would have to make up their minds to flee long before any evacuation could begin."

"They are rational," said Lloyd George. "If they see they will lose, they might attempt a retreat. Campaigns to reach their more remote conquests must also take years, so they might have the time to build the guns. I'd certainly welcome it if they did flee. To drive them out of northern Canada or Outer Mongolia, would be a nightmare logistically."

"A Norwegian ship recently confirmed the presence of Martians in Antarctica," said Churchill, nodding.

"Yes, exactly. Alaska and Greenland, as well. If we could force them to leave, we wouldn't have to have our grandchildren still fighting them when they are our age."

"The first step, however, is to convince them that they are going to be beaten," said Churchill. "We have some work ahead of us to reach that point, I think."

"And how is that coming, dear?" asked Clementine. "My friends ask me all the time, you know. Is Kitchener's drive on Khartoum going to bear fruit?"

"Not any time soon," growled De La Mare. "Speaking of grandchildren."

The others at the table chuckled, but Lindemann noted that Churchill did not. As much as he enjoyed the first lord's company, he did have some difficult personality quirks. He insisted on dominating any social gathering, and rarely laughed at any jokes but his own. And the man did have a temper. Lindemann had only glimpsed it, but the stories he'd heard made him very careful to do nothing which might unleash it on himself.

"Lord Kitchener is making steady, if slow, progress up the Nile," said Churchill. "But as David has said, these sorts of campaigns are as much a matter of logistics as they are of…"

Churchill broke off as a young naval officer entered the room and quickly made his way to the side of the first lord and handed him a slip of paper. The first lord, looked at it for a moment, frowned, and then sprang up and walked over the wall map. His finger poised over where the southern tip of Arabia was very close to Africa. He spun back to face the officer. "Has this been confirmed?" he snapped.

"Uh, no, sir. The message just came through. Admiral Carstairs is sending a request for confirmation, but he said you should see this right away."

"What's happening, Winston?" asked Lloyd George. "Trouble?"

"Could be… could be… blast!"

Lloyd George and De La Mare got up from their chairs and moved closer to the map. After a moment, Lindemann rose as well. The ladies did not look pleased.

"So what is it, *dear*?" said Clementine.

"The blighters are attacking our base in the Bab el Mandab strait. Not sure how since it's on an island and we have ships guarding it." He turned away from the map and ran his gaze over the guests. "Ladies, gentlemen, I'm afraid you'll have to excuse me." Pausing only to gulp down the last of his champagne, Churchill hurried out.

Lindemann looked after him for a moment, but then turned back to the map.

"If this turns out to be bad, that India convoy may have to take the long way round," said Lloyd George.

* * * * *

Advanced Base 14-3-1, Cycle 597,845.3

The night sky beyond the range of hills flickered and flashed with light and a steady rumble from the prey creatures' large projectile throwers could be plainly heard even from twenty telequel away. Kandanginar steered its travel chair up the ramp from the underground portions of the advanced base, accompanied by Lutnaptinav in its own chair. The reactor had just come on line and was functioning perfectly. Power would be available for the new heavy heat ray projectors which were even now being moved into position.

The attack on the island in the narrow strait of water was commencing. Over a hundred of the clan's fighting machines were moving down out of the hills where they had been concealed and advancing right to the water's edge. On the western side of the strait Group 18 was doing the same thing.

The prey creatures were responding as they always did when presented with targets; they were firing with their weapons as quickly as they could. Some of the weapons were mounted on the island, but most were on the water vessels nearby. There was little the fighting machines could do in return as their heat rays did not have the range to reach the vessels or the island.

There had been proposals to use the new explosive throwers in this operation, but that had been overruled by the Colonial Conclave. They had just gone into production and had not been deployed in large numbers yet and it was desired that they remain secret until they could be used decisively. But this was of no concern at the moment. In this operation the object was simply to provoke the prey to expend their ammunition. Observation had shown, and logic dictated, that the water vessels could only carry a finite number of the projectiles and the chemicals that propelled them. Firing at the rate which they did would eventually use them up, leaving them helpless. No doubt they could be resupplied somehow, but that would take time — critical time.

The tunneling machines had reached a point directly under the island and would soon be ready to emerge on its surface. Without the diversion provided by the fighting machines, the emergence would be extremely dangerous. The vibration of the machines would give the enemy warning that something was happening, and with the fully armed water vessels nearby, they could well concentrate enough fire against the tunnel mouth to make success impossible. But now, the firing of their own weapons should mask the vibrations, and optimally, when the emergence occurred, the water vessels would, have expended most of their ammunition. It was inevitable that there would be losses among the diversionary forces, but this was acceptable to achieve success.

They reached the command center of the base which had been constructed in an area excavated from the side of the mountain range. There had been no time, and no need, to construct an actual holdfast here, so the facilities were the bare minimum to conduct operations. Kandanginar and Lutnapnitav dismounted and placed themselves before a bank of video monitors.

"Things seem to be going well," observed Lutnapnitav. "The prey creatures are reacting as we anticipated."

"So far, but if we have learned anything in this long war, it is that the prey are capable of unanticipated actions. They are surprisingly adaptable for such primitive creatures."

"War. I have rarely heard this conflict referred to with that word, Progenitor," said Lutnapnitav. "That is normally reserved for conflict between... people."

Kandanginar waved its tendrils with amused irony. "Meaning we considered this merely an operation to remove an annoying infestation of vermin? So I thought when I left the Homeworld. So do far too many of us still. But it is a war, no matter what name we put upon it."

"As you say."

They turned their attention to the monitors. Using them they could receive video input from any of the fighting machines, the digging machines, or the hundreds of fighting drones which had moved into the tunnels. The small, remotely controlled drones would be the first to emerge when the digging machine broke through the surface. They were completely expendable and would be ideal to secure the area around the tunnel exit. Several score of the clan members were controlling the drones from another area of the advanced base.

Kandanginar activated a pickup on one of the fighting machines along the coast. The night was quite dark, the target world's enormous moon had not yet risen, but the video pickups had light amplification capabilities as well as infrared; the image was quite clear despite the darkness. The coastline and the restless body of uncontrolled water beside it was easily visible. The island, perhaps three *telequel* away, was a darker lump rising above the water, although not very far above. Except for a few higher projections, the island was low and flat.

As it watched, there was a bright flash from the island, followed quickly by two more. These were the prey creature projectile throwers. It did not know what, exactly, they were aiming at, but it did not see any explosions with the current viewpoint.

"Lutnapnitav, monitor the operational status of our fighting machines. Report to me if any are destroyed or become damaged."

"At once, Progenitor."

New flashes appeared out on the waters and Kandanginar could see they were coming from the prey creature water vessels. A moment later the whole area along the shoreline was lit up with a brilliant light. Tilting the video pick up it could see dazzling bright points of light in the sky. The enemy was using its artificial illumination munitions. In early battles it had become apparent that the prey creatures could not see well in darkness and apparently were unused to fighting under those conditions. The Race had taken advantage of that and attacked at night when possible. But the prey had adapted quickly and provided its warriors with these means of driving back the darkness. Several large light generating devices on the island and the vessels were also activated, projecting more light at the shore. No matter; if they could see the fighting machines more clearly, they would be all the more tempted to expend ammunition shooting at them.

"Progenitor," said Lutnapnitav, "a machine in Battlegroup 3-2 has sustained heavy damage and the pilot is injured."

"Is it still mobile?"

"Yes?"

"Have it withdraw immediately."

"At once."

Kandanginar touched the controls and put itself in communications with Andagmatu, the one controlling the digging machine under the island. "Report your status," it commanded.

"The machine is twelve *quel* below the surface, Commander," it replied. "Although with the shallow angle we must take to create a traversable passage, we have approximately one hundred and fifty quel yet to dig. Emergence should take place in 0.01 rotations."

"Understood, keep me informed of any delays."

Kandanginar quickly checked the status of the other digging machines, the ones which were creating the tunnels to where the heavy heat rays would be emplaced. Several had already broken through and were withdrawing to allow the constructor machines to begin their work. The rest were also close to their objectives. Things were going well. It then contacted its counterpart in Group 18. "Commander Ootjundapar, how goes your operation?"

"Satisfactorily," replied the other commander. "We have lost one war machine with the pilot killed, but no other losses. The enemy has only two small water vessels facing us. The rest are firing at you."

"So I have noted. They are concerned for the island. Will you be able to establish your heat ray emplacements per the schedule?"

"There have been some minor delays on two of them, but the rest will be operational on schedule. What is the status of your operation against the island?"

"It is proceeding as planned. Emergence will take place soon, and my attention is needed there. I will contact you again later." It broke its link with Ootjundapar and connected to one of the drones in the tunnel behind the digging machine under the island.

The initial view only showed the dimly lit far side of the cylindrical tunnel. The drones were parked in pockets dug into the side of the tunnel so they would not obstruct the operation of the digging machine or the carriers removing the spoil. This drone was in a newly dug pocket, as close to the front of the tunnel as possible. Hundreds more were waiting in other pockets spaced back along the way. There were larger pockets at intervals where the carriers might pass each other, full ones heading out with empty ones waiting to move forward. Other pockets had been made which were waiting areas for fighting machines which would follow the drones onto the island.

Kandanginar edged the drone into the tunnel and aimed it toward the front. All that could be seen was the rear of the carrier which was loading the material removed by the digger. The digging machine used a combination of heat rays and mechanical cutting bits to shatter, pulverize and remove the rock in front of it. This was then pulled through the machine and deposited in the carrier behind it. More heat rays fused the walls of the tunnel to prevent a collapse and hopefully seal out the overabundance of water on this planet which tried to seep into any underground space. The machine could move forward steadily. Smaller, more flexible machines would cut out the pockets as needed.

An alarm notified Kandanginar that the carrier was about to leave. It maneuvered the drone back into its pocket and watched it pass. After a short while, an empty carrier came forward.to take its place. Checking with Andagmatu, it was informed that emergence could be expected very shortly.

"Progenitor, the number of projectiles coming from the enemy water vessels is dropping off," said Lutnapnitav. "Not stopped, but there has been a reduction of almost sixty percent from the initial rate. Two more fighting machines have taken minor damage."

"Excellent. When our forces emerge on the island, we can expect an almost complete cessation of their fire against the shore as they try to analyze what is happening and then probably an increase to maximum levels as they try to respond. This should deplete their last reserves very quickly."

"Commander, the digging machine is breaking through the surface," reported Andagmatu. "It will take a short while to create an open passage. I am clearing the tunnel of the spoil carriers so your forces may advance."

"Very well." Kandanginar opened a circuit to address all those involved in the assault. "Prepare to attack per the plan." Scores of replies confirmed that all was ready. It has expected nothing less. Assured, it linked its video displays to a number of drones and fighting machines in different locations. It made no attempt to control any of them, it was merely observing and focusing its attention from one to another as events unfolded.

Looking through one of the drones which had moved up behind the digging machine, it could see that the enormous device had indeed broken through to the surface. It was still moving forward to create a smooth ramp for exit, but even before that was accomplished, drones were able to make their way over piles of rubble which had slid down into the tunnel behind the digger and reach level ground.

The positional locator showed that emergence had come exactly where it had been planned. The artificial satellite in orbit around the target world had provided accurate information about the prey creature installations and defenses on the island and a spot had been picked which was as distant from them as possible. It would take time to deploy the clan's forces and the longer it took for the enemy to respond, the better.

Swarms of drones were now emerging from the tunnel and spreading out to secure the perimeter. No sign of the enemy could be seen beyond the continuing flashes from their heavy weapons to the east. The digging machine finished its task and dragged itself clear of the exit. Several smaller constructor machines were at work behind it clearing debris and laying the transport track which would allow the fighting machines to be brought up. The fighting machines were too tall to walk through the tunnel, so they had to fold up their legs and sit on a small transport car which would carry them through the tunnel and deliver them to the surface. Fifty of them were on the way.

"Progenitor, one of the fighting machines on the shore has been disabled," reported Lutnapnitav. "The pilot is unharmed, but enemy fire is concentrating on it. It will be dangerous to try and recover the pilot. Should I order this anyway?"

"Wait. The prey creatures will become aware of our emergence shortly. This may divert their attention and allow a recovery."

"Understood."

Returning its attention to the drones, Kandanginar observed the approach of a small enemy vehicle, a pair of illuminators on its front, lighting the path before it, Kandanginar ordered the drone operators to hold their fire and the vehicle moved right in among the drones before coming to a halt. Prey creatures began to exit, apparently unaware of what they faced. It gave the command to fire and the small heat rays on the drones incinerated the creatures and set the vehicle on fire in moments.

A surprising amount of time then passed with still no response from the enemy. Kandanginar had feared a much quicker counterattack and was pleased at how long the enemy was taking to mount one. The constructor machines had now laid enough track to allow the carriers to bring the fighting machines to the surface and one by one they arrived, stood up, lifted the carrier off the track to make room for the next, and then strode out to join the perimeter.

It wasn't until twenty of them were deployed that the first response occurred. Several of the illumination munitions burst overhead lighting up the scene of activity. Even then, another ten machines arrived before the first heavy projectiles began to fall. Too late, much too late to cause serious problems.

"The attack force will advance," it commanded.

The fighting machine, accompanied by swarms of drones moved out toward their objectives. The primary objectives were the large projectile throwers mounted in several locations on the island. Secondary objective would be the structures, presumably housing warriors, supplies and communications equipment.

The island was only four *telequel* across at its widest point, so it took very little time to reach the objectives. Kandanginar, monitored the group that was assigned to destroy the large projectile throwers. These weapons were mounted behind ramparts made of a cast stone material that the enemy was using more and more frequently. It was highly resistant to the heat rays and had proved most troublesome against a number of the Race's recent offensives. But the ramparts here only faced the eastern shore and could provide no protection at all.

The prey creatures operating the weapons appeared to be taken by surprise by the sudden appearance of the fighting machines and drones. A few made attempts to turn their weapons around, but most tried to scatter. They did not get far as scores of heat rays stabbed out and quickly annihilated them. Ammunition stacked near the weapons exploded, completing the destruction in short order. The drones rapidly entered several underground chamber and slew more of the enemy. There was virtually no resistance.

Elsewhere the prey put up more of a fight. A sub-group led by Grafnagnatur encountered over a hundred of them on the north end of the island. They had no heavy weapons but fought fiercely with their smaller weapons and the explosive bombs they carried. Four of the drones were destroyed and one fighting machine damaged before they were wiped out.

A few other such areas of resistance were found, but all were quickly overwhelmed. As the defense crumbled, the interesting phenomenon which had been often observed occurred. Once the prey creatures became disorganized and retreat routes cut off, many stopped fighting and gave up. These were herded together and guarded by drones. They would be a welcome addition to the clan's food supply.

Others, however, refused to give up. Many were obliterated trying to flee and several groups of them retreated into the water and attempted to swim away. Some were killed by heat ray fire from the shore, while others disappeared beneath the water and presumably perished.

By this time the enemy water vessels were firing against the island, unmindful apparently that their fire was more likely to slay their captured comrades than hurt their enemy. Dawn was approaching and the operation had been completed successfully and with little loss. The enemy water vessels continued to throw projectiles against the island for another tenth rotation, but eventually drew off out of range. Kandanginar opened a circuit to address everyone.

"Stage one of the operation is complete. Commence stage two. We can expect an enemy counterattack within the next several rotations. We must be ready to meet it."

Chapter Ten

The Admiralty, London, October, 1912

"**W**e will have all our forces in place by the end of the week," said First Sea Lord Jacky Fisher, to the assembled officers and ministers of the Admiralty. The entire upper echelon of the body was there in the meeting room with Churchill presiding. Frederick Lindemann was thrilled to be included in such a gathering.

"*Agamemnon* will be the flagship for Admiral Beresford, with the leading squadron composed of *Swiftsure, Hibernia, Dominion, Commonwealth, Duncan, Hindustan,* and *Albemarle*. The supporting squadron will have the armored cruisers *Minotaur, Cochrane, Black Prince, Hampshire, Cornwall,* and *Essex*. The new dreadnought *Queen Elizabeth* is undergoing trials in the Med and I'm sending her along to give her crew some gunnery practice. We've also received a request from the French to have a few ships participate as observers and I saw no reason to turn them down, so the battleship *Bouvet* and the cruiser *Leon Gambetta* will be joining our forces. We will have about two dozen light cruisers and destroyers acting as escorts.

"The battleships will begin a long-range bombardment of Perim Island and the shoreline to the east. Depending on how the Martians react, the range will be decreased, and the support ships brought into action. Once all visible enemies have been dealt with the Marine force will be landed." Fisher was talking without notes and the old man seemed very energized to Lindemann.

The whole naval establishment had been energized for the last week, ever since word came that the Martians had seized the small island in the Bab el Mandab strait which connected the Red Sea to the Gulf of Aden and the Indian Ocean. This move threatened to cut the vital sea route from England to India and would render the Suez Canal nearly useless. The situation was unacceptable, and the Royal Navy was going to respond in strength.

"And what is the size of the landing force?" asked Churchill.

"About a battalion; all we could assemble from the ships in the force, I'm afraid."

"That's not much to send against Martian tripods, Jacky."

"I know, I know, but Kitchener wasn't willing to give me any of his troops on such short notice. We wait for him and it will be a month before we can move. We can't give those blighters that long to get dug in!"

"I agree, but..."

"And in any rate, we won't land anyone until the ships have blasted everything on that island," continued Fisher. "The Marines will have nothing to do but sweep up the debris."

"I have no doubt your fellows will do a splendid job," said Churchill, "but I'm still concerned about how the Martians got on that island in the first place. Louis, you were going to look into that, weren't you?" The question as directed at Prince Battenberg.

The second sea lord was a man in his late 50s, bearded and fit, although he limped a bit and was said to suffer from gout. He nodded toward the first lord but frowned. "Yes, sir, I received reports from the ship captains who were there at the time, but I'm afraid they were not able to shed any light on the subject. The Martian attack came at night in clear conditions and the ships and shore batteries began using star shells almost immediately. They observed large numbers of tripods on both the Arabian and African coasts. They could not determine what they were up to, but since standing orders are to engage the enemy whenever sighted, they did so.

"They fired on them for nearly an hour and a half, inflicting some damage, but then a single wireless message from the garrison on Perim was received stating that there were Martians on the island. Requests for more information, sent both by wireless and signal light, went unanswered. Shortly after that several large explosions were seen from the area of the shore batteries and then tripods were observed on the island. The ships closed to engage them, but they were running low on ammunition by then and could do little and were eventually forced to withdraw. As you know, we only had a single old battleship and two light cruisers on the scene as the risk to Perim seemed slight.

"None of the ship officers saw any Martians crossing over to the island; all agree on that. Three men managed to swim out from Perim and were picked up. Unfortunately, they could not provide any useful information. They were all enlisted men and simply state that they were attending to their duties until the Martian tripods and small spider machines appeared among them. There was nothing they could do but try to escape. I'm sorry sir, but that's all I could learn."

Churchill frowned. "It would seem that the demonstration on the coasts was merely a faint to distract our people and cause them to waste their ammunition."

"Yes, sir, that was my conclusion," said Battenberg.

"So how did they get there? If we are going to retake Perim Island — as we must — and then hold it, we need to know how it was taken from us in the first place. Ideas gentlemen?"

"Could they have just waded across the strait from the Arabian side?" asked Sir Graham Greene, Permanent Secretary of the Board of Admiralty. "How deep is the water?"

"Quite deep," said Admiral Fisher. "Nearly a hundred fathoms at one point."

"Could they go that deep?" asked Churchill. "Professor, you know as much about those machines as almost anyone, what do you think?"

Lindemann had been expecting such a question, so he was able to reply immediately. "The machines are sturdily constructed and have been observed on many occasions wading through water deep enough to nearly cover the top of them. They are clearly water proof at shallow depths. At greater depths? I really can't say. Nearly all of the tripods captured from the first invasion have been dismantled to one degree or another, but we do have one which has never been touched. We keep it as a reference model. I suppose the navy could have it taken to some suitably deep location and then lowered down by a crane to observe the effects of the higher water pressure."

"That could take months!" snapped Fisher. "We don't have the time for that now!"

"Yes," agreed Churchill. "A worthwhile experiment for some later date, Professor. But just based on what you know, do you think the Martians could have waded across the strait along the bottom?"

Less confident now, Lindemann answered, "I can't say that it is impossible, sir. But the Martians have, so far, shown themselves to be reluctant to do things like that. They've avoided large bodies of water when they could. And I'm also concerned that their smaller spider machines were sighted on Perim. In their attack on Memphis, Tennessee this past summer, they constructed rafts to transport them across the Mississippi River even though the tripods were able to wade. This might indicate that the spiders are not suited to wade across river or sea bottoms. Are the ship officers certain that nothing like rafts were used?"

Prince Battenberg made a growling noise and his beard seemed to bristle. "They have said that they saw none. And since they have been ordered to keep a special look out for such things, I am confident that there were none."

Lindemann realized that he might have offended the admiral, so he quickly said: "Then I'm sure they didn't get there that way, sir. I suppose if the tripods were able to walk across on the bottom, they might have been carrying the spider machines..."

"Well, they obviously got across somehow," said Admiral Charles Briggs, the Third Sea Lord. "And in significant strength. Presumably they couldn't have used the same sort of cylinders they use to come to Earth from Mars. Surely someone would have noticed that!"

"Unless they have developed flying machines," said Churchill. "God help us if that's the case."

"Flying machine would certainly have been noticed, too," said Battenberg.

"What about some sort of submersible vessel?" asked Fisher. "A large submarine which could have approached unseen and disgorged the invaders? I've warned about that sort of thing, you know!"

"We do keep a pretty close watch along the coastlines, Jacky," said Churchill. "There haven't been any signs of anything that looks like a shipyard anywhere. In fact, due to our naval strength, they've never even built one of their fortresses anywhere near the sea. But Martians with submarines would be as bad as Martians with aircraft, maybe worse. Professor, what do you think of those possibilities?"

"They certainly are possibilities, sir," said Lindemann. "We have speculated that we have not seen flying machines so far because the Martians evolved in an environment where the air was too thin for flying creatures, so they never attempted to emulate them as humans did with birds. There are no seas on Mars, so the Martians probably had no sea creatures to inspire them to build ships or submarines.

"But since arriving here, they have seen both and also seen how we make use of both the sea and the air to our advantage. They are clearly highly intelligent, and we have seen them introduce new devices like their scouting tripods and the spider machines. I suppose it is only a matter of time until they do start building air craft and water craft, and probably other machines we have not thought of."

The men in the room shifted in their chairs uneasily. These were ideas they probably did not want to think about. Enormous resources had been spent to give humans a fighting chance against the machines the Martians possessed when they first arrived. If they had to suddenly respond to new ones, would they be able to? *We have to be able to — which means we have to think about the possibilities.*

"Ah, yes, thank you, Professor," said Churchill after a bit. "As we have seen no evidence of flying machines or submarines, perhaps we should proceed on the assumption that the enemy did indeed walk their machines across the bottom of the strait to reach the island. If that is the case, what can we do to prevent them doing it again?"

"I would think that mines are the best bet, sir," said Admiral Pakenham, the Fourth Sea Lord. "Sow fields of mines in the shallow waters around the island and that would stop them."

"If they are really walking under the water, then standard sea mines would be so obvious they could just walk around them," said Battenberg.

"We'd need to develop a new type, perhaps link then together with cables, so they can't be gotten around without setting them off," replied Pakenham.

"That would take a great deal of time. We need to take the island back as quickly as possible and then hold on to it."

"Once we have it, we can establish a much tighter defense," said Fisher. "We only had a small squadron guarding the strait because it didn't seem like there was any danger. Now we know otherwise. If we keep a powerful squadron, close to the island, we can destroy the enemy as they try to emerge from the water, by God!" Fisher slapped his fist into his palm, his strange, oriental eyes were blazing.

"That does seem like our best course of action, Jacky," said Churchill. "I do like the idea of the mines though, too, William," he added, nodding at Pakenham. "If we are going to be facing the possibility of this sort of attack in the future, the mines could prove invaluable. I'll give orders to our ordnance people to start work on that. Oh, and there is one other thing. I'm bothered that we have no air reconnaissance in the region. The closest air bases are a thousand miles away in Egypt or on Socotra Island. The Royal Flying Corps refused to build a base on Perim, so we have nothing at all in the region. Jacky, the *Ark Royal* is finishing up her trials right now, isn't she? Could she be sent there with her seaplanes to give us some eyes in the sky, do you think?"

Lord Fisher blinked, opened his mouth as if to object, and then slowly nodded his head. "Capital idea, Winston! I'll have her dispatched at once! But she's slow so she won't be there in time for this operation."

"That's all right, but I'd like to get her out there anyway. Once we have the island back, we can build an air base of our own, but it will be good to have a mobile base, too. Well, I think that sums things up for now. We'll convene again once we've retaken the island to discuss how it all went. Good day, gentlemen."

The meeting broke up and the men dispersed. Churchill spoke with several of them individually before they left, but he made a little gesture to Lindemann indicating he should wait. Finally, he was free and came over to him. "Thanks for your help, there, Professor. I think you opened a few of their eyes."

"I hope so, sir."

"We have to keep in mind that things are going to keep changing in this war. We've adapted to the new conditions the Martians have created, but we have to assume that they will adapt as well. Nothing is going to stand still."

"Yes, sir, you are correct."

"So what did you think of Fisher's plan?"

Lindemann blinked. Churchill had often asked him questions on technical matters, but never one on specific operations. "Uh, well, the amount of firepower those ship represent ought to be able to sweep most of the enemy off that island, From what I understand, it's not very large and generally pretty flat, so their guns should be able to reach every part of it. But I agree that a single battalion of Marines doesn't seem like much of a force to seize the place."

"No, it's not. It's not sufficient at all. So I am going to twist Kitchener's arm and insist he give us a more substantial force and right quick."

"That seems wise, sir."

"All right, I must be off. Dinner on Wednesday?"

* * * * *

Aswan, Egypt, October, 1912

"So you will be heading out soon?" asked Vera Brittain.

"Yes," said Harry. "A few days at most. The fortress here is nearly complete and they are already pushing ships and troops farther up the river. I'm sure we'll be following along soon." He looked at the young woman who he'd come to think of as a good friend. "Do you think you'll be moving too?"

Vera shrugged, a small brown curl which had escaped her nurse's hat bobbed slightly. "I would imagine the hospital will relocate eventually. As long as you men keep getting hurt, you'll need us to patch you up so you can go out again." She sighed. "And again. Again, and again, until you don't come back."

Harry recognized that the you in her words was generic. It didn't mean him, just men in general. Vera had made it quite clear to him, after the third or fourth time he found an excuse to visit the hospital and accidentally run into her, that she was already engaged to some British fellow named Roland Leighton who was in the army somewhere in Mesopotamia. He'd been disappointed – but he kept finding excuses to visit her.

Aside from being pretty, she was... interesting. Smart and oh so talented; he might have kept coming back if she was sixty years old and ugly just to read her poetry. He suspected that it was his genuine interest in her writing that kept her from tossing him out on his ear.

The other officers in the company had found out about Vera and kidded him over wasting his time on her. But it wasn't wasted time, and the truth of the matter was that he wanted – needed – a friend who wasn't part of the 15th New Castle Battalion. He loved his chums in the company, but Good God, he'd been bumping elbows with them day and night for close to four years. Sometimes he got so sick of them. Burford's gloominess, MacDonald's cynicism, even Miller's good humor would rub him raw like the desert sand. Sometimes he just needed to get away from them. And wandering the wastelands alone had lost its charm quite a while ago. But Vera... Vera was different.

She was interested in everything, wanted to see everything, and thought deeply about what she saw and learned. He'd taken a certain satisfaction about being the best educated man in his company, but he'd met his match in Vera Brittain. She could hold her own in conversation about almost any subject — well, she didn't know anything about Mills Bombs or field maintenance for a SMLE Lee-Enfield rifle, but that hardly counted. She wasn't like any girl he'd ever met. Not that he'd met all that many, aside from his mother and sisters.

She was a very competent and conscientious nurse and obviously cared deeply for her patients. But she wrote poetry and essays and even sent articles back to England for some newspaper there. Harry liked her a great deal and he was certain that she liked him too — at least a little.

They were sitting at a table in the hospital's mess tent. There were plenty of other people around — it wouldn't have been proper for them to have been alone together — but they could ignore them. Vera pulled a sheet from a little leather folder she often carried and handed it to him. "I wrote this last night. What do you think?"

He took it and read:

> *The storm beats loud, and you are far away,*
> *The night is wild,*
> *On distant fields of battle breaks the day,*
> *My little child?*
>
> *I sought to shield you from the least of ills*
> *In bygone years,*
> *I soothed with dreams of manhood's far-off hills*
> *Your baby fears,*
>
> *But could not save you from the shock of strife;*
> *With radiant eyes*
> *You seized the sword and in the path of Life*
> *You sought your prize.*
>
> *The tempests rage, but you are fast asleep;*
> *Though winds be wild*
> *They cannot break your endless slumbers deep,*
> *My little child.*

"That's... that's lovely, Vera. But sad. So much of what you write is sad. Why?"

She took the sheet back, put it in her folder and shrugged, tilting her head charmingly. "A military hospital isn't exactly the place to find joy, Harry. There was a boy in the ward dying of pneumonia the other day calling for his mother and I wondered what she'd say if she could hear him calling, and this... this just came to me."

"Well, it is very good, even if it is sad."

"The world is a pretty sad place right now, wouldn't you say? More than half of it conquered by alien creatures who only think of us a food. Millions dead, more dying every day. Countless others driven from their homes — like you! I'm always amazed that you seem so chipper. You've got more reasons to be sad than I do. By the way, have you heard from your family recently?"

"I got a letter from my mother about a month ago. She's doing all right. Got a job sewing uniforms in one of the mills they are building there. My sisters are doing farm work. Ha! That's hard to picture; they wailed so much when Mum made them help weed her flower garden back home. Reading between the lines I think Sarah — she's the older one — may have a fellow. Not quite sure what to think about that."

"And how old is she?"

"Uh, she would be... Good God, she's sixteen now."

Vera snorted. "When I was that age, all that the girls thought about was getting married and having children. It had been drilled into us our whole lives."

"I... I guess it didn't take with you, though," said Harry, gesturing to her nurse uniform and then waving at the hospital around them.

"I always felt there had to be more than that to life. Oh, I plan to get married and have children, but I shouldn't be restricted to only that. Women are capable of more, even though most men don't think so. My father certainly thinks that way. I so wanted to go to university, but he wouldn't consider it. Waste of money, he said. I had finally managed to convince him to let me go, well, actually it was mostly my brother, Edward, who convinced him, and I had just started at Oxford when the Martians returned. Then the VAD was asking for volunteers and, well, here I am."

"Doing important work," said Harry nodding. "Hard to imagine Sarah being as determined as you, but war changes people. I'd probably scarcely recognize her if I saw her now."

"Do you miss her? Miss them all?"

"Sure. I haven't seen them for nearly two years and..." He paused; throat suddenly tight. "You trying to share some of that sadness with me, Vera?"

She grimaced, the corners of her mouth crimping in an interesting way. "Sorry. I do tend to do that to people, don't I?"

"Not always," he said, smiling. "When you get going on something that really interests you, you can light up the room. Like when we took that tour over to the Egyptian ruins the other week."

Vera blushed and laughed. "I did sort of get carried away, didn't I? But I'd read about them and then to actually see them... It was wonderful. There is so much wonder in the world. If it wasn't for this awful war..." She paused and looked at him with an odd expression. "Harry?"

"Yes?"

"I... I was thinking about writing an article for the paper. An article about you Australians. You've all suffered so much compared to the people back home..."

"They've suffered, too..." he answered automatically, startled. "The first invasion... do you remember that?"

"That was twelve years ago, Harry. I was eight at the time. I remember a big commotion, but I didn't understand what it was all about. My home is in Buxton in the midlands and they landed down south of London. We saw a few of the people who fled, but it was all over so quickly it really didn't affect me at all. But you, you've been driven out of your home altogether. I'm not sure the people in England can really imagine what that means. To be driven off your island completely. It would be like... like if everyone had been forced to flee to Ireland and France. Surely, it must bother you more than you let on?"

Harry bit his lip. This wasn't something he wanted to talk about, but Vera was looking at him expectantly. And he did like talking to her. "Yes, yes, it bothers me. We held onto Sydney for so long, years. All the time the Martians were taking the rest of Australia, we held Sydney. We knew a lot of folks were being killed and so many more were being forced to run. But we held Sydney and somehow it seemed like as long as we did, then we still held Australia. What was happening everywhere else was just temporary and we'd take it all back eventually.

"But then the decision was made to evacuate. We couldn't believe it at first. Leave? Run away? Leave *everything* to those... those monsters? We didn't want to believe it. And when we realized it was true we were all so angry. Angry at... England. They still had their homes. They had all the guns and tanks and ships that we needed to defend Australia, but they wouldn't help us! We had to give up and run, but they didn't!"

Harry found that he was quivering. All that pent-up anger that he'd had inside him for so long was breaking free like some rain-swollen river overwhelming a dam. He turned away from Vera and blinked back tears. Embarrassed, ashamed.

He flinched when she touched his arm. He turned back to look at her. "I'm sorry, Harry," she said quietly.

"N-not your fault. Not anyone's fault really — except the Martians'. We all understood the reasons. Australia was so far, so big. The Empire had other responsibilities like India and Canada and South Africa. They were a lot closer. They couldn't hold everything. Someone had to lose out and it was us. We understood but..."

"But that didn't matter to the people who had to lose their homes," said Vera.

"No, no it didn't. So, we were angry. But we still held on. Evacuating all those people took time, so we had to hold on. And we did. The Martians hit us, and we threw them back. We held until everyone was gone. I... we.... my battalion was with the rear guard. The last ones out. Had to swim to get to the boats. Most of the city was burning by then. The tripods were everywhere. I saw... I saw smoke coming from the neighborhood I grew up in." There were tears on his cheeks now and he angrily wiped them away. Vera was staring at him, wide eyed.

"I'm sorry," she whispered again.

He shook his head. "That wasn't the hard part, not really. By the time we left, the city was deserted. All the houses empty, most of the windows broken — there'd been a lot of looting, God knows why. Grass and weeds growing in all the gardens or poking up through cracks in the pavement. Trash everywhere. There were even 'roos roaming the streets, fleeing in front of the Martians, I guess. It had stopped bein' home even before we left, I think. Not how I remembered home, anyway."

"What... what was the hard part?" she asked.

"Not sure how to say it. But the way the Martians seem to destroy everything... All of us Aussies dream of going back, taking it back again. But there won't be anything to take back, will there? All the towns and cities will be gone by the time we can get back there. Everything covered with that damned red weed. It'll be like having to settle the place all over again. Starting from scratch. We all dream of going home, but we'll never be able to, will we?"

"I don't know, Harry. I hope you can go home again."

He sniffed, wiped his nose on his sleeve, and tried to smile, feeling, lighter somehow with this rambling confession to Vera. "Well, no matter whether I can or not, it isn't going to happen anytime soon. I guess that's what angers us the most: we're here, on the other side of the world, instead of trying to go back. Frustrating."

Vera nodded but didn't say anything. He was glad she didn't trot out the old saw about fighting the Martians anywhere would help eventually get them home. It might be true, but it was cold comfort. They stared at each other for a few moments and then she said:

"Would you mind if I wrote some of what you told me in my article? I wouldn't have to use your name if you didn't want?"

Harry shrugged. "I don't mind."

"Would any of your friends be willing to talk to me, do you think?"

"I... I can't see why not," he replied, not certain he really wanted any of them talking to her. "But we'll be leaving soon so I don't know that you'll have the chance. Well, maybe I can work something out."

"Thank you, that would be wonderful."

"Uh, have you heard anything from Roland, recently?" he asked, trying to change the subject, although this probably wasn't the best one to change it to. He wasn't sure what to make of this Roland Leighton. Vera seemed devoted to him, but she'd also admitted that she'd only known him for a few months before she joined the VAD and had not seen him since. To Harry it seemed like a rather tenuous relationship. She seemed much closer to her brother, Edward.

Vera's expression darkened. "Well, yes, I got a letter from him the other week but..."

"But what?"

"He sent me this." She reached into the leather folder and pulled out another sheet of paper and handed it to him. It was a poem, the man was a poet, too, blast him. Written in a clear, masculine hand:

> *Violets from Plug Street wood,*
> *Sweet, I send you oversea.*
> *(It is strange they should be blue,*
> *Blue, when his soaked blood was red,*
> *For they grew around his head:*
> *It is strange they should be blue.)*
> *Violets from Plug Street Wood,*
> *Think what they have meant to me —*
> *Life and hope and love and you.*
> *(And you did not see them grow,*
> *where his mangled body lay,*
> *Hiding horror from the day;*
> *Sweetest it was better so)*
> *Violets from oversea,*
> *To your dear, far, forgetting land,*
> *These I send in memory,*
> *Knowing you will understand.*

Harry read it through twice and shook his head. "It's nice, but I'm not sure I understand. Who's blood? Was some chum of his killed?"

Vera shook her head, looking very distressed. "I don't know. His letter was perfectly ordinary. Things are routine where he's stationed, guarding the Persian oil fields, he said. But then there was this."

"Maybe the words just came to him. You say that sometimes happens with you. It might not mean anything, Vera."

"I suppose," she said.

"Well, I have to be going. The colonel wants a dress parade this evening and I have to get ready. Wonderful talking with you Vera. I'll try to drop by again before we leave."

"Thanks for coming by, Harry. I do enjoy talking with you. Please take care of yourself."

* * * * *

Advanced Base 14-3-1, Cycle 597,845.3

"Kandanginar, the artificial satellite confirms that the prey creature water vessels are massing in great numbers a hundred *telequels* to the north of your position," said Jakruvnar, the leader of Clan Patralvus on the target world. "There are over fifty vessels, including one very large one. Are you prepared to resist their attack?"

Kandanginar regarded the image in the communications monitor and waved its tendrils in acknowledgement. "Yes, Commander. The emplacements for the super heavy heat rays have all been completed, the equipment mounted, and the power connections tested. Some minor adjustments to the targeting systems still needs to be finished, but I expect that to be done in a few tenths of a rotation. We are ready. I am concerned, however, that Group 18's preparations are not so far advanced."

"They have assured me that all is ready," said Jakruvnar.

"I am aware that Commander Xaxraltar has made this statement, but in my coordination talks with some of his subordinates, I believe that it overstates the situation and that some significant work remains to be done."

"That is disturbing," said Jakruvnar. "How serious a problem would this be if the attack comes soon?"

"Difficult to predict. I believe that at least some of their weapons are ready, but as you know, even with the extended range of the projectors, they still cannot fire effectively across the whole width of the strait. If the prey creatures could safely position themselves near the western shore, our own projectors could not engage them. To completely prevent passage, we must have weapons on both shores."

"Closing the strait to the prey creature vessels is a desirable, but secondary objective," replied Jakruvnar. "Protecting the tunnel, which soon will be completed, is the primary concern. It took considerable persuasion to convince the Colonial Conclave that this was a preferable method to a frontal attack against the enemy positions blocking the land route between Continents 1 and 2. If we were now to fail to protect the tunnel, it would be… unfortunate."

"I am aware of this, Commander. I am confident that we can protect the tunnel. Right now, it is unlikely that the enemy even knows of the tunnel's existence. This attack is probably aimed at only regaining control of the strait. In any case, we shall repel them."

"Very well. I am depending on you." Jakruvnar broke the connection and the screen went blank.

"The Commander seems… anxious about the coming battle," observed Lutnapnitav, from its seat nearby. "More so about possible criticism from the Colonial Conclave than from the physical consequences of the battle itself. Do I interpret this correctly?"

"I believe that you do. Falling out of favor with the council could have a greater effect on the clan than any material loss caused by a setback."

"I share many of your memories, Progenitor, but I must admit that the ones pertaining to the workings of both the Colonial Conclave here and the Council of Three Hundred on the Homeworld sometimes make little sense to me. Are we not all working for the good of the Race? Why is there so much strife among us?"

Kandanginar regarded its bud closely. Its curiosity was commendable, but its willingness to question, and even criticize, the methods and long-standing traditions of the clan and the Race could be disturbing. Many of those budded on the target world seem to share those characteristics. So far there had been no overt instances of disobedience, but it knew that the possibility of it had greatly upset the leaders on the Homeworld. Some said that this was a significant factor in the decision not to relocate the entire Race to the target world.

"Your questions are not easily answered, and this is not the time for it," it replied. "We must focus ourselves on the coming battle. I need you to assist me on the final preparations."

"Of course. Command and I obey."

As it happened, they had the rest of the day to complete their task. The prey creature fleet did not begin its approach until far into the night so as to arrive shortly after dawn of the following day. The long body of water to the north of the strait narrowed as it came to the strait so the enemy could be easily seen from both shores long before it got close enough to open fire so there was no risk of surprise.

Since capturing the island, the digging machines had worked without pause to construct underground shelters for the fighting machines and drones, so that none remained exposed on the surface. If things went well, they would have no role in the coming fight and there was no point in risking them. If somehow the enemy did manage to land forces on the island, the machines and drones could emerge to deal with them.

The primary defense of the island and the strait would the task of the new super heavy heat rays. Eight of them had been emplaced on the island and ten more along the eastern shore. Additional positions were being dug which would point to the south in case in the future the prey creatures would try to attack from that direction, but they would not be needed for the coming battle. Group 18 was supposed to have fifteen of its own projectors on the western shore. If the prey creature vessels came directly down the strait, they would be hit from three sides.

Unfortunately, as powerful as the new rays were, they still could not match the range of the prey creatures' largest projectile throwers. Under most conditions it was estimated that the rays would be able to inflict damage on the armored vessels at a distance of ten to twelve *telequels*. But the enemy weapons had been observed firing at fifteen or even twenty *telequels*. It was expected that the approaching fleet would open fire against the island at those ranges and there would be no way to fire back at them. The defenders would have to wait until the enemy came closer.

To avoid the risk of having the new heat rays damaged or destroyed by the expected long-range bombardment, they were emplaced in tunnels with many *quels* of rock around them and only a narrow opening through which they could fire. The projectors were set back from the tunnel mouths by a distance of twenty or thirty *quels* so that the enemy projectiles, which had to follow a parabolic trajectory, could not pass down the tunnels unless they were fired from extremely close range. This sort of mounting system necessarily limited the heat rays to a relatively narrow field of fire, but they had been carefully placed to provide full coverage of the strait. If the enemy could be lured in close enough, they would suffer heavily.

"Prey creature vessels have been sighted by Post 27, Progenitor," reported Lutnaptinav. The two of them were in the command post in the advanced base, out of any possible danger, but able to monitor everything that was going on. "They are advancing in several lines at a moderate speed. They should be in range to fire upon the island in a tenth rotation."

"Very good. All heat ray station, report your status."

Within moments all had reported that they were ready. The reactor was brought to full power and all energy conduits were functioning perfectly.

"We are ready," said Kandanginar. "Now we wait."

* * * * *

The Admiralty, London, October, 1912

"So now we wait," said Churchill.

"Yes, sir," said Frederick Lindemann. He glanced around the busy communications room in the Admiralty and despite his excitement found himself stifling a yawn. It was four in the morning and pitch-black outside. But in the Red Sea it was seven. The sun was coming up and the morning would bring battle. A telegram had arrived a few minutes before, that the fleet had sighted Perim Island and would begin the bombardment shortly.

"Rather amazing, isn't it?" said Churchill.

"Sir?"

"That here we are, comfortably waiting around in London and yet we are in almost instantaneous communications with our ships over three thousand miles away. Admiral Beresford sends out a wireless signal, our station in Cairo receives it, and then they send us a telegram by cable and mere minutes later it's in our hands."

"Oh, yes, sir, I see what you mean."

"Not like the old days, where messages could only be sent by ship. Back then you'd have to wait for weeks or months to get news. It's a good thing I didn't live in those times. I should think I'd go mad with the not knowing."

"Thank you for inviting me to be here, sir. It's… it's a real honor."

"Oh, glad to do it! I have to say I've gotten a great deal of good having you around, Professor. Not only do you know what you are talking about—a rare commodity indeed—but you have new ideas and aren't afraid to express them. Any organization as old as the Admiralty is going to become fossilized, so set in its ways that change is almost impossible. You've been like a breath of fresh air."

Lindemann was surprised and very pleased by the First Lord's words. This was exactly the sort of recognition he was hoping for when he first met Churchill. He was searching for some suitable reply when an orderly hurried up and handed Churchill another dispatch.

He read it and nodded. "They've opened fire."

* * * * *

Advanced Base 14-3-1, Cycle 597,845.3

The enemy was attacking. When someone opened the portal to the command chamber, it was possible to actually hear the bombardment, a low rumble in the distance. The prey creatures were unleashing formidable firepower against the island.

And accomplishing nothing.

Projectiles were striking all over the island, blasting craters and throwing plumes of dirt and debris high into the air. But aside from the hidden ray projectors, there was nothing there of any value which could be hit. All the fighting machines and drones were waiting deep underground in chambers which had been excavated for that purpose. Nothing could harm them there.

"No damage reported by any of the projector operators," said Lutnaptinav. "Of course, the enemy does not know of their existence. I suppose if they did and concentrated their fire against those locations, eventually they might smash through the surrounding rock."

"Given enough time and enough projectiles, that is possible," replied Kandanginar. "But that is not going to occur today. Still, it is a valid point. Perhaps we should construct additional firing positions and make the projectors mobile so they could be relocated if necessary."

"A wise precaution," said Lutnapnitav. "I am sure we will defeat this attack, but there could be more in the future."

"Perhaps, but if the coming operations are successful, the prey creatures may soon have more urgent matters to concern themselves about."

The bombardment continued for another hundredth rotation and then the observation posts reported that some of the prey creature war vessels were moving closer.

"They are in range of the northernmost ray projector," said Lutnaptinav.

"All positions hold your fire. We must draw them in closer. Fire only on my command."

"Will Group 18 also refrain from firing?" asked Lutnaptinav.

"That was the agreed plan."

More time passed and the bombardment slackened and then ceased entirely. Five of the smaller vessels drew closer to the island, but the others remained where they were. The closer vessels were in range of most of the projectors now and a message arrived from Commander Xaxraltar of Group 18.

"The others are not coming closer, Kandanginar. Shall we destroy the five vessels while we can?"

"Let us wait and see if we can attract better targets."

"What if these five moves past the island and into positions where we cannot fire on them?"

"What of it? They can do no significant harm by themselves. I advise that we wait."

It could tell that Xaxraltar was not pleased, but it agreed. The closer vessels did indeed cruise past the island, firing from time to time, at what Kandanginar did not know. But then they circled completely around and ended up back on the northern side.

"Progenitor, the other vessels are moving." declared Lutnaptinav.

Kandanginar checked the vision pickups from the observation stations and saw that it was true. Or partially true; not all of the vessels were moving, but over twenty of them were. "Very well, prepare to open fire on my command."

Closer and closer the enemy came. Kandanginar did not believe they were moving at their maximum speed, but the distance fell and fell. Perhaps one more telequel and...

"Progenitor, the Group 18 weapons have begun firing," said Lutnaptinav.

Kandanginar waved a few tendrils in irritation, but immediately said: "All weapons open fire."

In an instant, the enemy vessels found themselves being struck by over thirty of the new heat rays. The results were as effective—and satisfying—as it had hoped. Several vessels, struck by multiple rays at close range, exploded almost immediately, the intensely hot beams melting through their armor and igniting their stored ammunition supplies. Others, struck from farther away survived the initial attack, but caught fire or suffered minor explosions.

Five of the vessels were destroyed before there was any reaction from the prey. Then they, and the ones who had not come forward, began firing again and explosions erupted all around the places the ray projectors were mounted. The intensity of the rays made them easily visible and the enemy would have no trouble determining where they were coming from. Smoke and flying debris from their fire interfered slightly with the effectiveness of the rays but could not stop them. The rays which had destroyed their first targets now swiveled to find new ones. More enemy vessels exploded or burned and the ones who had closed now turned to escape from the trap they found themselves in. The prey increased their speed to try and get out of range, but vessel after vessel was destroyed.

"Progenitor, ray projector 16 reports that debris has blocked the entrance to their position and obstructed their field of fire. Constructor machines have been dispatched to clear the debris."

"Acknowledged. All positions continue to fire as long as you have targets."

Fifteen of the vessels were now obliterated or flaming wrecks. Most of the rest had fires burning on them. But they were pulling out of effective range and most of the ray projectors were in danger of overheating from this continuous operation. Kandanginar waited until two more vessel were destroyed and then ordered the fire to cease.

The surviving prey creature vessels continued to fire for another twentieth of a rotation, but eventually their weapons fell silent. They then sent a few small and fast vessels toward the location where the other vessels had sunk. Kandanginar, curious as to what they intended, did not order fire resumed until it realized the vessels were attempting to rescue prey creatures floating in the water. It then had the ray projectors that were in range destroy them. The enemy made no further attempts and their entire force retreated north before nightfall.

"A great victory, Progenitor," said Lutnaptinav. "We hurt the enemy badly and suffered no loss of our own. This island is now secure and the strait of water closed to the prey creatures."

"Yes," said Kandanginar, "but those are only secondary objectives. The main thing is that we can now safely complete the tunnel between the continents and protect it. We must bend all our efforts to that."

Chapter Eleven

The Admiralty, London, October, 1912

"*A*gamemnon sunk, *Dominion* sunk, *Hindustan* sunk, *Black Prince* sunk, *Essex* sunk..."

Prince Battenberg read off the litany of disaster in a voice fit for a funeral. But that's almost what this was, wasn't it? Frederick Lindemann sat off to one side of the large conference table, clasped his hands and bowed his head as though in church.

Most of the other men in the room looked as stunned as he felt. Churchill had the same pale, wooden expression as he'd had when the first telegrams had come through announcing the shattering defeat at the Bab el Mandab waterway.

"...*Challenger* sunk, *Boadicea* sunk, *Greyhound* sunk, *Doon* sunk, *Cherwell* still afloat, but probably doomed, *Hibernia* heavily damaged, *Hampshire* moderately damaged..."

Lord Fisher was the most physically distraught. He was huddled on a chair, rocking slightly forward and back, with tears streaming down his cheeks. It would normally have been his job to read off the list, but he was in no condition to do so.

"... and the French lost *Leon Gambetta* sunk and *Bouvet* seriously damaged. We have no word on casualties as of yet, but we have to assume they were very heavy with few survivors. Admiral Beresford is missing and presumed lost. Command has fallen to Admiral Gaunt. The fleet has withdrawn to a safe distance but is maintaining as close a watch on the strait as it can. Several ships from the Indian Ocean squadron are being sent to provide additional scouting from the south." Battenberg, finished, placed the paper on the table, slid it over to Churchill, and then sat down.

The First Lord did not touch the paper or even look at it. Instead he swept his eyes across the seated lords and admirals in the room and his expression sharpened and the color came back to his face. "Well!" he said loudly enough to make some people flinch. "A week ago, we sat in this very room and heard Professor Lindemann warn us that the Martians were capable of building new machines to adapt to changing circumstances. A shame that he was proved correct so soon. Even more of a shame that we didn't listen to him!"

"Winston, Winston, that's hardly fair!" moaned Fisher. "We had no way of knowing those damn... monsters, had built these new super heat rays! You can't hold us to blame for this!"

"No, I can't, since I am just as much to blame as anyone. More perhaps. But the King will surely hold me to account. And the Parliament. And the British people will as well." He looked again at the assembled men. "There is no doubt that we are responsible for this disaster. And yes, that's the word: a disaster. Sixteen ships lost, thousands of men killed and the strait still in the possession of the enemy. The short route to India is closed. What should I tell the King? What should I tell the people? 'These things happen'? 'Maybe we'll do better next time'?

"That won't do, gentlemen!" Churchill was on his feet now, the forgotten stub of a cigar in in his fist. "The blame rests on us, and we won't try to disguise the fact. But much more important than accepting the blame is answering the question of what do we do next? We cannot accept this. We will not accept this! The enemy has dealt us a hard blow; that cannot be denied. But we can deal out hard blows as well as take them!" His face was quite pink now and he thumped a fist on the tabletop.

"We've lost some ships, we've lost some fine men. But we have more ships and more men. Many more. The best in the world. We will take back Perim Island and secure the strait again. There is no question of that. The only questions that face us now are: how do we do it, and when can we do it? It is our job to answer those questions. So let us begin."

The mood in the room seemed to lighten a bit and expressions of agreement and determination appeared on many faces. Lindemann himself felt a small thrill pass through him. Churchill was an inspirational speaker, for certain. Fisher alone seemed unaffected by the First Lord's words and continued to blubber. Still, words would not take back the strait...

"We can certainly reinforce the Mediterranean Fleet and make up the losses in a few weeks, sir," said Battenberg. "But to simply make another attempt as we did the last one... well, I can't see it resulting anything different than the first one. I don't believe that ships alone can succeed."

"I agree," said Admiral Pakenham. "From the reports, the Martians have set up twenty-five or thirty of these new heat rays and have the strait in a cross fire. To try and run ships through there would be a bloody slaughter."

"But the range of the new rays is still shorter than our largest guns though, isn't that right?" asked Churchill.

"As near as can be determined, yes," said Battenberg. "They did not try to respond to the preliminary long-range bombardment. Now that may have just been meant to draw us into their trap—it almost certainly was—but even after the trap was sprung, they did not continue to fire once the survivors opened the range again as they retreated. Admiral Gaunt believes that against an armored target, the rays have an effective range of ten or fifteen thousand yards."

"Almost ten times the range of their normal rays," said Churchill, chewing on the remains of his cigar.

"Yes, sir."

"And our gun fire against the ray positions had no affect?"

"None that could be seen during the fighting. Detailed observations made later from a distance could not see anything that looked like normal weapons positions, just small openings cut in some of the rocky hillsides or cliffs. Apparently, the ray machines are deeply recessed in caves or tunnels. Shellfire against the rock isn't going to have much effect. Ark Royal is due there with her seaplanes in about four days, perhaps aerial observations will reveal more."

Churchill frowned. "Professor, what do you make of this?"

Lindemann straightened up in his chair. "Uh, well, sir, this new heat ray is probably just an enlarged version of the ones we've already seen. Just as it is possible to make larger and larger artillery with correspondingly longer range and greater destructive power, so it should be possible to make larger heat rays. No doubt the details of such an enlargement are more complex than making a larger gun, but obviously it can be done. It would appear that this new ray is too large to be mounted on one of their tripods.

"As for the way they are mounted, it is clear that the Martians are well aware of how our weapons work. They realized that since our shells follow a curved path, if they mounted their projectors set back in a tunnel, our shells could not reach them unless they were fired from a very close range. Their rays, of course, being pure energy, follow a straight path and can still hit distant targets even though they could not be elevated like one of our guns would need to be."

"So, trying to send ships against these things would be tantamount to suicide."

"Well, I imagine that if a ship could get near enough to put a shell directly down these tunnels with a flat enough trajectory then they might hit and destroy the ray projector. But the losses you would take getting that close would be…"

"Prohibitive," growled Churchill.

"Historically speaking, sir," said Battenberg, "shore batteries have always held an advantage over ships. Guns mounted in stout fortifications can only be destroyed by a direct hit. Near misses will do little but chip away at the body of the fort. Whereas any hit at all on a ship will contribute to its eventual destruction whether a gun is hit or not. This situation is about the same. If we were willing to commit overwhelming forces and accept heavy losses, we might be able to retake the strait, but I can't recommend such a course."

"No, no, of course not. If we equate one of these monster heat rays to a large piece of artillery, then simple arithmetic tells us that in the long run we shall run out of ships long before they run out of heat rays." Churchill paused, looked in disfavor at the stub of his cigar, took out a fresh one and lighted it. "So we can't do this job with ships alone. We shall require aid from the army."

"Didn't Kitchener already promise us some troops, sir?" asked Pakenham.

"Yes, but only a brigade to garrison the island. This is different. We shall need a major force to seize not only the island but both the eastern and western shores. It is obvious that we'll need troops and tanks to destroy the super heat ray positions and we can expect serious opposition from the Martians regular forces. At least naval gunfire should be able to help out with that. I have a meeting with the prime minister tomorrow and Kitchener will be there. I will hammer out just how serious a problem this is and get a commitment from both of them to deploy the forces we need to win.

"In the meantime, we must draw up our plans to reinforce the fleet in the Red Sea and start assembling the transports which will be needed to move an army there. I suspect most of the troops will be coming from Egypt and the campaign currently moving up the Nile, so the distances are relatively short. But we'll have to supply the army once it's there and that will take more ships. And after we secure the land around the strait we will need to hold it. That will mean the materials and equipment to construct major fortresses as we have done in Egypt. More ships. God knows where we'll find them all, but we must. That is your task, gentlemen. Get to work on it and we'll meet again after my meeting with Asquith."

The men rose and moved out of the room. Once again Churchill motioned Lindemann to remain behind. He did so, but when the rest of the others had left, Lord Fisher was still in his chair.

Churchill's face was filled with concern. He went over to stand in front of Fisher. "Jacky, are you all right?"

Fisher looked up; there were still tears on his cheeks. "All those ships! All those men! God forgive me!"

Churchill's expression slowly changed from concern to annoyance. "Jacky, pull yourself together man! You're the God-damned First Sea Lord!"

Fisher flinched as if he'd been slapped. In an instant his face went from dismay to rage. His mouth opened in a snarl and his eyes were blazing. He leapt to his feet.

"How dare you speak to me that way?! How dare you! I was serving in the Royal Navy before you were even born!"

"Jacky..."

"I won't have it! D'you hear me? I won't have it, you... you... *whippersnapper!*" He pushed past Churchill and stomped toward the door.

"Jacky..."

"I quit! You hear? I resign! I've had all of you that I can take!" He went out the door and slammed it behind him.

"Oh... dear..." gasped Lindemann.

Churchill shook his head. "Don't worry. He does this every few weeks. He'll be fine again in a day or two."

Lindemann had witnesses several of Fisher's outbursts in the past, but nothing like this. "It must be... difficult to deal with him."

"At times, but he can be brilliant, too. And people—the ones who don't see his tantrums—have confidence in him. That's worth a lot. But come with me back to my office. There's someone there I want you to meet."

He followed Churchill out of the meeting room and then up the grand staircase. A gentle October rain was tapping against the large windows. The First Lord's office was sumptuous, but just a bit shabby. Some of the furniture had worn spots and the carpet had clearly been there for a time. He realized that the place did not actually belong to Churchill and the décor was probably the work of some previous first lord, but obviously the present occupant had not made any changes. In his dealing with Churchill and his wife Clementine he'd come to the rather shocking realization that they were not at all wealthy. His line stretched back to the highest of the high nobility, his grandfather was the Duke of Marlborough, but being the descendant of a lesser son, he had not inherited any great wealth. Nor did he hold any titles beyond the temporary one of first lord of the admiralty, not even a knighthood. Amazingly, the bulk of his income seemed to derive from his writing. He was a prodigious writer with a number of books and many newspaper articles to his credit. Somehow, even in the midst of this great global war he still found time to write.

He did have some military rank and a few decorations, for in his youth he had been a gallant soldier—recklessly so sometimes. But his true passion was politics and even if he had been offered a title of nobility, he would have turned it down since that would have barred him from holding a seat in the House of Commons. He could have joined the House of Lords, of course, but that body had been stripped of nearly all power in recent years and that would not have satisfied Churchill at all.

As they entered the outer office, there was, indeed someone waiting for them. A tall, good looking man in an army major's uniform sprang to his feet. He looked to be in his late thirties and sported a small mustache and a sharp eye.

"Ah, Major Bridges," said Churchill. "Good of you to come." He motioned Lindemann forward. "Professor, let me introduce Major Tom Bridges, he's one of our military liaisons. Major, this is Professor Frederick Lindemann, my scientific advisor." Bridges immediately offered his hand and Lindemann took it. "We both served in the same regiment, you know, although not at the same time."

"Yes, the 4th Queen's Own Hussars," confirmed the major. His voice was a rich baritone. "Pleased to meet you Professor."

Churchill ushered both of them into his private office. "Major Bridges has spent some time in America this past year and he's come back with some very interesting information. I've asked him to tell us about it. Would either of you like something to drink?"

Lindemann and Bridges settled for tea, but Churchill had the steward provide him with a small glass of whiskey. "Need it after dealing with Fisher's tantrum," he muttered. Churchill seemed to be able to drink at any time of day or night. Lindemann had heard nasty talk about him being a drunk, but his own observations had been that Churchill could make a single glass last for a very long time and it merely looked as though he was drinking constantly. He had never once seen the man in any state of real intoxication.

After they were settled, Churchill said: "So Major, tell us about what our American cousins are up to."

"Oh, a great deal, sir." Bridges seemed completely at ease talking to the first lord. Lindemann suspected as a liaison, he must talk to a lot of high-ranking officials. "I spent quite a bit of time with one of their cavalry units. They are doing some novel things with horses, armored cars, and aircraft. But I imagine what you are really interested is their land ironclads. Am I right, sir?"

"Right you are," said Churchill. "The news stories and the official briefings I've seen say that they are amazing machines. You were actually stationed on one of them at Memphis, weren't you?"

"Yes, sir, the *Albuquerque*. The things are so large they give them names like ships."

"But that is what they are: land-going ships, correct?"

"Yes, sir. Here, I have some basic drawings of one of them." He opened his valise and took out several large sheets of paper which he unfolded and laid out on a table. They were standard mechanical drawings such as engineers or architects would use. Lindemann had done this sort of drafting himself from time to time. The sheets showed what was essentially a small warship, like a navy monitor, but mounted on two pairs of enormous caterpillar tracks similar to what an army tank would ride on. There was a bridge and observation tower, just like a navy ship, and then a turret with a very large gun and several others with smaller guns and a few more cannons mounted in casemates on the superstructure. From the dimensions on the drawing it looked like the thing was about two hundred feet long and fifty or sixty wide; rather small as warships went.

"They have boilers and coal bins like a ship," Bridges pointed out. "The steam from the boiler runs a turbine to produce electricity which drive electric motors down here in the tracks. They can go five or six miles an hour. They also have a propeller like a ship here in the back because the only way they can go long distances is by water."

"They can actually float?" asked Churchill. "Doesn't seem like they'd displace enough water to float."

"No, sir, they don't; not on their own. They can hook on large hollow tanks, 'floatation modules' the Yanks called them, to give them enough buoyancy to stay afloat. But the whole contraption is so unwieldy they have to have a larger ship tow them over any distance. I joined up with their first flotilla of them at Key West and stayed with them all the way to Memphis and then later to the Martian fortress near there. They're cramped, uncomfortable, mechanical nightmares, always breaking down, but they blew the bleeding hell out of the Martians when they encountered them. Captured a Martian fortress and that's something no one else has ever done."

"That's certainly true. What size is the main gun? Twelve-inch?"

"Yes, sir. The other ironclads have a seven-incher here, four five-inchers and a number of smaller guns. The one I was on, the *Albuquerque*, had replaced the seven-incher with an experimental weapon, some sort of lightning cannon which that Tesla fellow invented. Now that was something to see!"

"We've had some reports about that, but the Americans haven't seen fit to provide us with any details yet. Professor, what do you know about that?"

"Only what I've read in the press, sir," said Lindemann. "Apparently it is able to project an electrical charge of unprecedented intensity a considerable distance. I have no idea how it's done."

"So, would you advise that we build things like this, Major?" said Churchill, turning back to Bridges.

"There's no denying their effectiveness, sir. They can take heavy guns and heavy armor to places no ship can go. Of course, they are terribly unreliable mechanically, two out of the five sent against the fortress broke down after only twenty or thirty miles. And there was a sixth one which was damaged in a storm on the way to Key West."

"It's not unusually for a new machine to a lot of problems when first put into use," said Lindemann.

"True," said Bridges. "And the Americans are building more of them and they tell me they are using the experience gained from the first batch to make the next ones better. Their navy is building them, too, and theirs will be much more seaworthy. I got know one of the navy commanders pretty well during my stay."

Churchill continued to study the drawings, his new cigar had gone out, but he continued to chew on it. "We knew the Americans were working on these and we've done some studies on them ourselves, but we've never gone beyond the drawing stage. Damnation, I wish we had some now. This would be just the thing for down at Bab el Mandab."

"Perhaps the Yanks will let you borrow some of theirs, sir," said Bridges. "The first navy squadron is supposed to be completed fairly soon."

Churchill snorted. "I imagine they have their own plans for them, Major."

"I suppose so, sir."

Churchill stood back from the table. "Well, thank you Major, you've been most helpful. And do stay in touch, I'd love to hear any further thoughts you have on this subject."

"My pleasure, sir. Nice to have met you, Professor." Bridges folded up his papers, put them in his valise, made a small bow, and departed.

"Seems like a very competent fellow," ventured Lindemann.

"Yes, I'd heard about him and read his report, but I wanted to meet him in person. I always try to have contacts in as many places as I can."

Lindemann had noticed that. At the meals he'd shared with him, Churchill always had a wide range of guests from all branches of the government and services. A veritable spy network, it seemed. "So do you plan to build some of those things, sir?"

"I think so. They are little larger than a destroyer and our shipyards should be able to turn out everything but the caterpillar tracks in short order."

"The tracks will be the real challenge, I'm thinking."

"Yes. I know some people at Fosters and Metropolitan, who build a lot of our regular tanks and I'll see if they can come up with something." Churchill relit his cigar and then wandered over to the inevitable wall map, clutching his hands behind him. He stared at the Bab al Mandab.

"Well get our own land ironclads, but not soon enough to deal with this mess." He continued to stare at the map, but now his gaze was wider. "They are up to something," he muttered. "This wasn't just a move to deny the strait to us. There have been stirrings all over the Middle East. They tried to raid our oil fields in the Persian Gulf a few days ago. Unlike the Americans, our ships run on oil and that's where we get it. I wonder if the bounders have come to realize that? Do they have oil on Mars, do you think?"

"I don't know, sir..."

"And it looks like there's a new offensive brewing in the southern Ukraine." His hand swept up the map into Russia where there were a lot of red pins and not nearly enough white ones for the Russians. "We thought their next offensive would head up toward St. Petersburg to finish off the Tsar. He's concentrated what's left of his armies up there to try and stop them. But this seems to be headed southeastward, toward Romania. And the Turks report new attacks coming north out of Arabia. Blast, I wish we had better intelligence! Anything out of sight of the coast is just a huge blank to us. Once we do have Perim back I'm going to insist we put in an airfield and get some long-range aircraft based there."

"Don't we have some scouting parties in Arabia and Persia, sir?"

"A few. Takes a damn brave man to do that sort of thing, but we do a have a few wandering around the desert in there. I see their reports when they come in, but there haven't been any in a while." He thumped his fist in the center of Arabia. "What are they up to?"

* * * * *

Aswan, Egypt, November, 1912

Harry found Vera coming off her shift. He was glad to catch her because he only had a few minutes and somehow leaving without saying goodbye would have been just too painful.

"Vera!" He had to shout her name twice before she heard him, stopped, and turned.

"There you are," he said. "I was afraid I would miss you. We're finally going to be off. I know I've said good-bye about five times now, but it's for real this time, I'm afraid. And they're not even sending us up river, we've been ordered back to Cairo! Rumor has it that we're for some operation in the Red Sea. No idea what it's all about, but the boats are here to pick us up and headquarters is all in a tizzy and we've got orders to board in a few hours. I don't know if we'll be coming back here but I'll try to write to you and..."

He was babbling away when he noticed that Vera wasn't reacting at all. She was standing there like one of the stone statues dotting the Egyptian ruins. Her face was utterly blank.

"Vera? Vera, what's wrong?"

She flinched, seemed to see him at last. Her hands were shaking, and she fumbled one of them into a pocket and pulled out a piece of paper.

"I... I got this a little while ago," she said, her voice barely a whisper. "Roland's dead."

* * * * *

Advanced Base 14-3-1, Cycle 597,845.4

Kandanginar watched the image relayed by one of the construction machines. It showed the stone wall of a tunnel with piles of shattered stone lying about. Nothing appeared to be happening, but after a few moments some small pieces of rock fell off the face of the tunnel. More followed and some dust billowed up. Cracks appeared in the face of the wall and some larger chunks fell away. The image began to shudder as vibrations shook the machine carrying the vision pick-up. More cracks and more rocks fell and then the whole wall crumbled away and dust obscured everything. It quickly settled in the high gravity and it could see the front of the tunneling machine sent by Group 18 to meet their own. The meeting had been precisely calculated and the tunnel coming from the west met their own as perfectly as if it had been cut by a single machine.

"A successful operation, Progenitor," said Lutnaptinav.

"Yes, this has been most gratifying. We shall have the transport track laid and the tunnel open for movement in another three rotations. Then the clans on Continent 2 can send their forces through."

"And then?"

"Then the grand offensive can begin."

Chapter Twelve

Somewhere above Arabia, December, 1912

Major Erich Serno looked down from the control gondola of the zeppelin LZ-22 and watched the rolling dunes and strangely shaped rocky escarpments of the Arabian desert slide by below him. The region seemed utterly devoid of life although he supposed that was probably its natural state and had nothing to do with the fact that this was territory occupied by the Martians.

From time to time there would be a small patch of green; some oasis in the desert, but it was mostly just a sea of brown and tan with occasional patched of the red Martian lichen. Farther north, on the trip down from Constantinople, they had passed over the remains of some of the larger towns in the Levant and northern Arabia; Aleppo, Mosul, Al Jawl, and Medina. They were just ruins, of course, the Martians had been through those places, but at least you could tell that humans had once lived there. Out here, it was as if humans had never existed.

The zeppelin was cruising at nearly its maximum altitude, about four thousand meters, both to provide the maximum visibility and to assure they were out of range of any heat rays fired from the ground. Because there *were* Martians down there. They had cruised over one of their fortresses the day before and from time to time would catch the gleam of sunlight reflecting off the metal bodies of their machines.

Yes, the enemy was down there and the mission of the LZ-22 was to find out just where they were and in what strength. The Martians had overrun nearly the whole Arabian Peninsula in the first year after they arrived. For another year after that there had still been some people around to send periodic reports of what they had seen. But as time passed and the Martians grew more numerous most of the people had been killed or fled. Or captured, there were alarming reports of what they did to those they captured. There were still a few small bands of Bedouins wandering the wastelands, but any sort of reliable intelligence was very rare indeed.

It was Serno's mission to change that. He wasn't quite sure how his orders had changed from instructing Turkish pilots to commanding a pair of zeppelins. There had been no official written orders issued, but General von Sanders had told him he was a major and that for the time being this was his job and he was not about to argue about it.

The two zeppelins had arrived in November along with a shipload of equipment to support them. A large shed was being built to house them just west of Constantinople and several hundred men were there to perform maintenance and man the hydrogen generating equipment. Each of the zeppelins had its own captain, of course. Serno's job wasn't to command the airships, just direct their missions and make sure operations ran smoothly.

And from time to time take a ride with them.

There was no actual need for him to go along, but since no one had forbidden him to do so, he was perfectly willing to abuse his authority to this extent and have some fun. And he had to admit the zeppelins really were rather fun. They just cruised along, hour after hour—day after day! To be able to stay aloft so long was amazing in itself. With regular aircraft you had a few hours of fuel at most, but the zeppelins could carry enough for nearly a week of operations. At night they would turn off their engines and just drift with the wind. In the morning, they would get a navigational fix and resume their survey.

In essence, that was what they were doing: surveying. The Ottomans had maps of their sprawling empire, but they had not been the best, even before the Martians arrived. Now they were mostly obsolete with the human constructions destroyed and it was becoming apparent that even some of the natural features weren't quite where the maps showed them to be. In addition to the airship's crew, Serno had a four-man team of observers and a cartographical engineer to record what they were finding.

"Major?" Serno turned and saw one of the observers, Lieutenant Demm, beckoning to him. He went over and looked out the window. "According to the Turkish maps, we ought to be passing over the railroad line from Medina to Mecca, but there doesn't seem to be anything left of it. I think I can see some of the wooden ties scattered around, but the rails are all gone."

"Yes, they do seem to like to destroy the railways," replied Serno. "We don't know if they do it to deny us the use of them or because they want to salvage the metal in the rails. Maybe both."

"No one left around here to use them anymore. So, I guess they want the metal, sir."

"Yes, probably. When will we reach Mecca?"

"A couple of hours, sir. Bit of a headwind today. Oh, and we received a report from the British along the Nile that there is a considerable sandstorm heading this way. We need to watch out for that."

Serno nodded. Yes, bad weather was the only thing the zeppelins really needed to worry about. They were so long and had so much surface area that strong winds could possibly tear them apart.

"Are we getting regular reports from the British now? I know our ambassador in Constantinople passed along our request to them, but they didn't seem so happy with the idea."

"I wouldn't exactly call them regular, sir," said Demm. "But we are getting weather reports from time to time. Better than nothing, I guess."

Yes, it was better than nothing and it did signal an increasing measure of cooperation between the British and Germany and that was certainly a good thing. The only way they were going to beat the Martians was by cooperating.

After staring out the window for a while longer, he went over to the table where the engineer was carefully drafting the results of their observations onto a large sheet of paper. The man was meticulous, and his skills were like an artist. Eventually these notes would all be combined into a new map covering the whole area. Von Sanders should be pleased.

He watched the man work for a while, but then got up, stretched and decided to take a walk through the zeppelin, just to work the kinks out. There was a narrow passageway from the front to the back that ran under the huge bags which held the hydrogen gas. He was a bit nervous about the hydrogen. It was highly flammable, and one spark could set the while ship ablaze. There were very strict regulations to prevent any sparks; rubber soled shoes, no extraneous metal objects, and absolutely no smoking. Serno did like to smoke and he missed that.

He walked to the rear, stopped to peer out of a small observation window and then went all the way back to the front, ending in the control cabin. Captain Henrich Mathy was there, with his control crew. Mathy seemed like a decent sort and tolerated Serno's presence without a problem — although he made sure there was no doubt about who was in command of the airship. Serno was fine with that. He was a good pilot, but he knew little about controlling a zeppelin — but he was learning more with each flight.

"Good weather for flying today," he remarked.

"Yes, not bad, replied Mathy. "Once the sun gets up we encounter some significant updrafts, though, and we must be careful. I'm also a bit concerned about our hydrogen supply."

"Why? Are you having leaks?"

"Not leaks, but with the extreme temperature differences between night and day in this part of the world, we are losing more from venting than I like. During the day the sun warms the gas cells and they expand. If the pressure grows too high, we have to vent some gas. Then at night, everything cools off and the cells shrink again, and we lose lift. I have to release more hydrogen from our reserve cylinders to keep us aloft. The cycle repeats every day. It's not critical yet, but I need to keep my eyes on it."

"I see. How much longer can we stay out?"

"Maybe another two days and then we must head for home."

"All right. Keep me apprised, please."

"Certainly, Major."

Serno lingered a while longer, but then returned to the observation compartment. Nothing unusual was happening in there and he eventually fixed himself a cup of coffee. He was actually coming to like the Turkish coffee; when he had first arrived, he could barely force himself to drink the stuff.

"Major? We're coming up on Mecca. I... you can see where the big battle was, sir." Demm's voice had an oddly strained tone to it. Serno put down the coffee and went over to the window. He had to lean out to look straight ahead.

The holy city of the Moslems was up ahead but spread out on the plain before it was a blackened wasteland. When the Martians had first overrun the region and taken Mecca, the Islamic world had risen up in rage. Thousands, millions of them had taken it as a holy duty to recapture the place. Uncountable hordes had travelled to Arabia by rail, by boat, on horses and camels, or most often, on foot. They had assembled in the north and then marched on Mecca.

Sensible people had tried to stop them, but they would not listen. The Ottoman government has helpless to prevent the coming tragedy and probably would have been overthrown if they'd even tried. So, the Army of God, several million strong by some estimates, had marched south. Supplying them was an impossible task and many thousands died from hunger or thirst or disease before they got anywhere near their goal. Those that did survive had little in the way of weapons. A few had modern rifles, more had muskets, some had bows, but the bulk of them had nothing but swords and spears — or rocks and clubs.

The Martians slaughtered them.

No one knew what the enemy thought of this huge mass of people marching into their territory, but they let it come on all the way to Mecca — and then they struck. No details of the 'battle' had survived, but the few who escaped said that a hundred or more tripods had appeared and simply killed everyone in reach with their heat rays.

The tragedy had happened over three years ago, but the infrequent rains and blowing sands had not completely erased the evidence. Serno looked down and then got out a pair of binoculars. From this altitude it wasn't possible to see any small details and a person caught in the full force of a heat ray would be completely vaporized anyway, but he could still tell that something awful had happened here.

The Muslims called this *Majal Almawt*, the Field of Death and even from three thousand meters there was a feel of death to the place that made Serno shiver. Large blackened patches covered swaths across the plain which looked to be about twenty kilometers wide in places. Some low hills ringed the flat area, making it a perfect killing ground. Some of the black patches had a glittery quality to them; perhaps the heat had fused the sand to glass?

To make the horror of the place even worse, the Martian red weed covered most of the areas which hadn't been burned black. It wasn't exactly the shade of spilled blood, but the comparison was unavoidable. He'd been seeing more and more of the red weed as they'd flown south.

Too slowly the place slid by below him, but eventually they passed another set of hills and the ruins of Mecca lay just beyond. It had not been a large town, maybe fifty thousand permanent residents, plus the innumerable pilgrims. But being constructed mostly of non-flammable materials like stone and adobe, much of it still remained. Just the walls, of course, but you could at least tell that it had once been a city.

Before he left, Lieutenant Wulzinger, his aide and former archeology student, had suggested he keep a lookout for where the Black Stone of Mecca rested in the center of the Grand Mosque. Wulzinger had told him most of the legend of the stone before he could shut him up. Sarno looked, but while he thought he could identify the Grand Mosque just by its size and location, nothing resembling this stone was visible among the rubble.

One of the observers had a camera and was taking photographs. When they learned of this flight, some of the Ottoman officials had asked that this be done, and von Sanders had made it an order. Serno wasn't sure what they were hoping for.

Captain Mathy circled the city once and then continued on south. There was supposed to be another Martian fortress down that way, and they wanted to find its exact location.

Three hours of cruising brought them to what was left of the town of Al Bahah. There wasn't much there, but they did spot a group of tripods marching north. There were fifteen of them, the largest group they'd seen so far this trip. The enemy machines halted when the airship got closer and Serno would have sworn that they turned to watch as it flew past.

It was late afternoon when they reached Abha and it was just as destroyed as all the other towns they had passed. They still had not spotted the rumored Martian fortress, but they were flying down the western coast of the peninsula with the Red Sea barely visible on the horizon. Tomorrow they would go a hundred kilometers inland and parallel their earlier course but going north. It was possible they wouldn't find it this trip. The LZ-25 would be coming this way in another week and could continue the search. Serno estimated it would take three months to do a good survey of all of Arabia.

He stared off in the direction of the Red Sea, but he couldn't really see anything. They had gotten news the other week about some serious defeat the British had suffered down at the southern exit. But that was still hundreds of kilometers farther south and they wouldn't be going there on this trip.

He was just starting to think about dinner—the zeppelin had a small, flame-free electric galley—when a man came pounding into the cabin from the forward control room. "Major! Major Serno!"

"Yes?"

"We are receiving a wireless message!"

"From Constantinople?" If the atmospheric conditions were just right they could pick up a signal from that far, but usually they were not. But that was hardly an emergency...

"No sir! From the ground close by! It... it's in German!"

"What?" His eyebrows shot up. "We don't have any of our people down there!" He followed the man forward to where Captain Mathy was bent over the wireless operator.

"Ah, Major," he said when he saw him. "A bit of a puzzle here. A signal from the ground. By its strength it must be quite close. It just says: 'German zeppelin, please respond.' I haven't answered yet. Do you want me to?"

"Any tripods nearby?"

"None that we've seen."

Serno shrugged. "Why not? Go ahead. Ask them to identify themselves."

The wireless operator tapped out the message on his key and then listened for a reply. It came almost immediately, and the man wrote it out on a pad of paper. When it was finished, he handed it to Captain Mathy who looked at it and frowned. "The sender claims to be a Lieutenant Lawrence of the British army. He's asking us for a lift. Says he has vital information."

"A lift? He wants us to land and pick him up? Is he mad?"

Mathy shrugged. "Aren't all Englishmen? But the conditions are calm enough that we could probably manage it." He glanced out the window. "Depends on where he is down there."

"Really? You'd be willing to risk it?"

"We could try—if you order it, Major."

Serno rocked back in surprise. He would have expected Mathy to refuse. But was this worth the risk?

"It could be a trap, sir," said Mathy's executive officer, Leutnant Mueller.

"A rather remarkable one if it is," said Mathy. "The Martians have never communicated with any human before. For them to do so now..."

"And to know that this airship is German, and to somehow be able to transmit a Morse message in German," added Serno.

"And the sender used the English spelling for his rank," added the wireless operator.

"It's your decision, Major," said Mathy.

"Well," said Serno, "see if you can figure out exactly where he is and we'll see if it's practicable. And have everyone on the lookout for any Martians."

An exchange of messages managed to locate the mysterious Lawrence on a hilltop a few miles to their east. They circled it and found no sign of the enemy. "It's going to be getting dark soon," said Mathy. "If we are going to try this, we need to do it now."

"All right," said Serno at last. "Go ahead."

The zeppelin began descending and lining itself up to approach the hill going into the wind. The man on the ground had a mirror and flashed sunlight off it to give his exact location. Lower and lower, and slower and slower they went. Soon they could see a man standing in the open slowly waving his arms above his head.

"Too tricky to actually touch down," said Mathy. "I'm going to lower a rope and pull him aboard."

"Sounds reasonable."

Serno had to admire Mathy's skill in maneuvering the huge, bulky airship. They came in at little more than a walking pace about ten meters above the man. The rope was thrown down and he quickly tied it around himself and three crewmen hauled him aboard. The zeppelin's engines took on a louder tone, the nose angled up and some of the water ballast was jettisoned to allow them to regain altitude.

Serno went over to stare at their hitchhiker. He was a short fellow wearing a worn and very dusty British army uniform, but with an Arab-style headdress. He had several bags and satchels on his person and a case for binoculars. He was thanking the men who had hauled him up, speaking in accented, but very passable German. Serno went up to him.

"I'm Major Erich Serno," he said. "What can we do for you, Lieutenant...?"

"Lawrence, Tom Lawrence," the man replied. "Thanks so much for bringing me aboard. Thought I was a goner for sure."

"What on Earth were you doing down there?"

"Oh, same as you I expect: scouting. But I was doing it much more slowly and far more painfully, I image." He smiled and looked around the zeppelin's cabin. "Quite a machine you have here. We British would do well to build some of our own."

"You said you have vital information? Or was that just a ruse to get us to pick you up?"

"Oh no, although I might have done that, now that you mention it. But no, I do have information that you — and everyone — needs to know about."

"And that is?" asked Serno getting a little annoyed at the chatty Englishman.

"A bloody great lot of tripods heading north. Four or five hundred at least and more coming. I think they must be coming from Africa."

"What?! How can that be? We'd heard that the Martians had captured that island in the Bab el Mandab strait, but how could they have built a bridge across there so quickly? Or are they using boats of some sort?"

"Don't think it was a bridge or boats, old man," replied Lawrence. "I'd been out here knocking around Arabia for a few months when I received orders to head south and see if I could find out what was going on in the area around the strait. I had a half dozen Arabs with me then. Good chaps, but when they got sight of all the Martians they bolted and left me. Can't really blame them, I suppose.

"Anyway, I had gotten up onto a mountain near what's left of Taizz in hopes of surveying the area before I got closer. Couldn't actually see the strait from where I was, still sixty or seventy miles away, but when I got up there, I saw more than I wanted."

"What do you mean?" asked Serno.

"I was looking across a long valley toward another line of hills. The strait were on the other side of them. But the whole valley was filled with rubble. Like the tailings out of a mine. Big piles of it all over the place. And there was what looked like a hole drilled into the side of one of the hills. There seemed to be a lot of activity going on around it, but I couldn't see clearly over that distance even with my field glasses.

"But what I could see was rows and rows of the tripods standing off to the side of the hole. Every minute or so there would be another one of them appearing and marching over to join the others. There's no place they could have been coming from except out of that hole."

"Could there be a Martian fortress built under the hill?"

"Maybe, but if so, it was unlike any fortress anyone's ever seen before. But every hour or so the whole batch would suddenly start moving and march off toward the north east, into the interior of Arabia. I watched for nearly a day and there seemed to be no end to them. Some of them seemed to be of a type we haven't seen before. Smaller than one of their scouts, but much larger than their spider machines — of which there were large numbers too, by the way. Group after group came out of that hole and then moved off. My guess is that the blighters have dug a tunnel from there over to the African side."

"A tunnel! Is that possible?"

Lawrence shrugged. "When the Yanks captured that fortress last summer, they reported miles of tunnels underneath it. They clearly have some method of digging extensive tunnels. No reason why they couldn't dig one under the strait."

"And you say they were all moving northeast?"

"For as far as I could watch them, which wasn't all that far from where I was situated. As soon as I realized what was going on, I headed north. My radio doesn't have much range and I wanted to get to the coast and try to raise one of our ships. A risky venture as we've noticed the Martians do patrol the coastline pretty heavily. But then I spotted you chaps and decided I'd rather fly. And we'd best get going, old chap. Where is your base? We need to get word of this to both our governments."

Serno chewed on his lip. If what the man said was true then yes, they did need to get the word to von Sanders in Constantinople as quickly as possible. A force the size Lawrence was describing could slice right through the Ottoman defenses in southern Turkey. If that's where those tripods were going, of course. He could just see von Sanders asking him if he'd seen those tripods himself or just blithely accepted the word of this strange Englishman?

He turned to Captain Mathy, who had come aft to see the new passenger himself. "Captain, please steer us northeast. This man reports a huge group of tripods off in that direction. We need to see them for ourselves."

"Wait a minute," said Lawrence urgently. "I saw them three days ago! I have no idea where they are now."

"Well, we can make a guess about where they might be from their speed and the time you saw them," said Serno back gruffly. "Captain, please chart a course and get us on it at once."

Mathy frowned but nodded. "We would have had to turn for home tomorrow anyway and this course is not too far off our direction. Very good, I'll get us moving."

Lawrence protested for a few more moments, but Serno just directed that the man be given food and water and then left him to join Mathy at the navigation table. They studied the maps they had of the region which, since they hadn't surveyed that area yet, were of doubtful reliability.

"Town and road locations are suspect," said Mathy, "But they get the mountain ranges pretty accurately. If the tripods were heading off to the northeast, they'd almost have to swing around to the east of this range here." He pointed to an area on the map. "From there they'd be heading into the Al Rubal Khali Desert. They could follow that north toward Riyadh; it would be easier going for them than the mountains. From there, they could continue north toward Kuwait and the Persian Gulf, or bend northwest toward the Levant."

"Well, we ought to be able to overtake them before they reach Riyadh, shouldn't we?"

"I don't know," said Mathy. "Those tripods can go about thirty kilometers an hour on level ground, I'm told. If they kept moving without a pause, they could have almost reached Kuwait by now."

"Well, all we can do is try to catch up."

"Yes, we can try."

Instead of drifting as they usually did at night, the zeppelin kept its engines running and went northeast at its top speed. The desert below has utterly dark until the moon came up around midnight, which turned the dunes into a silvery seascape of amazing beauty.

"I've spent years in the desert," said Lawrence, looking out beside Serno, "but I've never seen it from this angle."

"Your German is very good," said Serno. "Where did you learn?"

"Oh, at university. I know German, French, Latin, Greek; seem to have a knack for languages. I was planning to be an archeologist before the war."

"Really? I'll have to have you meet my aide when we get back. That was his goal, too."

"You don't say! What's his name?"

"Wulzinger, Carl Wulzinger."

"Can't say I recognize it. University at Berlin?"

"So, he says. Well, I think I will try to get some sleep; I imagine we'll have a full day tomorrow. I'm afraid all we have are hammocks here, but I'll have one rigged for you."

"Thanks very much, I do appreciate it."

Serno didn't sleep terribly well. The hammock was comfortable enough, but his mind would not stop wrestling with the problem which had fallen in his lap. Hundreds of tripods heading north. The Martians already had a significant force arrayed against the Ottomans in Turkey and against the British in the Levant and Sinai, but this new force, if it stayed concentrated could probably smash through at any point it chose. So where was it heading?

It might be going for the oil fields around Basra. The British depended on that oil for their fleet. Did the Martians realize that? Or it could be heading for Sinai. The British were obsessed with keeping the Suez Canal open, although with the recent loss of control of the strait of Bab el Mandab, it wasn't quite so valuable as it once was, and an attack through Sinai could close it just as effectively as a strike through Egypt.

Or, they could be headed to Turkey. Of all the possibilities that was the one that concerned Serno the most. Only the rugged mountain terrain—and the Martian habit of stopping to consolidate after a victory—prevented them from smashing through the Ottoman army all the way to Constantinople. With a force like the one Lawrence claimed, there would be no stopping them. He worked the puzzle until finally he drifted off.

* * * * *

Holdfast 14-1, Cycle 597,845.4

Kandanginar was in a meeting with the Jakruvnar and Xlatangi-noor, the Clan Patralvus leaders and Xaxraltar, the commander of the forces sent from Continent 2, when the alert came. The subordinate who appeared on the communications monitor appeared distraught to have to interrupt so many of its elders.

"Commander Jakruvnar, forgive the intrusion, but a prey creature air vehicle has been sighted twenty *telequels* to the west of the holdfast. It is very large and matches the description of one reported by Group 13 to the north four rotations ago."

"Indeed?" said Jakruvnar. "Relay an image here."

The subordinate's image disappeared and was replaced with one showing the too blue sky of the target world and the mountain ranges to the west of the holdfast. An elongated dot floated above the mountains. After a moment the image zoomed in on the object and it could be seen as a long cylinder, pointed at one end and with projections at the other. A smaller pod was attached to the underside and four even smaller ones were attached at intervals down the length of the cylinder.

"Interesting," said Jakruvnar. "It is unlike the other air vehicles we have observed. It does not appear to have the large airfoils which provide the lift to keep them aloft."

"I theorize that considering its large size, this vehicle must be most-ly hollow and filled with some light gas, perhaps elements one or two," said Kandanginar.

"Does it pose any threat?" asked Jakruvnar.

"It could carry explosive bombs, but it seems unlikely it could carry enough of them to do more than superficial damage."

"But it is observing us," protested Xaxraltar. "It will be able to see the forces we have amassed here. "We have gone to considerable effort to conceal the transfer of forces in order to achieve surprise in the offensive. If this thing is able to report what it has seen, that will be lost."

Jakruvnar contacted the subordinate again. "Has the vehicle made any transmissions?"

"No, Commander. Not so far."

"At what altitude is it flying?"

"Slightly more than four thousand *quels*, Commander."

"Beyond effective range of the heat rays on our tripods," said Xlatanginoor.

"Perhaps," said Kandanginar. "But for this thing to stay aloft it must be very lightly constructed. Perhaps massed fire from our fighting machines, all concentrated on it, might be enough to destroy it."

"Unfortunate that you do not have any of the new heavy heat rays mounted here," said Xaxraltar.

"There was no apparent need," said Jakruvnar. "All production was directed to the operation at the strait separating the continents. But let us do as Kandanginar suggests. Order the fighting machines to close on this vehicle as quickly as possible and concentrate all of their fire against it."

"At once, Commander."

* * * * *

Central Arabia, December, 1912

"Well, there they are," said Captain Mathy. "Looks like we found one of their fortresses, too."

"My God, look at all those tripods," muttered Serno, staring through his field glasses. "Hectares of the spider machines, too, I think. Hard to tell for sure at this distance..."

"I told you so, old man," said Lieutenant Lawrence, who was looking through his own glasses. "Of course, I have no way of knowing if these are the same ones I saw, but I suspect they are."

"There are a hell of a lot of them, no matter where they came from. Can't really get a good count from here. Captain, can you get us closer?"

"I can," replied Mathy. "Not really sure I want to..."

"They can't hurt us this high, can they?"

"In theory, no. We're at almost four thousand meters and tests have shown the heat rays disperse and lose their effectiveness at about three thousand. But Major, let me remind you, those tests were made against armor plate and mannequins. They never tried it against a zeppelin!"

"Well, get us a little closer, alright?"

"Very well." Mathy gave the command and the airship, which had been cruising about twenty kilometers to the west of the fortress without getting closer now turned east to shorten the distance. After about ten minutes, they had cut the distance in half. "Close enough?" asked Mathy.

Serno squinted through his glasses. The Martian fortress was built along the same lines as all the others which had been seen: a ring of raised earth about four kilometers in diameter which acted as a defensive rampart. Towers were erected at intervals around the rim, each containing a heat ray projector. Inside the ring there weren't any structures, all of those were apparently underground. Here there were masses of tripods arrayed inside the ring but... "Still can't quite count the individual tripods. Maybe a few kilometers closer?" Mathy frowned and snorted but kept the zeppelin on course.

"Wait a moment!" cried Lawrence. "They're starting to move!"

Serno looked closer and sure enough a whole block of the ranked tripods had started to move...

Straight toward them.

"Got a bad feeling about this," said Lawrence. "I suggest we get the hell out of here, Major."

"Yes... I think you're right. Captain, turn us around!"

Mathy shouted orders and the airship went into a tight turn, banking a bit as it did so. The engines took on a sharper tone as they went to full power. Serno went from window to window as the view shifted. The tripods were marching over the ramparts of the fortress and moving toward them at their fastest pace.

"We can outrun them, can't we?" he called to Mathy. "Our top speed is higher, right?"

"We've got a head wind, but we should still be faster."

"Let's hope so. These bastards are coming on like they have a purpose." He turned his glasses back on the tripods. They were across the ramparts and there looked to be about a hundred of them. Some of the others back in the fortress were now starting to move, too, but they were well behind. Maybe they were just trying to scare...

The world turned red.

A blast of bright red light filled his vision and he could feel heat on his face and hands. He cried out, dropped the glasses, and turned away.

"They're shooting at us!" cried someone. *Really? Who'd have guessed?* Serno rubbed his watering eyes and was relieved that he wasn't blind. All around him the others who had been looking were in similar conditions. Those who had been spared were crouching down to avoid the red glare. It was getting noticeably warmer.

"Maximum climb!" screamed Mathy. "Jettison all ballast!"

The airship pitched its nose up sharply and Serno clutched a stanchion to steady himself. He pulled himself up and forward into the control cabin. The glare was less there as the windows were all pointed away from the enemy. Serno dared to look out and he could see that the skin of the ship bathed in the red glow. The lower part of the envelope had been coated with aluminum paint, which ought to give some protection, but what if it got hot enough to ignite the fabric?

"H-how high can we go?"

"I've never been above five thousand meters, but I'm going to break that today. All of those tripods are firing at us at once! Combining their rays. If we can't get clear we will burn—or the gas cells will rupture, which will kill us all the same."

The cabin was getting hot now and Serno's chest felt like it was in a vise. The air got very thin at five thousand meters and many men would pass out even below that. He had only been that high on a few occasions and he didn't like the effects at all, but they had no choice here. He gently slid down to the floor and hung on.

The engines took on an even higher pitch as Mathy had their throttles pushed to the limit and the whole craft was vibrating a bit. The heat coming through the floor of the cabin was becoming uncomfortable and he pulled himself upright but was instantly dizzy; only by clutching the stanchion did he avoid falling down. The helmsman staggered away from the wheel and collapsed, Mathy immediately seized the controls.

"Fifty-five hundred!" he cried. "That's as high as I can take it! Leveling out."

A puff of cooler air wafted through the cabin; not just cool, downright frigid, but it felt good. Were they getting away? Reeling like a drunken man, he stepped over to a window and looked down and back. There was still a dazzling red light coming up from the ground, but it seemed much farther away and the heat from it much less. Looking directly down, he saw they were over the mountains now and the tripods would have trouble following them quickly. After a few more minutes, the rays started to wink out and soon they were all gone.

"They... they've stopped firing," he gasped.

"Mathy nodded. "Taking us down," he mumbled. He fiddled with the controls and the nose of the ship angled downward, the motors throttled back a bit and it was suddenly very chilly in the cabin. Serno slid down the floor again which was now pleasantly warm. *Wow, I don't ever want to do that again...*

His eyes suddenly popped open and he muzzily realized that he had fallen asleep. *Asleep, yeah, that sounds better than passed out, doesn't it?* Looking around, he saw that he wasn't the only one. Several others of the control crew were still out. Mathy was not one of them, though and he was looking at him with an annoyed expression.

"I'm taking us back to base, Major." It was clearly a statement and not a request. "If we can make it," he added and Serno instantly came alert.

"Have we been damaged?"

"I don't think so, but I had to dump all of our water ballast and we vented a lot of gas with the heat and altitude. It's going to be a race to see if we can get home before we don't have enough lift to stay aloft."

"I understand. Well, do your best. And let me know as soon as your wireless operator can contact anyone. We need to pass on what we've seen whether we make it or not."

"Right." He turned back to his controls, kicking the helmsman to wake him up.

They did make it, but just barely.

With the daily heating and cooling cycle, they continued to lose hydrogen during the heat of the day and then at night they would lose altitude as the gas cells cooled again. By morning they would be a lot lower than they liked until the sun warmed things up again. After the first night Mathy had used up the last of their reserve hydrogen. Halfway through the second night Mathy had everyone awake and throwing out anything that wasn't vital. Clothing, food supplies, cooking gear, even the empty hydrogen cylinders all went overboard. Fortunately, with the engines running all the time they were burning up petrol at a furious rate and that lightened the ship, too.

But they made it over the mountains in Anatolia and it was all downhill after that. They got into radio contact with their base and passed on their report. This led to an endless stream of questions coming back from von Sanders, which kept Serno busy almost to the point that he stopped worrying about staying airborne.

Lieutenant Lawrence went from an amusing distraction to a serious annoyance. He asked, formally requested, and ultimately demanded to be allowed to send a message to his own people. Serno asked von Sanders and was told that under no circumstances should Lawrence be allowed to send any messages until they arrived back at Constantinople and he was interviewed. Late the second night Serno found Lawrence trying to pick the lock on the wireless cabinet.

"Major, the British really need to know!" he pleaded. "You can see that can't you? If we are ever going to beat these blighters, we need to work together!"

Serno *did* see that, but orders were orders. "We'll be back at Constantinople in another day," he told him. "Assuming we don't crash first, of course. I'm sure you'll be allowed to go about your business after the general talks with you. One more day can't make that big a difference, Lieutenant." Lawrence obviously thought otherwise but had no choice but to accept it.

But at last they were approaching their destination. The Bosporus sparkled in the distance and they were still five hundred meters above the ground. "We could land at my airfield in Skutari if we had to," said Serno to Mathy. That's where the zeppelin service used to go when I first got here."

"We've got orders to go to the new airfield," he replied. "I guess they want to get you and your report to the main headquarters right away. In any case, my hydrogen supplies are all there. Don't worry, we'll make it."

He was right, but it was near thing. They were down to a hundred meters by the time they were across the water and over the landing field. The ground crews were waiting for the ropes which were tossed down and they quickly had the airship locked to its mooring post. A few minutes later the gangway was let down and the crew stiffly debarked. An orderly came up to him and saluted.

"Major? A staff car has been dispatched to pick you up. It should be here shortly."

Serno thanked him and sighed. What he really wanted was a good meal and a bath, but he knew that wasn't going to happen until he had been debriefed by von Sanders.

"Major?" He turned and saw it was Lawrence. "I'm no stranger to how the high command works. They might detain me there for *days*! I simply must contact my own superiors about this. Those tripods we saw could almost be to Basra by now if that's their objective. And might I point out that you wouldn't even know about this but for me. You owe me that much."

Serno frowned. The man was right, they did own him. But what could he do? He glanced around, but no one was paying him any particular attention at the moment. He turned back to Lawrence.

"I'm afraid there isn't a thing I can do, Lieutenant. But you are a bit under foot around here. Why don't you just wait for the staff car to pick us up? Yes, why don't you wait right over there?" He pointed to the construction site where the zeppelin shed was being built, several hundred meters away. There were dozens of men scampering about and piles of materials. "Wait over there and don't go anywhere, do you understand?"

A smile crept across Lawrence's face. "Why yes, sir, I think I understand perfectly. And thank you, Major!" Serno extended his hand and Lawrence shook it.

"Good luck to you."

Lawrence strolled casually across the field, hands stuck in his pockets. He stopped and leaned against a stack of lumber. Serno turned away and did not look in that direction again. After about ten minutes the promised staff car arrived and Colonel von Falkenberg himself popped out.

"Serno! There you are! Come on, the general wants to see you right away. And that Englishman. Where is he?"

"He's right over there..." He turned and exclaimed: "Why the scoundrel has bolted!"

Chapter Thirteen

Admiralty House, London, December, 1912

"So, is your grand offensive all ready to go, Dear?" asked Clementine Churchill.

The First Lord of the Admiralty looked up from his discussion with Lloyd George and Frederick Lindemann and smiled at his wife. "I thought you had forbidden any talk about military matters on New Year's Eve, Dear." He gestured to the small holiday gathering of guests at his official residence. They had finished a very pleasant dinner and were now waiting for the clock to reach midnight.

Clementine snorted, "And what were you three talking about just now?"

"Caught in the act, gentleman! Egad, we've been found out!" Lloyd George and Lindeman chuckled, as did Clementine, but she persisted: "Well?"

Churchill leaned back in his chair and took a sip from his glass of Champaign. "Nearly, nearly. Another week or so and we'll be ready to go. This is going to be a very difficult operation for a number of reasons, and we have to get everything just right."

"I should think so! With half the newspapers in the country shouting for your head and the conservatives in the Commons demanding your resignation…"

"Ah! Ah!" interrupted Churchill, wagging a finger at his wife. "Military matters are one thing, but here you are daring to talk of *politics*! Even I drew the line at that!" Now Lloyd George and Lindemann laughed out loud, but Clementine looked nonplussed.

"Very well, then. So, go on with your planning, gentlemen. And feel free to go over to the map, I've seen you all staring at it from your seats!" She turned away and went over to the other guests.

Churchill chuckled, but then he did look at the large wall map. "Shall we?"

Without waiting for an answer, he got up and went over to it. His gaze centered on the cluster of red flags around Alexandria. Lloyd George gestured to them. "Will it be enough, do you think?"

"The experts seem to think so," said Churchill, but he shook his head slightly as he did so. "Six divisions of infantry, eight battalions of tanks, a brigade of cavalry, and as much artillery as Kitchener would spare.

Not as much as I would have liked, but with the fleet close at hand to lend its fire, I'm hoping it will do the job."

"You can't afford to lose any major ships, Winston, you know that you can't. Not after what happened last time. Another serious setback and Asquith will have to let you go."

"I know, David, I know. But our plan should avoid risks to the major units. We've been scouting the place using float planes from *Ark Royal* and even a few submarines, almost every day and we've plotted the locations of most of the super heat rays. Or at least I hope we have. I suppose they could have some more that are cleverly hidden, but there's nothing we can do about that.

"We'll land our forces on the Arabian shore well north of the strait. With the fleet on hand, we should be able to deal with any attack by the Martian tripods. Once we are firmly established, the army will work its way down the coast with the navy paralleling them. We'll take out the heat ray emplacements one by one. If the ships stay close to the Arabian coast, the rays on the African side won't be able to reach them, so we can ignore them for the time being.

"We haven't seen any sign of the enemy building any land fortification facing northward, so the only thing they can send against us will be their tripods. The army, with the fleet backing them up should be able to handle them. The tricky part will be when we reach the narrowest part of the strait, where Perim Island lies. Our troops won't be able to get at the rays mounted there, and yet they will come under fire from them as they work against the ones on the Arabian shore. Our plan is to get close enough to bring the army's big guns to bear on them from positions out of sight, so they can't be fired on in return. Those combined with the long-range guns of the fleet, should be able to silence the rays on the island and allow the troops to clear out all the ones on the shore. Once that's done, we can send troops across from the mainland in small craft and clear the bounders out."

"What about the African side?" asked Lloyd George.

"That may have to wait for a while," said Churchill shrugging. "If we take the Arabian shore and Perim, we'll have a clear passage through the strait again. We'll need to fortify the whole area so the Martians can't..." Churchill stopped in mid-sentence and whipped his head around. "Oh, bother! What now?"

A uniformed officer had appeared and been intercepted by Clementine. She looked quite put out, but the man was gesturing emphatically toward Churchill and shaking his head. Churchill strode over to them. "I'd given strict orders that there be no interruptions tonight except for a real emergency," he said.

"I'm sorry, sir," said the lieutenant, "but Prince Battenberg felt that this qualified as such." He held out a slip of paper.

"Very well. Thank you, Geoff, that will be all," growled The First Lord as he took the paper.

"Uh, Prince Battenberg seemed to feel that you might have a reply and instructed me to wait for it," replied the officer.

Churchill snorted. "I see." He opened the paper and read, his face growing redder and his scowl deeper with every passing moment. He turned and stalked back to the map. His hand brushed briefly on the Bab el Mandab strait, but then drifted northward. Up to the Persian Gulf, then westward toward Jerusalem, north again to Constantinople, and then finally up toward the top edge where the Danube entered the Black Sea.

"Well, what is it Winston?" said Lloyd George. "Don't leave us dangling!"

Churchill turned to face them. "Well! To quote the Duke of Wellington, the bloody Martians have humbugged us!"

Before Lloyd George could say anything else, Churchill beckoned to the Lieutenant. "Geoff, tell Prince Battenberg to send a signal to Admiral Carden to be prepared for new orders. And on your way out send in my secretary."

"Yes, sir, right away." The man left in a hurry.

"Well?" demanded Lloyd George.

"I'm going to request an immediate meeting of the War Cabinet, David. We have much to discuss."

* * * * *

Alexandria, Egypt, January, 1913

"Letter for you, Harry. I think it's from your girl."

"She's not my girl!" he snarled, but he rolled over on his cot and snatched the letter out of Burford Sampson's hand as quickly as a striking snake. He looked at the writing on the envelope and yes, it was indeed from Vera Brittain. Part of him was relieved; he hadn't heard from her since that awful day at Aswan when she'd learned that her fiancé had been killed. He could still remember the pain on her face and in her voice and the pain in his own heart that he couldn't do a thing to comfort her. He'd sent her several awkwardly worded letters since then, but this was the first reply. Looking closer at the envelope he realized that it had been posted in England. *She went home? Of course she did, you idiot.* The fact that she wasn't in Egypt anymore left him feeling oddly lonely.

"Go away, Burf," he said when he realized that Sampson was still standing there. "Why don't you see if you can find out when we are going to get moving?"

Sampson snorted. "What do you think I was doing at the headquarters tent when the mail came in? Still no word! They pull us out of Aswan and tell us we're going to recapture some damn island in the Red Sea, and then we sit and sit waiting to move! I swear no one knows what they're doing in this bloody war!"

"Go away, Burf," he said again and this time he finally did. Harry turned his attention back to the letter and carefully opened it. Inside were several sheets written on a light blue paper.

Dear Harry,

I am sorry for not writing sooner. Thank you so much for your letters. As you can imagine, my life has been a bit of a muddle lately. I'm back in England. The VAD gave me some leave and I needed to come home to see Roland's family and my own. We are all trying to make some sense of this. I've tried to get some information on the circumstances of his death but have gotten nothing but a vaguely worded message from his commanding officer stating that he died bravely in the line of duty and did not suffer. I suppose that's possible, but after all the suffering I've witnessed in the hospitals, I am not so sure.

This has been very hard on everyone. My brother, Edward, was very close to Roland, too, and two of his school chums, Geoffrey and Victor, have been devastated. All three are in the army, although Edward and Geoffrey are still here in England.

I'm not entirely sure what I shall do now. My initial decision to leave Oxford and join the VAD was a way of supporting Roland. As a volunteer I can quit any time I wish, but that seems like a cowardly thing to do. I feel so very empty right now; perhaps my work can help me as well as others. But I don't know. I have not felt much like writing, but a short poem did come to me the other night as I was watching the sunset. I enclose a copy.

I do hope that you are well. The newspapers are frustratingly vague about where the Australian units are right now. Keep writing, I do enjoy hearing from you.

Sincerely,

Vera

Harry sighed. Poor Vera. He couldn't quite imagine what she was going through. He'd lost people in his life; grandparents, his father, too many comrades, but to lose someone you were planning to marry. That was different somehow. Still she seemed to be bearing up pretty well. Then he looked at the poem.

Looking Westward

When I am dead, lay me not looking East,
But toward the verge where daylight sinks to rest,
For my Beloved, who fell in War's dark year,
Lies in a foreign meadow, facing West.

He does not see the Heavens flushed with dawn,
But flaming through the sunset's dying gleam;
He is not dazzled by the Morning Star,
But Hesper soothes him with her gentle beam.

He faces not the guns he thrilled to hear,
Nor sees the skyline red with fires of Hell;
He looks for ever towards that dear home land
He loved but bade a resolute farewell.

So would I, when my hour has come to sleep,
Lie watching where the twilight shades grow gray;
Far sooner would I share with him the Night
Than pass without him to the Splendid Day.

A chill went through him. It was beautiful and touching, but Vera was talking about her own death. He quickly went back and reread her letter. Was there anything in there indicating that she might... no, no, there wasn't any hint of anything like that. Still, it worried him greatly.

In frustration, he put the letter back in the envelope, locked it in his footlocker, and left the tent. January in Alexandria wasn't bad at all compared to summer in Sudan, but Harry scarcely noticed the pleasant breeze off the Mediterranean. He was worried about Vera and angry with himself for being worried. She wasn't his girlfriend, and that poem made it clear as crystal that her being suddenly un-engaged didn't change that a bit. He should forget about her and concentrate on his job.

Except at the moment his job seemed to be nothing but sitting around.

The Australian and New Zealand troops had all been withdrawn from the front and consolidated into what was now being called the Australian and New Zealand Army Corps—the ANZACs. They were better organized, trained, and equipped than they ever were back home, with ample artillery and tank support. But instead of doing something, they were sitting on their hands in Alexandria.

As Sampson had said, they had been pulled out of the drive up the Nile, sent back to Alexandria, reorganized and told that they would be part of a big attack to take back the strait at the southern end of the Red Sea. Harry vaguely remembered passing through there on the way from home to Egypt. The Martians had captured the place and now the British wanted it back. It sounded like it would be a hard fight, but the men—and Harry—were looking forward to really hurting the Martians. They were ready to go, the ships were there to transport them and then… nothing.

Harry wandered through the tent city where the troops were stationed, intending to go down to the harbor and watch all those waiting ships. But he'd scarcely started when two of his men, Privates Weaver and Falkes, found him, chattering excitedly. "Sir! Lieutenant Calloway!"

"What is it?" he asked them. "Something wrong?"

"No sir!" said Private Weaver. "Nothing's wrong sir, but he got it to work! It works!"

Harry looked at them in puzzlement. "What works?"

"Greene's contraption! His bomb thrower!"

"Bomb thrower…?"

"His bloody crossbow thing! You know sir, he's shown it to you!"

"Oh, that," said Harry remembering Private Greene's invention. "You say he got it to work? Really?"

"Yes, sir! He's been testing it out all morning on an old metal grain silo at the west end of the harbor. The bomb shoots out and sticks! Every time!"

"Almost every time," added Falkes. "He sent us to find you to get permission to use a live bomb."

"Well I don't know about that…"

"At least come take a look, sir. Will you take a look?"

"Why not? It's not like we've got anything else to do."

The men led him through the camps and then out along the waterfront. It was actually quite a hike. Finally, they arrived at a run-down complex of warehouses and storage bins and Harry spotted a group of about a half dozen men working on something. There was Private Greene, who saw Harry and ran over to him, grinning ear to ear.

"Hello, sir! I got it to work! I really did!"

"So I've been told. Can you show me?"

"Yes, sir!" He took him over to a crate where he had his stuff. The crossbow contraption was there along with a half dozen Mills bombs and several things which looked like thick broom handles with wooden fins on one end. Harry picked up the crossbow.

"Looks about the same as before," he said. "What's different?"

"Yes, sir, the bow hasn't changed much since you last saw it. The problem was the great bulbous end on the bloody Mills bomb. I couldn't figure out how to make that sit proper on the bow before I fired. Even when I added fins to the handle, the bleedin' thing would always tumble.

"But then we thought about addin' a longer shaft to the handle — it was Weaver's idea actually — so the end of the bomb would start out hangin' over the front of the bow! And it works, sir! Let me show you."

"All right, show me. Just a dud bomb, all right?"

"Yes, sir. Wouldn't dare use a real one without your say-so." Greene picked up a presumably dud bomb and one of the broom handles. "You see, the end of the bomb handle fits into this socket here in the end of the shaft. We cut a little notch in it so the armin' cord can hang out here where we can grab it. Didn't want to try pullin' the fuse and tryin' t'get everything put together and fired before it blew up."

"Seems like you've thought of everything, Greene," said Harry, impressed.

"Hope so, sir." He fit the handle of the Mills bomb into the socket and then strained to cock the crossbow. "If I could come up with a proper lever or pulley like the real ones had, I could probably make a stronger bow so would it throw farther, but for now this will do," he explained. He put the bomb and the broomstick into place and as he said the spherical part of the bomb projected just beyond the front, so the shaft of the broomstick lay flat in its launching groove. A notch in the end fit into the bow string. Weaver helped him take off the front cover of the bomb, exposing the sticky rubber.

"Okay, it's ready to go," said Greene. "I'm gonna fire at that old tank over there, sir." He indicated a rusted cylinder, thirty feet high and twenty in diameter about fifty yards away.

"Fine, go ahead."

Greene brought the outlandish weapon up and squinted along its length. Harry didn't notice any sort of sighting mechanism, but the man was aiming rather high; he must have practiced enough to know the bow's range and trajectory. Greene adjusted his aim a trifle and squeezed the trigger on the underside of the stock.

The arms of the bow jerked forward, and the bomb was launched outward with a sharp thwack. It soared upward in an arc which was just starting to come down again when it struck the tank. There was a loud hollow sound like a gong, but the bomb stuck to the side and didn't bounce off. Harry's eyebrows shot up.

"It worked! I'll be damned!"

"Yes sir," said Greene looking pleased "Tried it about a dozen times this morning and got it to stick nine times. Takes a bit of practice, but it does work. Uh, with your permission I'd like to try it with a real bomb."

"Hmmm," said Harry. He went up to the tank and looked it over. It was badly rusted and had dozens of small holes all over it. Clearly the thing was useless for any sort of storage. He doubted if anyone would be put out is they blew a hole in it. Then he strolled around the area trying to gauge whether the possible flying shrapnel would damage anything important. It didn't seem like it. Greene and the others followed him like anxious puppies.

"All right, I can't see any harm in giving it a try." He put up his hand as the men started to whoop. "But you need to build up some sort of barricade to give yourself cover when you do this. Don't want anyone getting hurt."

"Not a problem, sir!" said Weaver.

The men got to work and started hauling junk — of which there was no shortage — and soon had a rather substantial pile to shelter behind. Harry inspected it and gave his approval. They all got behind it and Greene, helped by Weaver, prepared to fire the bomb.

"Hold on a moment," said Harry, just before Weaver pulled the arming fuse.

"Sir?" said Greene.

"Not to cast any aspersions on your invention, Greene, but if you arm that thing and then for some reason it doesn't launch, we'll all be standing here with the bomb. You and Weaver can give it a try, but all the rest of us need to move a lot further back."

This produced some grumbling, but Harry herded the others off to a small shed about fifty yards away and took cover there. He then waved to Green to go ahead. The two men fiddled with their device for a few moments and then Weaver stood aside, Greene took aim and fired. The bomb soared upward toward the tank...

...and naturally bounced off.

The bomb fell to the ground and after a few seconds exploded, throwing a small geyser of dirt into the air. The men groaned in disappointment. Harry and the others walked over to where an embarrassed Greene was standing, holding his crossbow.

"I'm sorry sir," he said. "The dud bombs worked, they really did. You saw the one work!"

"Don't worry. I suppose it was inevitable that the first real test would fail. Do you have another live bomb?"

Greene's face lit up. "Sure do, sir! Three more!"

"Well then give it another go."

"Yes, sir!" Harry and the other watchers retreated to the shed while Greene and Weaver prepared another shot.

This time it went perfectly. The bomb shot up in its gentle arc, hit the side of the tank and stuck there. After a few more seconds it exploded with bang and the tank rang like a large bell. When the smoke cleared, there was a hole about four feet in diameter blown through the thin metal, Greene and all the other men cheered and ran forward to examine their work. Harry went over to Greene and patted him on the back.

"Well done. You really seem to have something there. Fifty yards isn't all that far, but it's a darned sight better than having to walk right up to a tripod."

"Sure is, sir! Can I get permission to make a few more of these?"

"A few more? I'm going to go get the colonel so he can see this. I bet he'll want the whole battalion equipped with these. When other folks see, they'll want them, too. I wonder if that ordnance captain, what was his name? Smyth? I wonder if he's still around anywhere? Greene? I think the whole army is going to be interested in your invention."

* * * * *

War Cabinet Offices, London, January, 1913

"Mr. Churchill, this is outrageous," said Field Marshal Kitchener. "First you insist that I suspend operations on the Nile so you can reopen traffic through the Red Sea. I could see the need, so I gave you all you asked for. But now, now you want to go haring off to Turkey! Turkey! And all on the say-so of some young lieutenant no one has ever heard of. Prime Minister, I strongly oppose this move."

Frederick Lindemann sat in a corner of the meeting room which was in a building next to the Prime Minister's residence on Downing Street. He was excited to be included in this meeting of the War Cabinet, but it looked as though things could become very contentious.

"Sometimes young lieutenants no one has ever heard of can be right about things, my lord," said Churchill, mildly. More than one person in the room winced. Churchill, just a young lieutenant during Kitchener's legendary Sudan campaign to retake Khartoum, had been a thorn in Kitchener's side. Kitchener, now the Secretary of State for War had never quite forgotten that.

Prime Minister Asquith looked over the dozen men in the room and tapped a finger on the tabletop. The War Cabinet was a relatively new creation, a select body of men from the government and military to advise the Prime Minister on the conduct of the war. Smaller than the regular cabinet and vastly easier to manage than Parliament, it was where the big decisions on strategy were made. Lindemann expected a rather big decision would be made here today.

Aside from Asquith, the top two men were naturally Kitchener and Churchill, the commanders of the army and navy respectively. But here was also Lloyd George, recently shifted from his post as Chancellor of the Exchequer to Minister of Munitions, his place at the Exchequer taken by Andrew Bonar Law, who was also here. And there was George Curzon — Earl Curzon of Kedelston — the House of Lords' representative on the council, Arthur Henderson, a representative of the Labour Party and minister without portfolio, and Jan Christian Smuts, who had once fought against Britain in the Boer War, but who was now a staunch supporter of the Empire and advocate for the defense of the what was left of South Africa. There were several other assistants and lesser ministers, but they, like Lindemann, would only speak when spoken to.

Asquith's gaze returned to Churchill. "Winston, I'm afraid I tend to agree with Lord Kitchener. Two months ago, we met in this very room where you convinced us that reopening the strait of Bab el Mandab was vitally necessary. The forces to do that have now been assembled and are ready to proceed. Why should we suddenly change direction and head off to Asia Minor? What about reopening the strait?" Henry Asquith was a big-nosed, distinguished, white haired man in his early sixties. He came from humble origins but had slowly and steadily risen through the ranks of the Liberal Party. After gaining national prominence as Chancellor of the Exchequer for devising the taxation plans which funded the vast armament programs needed for the war, he had been the natural successor to Prime Minister Campbell-Bannerman when he died. Some didn't feel that he really had the fire to be a wartime leader, but so far, he had survived every challenge.

Churchill appeared calm, but Lindemann knew that was a façade. The First Lord of the Admiralty had come under severe criticism in Parliament and in the press over the heavy losses of ships and men in the first disastrous attempt to reopen the strait. Many were calling for his resignation.

"Prime Minister, two months ago that would have been the correct decision. But the situation has changed, and we must be willing to change our own plans in response. And yes, I know that Napoleon once said that it was better to act boldly on a bad plan than to be constantly changing plans in hopes of finding the perfect one. But I say that that is not the situation here. To put things plainly, the enemy has outwitted us, and to expend our forces at Bab el Mandab would be doing exactly what they want us to do."

There were murmurs around the table and the shaking of heads. Lindemann had to admire Churchill's courage to take this course. The safe play, the play that almost anyone else in his position would make, would be to go ahead with the agreed plan, retake the strait, and redeem his earlier mistake. But he wasn't doing that—and it might cost him his career.

"And how do you know what the Martians want us to do, Winston?" asked Curzon. "Did this Lieutenant Lawrence, who you seem to think so much of, sneak into a Martian staff meeting and take notes?" Several men chuckled and even Churchill smiled briefly.

"No, my lord, Lieutenant Lawrence showed commendable initiative, and I believe he's earned a promotion for it, but no he did not provide me with any secret Martian communiques. Just the facts. And what can we deduce from those facts?" Before anyone could answer, he sprang from his chair and walked over to the inevitable map hanging on one wall. He jabbed a finger at the strait.

"We assumed that the enemy took Bab al Mandab to shut it down to our ship traffic. We arrogantly—yes, arrogantly—assumed that they were doing this to thwart our plans. We never stopped to think that this might have just been a side effect of their own plans. And from Lieutenant Lawrence's report it now becomes clear that their plan was not to cut our lines of communication, but to open up a new one for themselves! To allow them to transfer forces—enormous forces from Africa to Arabia."

"But to what end, Winston?" asked Asquith. "How can we know?"

"Absolute assurance is impossible, of course, but we can make some deductions." His hand moved from the strait up to the area south of Cairo. "For the better part of three years we've held this defense line here, protecting Cairo and the approach to Suez. The Martians in Africa have made several major attacks on it, but we've managed to hold them back. At the same time, we've built a line protecting the eastern approaches to Suez with our line through Sinai and Palestine. They've hit us there, too, but again we've managed to hold. Our central position has allowed us to shift forces from one line to another as necessary. We've managed to keep the enemy forces divided.

"Meanwhile the Martians in Arabia have gradually moved north into Iraq and Syria and are pushing into Turkey. And recently the enemy in Russia has begun a new offensive, not northward to take St. Petersburg and finish off the Tsar as we'd expected, but southward into Rumania and toward the Balkans.

"Finally, we have this recent development at Bab el Mandab. The enemy has shifted an enormous group of tripods from Africa to Arabia. What are they most likely to do with that force?"

Kitchener, frowned and shook his head. "We can't know for sure. They could hit our line at Sinai, they could be planning to wipe out our enclave at Basra..."

"Yes, that is possible, but this force could have reached either of those places by now and yet there has been no sign of an impending attack. Or they could be attempting the worse thing possible for us," His fist thumped down on another part of the map. "They could be aiming for the Bosporus and Constantinople! If they succeed in taking that and joining up with their forces in the north, they will have linked up Africa, the Middle east and Asia!"

Now all the men around the table were frowning. Some still shook their heads, but others were staring at the map intently.

"So far in this war," continued Churchill, "we've managed to keep the enemy's major enclaves separated from each other, and that has prevented them from assembling a truly overwhelming force. But if we allow this link up to happen, gentlemen, they can combine their forces and using their unprecedented mobility, to strike wherever they wish with power that we cannot hope to match."

He stepped over to the other side of the map. "They are trying to do the same thing in the Americas. They are assembling powerful forces for a strike on Panama. Again, we assume that they are doing it to cut the vital canal there, but in all probability, it is so they can combine their forces. Instead of facing attacks with five or six hundred tripods—as daunting as that is—we shall be facing attacks with one or two thousand. Unless we act boldly to prevent it!"

Kitchener was still shaking his head. "The force we have assembled for the Bab el Mandab operation is only two corps and some supporting units. Sufficient for a small operation. If we send it to Asia Minor, it would be like a pebble in a pond: far too small to have a decisive effect. And that assumes the Ottomans even want us to help! Have they asked?"

"There has been no formal request," said Asquith. "But there have been some inquiries by the German ambassador. They seem to be taking this threat very seriously. They have begun to shift major forces into Rumania to try and hold the line of the Danube."

"Let us hope that the Germans can hold the Martian northern force," said Churchill. "But if a thousand tripods cross the Bosporus into their rear, it will all be for naught." He paused and drew breath. Lindemann knew what was coming next. Churchill had used him and several others in his circle as sounding boards the past week to hone his argument for this meeting. He grasped the lapels of his coat and swept his gaze over the assembly. "But Lord Kitchener is correct: the Bab el Mandab force is not large enough. It must be reinforced."

"Reinforced?" exclaimed the Field Marshall. "With what?! We have no more troops to spare!"

"I'm not sure that it true," countered Churchill. "If the Martians have shifted major forces out of Africa, then the threat facing our forces there is diminished. We could safely pull some of them out and add them to the expeditionary force."

"If the Marians have weakened themselves in Africa then it is an opportunity to attack them there!" replied Kitchener. "We could attempt to destroy some of their fortresses and really hurt them."

"That would take too long, my lord. The threat in Turkey is happening right now. If we don't act immediately it will be too late."

Kitchener snorted. "At short notice, the most we could assemble would be another corps. Still not enough for what you are proposing."

"That is true," said Churchill, nodding. "And that is why the expedition cannot be made up just of our own troops. We must assemble an allied force which includes the French, the Italians—and the Americans. A truly international force, the likes of which we have not yet seen in this war."

The silence that followed lasted for perhaps fifteen seconds. Lindemann looked at the men around the table, mentally calculating which would be the first to air his protest. As it happened, nearly all of them exploded simultaneously, producing an unseemly uproar. It went on for another twenty seconds until Asquith raised his hand and quickly got things back under control.

"Winston," he said, "this is… this is…"

"Unprecedented? Yes, Prime Minister, exactly. Unprecedented, but exactly what is needed. Not just to meet the current crisis, but to win the war. For far too long each of the great powers has fought its own war on its own fronts with only the sketchiest cooperation with the others."

"There is that international committee," said Bonar Law, "The one President Roosevelt set up in 1909…"

"And what has it accomplished?" demanded Churchill. "Not a thing of significance. It was a noble idea, but no one—including us—has been willing to make the commitment to make a difference. That needs to end. Now."

"Winston," said Lloyd George, "I don't disagree with you on the need, but what you propose will take a great deal of time. Probably far more than we have, if this threat is as imminent as you suggest. How can you know that the other powers will respond quickly enough or forcefully enough?"

Churchill smiled. "The navy does have its own intelligence service, you know, David, and I've made some inquiries. The French are preparing to ship a corps to their outpost in Mexico. The Italians have a similar force assembled around Naples which they are trying to decide what to do with. They're embarrassed at being driven out of Libya and are looking for somewhere to strike. If we were to strongly urge them to join us in this expedition they might respond favorably. The Americans are another matter, of course. They are already heavily engaged on a wide front. We can't expect any significant troops from them, but I have hopes that a properly worded diplomatic request might convinced them to provide some naval forces and perhaps some of their new land ironclads. We are starting construction on our own version of these wonderful machines, but they can't possibly be ready in time for this. The American ironclads would be invaluable for this sort of operation.

"I might add that there are several smaller European powers like Belgium, Holland, Portugal, and Denmark who have been champing at the bit to contribute some forces to this war. They don't have much in the way of tanks or heavy artillery, but infantry always has a role. If shipping can be found, I believe their inclusion would be a good thing. Prime Minister, if the Foreign Office could put forth a proposal in the next few days, I believe that this could happen."

Another silence descended on the conference room as the men mulled over Churchill's amazing proposal. Surprisingly, it was Jan Smuts who broke the silence. The small South African Boer rarely spoke, but when he did, people listened.

"Prime Minister, my lords, gentlemen, I have to say that I agree with the First Lord of the Admiralty. Not only do I agree with his assessment of the likely Martian plans and the threat they pose, but I agree with the solution he proposes as well." He paused and looked into the eyes of the other men, one by one. "I come from South Africa, a home I have loved and bled for. Nearly all of it is in the hands of the Martians now. I and what remain of my people cling to a small enclave on the south coast. But we dream of taking back what is ours. I've talked with some Australians who are in the same situation. All around the world there are Russians and Brazilians and Americans and Chinese, and Arabs who have been forced to flee their homes, but who dream of going back. And there are as many or more who live in fear of losing their own homes — or their lives. No matter what language they speak, or what god they worship, or the color of their skin, they share these common hopes and fears.

"Individually we have little hope of retaking our homes or even defending the homes we still have. We must work together. All of us! Every nation, every man, woman, and child. So far, we have failed to do it. This proposal by Mr. Churchill may be how we start. I strongly urge the government to approve." Smuts, who had risen to his feet as he spoke, slowly sat down again.

This time the silence lasted longer. It appeared to Lindemann that even Churchill was surprised, and he returned to his seat without another word. Most of the men in the room looked down at the table, or their clasped hands.

Finally, the prime minister stirred. "Well!" he said, blinking rapidly and then rubbing a hand across his mouth. "Well, it seems we have a proposal on the table which has been seconded. We don't normally take votes here, and I'm not asking for one now, but, gentlemen, do you favor this proposal or oppose it?"

Half the men in the room rumbled assents or nodded their heads strongly. Nearly all the rest gave less assertive acknowledgements. None dissented. Only Kitchener remained unmoved. Asquith turned his gaze on him. "Field Marshall?"

Kitchener blinked and jerked slightly in his chair. He cleared his throat and growled: "I do not oppose it, Prime Minister."

* * * * *

Northern Area of Subcontinent 1-4, Cycle 597,845.4

Kandanginar looked at the mountain range to the north. The tall peaks were covered with frozen water and more frozen precipitation fell from the roiling gray clouds overhead. In some areas it was coming down so thickly that nothing could be seen beyond it. Some of the advanced scouts reported that in such condition's visibility could be reduced to zero. On rare occasions on the Homeworld dust storms could cause similar conditions, but apparently the target world's dynamic weather could cause this—and far worse—routinely. Some of the other clans had reported wind conditions so extreme that they could even destroy fighting machines.

The planet's size produced a strong gravity which had worked to retain a thick atmosphere and allowed enormous oceans of open water. It's closer position to the sun meant that the energy from it could drive a much stronger weather cycle. This had all been known before the first expedition had come here, but the practical consequences were still being discovered.

Other unexpected conditions were being revealed as well. The planet had also retained far more of the heat created during its formation. The crust was very thin compared to the Homeworld's and divided into separate segments floating on a molten interior. Where those segments met there could be volcanic eruptions or destructive shifting. Only a quarter cycle ago there had been a massive eruption in the far northern regions of Continent 3. Smaller eruptions were going on in other locations. Of more immediate concern to Kandanginar, one of these boundary regions existed where the newly created tunnel between Subcontinent 1-4 and Continent 2 had been dug. So far, the shifts had been minor, but they had still caused serious leaks from sea water seeping through the cracks. A major shift could destroy the tunnel entirely.

Such an event would not be an immediate crisis, since the forces from Continent 2 needed for the current operations had already passed through the tunnel, but it could be an important issue in the future...

"Subcommander Kandanginar?" The communicator in its fighting machine received a signal. It saw that it was from, Blatanitrav, the commander of Battle Group 14-21.

"Yes?" It replied.

"The enemy to our front has either fled or been destroyed. The passage through the mountains appears clear. Permission to advance?"

"Granted, proceed at once."

The advance northward from Holdfast 14-1 had initially been rapid. All the central areas of the subcontinent had been swept of prey creature resistance for over a full cycle. But now they were moving into areas still held by the prey creatures, and much of the terrain was very rough. Farther south there were some difficult areas, but these were mostly isolated clumps which could be bypassed. Here, a solid range of mountains, many *telequels* deep blocked every route toward their objective.

The attack force had been split into a number of subdivisions, each trying to force its way through the mountains and the defenses. Kandanginar had been put in charge of one of these divisions. Its own experience as a combat commander was extremely limited, being much more interested in scientific research, but its place in the hierarchy of the clan made it necessary. The unexpected and disturbing phenomena of the lack of instinctive loyalty in buds created on the target world required that members of the first wave—who could be assured of receiving loyalty—commanded every important expedition. There had not yet been any significant problems created by this phenomenon, but the Colonial Conclave—and the Council of Three hundred on the Homeworld—had insisted that no chances be taken.

So far, the terrain had proved more of a problem than the enemy. The prey creature armies they faced were not well equipped compared to some of the others; few of the armored gun vehicles, not many of the large projectile throwers and even the rapid-fire small projectile throwers were not numerous. But they knew how to make use of the mountainous terrain. There were only a limited number of routes which could be traversed by the Race's fighting machines and this allowed the prey to concentrate its forces along those routes. They were proving very adept at laying traps which could tumble a fighting machine to its destruction in this world's enormous gravity. In several areas they had used explosives to leave routes impassible, forcing time-consuming detours. So far, losses had been acceptable, but Kandanginar was becoming concerned about what might lie ahead.

The force advanced about twenty *telequels* before reaching another narrow point along their route which was defended. A halt was called so that fresh power cells could be brought up for the machines which needed them. Under normal conditions a fighting machine could operate for almost a quarter cycle on one set of cells, but the difficult terrain and repeated combats was draining them much faster than usual.

The extended nature of this present operation was also creating unaccustomed difficulties. Up until now, the Race's strategy had been to clear out an area of defenders and then build a holdfast to control that area. Then clear out a new area and repeat the process. As a result, most operations were conducted within a few hundred telequels of a holdfast. Repairs or replacements for damaged or destroyed machines and fresh power cells were always close by. Now, however, the closest holdfast, one of Group 13's, was many hundreds of telequels away and becoming more remote each rotation. By the time they reached their objective the distance would be more than a thousand.

This meant that all needed supplies had to be transported over great distances. And yet since there was no time to stop and thoroughly clear out all the prey creature defenders and build holdfasts, the vehicles transporting those supplies were subject to attack. The standard cargo carrier was a six-legged machine with a significant capacity, but it was unarmed, lightly armored, and usually unpiloted, simply following behind a single piloted machine. Such vehicles would be very vulnerable to attack and thus needed to be escorted. The greater the distance from a holdfast, the more carriers and the more escorts would be needed. A small advanced base with a reactor was under construction which would allow power cells to be recharged closer to the front of the advance, but it would not be operational for some time yet.

Kandanginar parked its machine and waited while one of those cargo carriers came up to it and a manipulator swapped out the power cells. While it waited, it fed from a preserved supply of food solution stored in its fighting machine. That was another thing which must be sent forward from the rear. As it ate, it received a communications from its commander, Jakruvnar.

"What is your status, subcommander?"

"We have halted at Coordinates 11387-21 to replenish, Commander. Prey creature forces are entrenched to our front. As soon as resupply is complete, we will resume the advance. How do things fare on the other attack routes?"

"The advance has been slower than anticipated."

"True, the terrain, the weather, and enemy resistance have all combined to slow us. Is this a major concern?"

"The force moving southward to meet us has also encountered unexpected resistance. A new prey creature clan—if I can use that word to describe it—has joined the battle. They are far better organized and equipped than those encountered previously. Their tactics are also superior."

"This force is from Subcontinent 1-1? The highly industrialized region we have not yet reached?"

"Yes," replied Jakruvnar. "Despite surveillance from the artificial satellite there is much we do not know about that region. If this encounter is a preview, we may be facing far more serious resistance than anticipated. The drive southward has been stopped along a major river line. Additional forces are being sent there, but success is uncertain. The Colonial Conclave is demanding that we increase the speed of our advance and strike the enemy from the rear."

"We are still over a thousand *telequels* away, Commander," said Kandanginar. "A great deal of difficult terrain lies before us and enemy resistance has not been broken."

"I am aware of this and I have so informed the Conclave. Their orders remain unchanged. And to make matters worse, the artificial satellite has also revealed a significant collection of water vessels to the west of our positions. Hundreds of vessels, many of them fighting vessels, but many more carrying ground forces. I fear that they mean to move against us."

Kandanginar considered this. "A major water obstacle lies before us where the subcontinent meets the main continent. If this force were to position itself there, our crossing it could prove difficult, perhaps impossible."

"That was my thought. What can we do to prevent this?"

"We had already planned to bring forward our tunneling machines to assist us in crossing the water obstacle, just as we did to seize the island in the strait to the south. I am wondering if we might not replicate the other aspects of that operation as well?"

"Explain."

"This force of water vessels must pass through a very narrow channel from the large inland sea to reach the water obstacle. If we were able to fortify the shores of that channel with the new heavy heat rays, as we did in the south, we might be able to block them and prevent them from interfering with our advance."

"Interesting. Could it be done? Just as important, could it be done quickly? We may have little time before this grouping water vessels moves our way."

"Perhaps. So far, we have been advancing on a broad front, sweeping all resistance before us along a score of parallel routes through the mountain. If we were to concentrate a significant portion and strike directly toward the area of that channel, without a pause, we might be able to arrive there quickly enough to establish a blocking position."

"The strike force would be far ahead of the rest of us, beyond easy supporting distance. That might be dangerous."

"True, there would be risks, but I see no other way to forestall this enemy force, Commander."

"What about a power source for the heat rays?"

"We could bring parts for a small reactor forward with us. Or, lacking time to assemble and install one, we could use massed power cells as a temporary measure."

Jakruvnar was silent for a moment and then responded. "Draw up a plan of action for my consideration. Include recommendations not only for the strike force, but the supporting resources you would need to accomplish your proposal; the tunneling machines, the heavy heat rays, and the cargo carriers needed to transport them."

"Yes, Commander, at once."

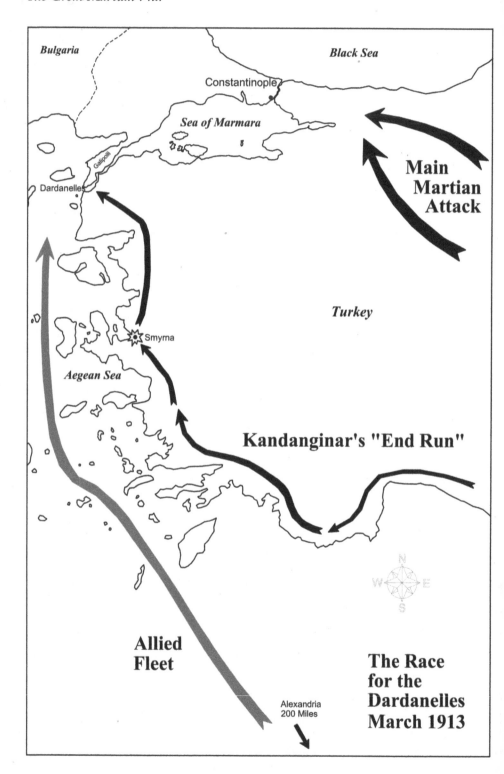

Bulgaria

Black Sea

Constantinople

Sea of Marmara

Gallipoli

Dardanelles

**Main
Martian
Attack**

Turkey

Smyrna

Aegean Sea

Kandanginar's "End Run"

N
W E
S

**Allied
Fleet**

Alexandria
200 Miles

**The Race
for the
Dardanelles
March 1913**

Chapter Fourteen

Washington, DC, February, 1913

"Mister President, this is totally unacceptable," said Admiral of the Navy George Dewey. "We've just completed these vessels and to turn them over to the British before we've even had the chance to use them is just... just..." the elderly naval hero sputtered to a halt.

Major Tom Bridges usually found an inconspicuous corner to hide in when witnessing contentious debates between men who vastly outranked him, but in this case he'd been thwarted: the American president's office didn't have any corners. Any spot he chose seemed to have a clear view of the desk and the person behind it. A visitor's eyes were drawn to the man—there was no avoiding it.

Not that Theodore Roosevelt wouldn't have been the focus of any gathering in any location. The magnetism of the man was, well, *magnetic*. He was a large, barrel-chested fellow with big arms, big hands, and those incredibly big teeth which created that trademark grin known around the world. Almost everything about him seemed larger than life and if his mustache was streaked with more white than it was in older photographs, he still radiated strength and energy. The other men in the room seemed almost like shadows compared to him.

Not that those other men were shadows. Admiral Dewey was the oldest one there, resplendent in his naval uniform, and the most famous American sailor alive. General Leonard Wood, the army chief of staff, tall thin, and graying had a more impressive record of victory against the Martians than anyone. Elihu Root, the Secretary of State, was an accomplished politician and diplomat. Even the British Ambassador, James Bryce, white haired and white bearded, had a record to be envied, but they all were eclipsed by Roosevelt.

The president adjusted the pince-nez glasses on his nose and cleared his throat. "Relax, George, James here isn't asking us to give them away! They'd remain American vessels under American command. They'd just be taking part in a combined operation with our friends the British. Isn't that right, James?" He looked to Ambassador Bryce.

"Absolutely, Mr. President," replied Bryce. "His Majesty's Government eagerly looks forward to the United States joining in this unprecedented example of international cooperation, something I know that you personally endorse so strongly."

"Yes, by thunder!" exclaimed Roosevelt, thumping his fist into the palm of the other hand. "I've been pushing for this since '09! About time we see something real rather than just words!"

"But sir," protested Dewey, "the squadron has barely finished its sea trials. There are still mechanical difficulties and the crews need more training, and you're asking them to cross the Atlantic at the worst possible time of year."

"He does have a point about the weather, Mr. President," said General Wood. "You'll recall the difficulties we had in getting the army's first land ironclads to New Orleans from Philadelphia. This trip would be potentially far more hazardous."

"Yes, but I understand that the navy versions are larger and much more seaworthy, isn't that true, admiral?"

"Yes, that is so," admitted Dewey, "but only relatively speaking. They still are not designed to sail through really heavy weather. One bad gale and we could lose the lot of them."

"Then we'll have to be careful. You get regular weather reports from almost every ship at sea, don't you? You ought to be able to avoid any really bad storm."

Dewey shook his head, looking very annoyed. "It doesn't really work that way, sir. And the ironclads are very slow. We are looking at a voyage of at least two weeks just to get from New York to Gibraltar; a lot can happen in that length of time and they are too slow to dodge a storm, even if we know about it."

"We'll just have to be careful and give them a good escort," said Roosevelt. "Root, what do you think of this?"

The secretary of state nodded his head slightly. "Assuming we can deliver them safely, I think this would be a wonderful opportunity to display solidarity with our allies. As you say, there has not been nearly enough of that."

"Leonard?" the president turned to look at General Wood. "Do you have any pressing need for the navy's help at the moment?"

"The army is always grateful for the navy's help, Mr. President," replied Wood. "We would have never won at St. Louis or Memphis without their gallant assistance. But now that we've pushed the enemy back from the Mississippi there are fewer opportunities for their ships to assist us..."

"But that's just what the ironclads were designed for!" interrupted Dewey. "Their amphibious nature allows them to go where regular ships can't."

"But the army has its own ironclads, George," soothed Roosevelt. "Their second squadron was just deployed."

General Wood continued. "The only potentially immediate need I can see would be in Panama, Mr. President. The Martians are massing their forces to the north and south of the canal. We expect a very powerful attack there sometime in the near future."

Roosevelt shook his head. "The Panama Canal is the most heavily fortified area in the entire world—as you well know, Leonard; I've browbeaten you often enough about it—and I can't see six land ironclads making much difference down there among all those mountains and jungles. Half the fleet is already positioned there with a hundred times the firepower the land ironclads possess. I don't see any urgent need."

"Mr. President," said Ambassador Bryce, "His Majesty would be happy to lend the use of our Caribbean squadron in the event of an emergency to make up for the lack of the land ironclads."

"See?" said Roosevelt, smiling. "International cooperation! That's what we need. There are French and German warships in the Gulf as well. I'm sure we could count on them for aid if necessary. Good Heavens, but the Germans owe it to us after we helped them out when I was there in '09. Yes, we can do this. George, send orders for your vessels to prepare to cross the Atlantic and join the forces being gathered in the Mediterranean."

Dewey sighed but nodded. "Yes, sir, right away."

"Excellent! David, was there anything else?"

"That was the main issue. Oh, if you are agreeable, I'd like to have Major Bridges, here, attached to your squadron as a liaison. He was aboard the squadron that fought at Memphis. He knows his way around the ironclads, and he could help with coordinating activities."

Bridges came to attention, stepped forward a pace, and bowed slightly at Roosevelt.

"Of course! Of course!" boomed Roosevelt. "I envy you, Major! Wish I could be there with you!"

* * * * *

Alexandria, Egypt, March, 1913

"Well it's about bloody time!"

Harry glanced back, but he already knew who had made the exclamation. Everyone in the battalion—hell, everyone in the whole expedition—had been griping about the delays, but Ian MacDonald had been one of the loudest and the most unrelenting. Of course, MacDonald complained about nearly everything. Still, it was about bloody time.

After more false-starts than Harry could count, it looked like they were finally on their way. The troops were formed up and boarding the ships in Alexandria's harbor and if the rumors were correct, they would be sailing not to the Red Sea to recapture some island, but off to Turkey to help out the poor Ottomans. Harry had long since learned to take every rumor with a large grain of salt, but the mere fact that they had all been issued overcoats had given this rumor more credence than most. Northern

Turkey was cold this time of year.

They had assembled and stood to before dawn and then marched down to the docks. Lorries, loaded with the gear and supplies they couldn't carry themselves, had followed along. They had waited hours, but now it was finally their turn. The troops were starting to march up the gangplank of the *S.S Bridlington*, while cranes lifted up huge net bundles of gear to then lower into the hold. The line inched forward and soon it would be their turn.

"Sir? Lieutenant Calloway?" He turned and saw it was Corporal Scoggins, their dogrobber.

"Yes, Ralph? What is it?"

"It's Abdo."

"What? What about him?"

"He's here."

"What? How? We left him in camp!" The native man they had rescued from the Martian 'farm', had been hanging around for months, acting as a servant to the company officers. But they had explained to him that he could not come along on this expedition. The man had been devastated, but there was nothing for it. Native servants were common around the camps. They were unauthorized, but no one made a fuss about them. But there was no way they could smuggle him aboard a ship. They'd given him some money and as much encouragement and praise as they could muster and left him behind.

"He must have hidden himself on one of the lorries, sir," said Scoggins. "I just saw him a moment ago climbing into one of those cargo nets. Before I could do anything, they hoisted him up!"

"You mean he's already aboard?"

"Yes, sir."

"Hell... bloody hell!"

"What should we do?"

Harry's eyebrows raised. Scoggins almost never asked what to do. The old scrounger always seemed to be one step ahead of everyone around him. Not this time, apparently. But what should they do? Raise an alarm and risk delaying the embarkation while they tried to find one lone native? That would go over well! No...

"We do nothing, Ralph."

Scoggins frowned. "Really, sir?"

"If they find him and toss him off, fine. If they don't find him and he comes along... well, that's fine, too. Let's not start a row over this, eh?"

"If you say so, sir."

"I do. Look, it's our turn. Let's go."

As they neared the gangway, a battalion marched up to board another ship tied to the opposite side of the wharf. They were singing lustily.

Harry recognized the tune at once, but somehow the words were different than he remembered...

> *Hark! I hear the foe advancing,*
> *Three-legg'd steeds are boldly prancing,*
> *Metal heads in sunbeams glancing,*
> *Glitter o'er the land.*

> *Men of Harlech, lie ye dreaming?*
> *See ye not their heat rays beaming,*
> *And their monstrous tripods streaming,*
> *Where we make our stand?*

"Damn comedians," growled Scoggins. "I'll never be able to hear that song again proper now!"

"Welshmen, I guess, said Harry. "Well it is their song, they can sing it however they want." They were still singing as Harry reached the top of the gangway and was directed toward his quarters.

> *From the rocks rebounding,*
> *Let the war cry sounding*
> *Summon all at Cambria's call,*
> *The haughty foe surrounding,*

> *Men of Harlech, on to glory!*
> *See, your banner famed in story*
> *Waves these burning words before ye*
> *"Britain scorns to yield!"*

The *Bridlington* was a bigger ship than the one which had brought them from Australia, and it was better arranged and organized, so the accommodations were not bad at all—at least for the officers. Even the men didn't have it too bad below decks and everyone was excited to finally be off. Of course, even after boarding there were still more hours of waiting while other ships were loading. But their transport moved out of the harbor to join the rest of the fleet and Harry marveled at the size of the force. Dreadnoughts and older battleships, huge gray shapes like floating mountains, bristling with guns; cruisers, large and small, sleek and dangerous-looking; destroyers darting about like sheep dogs, keeping watch on their charges. He'd never seen anything like it.

And not all the ships were British. Alongside the White Ensign, there were French flags and Italian flags and even some from Spain, Belgium, and the United States. Harry spotted a few he couldn't even place. "God in Heaven look at them all!" he said.

"Quite a show, that's for sure," said Burford Sampson from the rail beside him.

"Think what we could have done with this back home," growled MacDonald.

"Someday, Ian," said Lieutenant Miller. "Someday we'll be a part of a fleet like this heading for Australia."

It was a pleasant idea, but Harry knew, that just like him, they were all wondering if they would ever live to see it.

Eventually, the armada finally began to move. They turned north and the Egyptian coast slowly fell below the horizon behind them. The sea was calm and puffy clouds drifted past. That evening Colonel Anderson called all the officers together after dinner to let them know what they were heading for. He had a map spread out on a table and they gathered around it.

"All right, gentlemen," he said, "I know that you've all been hearing a hundred different rumors about our mission, but I finally received some real information from headquarters and now that we are under way I can share it with you." He pointed to the map, which showed Turkey and the regions around it. "As you've probably heard, the Martians are launching a major offensive. There's a big force of them heading south out of Russia into the Balkans and there's another great bunch of them heading north into Turkey. The generals believe they are all trying to join up around Constantinople. And we are talking about a bloody lot of them! A thousand or more tripods in each group."

"A thousand, sir?" gulped Lieutenant Hunter of B Company.

"At least," said Anderson. "Maybe more. Not like back home, eh? This is the big times boys." Harry shook his head. Defending Australia, they'd never had to deal with more than a few hundred—and they hadn't been able to deal with them in the end, had they?

"And if they do manage to join up there will be hell to pay," continued the colonel. "As we found out to our loss, these blighters can move around like lighting. Imagine the havoc two or three thousand of them could cause if they could concentrate anywhere, they liked."

"So, our job is to keep them from joining up, sir?" asked Sampson.

"Yes, exactly. The Germans are finally getting themselves into the war and trying to hold the northern force along the Danube. But we need to stop the southern force from coming north. It's plain as plain that the Turks can't do that on their own, so we're going to help them out."

"We ought to be able to stop them along here," said Major Stanford, drawing his finger along the line of the Dardanelles, Sea of Marmora, and the Bosporus. "Just dig in on the north shore and with all these warships to help out, we can stop even a thousand of them."

Colonel Anderson shook his head. "Not quite that simple, Reggie. The generals and admirals want the water route into the Black Sea kept open. We can't let the Martians hold the southern shore and take pot shots at our passing ships. No, we need to form our line on the south shore and hold there. The navies will still be able to support us, but we'll have to fight the Martians face to face when they arrive."

"Surely not along the whole south shore of the Sea of Marmora, sir? It's got to be forty miles across. The blighters can't fire that far!"

"No, no, you're right. We only need to hold the south side of the Dardanelles and the Bosporus. Maybe eighty or ninety miles altogether."

"Where will we be going in, sir?" asked Captain Berwick.

"We don't know that yet. I'm guessing that the general doesn't know exactly how many Turks there will be left when we arrive. Once he gets a better idea of the situation, he'll announce our dispositions. It's about a three-day trip to get there from here, but once we get there, we might be put ashore on short notice, so have your men ready, right?"

"Yes, sir."

"Good. So, enjoy the voyage, it might be the last easy time we have for quite a while."

* * * * *

Coordinates 12943-08 of Subcontinent 1-4, Cycle 597,845.5

Kandanginar stared down at the broad expanse of water with satisfaction and no small measure of relief. They had reached their objective and there were no substantial prey creature forces waiting for them. Its plan to strike ahead with only a portion of the attack force and seize the vital waterway appeared to have succeeded. The large inland sea held only a few small water vessels, which clearly were not a threat. The entrance to the narrow strait was only a few *telequels* ahead.

The journey here had been harrowing with difficult terrain, terrible weather, and stubborn prey creatures to contend with. Six fighting machines and two pilots had been lost to mishaps alone, while fifteen more had been destroyed by enemy action.

Still, things could have been much worse. They had been forced to take a route which at several points came very close to the shoreline of the inland sea. If the prey creatures had massed their war vessels along a few of those points, they could have inflicted serious losses. Kandanginar had attempted to pass through those points during the night when the prey were the least dangerous, but the column of fighting machines and cargo carriers stretched for many *telequels* and it sometimes took nearly a full planetary rotation for them all to pass a given point. But the most dangerous points had been traversed without interference. This was puzzling since the artificial satellite had reported that the gathering of war vessels to the south had grown even larger. The enemy clearly had the forces to interfere if they so wished. Why hadn't they? Had this move taken them completely by surprise?

Perhaps, because it also appeared that the speed of the advance had thrown the enemy land forces into disarray. The first few rotations had seen the same sort of resistance as had been met all along the line of advance, but then the attack force had broken through another defense point and encountered nothing more beyond it. They were then able to advance hundreds of telequels with virtually no resistance. Habitation zones, large and small had been taken by surprise, their non-warrior populations fleeing in panic at the approach of the fighting machines. There had been no time to completely destroy them but there had been much slaughter.

And now they were here. Three hundred fighting machines and over a hundred cargo carriers holding extra power cells and the components for twenty of the heavy heat rays, three tunneling machines, and a power reactor.

"Progenitor," said Lutnaptinav over the communicator. It was with an advanced scouting party. "There appear to be a number of defense installations ahead, but they seem to be constructed to point at the entrance to the water passage rather than at us. That is very odd, is it not?"

"Perhaps, and perhaps not. The first expedition which failed reported that even though they had taken the prey creatures completely by surprise, they did encounter warriors and weapons and fighting vessels at sea. If those things existed, it must have been because the prey creatures sometimes fight each other."

"Just as we do?"

Kandanginar paused before answering, but since Lutnaptinav shared many of its memories, there was no point in denying it. "Yes, just as we sometimes do. What are the defenders of these installations doing? I assume they have seen you."

"Yes, they have. There are not many of them and most appear to be fleeing rather than attempting to fight. A few are trying to turn around some of the large projectile throwers. If we attack at once we can destroy them before they can succeed."

"Excellent. That is what we shall do." Kandanginar set its communicator to an open frequency. "Battle groups 14-12 and 14-21, advance immediately and secure the enemy defense sites."

The leading elements moved forward rapidly and quickly captured the nearby positions. They soon discovered that there were more of them further east and forces were dispatched against them as well. Before long they came under fire from similar positions on the other side of the water passage. They were out of range of the heat rays and the water was much too deep to cross so there was nothing which could be done about that, but the fire was neither accurate nor heavy.

By nightfall scouts had reached a large habitation zone about twenty *telequels* to the east of the mouth of the passage. There was a great deal of panic evident, but little in the way of organized military units. Kandanginar ordered the scouts to pull back. They had more important things to do than destroy the place.

As soon as the cargo carriers arrived, the technicians were set to assembling the tunneling machines. They would be needed to dig the emplacements for the heat rays and for the reactor. Seismic probes discovered that the water in the narrow passage was about a hundred quels deep at most points; not too deep to preclude digging a tunnel under the channel. This would allow them to send forces to the northern shore. But that would have to wait.

Work proceeded through the night and by dawn encouraging progress had been made. But only a short time later a message arrived from Commander Jakruvnar. "Kandanginar, the artificial satellite has revealed that the prey creature fleet in on the move. It appears to be heading directly toward your position."

"At what speed? How long until it arrives?"

"At the current speed, less than three full rotations. Can you be ready to receive an attack before then?"

Kandanginar thought quickly. "There is no hope of having the reactor ready by then, but we could have four or five heat rays in position. We could power them for a time with the spare power cells. That might hold the enemy off long enough for us to complete our defenses."

"That would be a considerable risk. If they attack aggressively you could take heavy casualties and be forced back with the loss of all the equipment."

"True, but if we do not hold them off their entire force will soon be in position to oppose our offensive."

Jakruvnar did not immediately answer.

"Commander? What are your orders?"

"Hold as long as you possibly can."

* * * * *

Near Lemnos Island, March, 1913

Major Tom Bridges strode out onto the platform projecting from the bridge of the *USNLI Yellowstone*. The sun was just coming up, silhouetting the rocky shoreline of the Turkish coast in the far distance. Off to the left was the island of Lemnos, Greek territory. The nearly level sunlight made it fairly gleam in white and green and gold. By all rights, that should have been friendly territory, but the absurd war the Greeks recently fought against the Turks, made their attitude toward this huge armada sailing to help the Turks questionable.

A gentle breeze was blowing up from the south and promised a warm day. A hundred other ships surrounded them, black smoke wafting up from their stacks. Over a hundred more were out of sight behind them. The fleet would be approaching the Dardanelles in an hour or so, and the commander, Admiral Carden, had timed their arrival for just after dawn. The narrow passage was a tricky one and they wanted full daylight to go through. Especially since they had been getting some very confused signals from the Turks about what was going on in the vicinity. Martian forces were driving quickly up from the south, but no one seemed to know exactly where they were.

"Good morning, Major, up bright and early I see,"

Bridges turned to see the ironclad's skipper, Commander Drew Harding, coming out through the bridge door.

"Yes, sir. And a beautiful morning it is, too. Very welcome after the terrible weather we had getting here."

"Yes, it hasn't exactly been a pleasure cruise, has it? But we made it and that's the important thing."

Bridges looked at Harding's face. He seemed relaxed and in a good humor. He'd spent about a week with the man before this current assignment, during that extraordinary campaign at Memphis and against the nearby Martian fortress. At that time Harding was recovering from injuries he'd suffered when his ship had been sunk trying to stop the Martian attack across the Mississippi. He'd been physically hurt, but that had seemed minor compared to what the loss of his ship had done to his spirit. He'd been the only survivor and that would gnaw at the soul of any man. He'd been exonerated of wrongdoing and given command of one of his navy's new land ironclads and to all appearances was fully recovered.

Bridges glanced around the ship. "I must say your navy version of these contraptions is a lot more seaworthy than the ones your army has. I only was aboard the Albuquerque at sea from Key West to New Orleans and it was the clumsiest tub I've ever sailed on. Not that it didn't prove itself once it got ashore, of course."

Harding laughed, "Well, what can you expect when the army tries to design a ship? They just considered the things huge tanks which also needed to be able to float. The navy looks at them as ships, which could also drive on land when necessary."

Bridges nodded. The navy version was significantly larger than the army version and nearly all the extra size was devoted to giving it better sea-keeping qualities. The army ironclads couldn't even float without having additional flotation modules attached. The navy ones could stay afloat on their own — but just barely. For long distance travel they, too, had additional floatation modules attached. But they had larger engines, better propellers and rudders, and all the extra space gave them room for real quarters for the crews. How well they would do once ashore remained to be seen.

Despite being larger, they had almost exactly the same armament as the army version; a twelve-inch gun in a turret forward of the bridge, four five-inch guns mounted individually in pairs of turrets on each side, four four-inch guns in small casemate mounts on the superstructure, and a dozen or so machine guns anywhere there was room to mount them. And just forward of the twelve-inch turret was another turret with the Americans' wonder weapon, the Tesla lightning cannon. Bridges had seen the thing in action and it really was a wonder. It could project a bolt of electrical energy which was fully capable of destroying a Martian tripod — and not just one at a time. The bolt would leap from tripod to tripod — and to the spider machines as well — and take out a whole group of them at once. The only drawback was that it took about ten minutes to recharge the thing's batteries after it shot.

The six ironclads, *Yellowstone, Cimarron, Laramie, Escalanta, Sheyenne,* and *Big Sioux,* all named for rivers in territory occupied by the Martians, made up the 1st Navy Land Ironclad Squadron (not to be confused with the army 1st Land Ironclad Squadron). Bridges had joined them in New York and been assigned to Harding's vessel due to their earlier acquaintance. Just like when he'd been with the army squadron he had not been put on the flagship, Big Sioux. Apparently, the navy commodore was no more eager to rub elbows with an observer than the army brigadier had been. That didn't bother Bridges; Harding was a pleasant enough chap and with all the other staff on the flagship he would have ending up sleeping in the coal bunker instead of a small, but comfortable cabin aboard *Yellowstone.*

The Atlantic crossing had been a bit harrowing. No really severe storms, but enough foul weather to keep the ships rolling and the pumps pumping, nearly the whole way. Even though the ironclads could make about eight knots on their own, each was also towed by a larger vessel to increase the speed. They'd made it across in twelve days and put in at Gibraltar for rest and repairs. Then it was across the Med to join up with the other ships assembling for the big operation. But even the weather in the western Mediterranean had been wet and cold. It wasn't until they'd passed the Strait of Messina that things became more spring-like. They made the rendezvous just north of Alexandria and then entered the Aegean and now here they were, approaching the Dardanelles.

"Quite a thing, isn't it?" said Harding.

"Sir?"

"This fleet," replied the American, waving his hand out toward the ships all around them. "I suppose there have been bigger ones, but so many different countries are involved. I don't think anything like this has ever happened before."

"Perhaps not, but it's about time if we're ever going to win."

"Have you ever been to Constantinople, Major? I know you've done an awful lot of travelling."

"No, I can't say that I have. Managed to miss that one somehow. India, Egypt, South Africa, all over Europe, and then America, of course, but never Constantinople."

"I guess the locals call it Istanbul."

"Ever since they took it from the Greeks, yes."

"And the Greeks still want it back, don't they?"

"I suppose so. After five hundred years you'd think they'd have given up on that. But for right now the only thing that matters is to keep the Martians from getting hold of it."

"That's for sure," said Harding. "Well, I have some things to do. See you later." The American went back onto the bridge, leaving him alone with the sun and sea and the fleet.

Harding was right, though: it really was quite a thing. He watched the ships steaming along so splendidly. Most of them were painted various shades of gray, but there were a few, probably from the smaller European navies, that still wore their peacetime colors. Black hulls and white or tan upper works, a few even painted shades of green, making them look oddly out of place, like some carnival clown wandered into a funeral. Wartime gray was intended to make the warships harder to see and thus harder to hit. He wondered if the Martians really saw things the same as humans did. The color of the ship might not make any difference at all.

After a while he wandered down to the wardroom to get a cup of coffee. Or at any rate it was something they called coffee. With South and Central America in the hands -tentacles? -of the Martians, there was a worldwide shortage of coffee. Bridges wasn't sure what this stuff really was, but it was pretty awful. Thank God India was still able to produce tea!

He was just starting to think about breakfast when a commotion caught his attention. People were bustling about, and he thought he could hear some ship's horns sounding in the distance. Leaving his ersatz coffee behind, he hurried up on deck and looked around.

The orderly columns of ships were falling into confusion with ships turning this way or that. What was going on? A sudden rumble in the distance caught his attention. Gunfire! He climbed up to the bridge and found Harding and his officers all staring out through the windows with field glasses. Finding an unused pair, he stared out in the direction of the shooting.

The rugged Turkish coastline was closer now and with the sun higher it was easier to see in that direction. There seemed to be smoke drifting along, both on the shore and from some of the ships. As he watched, there was a flash of yellow from one of those ships and after a number of long seconds, the noise of the guns reached his ears. Yes, definitely firing - but at what? The only possible answer to that question was not good. He peered at the coastline, but it was still eight or ten miles away and he couldn't see much of... Sunlight glinted off something and focusing on it, Bridges thought he could see a few tiny shaped moving.

"Martians?" he asked aloud. "Are those Martians?"

Commander Harding lowered his binoculars and looked over at him, his face grim. "Yes. The leading destroyers report a large batch of Martians near the headlands of the Dardanelles." He took up the glasses again and looked forward.

"They've beaten us to it."

* * * * *

Admiralty House, London, March, 1913

"A signal from Admiral Carden, my lord," said an orderly, holding out a silver tray with a piece of paper on it to Winston Churchill.

Frederick Lindemann looked up from a report he was pretending to read. Jimmy Chadwick continued to send him updates from the project he'd been working on at the National Physical Laboratory, and Eccles was still pretending that he worked there, but these days he barely spent one day a week at his actual job. His position as science advisor to Winston Churchill was now his first priority even though it didn't actually pay anything. Not that his salary at NPL was much, either; without the allowance from his father he'd not be able to get by.

His real boss had been pouring over a map when the orderly arrived, but now he straightened up and took the proffered signal. "Probably to let us know he's reached the Dardanelles," mumbled Churchill through the cigar clenched between his teeth. He feigned nonchalance, but Lindemann knew that the man was very keyed up. The mere fact that he was in his office at this very early hour proved that. Churchill's working hours were a bit... odd. Normally, he would stay up far past midnight, working until two or three in the morning. Then he would go to bed and usually not be up until after ten. Lindemann, with some difficulty, had adjusted his schedule to match. Not only did he enjoy Churchill's company, but he was doing all he could to make himself indispensable to the man and that meant being available at any hour day or night.

Churchill looked at the dispatch and then stiffened. "Damnation!"

"Trouble, sir?" asked Lindemann, putting aside his report and rising from his chair.

"Yes, the damnable Martians have…"

"Beaten us! They've beaten us there!"

Churchill and Lindemann both twisted around as Lord Fisher burst into the room, slamming open the door, and waving a dispatch paper in his hand. "Winston! Have you seen this? The bloody Martians have beaten us to the Dardanelles!"

"Yes, yes, Jacky, we both get copies of these signals, you know."

"What in hell are we going to do," continued Fisher. "They've sealed the straights against us!"

"Now we don't know that," said Churchill. "Carden's message just says that they've spotted some tripods on the south shore of the Dardanelles. We don't know in what strength or if they've…"

"If they have set up their awful super heat rays we're done! The fleet can't get through in the face of those! You know that! After what happened to us ad Bab al Mandab, we can't try something like that again!"

"The tripods may just be a scouting detachment," said Churchill. "We heard some rumors that a force was moving rapidly along the coast, but they can't possibly have reached the Dardanelles more than a few hours ago or we would have heard something from the Turks. If we tell Carden to move boldly we can probably push right on through."

"And if you're wrong, we could lose the whole fleet! No! I cannot approve this; I cannot, and I will not!"

Lindemann had gotten used to Fisher's temper tantrums, just as Churchill had, but this one seemed especially bad — and very poorly timed. A delay now could be fatal to the whole operation.

"Jacky," said Churchill in a soothing tone, "we can't call the whole thing off just because a few Martians have been sighted. You know how much trouble we went through to set this all up. And what about all the ships from the other powers that are there? What will they think if we turn back without even trying? They'll think that British admirals and British sailors are cowards. We can't have that, can we?"

That seemed to get through to Fisher, who stopped ranting and then sat down, with a puzzled expression on his face. "No… no, I suppose not. But we can't just go barging in there! At the very least we need to do some scouting. Send in a few destroyers, first. Put some men ashore. And *Ark Royal* is there! Get her float planes up to take a look!"

"That could take time," said Churchill, his soothing tone gone. "The longer we delay, the more time we give the enemy to prepare…"

"I insist!" snapped Fisher, fully belligerent again. "I refuse to give any order to Carden unless you agree to this!"

Churchill sighed. In theory, as first lord of the admiralty, he could just order Fisher to comply. The civilian head of the fleet outranked the naval head. But Lindemann understood that this was just almost never done. Not in tactical matters where the professional officers were assumed to know better than their civilian masters. So, the two men went back and forth for a quarter of an hour, Churchill wheedling and Fisher whining until they had come to a compromise. Admiral Carden could take one day to evaluate the situation but then must launch an attack and push through the strait unless he judged the situation to be completely impossible. Lindemann could tell that neither man was happy. A message to Admiral Carden was composed and sent off.

Fisher finally clumped out of the room and Churchill sagged back in his chair. "God in Heaven," he growled, "he can be such a child sometimes." After a moment he looked directly at Lindemann. "You never heard me say that."

"Of course not, sir. Do you think the operation can still succeed?"

"Well, this does throw a wrench in it. We didn't think the Martians could be there so soon. And why in blazes didn't we hear anything from the Turks about this? How could a large force move five hundred miles through their territory without them noticing?"

"Well, they're not up to Europeans standards of efficiency, sir. Moslems and all. There might be reports slowly working their way through their bureaucracy. They'll reach the top and get passed on to us after it's too late to do any good."

"Yes, I suppose. But Carden simply must act boldly. We've staked everything on this operation."

Churchill didn't add that *he* had staked everything on this operation. After the disaster at Bab al Mandab, a failure here would be the end of his career. And if Churchill lost his post, he wouldn't need a science advisor...

Lindemann took up the report again. He supposed he better not get too far out of favor with the National Physical Laboratory. He might need that job again soon.

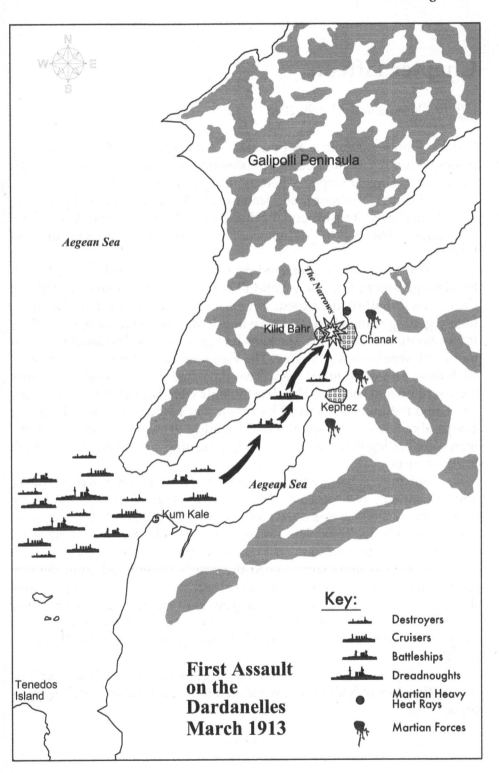

Galipolli Peninsula

Aegean Sea

The Narrows

Kilid Bahr

Chanak

Kephez

Aegean Sea

Kum Kale

Tenedos
Island

**First Assault
on the
Dardanelles
March 1913**

Key:

Destroyers

Cruisers

Battleships

Dreadnoughts

Martian Heavy
Heat Rays

Martian Forces

Chapter Fifteen

Off the Dardanelles, March, 1913

"Looks like something's happening," said Harry Calloway, peering through his binoculars. "Some of the destroyers are moving forward and it looks like the bigger ships are getting ready to move, too."

"Damn well about time," said Ian MacDonald. 'Y'know I'm getting bloody tired of waiting around for these generals and admirals to make up their minds. The stinkin' Martians are over there, let us go fight the bastards!"

The other officers clustered near the rail of the *Bridlington* all muttered in agreement and Harry couldn't help but feel the same way. After all the delays in putting the expedition into motion it seemed like they were finally getting somewhere and then suddenly they were stopped in their tracks again. Seemingly the Martians had gotten to the Dardanelles before them and were blocking the way. The vanguard of the fleet had skirmished with them and then pulled back. Two days had gone by while seaplanes were sent up and some cavalry detachments were landed farther down the coast, and naturally not a word had been sent to the thousands of waiting troops about what was going on. A steadily growing percentage of the men were betting that they would end up turning around and sailing back to Alexandria.

But now something was going on. As they continued to watch, smoke suddenly blossomed from some of the battleships and the heavy concussions echoed across the water to where the transports lay at anchor. Harry focused his binoculars on the distant shore and saw explosions erupting there, but it was too far to see what they were shooting at.

More and more ships joined the bombardment, although the majority of the warships were still not involved. The roar of the big guns and the rumble of the distant explosions grew loud enough that conversation was difficult and the watchers fell silent. An easterly breeze blew some of the gun smoke in their direction and the sharp tang of cordite filled their nostrils.

Harry had seen what large naval guns could do to the Martians during the siege of Sydney and wondered if they were accomplishing anything here?

* * * * *

Coordinates 12943-08 of Subcontinent 1-4, Cycle 597,845.5

The impact of a heavy projectile shook the underground chamber and a small stone broke loose from the ceiling and fell to the floor. Kandanginar glanced upward from its travel chair, but nothing more followed — for the moment. The chamber was not nearly as deep or as heavily reinforced as it would have preferred, but there was no choice. To have constructed it perfectly would have taken far too much time. Time they did not have.

They had reached the narrow water passage ahead of the prey creature fleet, and managed to hold them off for two rotations by little more than bluff, but now they appeared to be making a serious attack and unless the new heavy heat rays could be made operational soon, it might prove impossible to stop them.

An ideal deployment would have seen the twenty ray projectors they had brought with them positioned in twenty separate locations, creating an interlocking field of fire, but with an attack imminent, all that could be accomplished was to use the digging machines to excavate a single position which had firing ports for six of the projectors.

Fortunately, the water passage grew very narrow and made a sharp turn a few *telequels* east of its mouth, just beyond an abandoned prey creature habitation. Not only could the chamber be placed in a location out of direct sight of the open water to the west, but if the enemy tried to close on it, the range would be so short that the fighting machines could use their weapons effectively and support the heavy heat rays. Granted that this positioning gave up the much longer range of the heavy heat rays, but the multiplication of effective forces would make this worth it.

Even so, the land was not hilly on the south side of the passage and the chamber could not be deeply buried. Random projectiles could still strike the surface above the chamber and enough of them might bring about a collapse. The mountainous northern shore would have been a far better location, but until a tunnel could be dug there was no way to reach it. *Some of the clans on Continent 3 have constructed crude water craft to cross major rivers. Perhaps we should think about doing the same.*

"Progenitor?" Lutnaptinav approached in its own travel chair. The bud was assisting in the construction.

"Yes?"

"Two of the projectors are in place. We can connect the power cells to them now."

"Very well, proceed."

It would take at least eight more rotations to set up the reactor and bring it online, so all efforts had gone into creating the firing positions for the heat rays. They would be powered by groups of the spare power cells for the fighting machines. Hundreds of them were stacked in the chamber. Other clan members, operating manipulators were hooking them into a series of conduits. It was not the most efficient method and an extended battle might use up the cells, leaving the heavy heat rays useless and depriving the fighting machines of replacement cells. A considerable risk, but there was no choice. If the enemy water vessels came on in strength, only the heavy heat rays could stop them.

Kandanginar moved its travel chair into one of the tunnels where the projectors were located, Lutnaptinav following. It led several hundred quels beyond the main chamber and then turned enough that no projectile could pass along it all the way to the main chamber. The ray projector sat there pointing out through the opening, another thirty quels down the tunnel. The waters of the passage could be seen in the distance. A manipulator was already connecting a power conduit to the device.

"How long to complete?"

"Point zero-two-five rotations for the first two, another point one rotations for the rest."

"Let us hope that we have that much time." It opened a communications circuit. "Battle Group Leader Galmattinar, report your status."

"Subcommander, the enemy continues to bombard the area around the entrance to the water passage, responded Galmattinar immediately. "Our fighting machines emerge from cover at random intervals to draw their fire, as you ordered. We have lost three machines so far, with one pilot killed and one injured.

"Acceptable losses."

"Yes, Subcommander, but now the enemy appears to be advancing. Eight of the smaller vessels are moving into the mouth of the passage and many more of the larger ones are forming up to follow. We cannot stop them with the current tactics. Do you wish us to engage closely?"

Kandanginar considered the options. A general engagement on the open plains on the south side of the passage could be very costly, but it could buy time to get the heavy heat rays into operation. Would it be worth it? "How quickly are the lead vessels moving?"

Galmattinar supplied a figure and Kandanginar calculated time versus distance. At the given rate, there would be time to complete the work, but only if the prey creatures did not increase speed. Study of the enemy water vessels indicated that the type now approaching were capable of greater speed than these were using. Still, a general engagement, if it became necessary, could be more advantageously be fought in the narrowest part of the passage.

"Withdraw our forces to the vicinity of the heavy heat ray position. Put half in the habitation and the rest farther east. Have all make ready for battle, including the bombardment drones."

"Subcommander, we have not yet received permission to employ the new drones," said Galmattinar.

"I am aware of this. If it becomes necessary to use them I shall take full responsibility. Have all of the smaller drones move to a safe location, they will be of no use in this sort of a battle."

"Very well, Subcommander. We shall begin the withdrawal immediately."

Kandanginar broke the connection and turned its travel chair to face Lutnaptinav. "Continue the work here at the fastest possible pace. I am going to take a fighting machine and directly observe the battle."

The bud seemed surprised, but waved its tendrils in acquiescence. "As you command."

* * * * *

Admiralty House, London, March, 1913

It was another unusually early morning for the First Lord of the Admiralty. Frederick Lindemann watched Churchill prowling around the operations room, chewing on cigars and drinking coffee, waiting for signals from Admiral Carden to come in. The admiral had taken two days to make his reconnaissance, rather than the one day agreed to by Churchill and Fisher, but this morning he was making his attack. Everyone was waiting to hear the results.

Lord Fisher hurried into the room, still fiddling with the buttons on his trousers and asked: "Anything?"

"No," replied Churchill, "Nothing since that last signal that the enemy was withdrawing and that Carden had ordered the 23rd Destroyer Flotilla into the Narrows."

Both men leaned over a large detailed map of the Dardanelles spread on a table which had colored wooden blocks set on it to denote the ships in the fleet. A blue block with the notation '23 DD' painted on it was leading the way into the strait. A great many other blocks, of various colors were massed outside the strait, with a few following the destroyers in.

"Good! Good!" said Fisher. "The destroyers will flush them out and the battleships can smash them!"

Lindemann studied Fisher. The First Sea Lord had gone through one of his frequent mood swings and was now bubbling with confidence and enthusiasm. But he knew that even the tiniest thing could send that all crashing down and turn him into a broken pessimist. He couldn't see how Churchill could put up with the man so patiently — or why the Prime Minister could tolerate having the fleet in the hands of someone so erratic.

If it had been Lindemann's decision, he'd relieve the old man and replace him with someone else, Battenburg, say.

Another message arrived which Churchill and Fisher read without any visible reaction. They handed it to one of the junior officers who was in charge of the map. He pushed the block for the destroyer flotilla a little farther into the channel and adjusted a few of the other blocks as well.

The old clock on the wall rang out six times.

* * * * *

Coordinates 12943-08 of Subcontinent 1-4, Cycle 597,845.5

Kandanginar piloted its fighting machine to the end of a long row of prey creature structures and extended a vision pick-up. The small city had been abandoned and had not been significantly damaged. Normally when the Race occupied, or even passed through, such a place it would be destroyed as a matter of routine. Kandanginar had ordered that this not be done in this case, calculating that the buildings might provide useful cover in the event of a battle. So it was proving.

The five battle groups which had been delaying the enemy at the mouth of the water passage had withdrawn to the city and were concealed as best as could be managed. Heavy projectiles from some of the more distant prey-creature vessels were starting to fall on the place, but so far not in great number. Four more battle groups were positioned in the area around the chamber containing the heavy heat rays. The last battlegroup which had come north was deployed as scouts farther to the east. Enemy forces were massing there, but not in dangerous numbers so far. Hundreds of drones were concealed in the city or in other places of concealment. The small machines were useful against the prey creature ground forces, but with their very small heat rays, they would be of little use against the enemy water vessels.

From its position it could see down the length of the passage, all the way to where it met the open sea. A great many vessels were visible, although some were concealed by the smoke from their own weapons. Eight of the smaller ones were advancing slowly and had almost reached the point where the channel turned sharply north and became very narrow. The heavy heat ray position was just beyond that.

It had been a risk to set up them up in that location. It negated the long range of the weapons and meant that any engagement would be at extremely short range. So close that the prey creatures would have the opportunity of firing directly down the tunnels and destroy the heat rays if they were quick enough.

The advantage was that at such a close range, the heat rays would be extremely effective, able to burn through even the thickest armor in a short time. The enemy vessels could be destroyed quickly. Equally important, the channel was so narrow that the fighting machines would be close enough to engage as well. Kandanginar hoped that such a concentration of force would be more than the prey creatures could endure.

It would shortly discover if its calculations were correct.

The leading vessels, which were firing their small projectiles from time to time, reached the turn and followed the passage north. More vessels were coming up behind them. Several of the battle group commanders asked for permission to open fire, but Kandanginar ordered them to remain concealed. Shells from the more distant vessels were falling in the city more frequently now and several fighting machines reported damage.

"Lutnaptinav, report your status."

"We are nearly ready, Subcommander," replied the bud. "Another zero point zero-zero-five rotations."

"Very well, stand by."

The first group of small vessels were moving past the heat ray position. A second group of somewhat larger vessels were approaching the turn. Some of the biggest ones were now entering the mouth of the passage. It was tempting to allow those to come all the way to the turn, but that would mean that significant numbers of the enemy would be past the main defense positions and be free to travel all the way to the small inland sea if they wished. No, best to stop them here.

"Kandanginar to all battle groups, engage the enemy."

* * * * *

USNLI Yellowstone, The Dardanelles, March, 1913

"Looks like we're getting through," said Tom Bridges, peering through his binoculars. "The Martians have buggered off."

Commander Drew Harding stood away from a more powerful set of glasses on a pintle mount and shook his head. "Don't be so sure. The bastards can move so fast there's no telling what they are up to. The very first time we Americans fought them, they pulled back, our troops followed, and then they attacked and wiped out the whole army facing them before they could get their artillery unlimbered. You remember Andy Comstock? He was there when it happened."

"I do seem to recall hearing something about that," said Bridges. "Ships are a bit different from field artillery though, their guns are always ready."

223

"True." Harding put his eyes to the glasses again. "Still, you are right, the destroyers are in the Narrows. Some armored cruisers are following and some of the older battleships after them. Admiral Carden seems to be skittish about committing any of the dreadnoughts, though."

"Will we be going in soon, do you think?"

"I doubt it. In spite of what the navy might like to think, we're not actually warships. Too slow, too clumsy, and not really all that well armed or armored when you come right down to it. Not compared to a battleship, anyway. On land we'll do alright, but in a situation like this, why make us fill the role of a warship when you've got plenty of the real thing handy?"

"So we'll wait here until the fleet is sure the way is clear?"

"I imagine so. We'll probably go through with the army transports since we're supposed to be supporting... Hell's bells, what's going on there now?"

The sharp tone in the American's voice brought Bridges attention back to the image through his binoculars. He couldn't really see much as the distance was at least fifteen miles from where they were waiting at the mouth of the strait to the Narrows, but new clouds of smoke were billowing up and he thought that perhaps he could see things moving on the shore. The distinctive red glow of Martian heat rays flickered through the clouds of smoke. Over the distance, the rumble of gunfire and the heavy thud of explosions, shook the *Yellowstone* slightly.

"Looks like you were right, Commander, the blighters haven't given up!"

"No, I think they may have suckered us into a trap."

* * * * *

Coordinates 12943-08 of Subcontinent 1-4, Cycle 597,845.6

The beam of the heavy heat ray, so much wider and brighter than the standard ones, burned its way vertically through the enemy vessel from the top down to the waterline. Clouds of black smoke boiled upward around the cut, punctuated by puffs of white as the propellant for the prey creature weapons ignited, and red and orange droplets of molten metal splashing outward. When the ray reached the water, a huge blast of white steam erupted. The water reduced the effects of the ray, but the damage was still sufficient. The vessel broke into two pieces and quickly sank into the depths, the severed ends pointing nearly straight up before vanishing. The ray winked out as the projector traversed to find a new target.

Kandanginar looked on from its observation point. The eight enemy vessels which had led the prey creature attack were all sunk or burning. The heavy heat rays had destroyed five of them and the massed heat rays of the fighting machines had done for the other three. The prey creatures had only been able to fire a few ineffective shots in return.

A nearby explosion showered Kandanginar's machine with dirt and small rocks, reminding it that the battle had barely begun. The second group of enemy vessels were firing now and they mounted many more weapons than the first group. Explosions erupted around the position where the heavy heat rays were mounted and others among the fighting machines. As it watched, one of the machines had a leg blown off and it crashed to the ground.

More vessels were joining the fight and the volume of fire was becoming alarming. In just a few moments three more machines were disabled and the constant explosions were interfering with the fire from the heavy heat rays. Very large projectiles, apparently from the largest war vessels, still outside the strait, began falling on the city, blowing groups of buildings to rubble with a single shot. Any fighting machine caught in such a blast would have little chance of survival.

It had been observed on a number of occasions that the prey creatures had become very adept at directing the fire of their long-range weapons. If a target was identified, in a short amount of time projectiles from many different weapons, often separated by *telequels* of distance, would all start to converge on it. While the individual weapons were not particularly accurate, the sheer number of projectiles often assured the destruction of the target. So even though only a few score of vessels could engage at a time here, the others could aid them with long range fire.

"Progenitor." It was Lutnaptinav. "One of the heavy heat rays is currently unable to fire due to debris blocking the tunnel. I have a manipulator working to clear it."

"Understood."

The second group of vessels was approaching the turn now. Several of them were burning due to shots from the fighting machines along the shore, but they were still moving and firing. The leading one came into view of the heat ray position and four beams stabbed out almost simultaneously to strike it. The front of the vessel was bathed in a dazzling red light and then a moment later an explosion tore the forward third of it to pieces. It lurched and slewed around almost sideways. The beams moved along its exposed length causing more explosions and leaving the remains burning from end to end. A few of the prey creatures flung themselves into the water on the side opposite the heat rays. Several of them were on fire.

The next vessel in line, unable to turn quickly enough, collided with the burning wreck, its pointed front slicing deeply into its ill-fated companion. It was partially shielded from the heavy heat rays, but dozens of lighter ones stabbed out from the fighting machines along the shore and it was soon afire in a score of places. Still, it continued to fight back, claiming several fighting machines, until a huge explosion ripped through it and both vessels slid beneath the water.

The other following vessels managed to turn away without collisions and pulled back out of line of sight of the heavy heat rays. They, and the other vessels behind them continued to fire at the fighting machines along the shore and among the buildings. The fighting machines fired back, but it quickly became apparent that this was a battle that could not be won with the fighting machines alone.

"Kandanginar to all battlegroups, fall back to positions around the heavy heat rays. Find cover and wait for my orders."

The fighting machines pulled back and the smoke from the enemy's bombardment provided concealment. Kandanginar piloted his own machine through the streets, maneuvering around piles of rubble, and eventually emerging into open ground on the eastern side. The status display showed that twenty-one machines had been lost and thirty more had sustained damage. Not critical losses yet, but if the enemy continued its attack they might become so.

Lutnaptinav reported that the blocked passage on the heat ray had been cleared, but the enemy's bombardment seemed to be concentrating on the position, and more blockages could be expected. "Several of the prey creature flying machines are circling overheard, Progenitor. I believe that they are helping to direct the fire from the largest vessels. The fire is disturbingly accurate."

"When we have time to build a proper base, we must give thought to mounting a few of the rays so that they can fire upward to deal with this nuisance."

"If we have time to build a proper base," replied the bud. "If they press their attack we may be forced to withdraw."

Kandanginar did not reply, but what Lutnaptinav said was true. So far they had only destroyed ten of the prey creature's smaller vessels. If they were willing to sustain the losses, and attack aggressively, they might well force their way through and inflict crippling losses.

The battlegroups were reassembling in sheltered ground to the east of the heavy ray position. But they quickly discovered that it was too vulnerable to falling projectiles and Kandanginar ordered them to disperse as much as possible while still remaining close enough to reengage if the enemy came on again.

Fortunately, the prey creatures did not immediately resume the attack. Instead they continued to bombard from long range, while their vessels beyond the narrows reorganized themselves. This went on for some time, but then a new message came from Lutnaptinav. "The bombardment has collapsed the roof of the chamber holding heat ray number three. It has been completely destroyed. Heat ray five may soon suffer the same fate. I have lost two manipulator machines trying to keep the firing tunnels cleared of debris."

"Make every effort to keep the rays in operation. I do not believe that the enemy has given up."

"As you command."

The bombardment continued and Kandanginar was forced to frequently shift the position of the battlegroups as the prey creature fire sought them out. Clearly the flying machines overhead were spotting for the enemy vessels. *Yes, we need to devise a solution to this problem.*

During one short lull, Kandanginar reported the situation to Commander Jakruvnar. It approved of the course of action being followed, but warned against excessive casualties. "Do I have permission to withdraw if the situation grows unacceptable?"

"The decision is yours, Kandanginag," it replied. "The main attack force is still at least four planetary rotations away from the water barrier and resistance is stiffening. If the force you are facing is allowed to reinforce the defenses, our advance may be brought to a halt."

So my defense here is critical, but I will be held accountable for the losses I sustain. Not an ideal situation. Orders had to be obeyed, but it seemed to Kandanginar that it had been given two conflicting orders. Still, there was nothing for it but to try to obey both.

"Subcommander, the enemy vessels are advancing again." It was Battle Group Commander Galmattinar. Kandanginar broke the connection with Jakruvnar and returned its attention to the battle.

The enemy had reorganized the forces in the passage. Eight of the larger vessels, although still not the very largest ones, were now leading the attack, with many others following along. The leading vessels were in pairs this time rather than a single long column like before. They were coming on faster than the first attack and would reach the narrows very soon. The long range bombardment was intensifying, and Lutnaptinav reported another heat ray was blocked from firing.

Kandanginar had to make a decision and make it now. The five heavy heat rays alone would not be able to stop this force. Only by committing every available fighting machine would there be any hope. Even with them, there was no guarantee of victory, and if the prey creatures were willing to continue the attack no matter what their loss, Kandanginar could face annihilation. *The decision is mine, no one else's.*

"Kandanginar to all battlegroups... attack."

The leading pair of vessels reached the turn, but only three of the heavy heat rays were able to fire. They concentrated their beams on the closest vessel, but this one appeared to be much more heavily armored than the previous ones. Flames erupted from several points, but it kept moving and continued to shoot. As the following ships moved around the turn, they all concentrated their fire on where the heat rays were emanating. One of the rays cut off, but almost immediately it was replaced by another. Lutnaptinav and its team were working diligently to keep the weapons in operation. The target ship was burning furiously now and over a hundred fighting machines were approaching the shoreline and adding their fire. The vessel slewed out of formation and headed toward the shoreline.

This only gave the other vessel in the pair a better field of fire. Dozens, hundreds, of projectiles flew from the enemy weapons and the shoreline was blanketed in smoke. Fighting machines blew apart or crashed to the ground. All but two of the heavy heat rays were soon put out of action. But Clan Patralvus flung itself into battle, matching heat rays against projectile throwers. In a short while most of the leading enemy vessels were burning or damaged to some extent, but they were still fighting back—and more were approaching the narrows. Losses among the clan were mounting alarmingly. Something had to be done and there was only one option left to try.

"This is Commander Kandanginar, have the new bombardment drones open fire at once."

Fifty of the devices had accompanied the force and they were dispersed in areas of low ground all along the water passage. A few had been destroyed or damaged by random projectiles, but all of the rest now went into action. Each drone had a launcher and each launcher was fed by a magazine holding twenty of the small explosive bombs. The bombs, fully charged miniature power cells, were loaded into the launchers and then a powerful magnetic field flung them out with great force along a calculated parabolic trajectory. Aiming data was supplied by the fighting machines and although some deviation was caused by local atmospheric conditions, the accuracy was still very good.

The bombs arced down and exploded on or near the prey creature vessels, each blast a dazzling pulse of blue light. The bombs had been tested on captive prey creatures and had proved deadly for fifty or sixty *quels* against unprotected enemy in the open. There was some debate on how effective they would be against armored ground vehicles or armored water vessels. The bombs had limited ability to penetrate armor with anything less than a direct hit, but in the current situation any damage they could do would be important.

Most of the bombs were directed at the vessels in the narrows, but some were also targeted at the following ones. Geysers of water rose up from near misses and blast after blast appeared on the ships themselves.

As Kandanginar had expected, the explosions were not penetrating the armor of the vessels, but there many unarmored and even flammable items and structures on the upper parts of them. The bombs tore these to bits and started many fires. The fire of the leading vessels slackened off to almost nothing and some of the following ships began to maneuver erratically to escape the bombardment.

Still, some enemy fire continued and fighting machine after fighting machine was destroyed. The clan could not sustain these losses for long. Perhaps it was time to…

Just at that moment, one of the vessels in the leading group exploded in a massive ball of fire and smoke. Large pieces of wreckage were flung high into the air to come crashing down on the shore, in the water, or on other vessels. The others began to turn away and amazingly one of the more heavily damaged ones leaned sharply to one side and then simply rolled over until it was upside down, the screw devices which propelled it still spinning uselessly in the air. Kandanginar stared at it on the video display in fascination, as it slipped lower and lower in the water.

"Subcommander! The enemy is retreating!" said Galmattinar over the communicator.

It was true, the prey creature vessels were all turning around. Some of them began spewing thick clouds of black smoke even though they had not been damaged. The volume of enemy fire decreased significantly.

"Subcommander, should we pursue?"

It was tempting, but no, the enemy was now out of sight of the remaining heavy heat rays, and the bombardment drones would soon run out of bombs and the widening waters of the passage would quickly put the fighting machines' weapons out of effective range.

"No," it replied. "No pursuit. We have done enough for now."

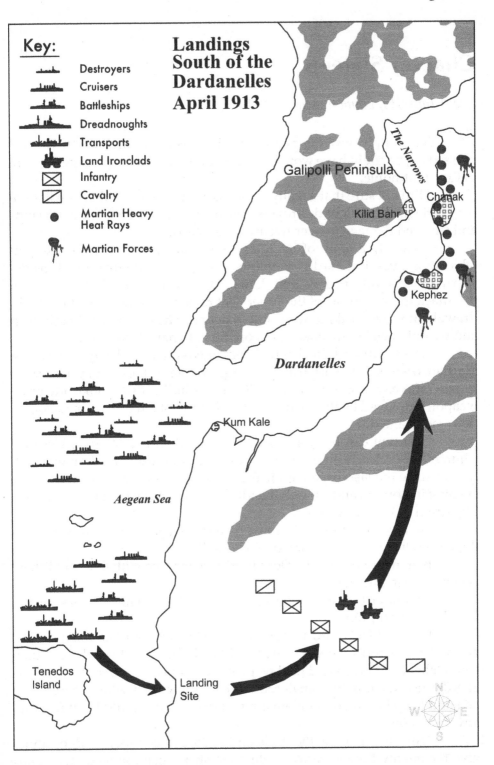

Key:

- ⊶ Destroyers
- ⊶ Cruisers
- ⊶ Battleships
- ⊶ Dreadnoughts
- ⊶ Transports
- Land Ironclads
- ⊠ Infantry
- ⊡ Cavalry
- • Martian Heavy Heat Rays
- Martian Forces

Landings South of the Dardanelles April 1913

Galipolli Peninsula

The Narrows

Chanak

Kilid Bahr

Kephez

Dardanelles

Kum Kale

Aegean Sea

Tenedos Island

Landing Site

Chapter Sixteen

The Admiralty, London, March, 1913

"Carden simply lost his nerve," said Winston Churchill. "If he had pressed on, he could have won the victory and secured the passage through to Constantinople."

"I'm not sure that's really a fair assessment, sir," said Prince Battenberg. "He had lost eight destroyers, five armored cruisers, four battleships and suffered damage to over twenty other ships…"

"Scarcely a tenth of his total force!" snapped Churchill. "Regrettable losses, yes, but hardly crippling. Reports indicate that our ships destroyed nearly fifty tripods and damaged a lot more. And at the start of the attack there were six of the super heat rays, and at the time of the withdrawal, only two or three were still in action. The enemy was badly hurt and we only needed to make one more push to have broken them!"

"And, Admiral Carden had encountered a completely new sort of Martian weapon," persisted Battenberg. "While it does not appear to be as powerful as the super heat rays, it can fire indirectly — unlike any other weapon employed by the enemy. Until we understand its capabilities, caution is warranted."

"Caution can be warranted, but not when it costs us a victory!" Churchill was clearly angry. Lindemann had been watching him worriedly ever since the last dispatches had arrived. It was now ten o'clock in the evening in London and Churchill hadn't slept in nearly twenty-four hours. The strain as beginning to tell.

"In any case, the attack must be resumed at once. If Carden won't do it, I'll relieve him with someone who will!"

Battenberg frowned. "Does Lord Fisher agree with this, sir? Where is Lord Fisher, anyway?"

"Admiral Fisher is… indisposed," said Churchill. "It has been a very long day for him."

In actual fact, Lord Fisher was in a state of complete collapse. The news of this latest reverse seemed to have been more than the old man could take. He'd raved and he'd wept and eventually Churchill had several orderlies take him to a small room on an upper floor where there was a bed and keep him there. Lindemann wondered if he would be fit for duty any time soon.

"And in any case, the decision to proceed is mine. Carden cannot give the enemy time to recover. He must strike again immediately. Start landing his troops if he thinks they will be necessary, but strike! I've sent him orders to that effect, but he has not replied. I'm giving him until midnight, but if I have not heard from him by then, I will relive him of command and turn things over to… to…. who is his second in command?"

"De Robeck, sir."

"Yes, yes, I'll give the fleet to de Robeck."

Battenberg clearly disagreed with the First Lord's decision, but all he said was: "Yes, sir."

Battenberg moved away and Churchill paced for a bit before stopping next to where Lindemann was sitting, trying to stay awake.

"If we strike quickly we can still salvage the situation," he said.

"It's one in the morning there, sir. And if you have to appoint a new admiral, won't it take some him for him to assume command?"

"Yes, yes, I know. To a normal person 'immediately', means right now. But to admirals and generals it means some time in the next week—or month. A day or two I can tolerate, it will take the enemy time to recover, too, after all. But we simply cannot wait any longer than that!"

* * * * *

Skutari Airfield, March, 1913

Major Erich Serco walked from plane to plane, looking them over with an experienced eye. What he saw did not please him. Torn fabric, oil stains, bent tail skids. Some of the deficiencies could be blamed on the age of the second-hand Rumplers the squadron was equipped with, and some on the fact that the Turkish mechanics were still only half-trained. But most of the problems could be blamed on the fact that there was simply no time to fix them.

The Martians, those same Martians he had seen in southern Arabia from the zeppelin back in December, were now less than two hundred kilometers away. A huge number of tripods, some estimates said as many as a thousand of them, had driven north, smashing their way through the Taurus Mountains, the highlands of Anatolia, and now through the Pontic Mountains east of Constantinople. The Ottomans were throwing everything they had against them, trying to slow them down.

Unfortunately, the Ottomans didn't have much left to throw. At least not in the mountains. Some of the promised equipment from Germany had arrived. Some heavy artillery, some tanks, a few more aircraft, but there was no way to get it to the mountain passes where they might have a chance to bottle up the enemy advance. As incredible as it might seem, there was no direct rail connection between northern Turkey and the southern parts of the Ottoman Empire. A single rail line wound its way from Constantinople to Ankara and then southeast to the Taurus Mountains, but from there anything heading south had to be carried up over the heights by horse-drawn wagons—hundreds of kilometers—and then loaded back onto trains on the other side. Before the war, a German company was working on constructing a rail line from Berlin to Baghdad, which would have required a very long tunnel through the mountains, but it was never completed.

The soldiers defending the passes had little more than some light field artillery, machine guns, rifles, and raw courage. From what Serno had heard, they had made good use of all four. They had delayed the Martians, hurt them, even, but they couldn't stop them. Position after position had been overrun and the defenders forced to fall back to the next one.

But they were running out of mountains.

The Martians, advancing on a broad front, were now nearing the fertile northern plains leading down to the Bosporus and Constantinople. The tanks and heavy guns which had been given to the Turks would be there waiting for them, but everyone knew it wouldn't be enough. With room to maneuver, the Martians would blast their way through.

Serno had no doubt the Turks would fight bravely. Everyone realized this was a war of annihilation. There would be no truces, no negotiations, no treaties where a few border provinces changed hands. No, if the Martians won everyone would die. Every town and village, every palace and mosque would be destroyed. Any humans spared would be reduced to cattle. Fight or die.

More probably fight *and* die.

Now that the enemy was closer, Serno's air squadrons were being thrown into the fight. Not so much in direct attacks on the Martians, which would have been suicidal, but for reconnaissance. Direct communications with the front lines was sketchy at best. The Turkish troops had few radios and depended on the undependable telegraph service.

Trying to keep track of where the enemy was and what forces were there to oppose them was difficult and General von Sanders was demanding that Serno's men provide the information that was needed. His fliers were in the air from dawn until dark every day. Shuttling endlessly to the front and then back again. The machines were wearing out and so were the men. They had lost a few to the enemy, but more to accidents and equipment failure. Less than half his planes were still serviceable, and the enemy was getting closer and closer.

A single division of German troops had arrived, along with an Austro-Hungarian one. They were good men and well equipped, but there weren't enough of them. Most of them were being held north of the Bosporus as a last defense for the city. Everyone had hoped there would be more, but instead of coming to Constantinople, the Imperial Army was now defending the line of the Danube in Romania.

The news coming from there was mostly good. German and Austrian forces—committed to the fight at last—had rushed south and east and beaten the Martians to the river. Aided by Romanian troops and supported by a mix of Russian, Romanian, and Austrian gunboats they had thrown back the first Martian attempt to cross near the river's mouth. From there the battle lines had spread back west along the line of the river, the Martians trying to flank the defenders and get across, but the defenders extended their lines with arriving troops as fast or faster than the Martians. The line stretched all the way from the Black Sea to the Carpathian Mountains. If the dispatches could be believed, the enemy was being stopped at every point and hurt badly in the process.

That was all very heartening, but it wasn't going to matter a damn if the Martians got across the Bosporus and took Constantinople. From there, they could strike north and take the defenders of the Danube line in the rear and link up with the other Martian forces. It would be a disaster of major proportions.

Fortunately, people in high places did seem to realize that. More help was on the way, they'd been told. German forces were said to be coming south and amazingly, a multi-national force of British, French, Italians, and Americans were coming by sea to reinforce the defenses along the Bosporus and Dardanelles.

Or at least they were trying to.

Word had come that a fast-moving Martian column had raced up the western coast, destroying the ancient city of Smyrna, and reached the Dardanelles ahead of the allied fleet. It was a measure of how confused and inadequate the Ottoman defenses and communications were that the first knowledge of this force had arrived at headquarters at about the same time the Martians reached the Dardanelles.

The Allies had attempted to break through once or twice (no one at headquarters was sure how many attempts had been made) but they had been beaten back each time. The appearance of this Martian force had thrown the Ottoman government into a panic. Or at least a worse panic than they were already in. If the Martians got across the Dardanelles, then they could outflank the defenses along the Bosporus by moving east up the Gallipoli peninsula. Forces were being rushed to Gallipoli to reinforce the small garrisons in the forts along the north shore of the Dardanelles. In the city it was said that the Sultan and his harem had a special train, packed with treasure, standing ready to evacuate them. Exactly where they could flee to if the city fell was anyone's guess.

A low rumble from off to the southeast reminded Serno that he had more immediate concerns. The Martians were now close enough that the defending artillery could be heard. Or maybe that wasn't just human artillery. In the last few days the Martians had begun using a new weapon, never seen before. No one was quite certain what it was, but it acted like artillery. Projectiles were being fired from hidden positions which then exploded when they reached their target. This had come as a nasty surprise. So far in the war, the humans' monopoly on indirect fire weapons had been a big advantage. It appeared that advantage had been lost. So far no one had gotten a good look at what was firing the projectiles. Today's mission was to try and find out.

Serno completed his inspection and waved the pilots into their cockpits and then swung up into his own plane. "Switch is on!" he called, and a moment later the engine roared to life, followed by those on the other planes. Except for the one on Number 11, that one refused to start and after a minute Serno shook his head and then signaled for the rest of the squadron to take off. Soon they were airborne and heading east.

It shocked Serno how quickly the battlefield came into sight. A mere thirty minutes in the air and he could see of smoke in the distance. *Only sixty or seventy kilometers from our base! We may have to shift operations north of the Bosporus if we can't stop these bastards!*

The approach to the Bosporus was through a long narrow peninsula running east and west. The Black Sea was to the north and the Sea of Marmara to the south. A defensive line about 40 kilometers long was being built across the base of the peninsula, from Agva Merkez on the Black Sea to Alikahya Fatin on the Marmara. It was an admission that the rest of Anatolia, nearly all of Turkey, was being abandoned to the Martians, but there really was no choice. There simply weren't enough troops to defend a longer line. And with naval support at both ends of the line, maybe it could be held.

Below him, streams of refugees fought for space on the road with troops moving to the front. The civilians were desperately trying to get to the right side of the defense line, while the troops were going to the forward lines, trying to buy a few more days for the defenses to be solidified.

Looking closer he saw that some of those troops were German, their field-gray uniforms much different from the mix of tans, greens, and browns worn by the Ottoman troops. There was some heavy artillery in the column, and even, to his surprise, a few of the armored tanks. In the last staff meeting with von Sanders, it had been said that all the tanks they'd received (not nearly enough) would be kept close to Constantinople, but apparently someone had changed their mind. Probably pressure from their Turkish hosts. The Turks were grateful for the German help, but they had ceaseless demands for more and more.

They were getting close to the front now and Serno put his plane into a steeper climb and signaled for the others to follow. With tripods close by they needed to be at a safe altitude. Of course, there was no way to be sure what was safe. The close call in the zeppelin was always in the back of his mind. He levelled out at twenty-five hundred meters. He'd have preferred to be higher, but they had to be low enough to actually see things, so this was a compromise.

He could see the flashes of guns below and the garish red glow of heat rays through the clouds of smoke and dust. The thud and crack of explosions could be heard even above the roar of his engine. In a few spots the clouds were an inky black; the Martians were using their hideous black dust weapons, it seemed. They produced clouds of fine dust, which carried on the wind. Landing on bare skin it caused terrible burns, and if any were inhaled, it guaranteed a quick and awful death. Most armies had developed breathing masks and other protective gear, but the Turkish troops had little of that and were terribly vulnerable.

They passed over the lines and then circled back, Serno making some notes on a pad of paper he carried in the cockpit. Trying to count tripods in a situation like this wasn't easy, but he did his best. The force below looked like a fairly typical one, maybe forty or fifty of the war machines. There was no way to count the small spider machines from this altitude, but there were sure to be some down there.

To the north and south he could see the smoke from more fighting. The broad front at the start of the Martian advance was narrowing down and down as it neared Constantinople. If they didn't find any evidence of the new weapon here, they would have to try some other spot along the line.

As he came back over friendly lines and started to turn toward the enemy again, he saw flickers of blue light below. He banked his plane more sharply to get a better look. There was a battery of artillery down there and it was suddenly smothered by a blanket of bright blue flashes. Dazzlingly bright, even at this altitude, they must have been blinding close up and after each flash, there was a billowing cloud of smoke and dust. A series of sharp cracks, much different from the sound of normal artillery, filled the air. An instant later, the blue explosions were joined by much more normal ones, probably the battery's ammunition going up.

So there's the result, but where's the cause?

This was clearly the new weapon the generals had told him about, but where was it coming from? There needed to be a gun or launcher of some sort that was firing this stuff. The obvious place to look for it was behind the Martian lines. It was artillery, wasn't it? And that's where you found artillery. He levelled out and headed for the enemy rear.

Of course, the Martians didn't have regular battle lines the way a human army would, but they did have a front and a rear. With them forced to follow the passes through the mountains and rough terrain, he had a pretty good guess where their rear was. The road to Akyazi was over that way, and the Martians had passed through there only yesterday. He steered in that direction.

He passed over the main part of the battle and beyond the smoke clouds. Visibility was better here and he strained his eyes to see what was down there. He spotted a new batch of the regular tripods coming forward, but was there anything else? He didn't see anything... wait, what was that?

Squinting, he thought he saw something in a little valley a few kilometers east of where the main fighting was going on. Tripod shapes, but different somehow. They were not moving, but that didn't prove anything. The Martians sometimes brought reserve tripods with their forces which could then be used to replace damaged ones. Was that what these were, or were they something different?

Only one way to find out.

He waggled his wings to get the attention of the squadron and when he had it, he pointed down. He couldn't see the reactions of the men piloting those planes, and he had no way to know if they would follow him, but he put the nose of his Rumpler down and descended in a curve that would bring him over his target and then away in a direction which he hoped would not take him too close to any other enemies. Glancing back, he saw that nearly everyone else was indeed following him, although some had clearly hesitated and were well back, just starting their dives.

For a moment he lost track of where he'd seen the strange tripods, but then he found them again and adjusted his course. Three thousand meters, two thousand meters, fifteen hundred... the ground was coining up fast. The Rumpler was a bit of a slug, but it did dive well. As he got closer, he realized that he had found what he was looking for. The cluster of tripods in the valley were different than any he'd ever seen before. They were smaller and shorter than the usual ones. Three legs, of course, joined at a central cylinder, but the body above the legs was much smaller and strangely elongated. A long object, looking for all the world like a gun tube, although box-like rather than cylindrical, was mounted on an arm projecting up from near the rear of the main body. A smaller box stuck out of the top near the rear of the gun tube. As the range closed rapidly, he got confirmation of what the long boxes were; something spat out of the ends, almost too fast to see, and the machines rocked back in recoil.

Yes, guns of some sort, although there was no flash or smoke when they fired. Clearly, these where what he had been sent out to find. As his

Rumpler came out of its dive and roared past, he twisted around for one more look. He did not see any other weapons or arms, or tentacles like on a normal tripod and oddly, these things did not react to his aircraft at all, even though he couldn't have passed more than a hundred meters above them.

He banked to the right and pulled back on the control stick, using some of his momentum to gain altitude again. Should he come back around for another look? He was flying a single-seat version of the Rumpler and did not have an observer. Two of the planes in the squadron were the observer type and one of the observers did have a camera. Did he get a picture? Probably not. Maybe if they came back around...

The shriek of a heat ray reached his ears from the ground. Looking back, he saw one of the planes—one of the ones which had lagged behind—explode into flames. More heat rays stabbed upward from a group of the standard tripods which had appeared on the lip of the valley. Another plane was caught by one; its wing was sliced off and it corkscrewed into the ground and shattered into a million pieces. Then they were up and away and out of range.

Come back again? I don't think so!

He climbed slowly back to three thousand meters and circled until the survivors of the squadron had joined him. Then he turned west and headed for the base.

* * * * *

Advanced Base 14-5, Cycle 597,845.5

"The reactor is operation, Progenitor," reported Lutnaptinav. "Power is now available for all the heavy heat ray positions and the power cell recharging station."

"Excellent," said Kandanginar, "well done. You and your crews have performed most efficiently."

"Some of the heat ray positions are not well protected. I suggest that they should be relocated. Do you believe we will have the time to do that before another attack comes?"

"That is difficult to predict. The fact that the enemy vessels have not departed would indicate that they do intend to attack again. But if that is so, the delay in doing so makes no sense. It has been ten planetary rotations since the last attack and the time has been invaluable to improving our defenses."

"Perhaps they are waiting for reinforcements," said Lutnaptinav.

"That is possible, although the artificial satellite does not report any significant number of additional water vessels heading in this direction. The prey creature land forces on this side of the water barrier are in full retreat far to the east of us and pose no threat to our rear. The only significant reinforcements moving against us are the forces taking up position on the opposite shore."

"Will that affect our plans to dig a tunnel beneath the water and seize that area?"

"It may, if forces continue to arrive. Especially if they have many of their large projectile throwers. We only have the three tunneling machines so if we are restricted to only two or three exit points, the prey might be able to thwart us. If they are aware of how we captured the island, they will be on their guard against such an attempt."

"Is not the Colonial Conclave urging us to make the attempt?"

"They are, although they care not whether we do so here, or if the main force to the east accomplishes it. The vital thing is to get across the water barrier and move north to the assistance of the clans coming down from Continent 1."

"Is it true their advance has been halted?"

"Where did you get that information?" Kandanginar was surprised. It was true, but the information was supposed to only be known by the clan leaders.

"There have been rumors..."

"Among the buds?"

Lutnaptinav took far too long to answer such a simple question, but finally said: "Yes."

"What else is being said among the buds, Lutnaptinav?"

"It would take considerable time to relate all that I have..."

"Do not be evasive!" said Kandanginar sharply. "You know quite well what I mean. It has become fully apparent that those of you budded on this world, the so called *Threeborn*, share information—and opinions—among yourselves that you keep secret from your progenitors. This is... disturbing behavior. It must stop."

"Do you order me to cease communications with the other... Threeborn? I will obey, of course, but that could prove awkward when tasks need to be done which involve them."

Kandanginar paused and regarded its bud. The conversation had taken an alarming turn. There had been rumors circulating among the higher-ranking members of the Race on the target world that the buds engendered here had created networks among themselves which they concealed from their elders. Networks which might be considered... subversive. Kandanginar had been skeptical that this was happening, at least in any significant way. Had it been wrong? Lutnaptinav's behavior and... prevarication indicated that the rumors might actually be true.

"Progenitor, I assure you that my actions are taken with the best interest of the clan and the Race in mind. You need not doubt my loyalty."

The best interest as determined by who?

"In any case, I suggest that we have more urgent matters demanding our attention," said Lutnaptinav.

On the Homeworld such impertinence would be grounds for a quick termination, but here, here every member was needed for the urgent tasks facing them. Lutnaptinav's work had been exemplary. And much work remained to be done.

"We will discuss this later," said Kandanginar. "For the moment, proceed with relocating the heavy heat rays you are concerned about. But only one at a time. The prey creatures could attack at any moment and I do not want more than one weapon inoperable."

"I hear and obey, Progenitor," said Lutnaptinav.

* * * * *

USNLI Big Sioux, The Dardanelles, April 1913

The wardroom aboard the flagship of the American Navy's land ironclad squadron was not large. None of the human amenities on the outlandish ships/vehicles were anything other than small or tiny. The squadron commander, Commodore William Bullard, was briefing his officers on the coming operation. The six land ironclad commanders, including Commander Harding, just managed to squeeze into the wardroom with the commodore. Subordinates or lookers-on, like Tom Bridges, were clustered in the corridor outside, trying to hear.

"Is this the real thing, sir, or just another false alarm?" asked one of the skippers. "They've been saying we were going to land soon for almost three weeks."

"I've been assured by Admiral de Robeck that we will be landing in the morning, John," said Bullard. "I know the delay has been frustrating for you and your crews. Hell, I've been frustrated, too. We've given the enemy far too much time to make preparations. If we'd attacked all out the day after the first repulse, we'd all be in Constantinople now."

"The Brits have been leery about attacking land forts with ships ever since Fort McHenry!" quipped another commander, getting a laugh. Bridges, after spending over a year with American military units, was used to that sort of thing and was not offended. Well, not much, anyway.

"There's no doubt the Martians have been using the time to get thoroughly dug in," said Bullard, "but it has allowed us build up our strength, too. When the Greeks got the word that the enemy had destroyed Smyrna on their way here, it finally knocked them off the fence. The people there were mostly Greeks and it's really riled them up. They are allowing us to use their port facilities and the island of Lemnos as a forward base. Greek troops are being offered, although we're not sure how much use they will actually be. And just two days ago a German squadron, led by the battle cruiser *Goeben*, showed up with almost no advanced notice. They want to help us push through so they can get into the Black Sea and help out their armies fighting on the Danube.

"So, we have a hell of a lot of strength piled up here. Now we just have to use it properly. Tomorrow, there will be a major landing to the south of the Dardanelles. We already have some cavalry in that area, although they've been forced to retreat a fair way south by Martian patrols. That's fine as it should draw them away from where we are going to land, right here." There was a map on the small table in the wardroom, but Bridges couldn't see it.

"Our mission will be to land, and then strike north to attack the Martian defenses along the Dardanelles from the rear. The fleet will delay its own attack until we are in position to hit them. Information coming from air scouting estimates there are three to four hundred tripods in the area. We have to assume they will make every effort to prevent us from doing this.

"As you know, up until now we have been under the command of the senior British admiral, if you can keep track of them as they come and go. But once ashore we will be under army jurisdiction. Yes, yes, I know, but we all knew that would often be the case when we took control of these amphibious monsters. So, we will be getting our orders from General Archibald Murray. I shall attempt to keep you insulated from as much nonsense as possible.

"The infantry is going ashore in small boats, but sadly there are no proper port facilities anywhere along this stretch of coastline, so getting the artillery and tanks landed is going to a real problem until the engineers can work something out. The fleet can make up for the lack of artillery, but gentlemen, the only ones who can make up for the tanks is us." Bullard paused and looked at his commanders.

"Gentlemen, we will be the first ones ashore."

* * * * *

SS Bridlington, Off the Dardanelles, April 1913

The guns had been roaring since before dawn. Bright flashes of light lit up the skies and distant coastline. The concussions thumped against the ship and rattled loose items. A half dozen battleships, a score of cruisers, and flocks of smaller craft were pouring shells into the Turkish coast. And this was only a small portion of the armada which had assembled. Word had it that nearly half of the ships were preparing for the push through the strait, and the remainder were waiting in reserve to replace ships who ran low on ammunition.

Lieutenant Harry Calloway was up before the bombardment began. After weeks of sitting around, they were finally landing today. The 15th New Castle Battalion was not part of the first wave, but it would be going in shortly afterwards. The men had to be awake and ready to go before the sun rose. Harry had his platoon assembled and inspected and prepared an hour before they were actually called. But the men were as eager to get going as he was; as everyone was. They were sick of the ship and sick of waiting. Every man jack of them was itching to see some combat.

The many delays had had at least one good result. Private Greene's amazing crossbow bomb thrower contraption had been copied and now every platoon in the battalion had two of the outrageous things. They were starting to appear in some of the other battalions as well. Of course, they had never been tested in combat.

The order finally came, and they filed up the ladders and came out on deck where they were mustered next to the rope nets which led down to the boats bobbing in the water. The eastern sky was a soft pink seen through the haze thrown up by the bombardment. Off to the south was a small island called Tenedos, only a few miles off the Turkish coast. Troops would be landing there, too, they'd been told. It had not been seized up until now because it was in range of the new Martian weapons.

"What are they shooting at?" asked one of the men, staring at the tortured coastline. Shell after shell exploded, but no tripods could be seen in the growing light.

"Just making sure there aren't any unfriendly strangers waiting for us," said Burford Sampson. "Be damned awkward to get caught by a tripod while we were bobbing around in a boat."

"God's truth, sir!"

"Looks like it's starting," said Ian MacDonald, pointing. "There go the Yank land ironclads."

Everyone crowded closer to the rail and stared out toward the shore. The Americans had invented amazing vehicles which could sail on the water like ships and then crawl up out of the water and drive on land like enormous tanks. Heavily armored and carrying many large guns, they could slug it out toe to toe with the enemy tripods—and win.

Right now six of them were heading toward a stretch of beach a little to the north of where the *Bridlington* was anchored. Black smoke belched from their stacks and their trailing wakes were like six arrows pointing at the enemy.

"Hope they don't sink," said someone. "They look awfully low in the water."

"I read that for long voyages they have additional hull pieces hooked to them to make them more seaworthy," said Sampson. "They jettison them before going ashore."

"Bloody clever."

"Why don't we have any of the bloody things?" asked Sergeant Milroy.

"They're building some in England, I hear. Not ready yet, I guess."

The ironclads were very near the shore now and Harry pulled out his binoculars to see better. The strange things had reached water shallow enough for their caterpillar tracks to touch bottom. They jerked and shuddered and lurched upward. Water poured off them and with a sort of side to side motion caused by the uneven ground, they reminded Harry of a dog emerging from a pond and shaking the water off itself.

After a minute or two they were all ashore. Their turrets swiveled back and forth but could find no targets to shoot at. And nothing appeared to be shooting at them. The naval bombardment had shifted target to regions further inland.

"No welcoming party, it seems," said Sampson. "Bloody rude."

"There goes the first wave of infantry," said MacDonald. Small steam tugs, towing lines of boats were now following in the wake of the ironclads. "It should be our turn soon."

As if in reply to MacDonald's words, whistles started blowing aboard the *Bridlington* and sailors shouted: "Get in the boats! Get in the boats!"

Now the heavily laden infantry awkwardly swung over the rails, grabbed the rope netting and slowly lowered themselves down into the boats. Each boat could hold about a platoon and Harry had to make sure all his men got into the right boat. Climbing down wasn't easy and there was a great deal of jostling and cursing. When it was his turn, Harry, not burdened with a rifle, managed it without any real difficulty.

But as his feet touched the planks, there was a shout and cry from the next boat over and he twisted his head just in time to see a man fall. He plummeted twenty feet and landed squarely in the boat with a sickening thud that shook the small vessel. Shouts of alarm and a cry of pain could be heard above all the other noise. Someone in Paul Miller's platoon had been badly hurt it seemed.

Harry got his men arranged safely and the boat cast off along with the others. A steam tug rounded them up into a long string and pulled away. Miller's boat was left behind, and Harry could see that the injured man was being pulled back aboard the *Bridlington* with a rope.

"Poor sod is gonna miss all the fun," said one of the men.

"Nah, the lucky bastard will spend a few weeks in hospital with the pretty nurses," said Private Killian.

The mention of the hospital suddenly made Harry think about the letter he'd received a few days ago. Vera was back! The army had set up a hospital on the nearby island of Lemnos and Vera was there. Her letter was strangely emotionless, just some bare facts, and there was no attached poetry. He wondered how she was. Was she recovering from the death of her fiancé? Well enough to continue on as a VAD nurse, apparently, but that didn't really tell anything. Lots of people dealt with tragedy by immersing themselves in familiar routines. With the battle looming there had been no time to visit her, but maybe there would be a chance later on.

A toot from the tug's whistle jerked his attention back where it belonged. The string of boats was getting close to shore and the soldiers were expected to help row the last few hundred yards. There was one sailor at the tiller and two others to help get things organized. With a lot of shouting they managed to turn a dozen men into rowers and at the proper time the boat was cut loose from the string and headed — not quite directly — toward the beach.

If the sea had been rough, Harry wasn't sure they would have made it, but on a calm morning like this, there was no trouble. A few minutes of pulling lustily on the oars and the boat lurched to a halt on the sand. Harry jumped out and looked for trouble, but while there was a great deal of noise and confusion, there was nothing shooting at them, so the men were able to debark and help shove the empty boat back into the water, so the two sailors could row it back out to the tug and go back for the next load.

The battalion was forming up — except for Miller's platoon — and was soon marching inland behind the first wave of infantry and the land ironclads which were over a mile ahead of them now. Captain Berwick left a man behind in the optimistic hope that he could find Miller when he arrived and guide him to rejoin the rest of the battalion.

The land rose in front of them into a series of low hills, brown and dreary with only a few bits of green here and there as the first new growth of spring burst through. There were some houses scattered about, some untouched and other blown to bits, but all the inhabitants long fled. There were some vineyards and olive groves here and there, and like the buildings, some were untouched while others had been shredded by shellfire. The navy guns were now firing at targets off beyond the hills, but smoldering craters showed that their fury had been focused here not long ago.

They had been told that their objective was to move against the enemy strongholds along the Dardanelles and help the navy take them out. It was over fifteen miles to the closest of them and Harry doubted they could get there until well after noon—even if there was no opposition from the Martians.

So far there hadn't been any opposition, but that couldn't possibly last.

"Keep it closed up," he ordered. "We've got a long way to go."

* * * * *

Advanced Base 14-5, Cycle 597,845.5

"Subcommander, the enemy is landing in strength eighteen telequel to the south of ray emplacement seven," reported Lutnaptivav. "The leading element is composed of six very large armored vehicles of a type we have not encountered before. They were not unloaded from larger water vessels; they appear to be able to float on water and then drive on land."

"Yes, I was concerned that this might be the case," replied Kandanginar. "We have received reports that similar devices were used against the clans on Continent 3 with devastating effect. Images from the artificial satellite indicated that some of the assembling water vessels might be of this type."

"How much danger do they pose?"

"It is hard to know precisely. They are much more heavily armored than the standard small vehicles the prey creatures use and can withstand our standard heat rays for a considerable time. They carry larger weapons, as well, which are capable of destroying our fighting machines with a single shot. Used in groups and supported by their other forces, they could prove a significant danger."

"But they have not been tested against our new heavy heat ray," pointed out Lutnaptinav. "Those should be able to destroy them."

"So we can hope. But at the present the majority of our heavy heat rays are positioned to fire upon the water passage rather than inland. It would appear that the prey creatures are attempting to attack them from the rear."

"I was ordered to place the rays to cover the water passage..."

"My statement was not a criticism of you, Lutnaptinav. You did as I ordered and did it well. We responded to the imminent threat, attack from

246

the water. Now we must adapt and respond to this threat from the land. Can any of the rays be repositioned?"

"Not quickly. The slope of the land is not conducive to constructing emplacements firing in that direction. We may be able to find a few suitable locations, but they could not cover all approaches and it will take considerable time to construct them. If the enemy advances quickly they will not be ready."

"Yes, and that seems likely."

"If we had been able to finish the tunnel to the north shore and seize that, we could have placed heat rays there which could fire across and cover the approaches from the south."

"Yes, but we did not have the time. And in any case the prey creature strength on the north shore is growing every rotation. Do not waste your thoughts on what might have been, focus, rather, on what is."

"Yes, Progenitor. It appears to me that we must either defeat this attack with our fighting machines and drones or withdraw and avoid taking useless losses."

"Our main force is only now reaching the shores of the water barrier to our east. The remnants of the prey creature army have gathered there and resistance is stiffening. It will be some time before the defenses can be overwhelmed and probably much longer before they can manage to cross the water. We have been ordered to prevent the force we face here from interfering."

"Then it seems that we have no choice at all. We must hold here as long as we can."

"Yes, with our earlier losses we still have almost three hundred fighting machines and nearly a thousand drones we can use to engage the forces the prey creatures are landing. But we must attempt to do so as far from the sea as possible to reduce the effect of the weapons on their watercraft."

"If we position our forces to defend the heavy heat ray positions, that will not be possible," said Lutnaptinav.

"True, but if we defend the direct approaches primarily with the standard drones and keep our main force of fighting machines to the south and east, we might be able to strike them unexpectedly from the flank and rear."

"That seems like a wise strategy, Subcommander. Even if it fails, we will still have a line of withdrawal."

"Position our forces as I have described."

"At once."

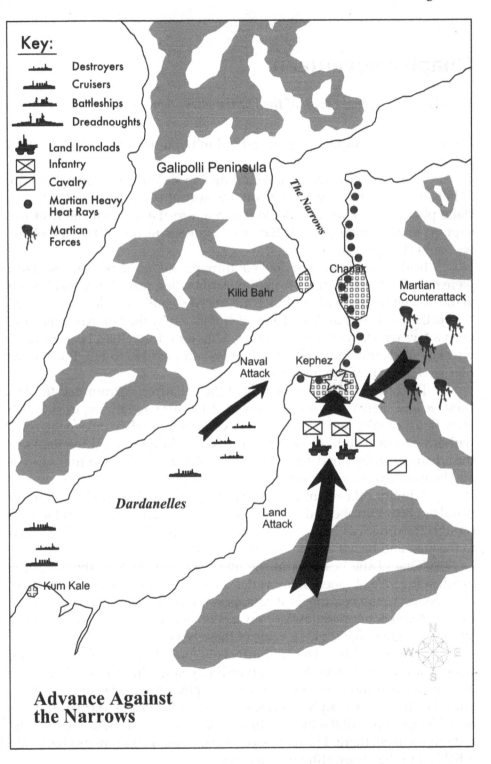

Key:

- Destroyers
- Cruisers
- Battleships
- Dreadnoughts
- Land Ironclads
- Infantry
- Cavalry
- Martian Heavy Heat Rays
- Martian Forces

Galipolli Peninsula

The Narrows

Chanak

Kilid Bahr

Martian Counterattack

Naval Attack

Kephez

Dardanelles

Land Attack

Kum Kale

Advance Against the Narrows

Chapter Seventeen

USNLI Yellowstone, South of the Dardanelles, April 1913

"No sign of the blighters. Seems odd, don't you think?" said Major Tom Bridges.

Commander Harding lowered his binoculars and glanced at him. "They aren't fools. They must know the sort of firepower the land ironclads possess. And we're still close enough to the sea that the fleet can support us with their guns. If they try to engage us out in the open here, we could slaughter them."

Bridges nodded and looked through his own binoculars. They were only four or five miles from the Dardanelles, now. They had landed at dawn well to the south and then advanced steadily – if slowly – toward the north east. They had found a lot of craters left by the bombardment and even a few wrecked enemy machines, although if they had been recently wrecked or during the earlier fights it was impossible to tell. But no live Martians had shown themselves.

The other five land ironclads of the squadron surrounded the *Yellowstone* and behind them were waves of infantry advancing in skirmish lines. Some cavalry had been landed days earlier, but they'd been forced to withdraw to the south. Now they were back, flitting around the flanks of the advance. Bridges had served in the cavalry himself earlier in his career and he watched their movements with a critical eye.

A junior officer came up to Harding and spoke with him. Bridges could not hear him above the racket the ironclad made, but it didn't look as though Harding was happy with whatever he was being told. He replied to the man and he left again. "Trouble?" he asked.

"One of the bearings in the motor for the number three track is overheating. We shipped some water when we came ashore, and it may have gotten to the bearing. Not serious yet, but I hope we get a chance to stop and run some maintenance on it. We've come almost twenty miles since we landed, that's a lot for one of these beasts.'

Bridges nodded. The land ironclads could travel long distances by water with no more trouble than an ordinary ship. But ashore, their huge weight put enormous strain on their caterpillar tracks. When he'd been with the American army's ironclads which captured the Martian fortress near Memphis two of the five machines had broken down just covering the sixty miles to get there. The navy's version seemed a bit more mechanically reliable, but they were still monstrosities.

He scanned the terrain in front of them and there was still no sign of the enemy. There was a ruined town up ahead; Kephez on the map. It was a suburb of the larger town of Canakkale a little to the north, right at the Narrows. Both had been in the thick of the fighting during the first attempt to force the strait and they'd mostly been reduced to rubble. Supposedly the bulk of the enemy super heat ray positions were beyond in tunnels which looked out on the water. "How are we supposed to find the rays, commander? I can't see anything of them from here."

"Our orders were a bit vague about that, Major," replied Harding. "I suppose the infantry will be the ones who have to search them out and destroy them. We're here to keep the damn tripods off their backs while they do it."

The squadron rolled on. Out in the countryside they had managed to steer around any buildings they encountered and limit the damage they did to garden walls, sheds, and the occasional grape vine or olive tree. But now, the structures were closer together and it was impossible not to crush some of them. Many had already been damaged in the fighting, but a few were relatively untouched. It was a shame to destroy them, but there was no choice. Bridges wondered who the owners were and if they had fled, been killed, or if they'd been 'harvested' by the Martians for food? Far better to be killed outright than that!

"Sir! Signal from the commodore to halt here!" shouted a young ensign who dashed onto the bridge.

"Right," replied Harding. "Helm, full stop!" The man at the controls adjusted the engine room telegraph and the huge machine jerked to a halt. Its top speed on land was only about five miles per hour, so it only took a moment. A few seconds later one of the other ironclads let off a shot from one of its secondary guns. Bridges saw the puff of the explosion where it hit, perhaps a mile ahead, and brought up his binoculars.

"What are they shooting at?" he asked. "I don't see anything."

"Not sure..." said Harding, also using his binoculars. "A tripod ought to be easy to spot." The buildings of Kephez were mostly small adobe structures, few over two stories tall. One of the Martian war machines would tower over them.

"Another signal, sir," said the same ensign breathlessly. The boy was running back and forth between the bridge and the wireless compartment. He handed a small slip of paper to Harding. The man frowned.

"The lookouts have spotted some of those spider machines among the buildings. The commodore is going to wait here and let the infantry catch up with us and then go in ahead. Thank God, he actually listened to me!" The look on the commander's face was one of relief mixed with anxiety.

Oh! Oh, that's right, his first ship was destroyed by a batch of those things. Bridges had first met Harding after the Battle of Memphis. He had been in command of a large navy river monitor which had tried to stop the Martians from crossing the Mississippi. They had collided with a raft full of the spider machines and they had swarmed aboard and ultimately destroyed the ship. Harding had been thrown overboard and was the sole survivor.

"I... I told the commodore about how the spiders tried to swamp one of the army ironclads when we attacked the fortress. If those things can get in close, our guns won't be able to shoot at them and... I was worried that he had ignored me."

"I remember that," said Bridges.

"Of course you do," said Harding. "You were there, too, weren't you?"

"Right next to you, sir. But I also recall that that amazing lightning gun on *Albuquerque* did a handsome job on the blighters. Each of your ironclads has one of them, don't they?"

"Yes, but they take ten minutes to charge up after they fire. If we get caught in a town full of those damn things, we could be in real trouble."

"Seems the commodore agrees with you."

"Yes. He's a smart man."

"So, we wait here for the infantry?"

"Yes. Let them get in front and then we'll follow behind and deal with anything they can't."

Bridges looked at the way ahead. Ruined houses, narrow streets, hundreds of places where the spiders could be lurking.

"I don't envy them."

* * * * *

Kephez, Turkey, April 1913

"Keep a watch on our flank, sergeant!" ordered Harry Calloway. "I don't know where the hell D Company has gotten to and we can't depend them to watch out for us." Milroy waved his acknowledgement to him and headed down an alley toward where the right end of the platoon ought to be. Harry gathered the section of men nearest to him and pushed forward along a narrow street, until they reached the next intersection where they paused.

The streets of the town were deserted but it seemed obvious that when the inhabitants had been forced to flee a month or so earlier, they hadn't been given much warning. Possessions of all sorts, clothing, blankets, pots and pans, vases and candlesticks, children's toys, framed pictures, everything you might find in a home, had been dragged outside—

and then abandoned. Subsequent bombardments had strewn the items about and in places mixed them with the rubble of the collapsed buildings, but it was clear what had happened.

"Looks like Sydney the last time we saw it," muttered one of the men.

Harry started. Yes, despite the vastly different architecture, and the style and make of the possessions, it did remind him Sydney during the frantic evacuation. *Except this time, we're attacking instead of retreating!*

Yes, that was the difference—the big difference. They had been marching all day in the wake of the big land ironclads, but they were marching toward the enemy, not away from them. It was getting on now, the sun was far in the west, but at last they had found the enemy.

Or at least some of them. No tripods had been sighted yet, but word had come back that the town ahead of them was infested with spider machines. The ironclads didn't want to tangle with them alone, so they waited for the infantry to come up. The first wave had gone in and the 15th New Castle, part of the second wave, had come up behind. The troops in front of them, a British battalion, had disappeared into the town and after a short wait the 15th had followed them. Navy guns were blasting the town ahead of them and clouds of fine dust drifted past them, reducing visibility, sometimes to just a few yards. Intermixed with the roar of the big guns they could hear the rattle of rifle and machine guns and the strangely toned *crump* of the Mills bombs, so the first wave had clearly encountered something. But so far Harry and his platoon had found nothing.

The streets of the town were narrow and twisting and formed a virtual labyrinth. The platoons and sections needed to advance down parallel streets, but the streets weren't parallel. They kept losing contact with the troops on their flanks and then suddenly encountering them again when the streets converged unexpectedly. Harry looked right and left at the intersection but couldn't spot MacDonald's platoon to his left or D Company to his right. Looking back, he caught sight of one of the ironclads, towering like a bloody cathedral a few hundred yards to their rear. The monstrous machines weren't bothering with streets, they just crushed whatever was in front of them and made their own.

The rattle of a Lewis Gun not that far ahead caught his attention. They ought to be catching up with the battalion ahead of them soon. He put his men in motion again and advanced to the next intersection. The troops in front of him halted suddenly and began talking excitedly. Harry pushed through them and found what had caused them to stop: a wrecked spider machine.

He'd never actually seen one before, although he'd seen pictures of them. The Martians hadn't had them yet when they attacked Sydney, and seeing one now, Harry was extremely glad of it. The damn thing did look like a spider; a fat elongated body, about the size of a cow's, three long spindly legs projecting from a small cylinder beneath the body, and two appendages from the lower front of the body. One held something that for all the world looked like an oversized human pistol. That would have to be the small heat ray they'd been told of. The other was a long tentacle with a cutting blade on the end of it. When working, the blade would whip around at high speed creating a deadly zone around the front and sides of the machine.

Fortunately, this one wasn't working. It was crumpled on its side, with a blackened hole punched through the top, near the rear. Little scuff marks pocked its skin, caused by bullets, Harry presumed. The big hole might have been caused by a Mills bomb. At the front there was a hemispherical knob that all the Martian machines seemed to have. When active, it glowed a bright red, but this one was just the same color as the metal body. Dead. The men gathered around gawking at it, until Harry ordered them away. "Come on, we need to keep moving. But be on your guard! The next one of these we meet might be alive."

"How we supposed to kill the bleedin' things?" asked one of the men.

"The same way you kill the tripods," snapped Sergeant Milroy.

"What? You mean get into the deepest 'ole you can find and call for the artillery?" That got a laugh, but Milroy wasn't amused.

"Shoot it with everything you've got until someone can get a bomb on it, you sod! Now spread out and stay alert!"

"The briefing we got said that the metal on them is a lot thinner than on the big tripods," said Harry, loudly so they would all hear. "Concentrated rifle and machine gun fire can bring them down. But bombs are best. Greene, you still got your contraption?"

"Yes, sir!" replied Private Greene holding up his crossbow. "All ready for action."

"Good, let's go."

At the next intersection he ran into Captain Berwick and he was relieved. He'd been advancing for nearly a mile with only the vaguest notion of what he was supposed to be doing. Berwick looked harried; he had to keep a whole company in order, not just a platoon, like Harry. "Everything square, Harry?" he asked.

"So far, sir. The only thing we've run into so far is a dead spider machine. Sounds like there's fighting up ahead, though."

"Yes, the Royal Scots have run into a bunch of the damn things and we've been ordered to move up and help them. So, get moving and keep your eyes peeled. We've gotten reports that some of the spiders are hiding in the rubble. They let us pass and then emerge and hit us from the rear."

"Oh joy..."

"So always have a few men looking behind you."

"Yes, sir."

"Move them out, Harry." Without waiting for a reply, he turned and headed off to the left, presumably where the rest of the company was deployed. Harry passed on the warning and got his platoon in motion. The firing ahead was getting louder and the men's mood was getting more serious. Rifles at the ready, some even had their bayonets fixed, although they were useless, Mills bombs where they could be grabbed quickly. The Lewis gunner had his weapon ready to fire from the hip if necessary, his two assistants close by with spare ammunition drums. Harry pulled his Webley revolver out of its holster even though it would be scarcely more useful than a bayonet.

The firing was louder and the naval bombardment closer. The navy had sent spotting teams with the infantry, equipped with wireless sets to direct the fire from the ships. Harry hoped they knew what they were doing. He still remembered those short rounds during the evacuation from Sydney. Had any of the men from that other tank crew made it out?

Clouds of smoke and dust drifted past making it hard to see. Now there was another sound mixed in with the others, a high-pitched squeal which he suddenly realized must be the small heat ray on the spider machines. The big tripods' rays made a sound like a buzz saw cutting wood; this was similar but different. They must be getting close.

But where were the Royal Scots, the troops they were coming to help? They had to be just up ahead, and they ought to be running into their rear elements: officers, ammo carriers, stretcher bearers, wounded... and the dead.

His platoon suddenly emerged into an open space. A town square or market or something. It was a paved plaza maybe a hundred paces across with a wrecked fountain in the center and ruined buildings along its side. A few craters had been blasted in the ground and paving stones were scattered everywhere. Harry peered through the smoke but did not see anything moving. He waved to his men and they moved forward.

They were about halfway across when the Martians hit them. With no warning, heat rays stabbed out and men screamed and fell. The heat rays on the big tripods would blast a man to ash and steam in an eyeblink, but the smaller rays on the spider machines weren't nearly so powerful. They could burn a hole through man, or set him ablaze, but they left a body afterward.

In just a few frantic seconds the rays claimed a dozen victims and then Harry and his surviving men were on the ground, behind cover or in shell craters, firing back. He crouched next to a low wall and desperately tried to see how many spiders there were and where they were located, but he could only see two for sure on the far side of the square. There had to be at least a couple more off to the sides. Someone was screaming loudly; it was the sort of scream that told you they were on fire.

A man was kneeling next to him working the action of his Lee-Enfield as quickly as he could, but he wasn't charging the magazine. He was just working the bolt and pulling the trigger, but the empty rifle wasn't firing. He saw that it was Dunning, one of the replacements they'd gotten in Egypt. This was his first action. He reached over and gripped the man's shoulder. "Dunning! You have to load your gun to make it work."

Dunning looked at him, eyes wide, mouth twisted. "What?"

"Load your rifle! It's empty!"

"Oh! Oh, yes, sir!" The man—boy, really—fumbled a clip out of his belt and pushed the cartridges into the magazine. Then he went back to work. But an instant later a heat ray swept along the top of the wall, catching Dunning full in the face. He tumbled backward and sprawled on the ground, his face a blackened ruin, steaming and smoking. His arms twitched a few times and then he was still.

Harry stared for a moment, a red anger growing in him and he clutched his pistol tightly. His men were being killed and he had to do something! But what? A rush across the open space would see half of his men—half of his remaining men slaughtered. But to stay here…

Explosions started to erupt near the far side of the square. Men were throwing Mills bombs and he saw one of the crossbows toss a bomb all the way into the houses on the far side. The Lewis gun was set up and blazing away. After a minute or so, two spider machines emerged from their cover and started scuttling toward them. An instant later another one appeared from the left side of the square. Their heat rays stabbed out, searching for more victims. The pair from the far side looked to be heading directly toward him and he suddenly realized that he couldn't retreat without becoming totally exposed. He reached for the one mills bomb he always carried…

"Stay down, sir!" he heard someone shout off to his right. Looking that way, he saw Private Greene rear up and let loose with his crossbow. The bomb soared through the air… and bounced off one of the spiders. Harry groaned, but the errant bomb tumbled right beneath the second spider and then exploded, flipping the thing onto its back. It waved its legs futilely for a moment and then went still. But the other kept coming and Harry pulled the cover off his bomb.

Suddenly there was the high-pitched trill of an officer's whistle and a body of men emerged from the left side of the square. It was Miller's missing platoon! They had caught up! A swarm of khaki-clad men, led my Miller himself, swept into the square and rushed toward the spider machines. The one coming toward Harry didn't seem to notice them and before it did, a bomb was slapped on its back and the explosion tore it apart. Meanwhile Private Greene made up for his earlier miss by sticking a bomb solidly to the third spider. The explosion tore off a leg and the heat ray. The hideous thing kept moving, until a hail of rifle fire finally put it down.

Harry let out the breath he'd been holding and staggered out of his cover to meet Lieutenant Miller who was grinning ear to ear. "Thanks, Paul," he said, transferring the Mills bomb to his left hand and holding out his right. "I'd have been toast if you hadn't come along."

Miller shook his hand. "Our pleasure, Harry. Hell, I never thought we'd catch up with you fellows. Been eating dust ever since we made it ashore. And then no one seemed to know where the battalion was. Glad we caught up when we did, though."

"In the nick of time."

"So those are the spider machines they were telling us about," said Miller strolling over to look at the one lying on its back. "Ugly things, aren't they?" He kicked the inert lump of metal.

The spider suddenly moved and drove the metal blade on the end of its tentacle through Paul Miller's body.

Harry screamed in outrage. Miller's hands had instinctively clutched the tentacle and his eyes were wide open as the Spider tried to shake him loose. Harry leaped past Miller's convulsing body and slammed the Mills bomb against the Martian killing machine and pulled the arming pin. He threw himself to the ground as the blast blew a huge hole in the thing's center. It finally stopped moving. At last it was dead.

So was Paul Miller.

"Damn, damn, damn..." moaned Harry and he knelt over Miller. Some of Paul's men gathered around, but there was nothing they, or anyone could do. Sergeant Milroy appeared and pulled Harry away. He realized he was crying, and he angrily wiped away the tears on his cheeks. "He... he saved my...our lives..."

"Not a bad way to go then, sir. He was a good man," said Milroy. "But we've got eight dead in our own platoon and four more wounded bad."

"Right... right..." said Harry. He had responsibilities. He could mourn later. He pulled himself together and did what had to be done; saw the wounded tended and sent to the rear, posted pickets on the flank, made sure the men had ammo and water. The routine settled him down. They needed to be ready in case there was another attack, but the whole battle seemed to have quieted down for the moment.

While he was doing that, more men came into the square. He was surprised to see not only Captain Berwick, but also Colonel Anderson and the brigade commander as well. A number of other staff officers accompanied them and a small group of naval personnel with a portable wireless set. They must have been the ones calling in the gunfire from the ships. Having nothing more to do immediately, he drifted over where he could hear.

"Sir, we've been pushing through these damn streets for hours," said Anderson angrily. "I'm losing men to these bloody spiders, but where the hell are these super heat ray positions we are supposed to destroy? We could wander around these ruins for days without spotting them."

"Yes, I know, Jimmy, I know," replied the Brigadier. "I'm getting the same complaints from my other battalions. Well, it seems to me that if the damn rays are here to shoot at ships, perhaps we should give them some ships to shoot at!"

"My thinking exactly, sir."

"Right. Well, let's give it a go. Lieutenant!" He turned and shouted at the naval officer.

"Sir?" said the man, running up.

"Can you still contact the fleet on that wireless of your?"

"Yes, sir. Loud and clear."

"Good, then you get a message through to your admiral. Tell him that we need him to send in some ships to draw the fire of the Martians. We can't knock out those ray positions unless they reveal themselves. Understand?"

"Yes, sir," said the man, although he looked rather skeptical.

"Good. Get on with it." He turned back to Colonel Anderson. "It will probably take a bit for them to get moving, but with any luck we can still hit them before dark. You have your men get some rest in the meantime."

"Yes sir, thank you sir." The brigadier moved off and Anderson had some words with his company commanders who had assembled while he was talking. Harry turned away and went back to his platoon. He pulled out his canteen and took a drink from it, which left it nearly empty.

"Can I fill that for you, sir?" He turned and saw that Ralph Scoggins was there.

"Is there somewhere to fill it?"

"There's a well back over that way, sir. I've got Abdo filling everyone's".

"Is he still with us? How'd he get ashore?"

"Not sure, sir. He just showed up an hour ago. Must have snuck aboard one of the boats."

Harry shook his head in wonder. He handed Scoggins his canteen and the man walked off with it. Harry sat down in the shade created by a half-destroyed building and rested his back against it. He really ought to eat something, but his stomach didn't feel like it could hold anything. He kept seeing Miller's dead face... Tired... he was so tired...

He started when Burford Sampson sat down beside him. "You all right, boy?"

"Don't call me boy. You... you hear about Paul?"

"Yeah."

"A damn shame. He made it through the whole siege and everything else only to die in some damn Turkish village! What the hell are we doing here, Burf?"

"Same thing we were doing back in Sydney: fighting Martians. But, yeah, it is damn shame. But you know we've been awful lucky. Not another company in the battalion that still has the same officers it started with."

"Yeah... yeah, I guess that's true. Who... who's taking over Paul's platoon?"

"His platoon sergeant for now. He's a good fellow." Sampson stared at him for a bit. "So, what happened?"

Harry was certain that Sampson had heard exactly what had happened, but he was giving him the chance to get it off his chest. "We were pinned down here and then Paul hit them from the flank. Two of the spiders were destroyed and I though the third one was, too. It wasn't moving, but when Paul got to close it... it killed him."

"And then you killed it. That was quick thinking, Harry."

"I should have done it sooner! That bloody briefing pamphlet they sent around said that sometimes the spiders would freeze for a while and then start moving again later. I should have remembered!"

"Paul didn't remember either. I doubt I would have in the heat of the moment. Don't beat yourself up over it. When a bloke's number is up, it's up."

Harry didn't have any answer to that simple truth and then Scoggins returned with his canteen and Sampson cajoled him into eating something. "About two hours until sunset," he said, looking at the sky. "I hope the damn navy moves soon. Hate fighting those buggers in the dark."

"That's for sure."

They waited.

* * * * *

The Admiralty, London, April 1913

259

"The army is asking that the fleet move into the strait to get the enemy to reveal their heat ray positions," said Admiral Battenberg holding a dispatch. "They are having trouble finding them. De Robek is asking permission to proceed."

Frederick Lindemann stifled a yawn. It had been another very long day. He'd managed to take a short nap after they got word that the landings had gone off without trouble, but now the fighting was heating up again. It was still amazing that they could be here, fifteen hundred miles from the battle and get reports quickly enough to actually make decisions. Sometimes he wondered if that was such a good thing. He was not a soldier or a sailor, but shouldn't the man on the spot be the one taking the initiative?

Churchill seemed to think so too.

"For God's sake tell him to go ahead! He's wasting time."

"Are you sure, sir?" asked Admiral Pakenham, the fourth sea lord. "We could lose more ships. I'd think if the army just spent some time looking, they'd be able to find those things."

"You do? Well, you'd be wrong, William. At sea you've got a flat billiard table for a battlefield. Everything's right there in the open. On land it's not nearly so easy. Why at Omdurman, when I was with the 21st Lancers, there was a gully with three thousand fuzzy-wuzzies in it not a hundred yards off and we didn't even see them until we stumbled right into them. Tell de Robeck to go ahead—with some lighter ships."

"Very well, sir," said Pakenham.

* * * * *

Advanced Base 14-5, Cycle 597,845.5

"The prey creature ground forces have paused in the ruins of the habitation, subcommander," reported Lutnaptinav. "However, it now appears that their water vessels are advancing into the strait again."

"What losses have our drones suffered?" asked Kandanginar.

"One hundred and four have been destroyed or rendered inoperable. Three fighting machines have also been damaged, apparently by badly targeted heavy projectiles rather than deliberately. There is no sign the enemy has discovered where the fighting machines are waiting in reserve."

"That is good."

"What of the water vessels. Progenitor? They will soon be in range of the westernmost of our heavy heat rays. As before, only smaller vessels are in the lead. Should we fire upon them? It occurs to me that they may be doing this to get us to reveal their positions."

"That is a very likely possibility. And if we were to do as they wish? What would their likely response be?" asked Kandanginar.

"I calculate that they would send their ground forces against them. That is clearly what the ground forces are here for."

"And that would draw those forces deeper into the habitation area and engage them more heavily with our defending drones."

"Ah, I see," said Lutnaptinav.

"Yes. Open fire on the vessels when they are in range."

* * * * *

Kephez, Turkey, April 1913

They were moving again, deeper into the ruined town. The land ironclads were rumbling forward and two divisions of infantry were surrounding them. Supposedly the navy would be coming into the strait to make the enemy reveal their super heat ray positions. Exactly how the army was then supposed to take them out, they weren't sure. They said they were in caves of some sort.

The pause had allowed the troops to get themselves organized and for some of their support units to catch up. They'd managed to land some of the field artillery, but no tanks or heavy guns yet. So when the advance resumed, it went better, at least at first. They started encountering more of the spider machines right away, but they were ready for them now. They lost men, but they killed machines. They quickly learned that a man could squeeze through spaces much narrower than the spiders could. They could send scouts ahead, worming their way through the rubble or the spaces between buildings, to search out the enemy hiding places. Once found, they could draw their fire from the front, while men with bombs worked around their flanks to destroy them. Harry's platoon killed two that way and only lost one man wounded.

But it was slow going. They were still a mile short of the water when they heard the navy going into action, and the rather intimidating snarl of what had to be the big heat rays. From where they were, they still couldn't spot the enemy weapons. And night was coming. The sun was dipping below the horizon and they wouldn't have long before it was completely dark.

"Maybe that will make it easier to spot where the heat rays are," said Harry.

"Maybe," replied Sergeant Milroy. "But we better hope the navy can provide enough star shells to light things up. Hunting these buggers in the dark ain't gonna be fun, sir."

"True, but we've got some artillery of our own here now. Maybe they can help out."

"If they thought to bring star shells."

"Yeah, well, let's kill as many of them as we can while we still have light."

They pushed on through the gathering gloom. They encountered a group of spiders clustered around what must have been a mosque; the minaret was still standing. The Martians seemed to be learning the tactics better, too. Now instead of spiders in ones and twos, they had them in larger groups, where they could guard their flanks. Harry lost two men, trying to get around them and was momentarily stymied, until Ian MacDonald brought his platoon into action on one side and D Company appeared on the other. A sharp action ensued and by the end of it they had a half-dozen dead spiders, and a dozen dead or wounded men.

"I never thought I'd hear myself say it," said Milroy, "but I think I prefer fighting the big tripods to these little stinkers."

"Yeah, I think you're right," said Harry wiping the sweat off his face and taking a long drink from his canteen. "Damn odd we haven't seen any of those so far, though. We know there are a bunch of then in the area."

"If they want to sit this one out, I won't complain, sir."

"No, me neither. Well, back to work." He got his men reorganized and then was told they could rest for a few minutes before moving out again. He decided to climb the minaret to see if he could get a better view; maybe even spot their targets.

It was awkward and a bit scary, since it was almost completely dark inside the needle-like tower. Keeping one hand on the wall, he follower the spiral staircase up and up, reminding himself that the passage was far too small for a spider machine to fit into. There was some damage near the top and he stumbled over loose rubble and nearly gave up and went back down, but he could see a faint light filtering down from above and he kept going.

Puffing hard, he emerged at the top and grasped the ornate railing and looked toward the north. The Dardanelles seemed closer than it had all day. He looked off to the west and caught his breath. There was still a bit of sunset glow which reflected off the water and silhouetted the dozens of ships steaming his way. Small ones were leading but larger ones were right behind. As he watched, flashes came from some of the guns and moments later explosions erupted along the shoreline.

Then the Martians answered back.

A red beam stabbed out connecting the shoreline with one of the leading ships. Flames leapt up, but the ship, probably a destroyer, turned immediately at high speed and clouds of black smoke poured from its stack, trying to conceal it. A few small explosions glowed through the smoke, but the ship still seemed to be alive. A second beam lashed out against another destroyer, but this one wasn't as lucky as its comrade. It tried to turn, but the bean stuck to it like glue and before it could complete its maneuver a fiery blast appeared right in the middle of it. Just as the initial noise reached Harry's ears, the ship broke in two.

But the fleet was firing steadily now, and more and more explosions blanketed the shore line. It was an incredibly grand spectacle and Harry found himself thumping his fist against the railing.

After a few moments, he realized, that he had spotted two of the ray positions. One didn't seem all that far away. Perhaps he should go down and report what he'd seen. As he turned to find his way back down the steps, he noticed a cluster of red lights off to the southeast which froze him in his tracks.

Oh my God...

He snatched out his binoculars and focused them on the lights. Dozens, no hundreds of red sparks were out there, a couple of miles away, maybe. It wasn't quite dark, and he could see the last light reflecting off metal. He'd seen those lights before and there wasn't a doubt about what they were. *All those missing tripods! And here they come! I need to warn the colonel!*

But before he could turn thoughts into action, the world seemed to explode in a hundred eye-aching blasts of blue light.

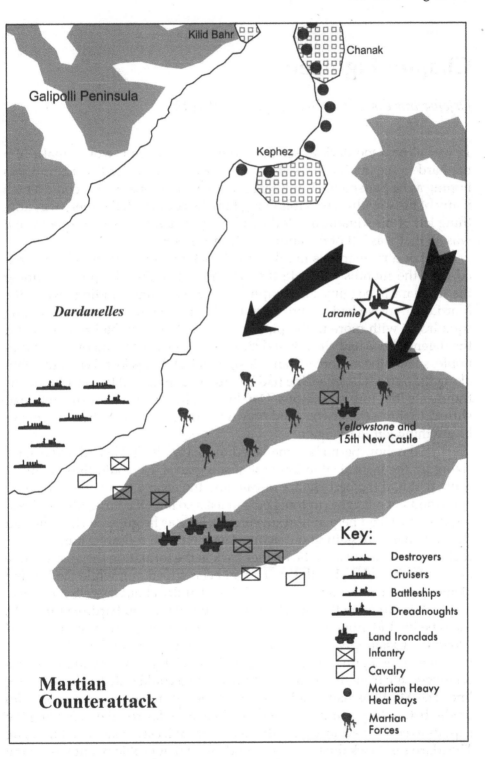

Key:

⚓ Destroyers

🚢 Cruisers

🛥 Battleships

🛳 Dreadnoughts

Land Ironclads

⊠ Infantry

▱ Cavalry

● Martian Heavy Heat Rays

Martian Forces

Martian Counterattack

Chapter Eighteen

Defense line east of Constantinople, April 1913

It was almost too dark to see the targets, but maybe it would make him too hard to see in return. Or at least that was what Major Erich Serno was hoping as he banked his Rumpler and dove on the enemy. He couldn't tell if any of his squadron was following him; he couldn't tell if there was any-thing left of his squadron *to* follow him. *Squadron!* It wasn't a squadron; it was all that was left of the entire Turkish Air Force.

For a moment his mind flashed back to all the effort he'd expend-ed over the months to create that air force. Training the pilots, training the mechanics, begging for equipment and bases and funding. When the Martian offensive had begun, he'd managed to build a dozen functioning squadrons, with more in the pipeline. But as the army had retreated and the defense lines had shrunk and shrunk as they converged on Constanti-nople, so had the air force. Planes lost, men lost, bases lost. When the fight along the current defense line had begun, he'd managed to consolidate the fragments into four squadrons. Day by day, hell, sortie by sortie, that had shrunk to three, then two… and now one. After this attack there might not be anything left to try again.

Somehow Serno had managed to survive it all. He had a knack for sizing up the tactical situation with just a glance. He could find an attack route that had the best chance of catching the enemy unawares. He could get in and get out again untouched — at least so far. Of course, always lead-ing the attack had helped him survive. As long as he guessed right, he had the best chance of getting out again. The men who followed him in, well, their chances diminished the further back in the formation they were. Time and again the tail end of the attack had been wiped out, while the leading elements made it through. Serno didn't feel guilty about it, well, not much.

His target on this attack was a group of the bombardment tripods, the type he'd identified a few days ago. These new Martian weapons had proven devastatingly effective against dug-in infantry and artillery. Until now, a man or a gun out of sight behind a thick layer of dirt and rock was relatively safe from the enemy heat rays, which could only fire in a straight line. The Martians had to advance until they were nearly on top of a de-fender before they could fire down on them and destroy them. Forcing the tripods to come that close gave the defenders at least a change to kill them. The Martians' black dust weapon could avoid that problem, but the enemy never seemed to have all that much of the stuff to use. The new bombardment tripods threw small bombs, which exploded with a bright blue flash, killing anything caught in the blast and stunning or blinding men close by.

The new tripods were hard to spot since their weapons made no revealing flash and created very little noise when they fired. And they could move around quickly to new firing positions, making counter-battery fire almost impossible for the human artillery. The generals had decided that the best countermeasure was aircraft. Serno had lost track of how many sorties he'd made. Seven? Eight? At least that many. He and his pilots had killed some of the tripods, too. He didn't know how many. Fewer than the number of men and planes he'd lost doing it, though, he was sure of that much. But for the moment the defense line was holding. It had been holding for several days. Maybe all those men he'd lost had accomplished something.

His dive steepened and the speed built up. He hoped he wasn't asking too much of the battered Rumpler. The planes needed more maintenance than they were getting. They were worn out, just like the men flying them.

He momentarily lost sight of his target, but then a batch of star shells burst nearby, lighting up the battlefield. The bombardment tripods gleamed in the harsh, white light of the burning magnesium. He adjusted his course slightly, lining up on the tripod he'd chosen. His left hand grasped the lever that would release the pair of hundred-kilogram bombs carried under the wings.

He pulled out of his dive and skimmed just a few dozen meters above the ground as the target grew rapidly. It seemed oblivious to his presence. At the proper moment he jerked the lever, felt the bombs detach, and pulled back on the stick to climb away. Twisting around in the cockpit, he looked back just in time to see his bombs explode against the tripod. His aim had been perfect, and the machine was torn apart, legs, body, weapon spinning off into the dark. Yes!

He banked his plane west, heading back toward friendly lines. He didn't look forward to landing in the dark, but it was still a lot safer than...

A red glow engulfed him. *Heat ray!*

He couldn't tell where it was coming from, but he instantly rolled the plane and dove for the ground. Climbing was no good, he would lose speed and be hanging up there a fat, slow—dead—target. Low and fast was his only hope. The mere fact that he was still alive to try told him he hadn't been hit yet. A heat ray would burn the wood and canvas aircraft to ashes in an instant, but even a near miss could set one on fire. The ground was coming up fast and he had to level out, but he kept twisting and turning to try and throw off the enemy's aim. He could feel the heat on his face;

it was close. He hopped over a line of trees and the glow faded and died. He'd made it!

Well, almost.

A shudder in the Rumpler made him look back. The fuselage, just behind the cockpit, was burning. He juked and twisted right and left to try and blow out the flames, but it was no good, the wind just spread the fire back toward the tail and the vital control surfaces there. Shortly he was going to lose control; he needed to land, but where?

His evasive maneuvers had taken him right into the midst of the battle raging along the defense line. Shells exploded, heat rays blasted, smoke and flames were everywhere. Tripods flashed by on either side, but none wasted a shot on an obviously doomed aircraft. Up ahead he could see the start of the trench lines, sparkling with the blue flashed of the Martian bombardment. If he could just get past them and then crash without breaking his neck...

Machine gun bullets zipped past and a few stitched holes in the upper wing. Damn it! To make it this far only to be killed by his own side! He veered to the left but then had trouble straightening out. Looking back, he could see that the rudder was on fire. He swooped over several wrecked tripods and then he was over the trenches. A blue explosion dazzled his eyes and nearly swatted the Rumpler into the ground, but he recovered somehow and stayed airborne for a few moments longer. Up ahead there was ground that looked reasonably flat and was not currently under fire. He eased back on the throttle, lifted the nose a bit and...

Crunch!

A tree trunk, completely stripped of branches, which he had not noticed, ripped off the left wings of the biplane and tossed it into a flat spin. It slammed into the ground, tearing off the undercarriage, and slid along for an amazing distance before coming to a halt. Serno was dazed, but he knew he had to get out of the burning craft. He fumbled the restraining harness off and half climbed, half fell out of the cockpit onto the hard ground.

In the flickering light of his burning plane. He pulled himself up, staggered a few dozen yards away, and then collapsed. He was all alone and he wondered if any of the rest of the squadron had made it out. Was he the last survivor of the Turkish Air Force? After the frantic escape, he was left with no strength at all; he just sat and watched his plane burn. It blazed up when the fire reached the fuel tank and he was forced to drag himself further away when the machine gun ammunition started to cook off.

By then he heard voices approaching and soon a small party of Turkish troops arrived. He had enough of the language now to identify himself. The men didn't seem particularly glad to see him and he wasn't surprised. The popularity of the Germans had been falling with every kilometer the Martians advanced. Apparently, they had been expecting the Germans to pull some miracle out of their hats and stop the enemy cold. When that hadn't happened, they had turned sullen.

"I need to go to the rear," he told them, speaking very slowly and pointing west.

This produced a torrent of rapid speaking that he couldn't follow, but from the shrugs he gathered they were saying: *Fine, go ahead. Suit yourself.*

"Do you have a vehicle to carry me?"

Some laughed, several turned away, others shook their heads. *March, infidel, march!*

One of them seemed angry rather than uncaring. He spoke loudly and slower than the others and Serno could just make him out. "Where are the rest of you Germans?" he demanded. "And the British and the French? You tell us help is coming, but where is the help? Where are the allies?" he waved his arms angrily.

Serno restrained himself from saying that he hadn't promised them any help, but he gestured to his burning plane. The man snorted and turned away. Yes, that was the other thing, word had come that a huge allied fleet of British, French, American, and other European forces were on their way to help. But where were they? Stalled at the mouth of the Dardanelles from what Serno had heard.

All the time they had been talking the roar of the battle off to the east had not stopped. Now, though, it seemed to be growing louder. And a few of the Turks stopped and stiffened and looked that way.

Out of the dark, some men came running. The men near Serno shouted at them, and they shouted back—but didn't stop. Then more appeared—and more. The ones he had been talking with became agitated and started moving—in the same direction as the running men.

"What's happening," cried Serno. But even as he spoke, he knew what had happened. *The line has broken.* Swarms of men were now streaming past. Men on horseback, a horse team pulling a field gun, supply wagons, all streaming west. Looking beyond them, he thought he could glimpse the red eyes of tripods.

Time to go.

He forced his weary legs to move and he joined the retreat. It was sixty kilometers to the Bosporus, and he doubted the defenders would rally before they reached it. As he quickened his pace, he found himself wondering the same thing as the angry Turk: *Where are the allies?*

* * * * *

USNLI Yellowstone, *Kephez, Turkey, April 1913*

It was night, but it wasn't dark; not nearly dark enough. Major Tom Bridges peered out through a vision slit on the armored pilot house of the US Land Ironclad *Yellowstone* at an image of hell.

After landing without incident that morning, the ironclads had rumbled northeastward toward the strait all day. In late afternoon they had reached the built-up area just to the west of the Narrows and then slowed to let the infantry catch up and precede them into the town. The Martian spider machines had infested the place and they needed the infantry to dig them out. With the ironclads only able to provide sporadic support, it had been bloody work, but by nightfall they were close to the water. The fleet had moved up and some of the enemy super heat ray positions had been spotted. They were preparing to advance on them and destroy them, when all hell had broken loose.

The Martian tripods, which had been suspiciously absent all day had appeared behind their right flank in large numbers; perhaps as many as three hundred. They were supported by the new bombardment tripods which had surprised the navy in its first attempt to force the Narrows. The explosive bombs they threw had played Hob with the infantry, although they didn't seem to be a major danger to the ironclads. The spider machines lurking in the town had attacked at the same time and the human forces had been thrown into confusion.

Flares and heat rays, star shells and the blinding blue flashes of the Martian artillery lit up the night. Explosions from the navy guns and burning buildings filled the air with smoke which caught the light or blotted it out depending on wind and circumstance. Searchlights stabbed out from the ironclads, trying to pinpoint targets. When they caught a tripod, the heavy gun turrets would swivel and try to blast it before it could slip away. As Bridges, watched, exactly that happened. The big twelve-inch gun in the main turret roared out, shaking the whole vehicle, and an instant later a tripod half a mile away disintegrated as the heavy shell tore it to pieces.

The flank attack had bent back the infantry's line. It might have broken completely except reinforcements were hurrying up from the landing site twenty miles to the southwest. These arrived in time to bolster the defense, but they were nearly all infantry and the pressure was still severe. The line was forced back until it was now nearly facing due east. The six ironclads had become bastions around which the infantry could rally. What they really needed were tanks, but none had arrived so far.

Bridges flinched away from the view slit as a heat ray passed across *Yellowstone*. The slit had a thick block of tinted quartz which gave some protection, but you still didn't dare to keep looking when it happened. The ironclads were remarkably resistant to the Martian rays. Heavily armored and, unlike most warships, totally stripped of anything that might catch fire the machines could withstand punishment which would have wrecked a tank in short order. Still, concentrated fire at close range by multiple heat rays could burn through the armor. They'd seen that during the fight to capture the Martian fortress near Memphis. The Martians kept trying to do that here and the ironclads had been forced back and back to keep the distance open.

Commander Harding entered through the rear door of the pilot-house shaking his head. "Hoo! Nearly got me that time!" he said. "If I'd been a second slower, I'd be ash."

"You need to be more careful, sir," said the officer of the watch, a young lieutenant named Pickering.

"Yes, yes," said Harding, brushing off the scolding. "Get ready to move, the commodore has signaled that we need to fall back again. The bastards are swarming all over the infantry and they can't hold."

"Yes, sir." Pickering turned to the engine room telegraph.

"Things getting sticky?" asked Bridges.

"You might say that. Despite what we can do and what the navy ships can do, the infantry is getting shredded. We need to get out of the town and find some defensible ground."

"I'd think the town would be a good place to hold."

"If it was just the tripods, you'd be right. But it's those damn spiders. In the dark, among the ruins, they can get in among the infantry and be too close for any supporting artillery to fire at them. At close quarters those things are murderous." Yes, as Bridges remembered Harding had faced the spiders at as close a range as it was possible to be and live to tell about it.

The ironclad shook again as they let off another salvo. "How is our ammunition holding up?" asked Bridges.

"Yeah, that's the other thing, we've used up a lot and got no way to resupply until they can get the landing site organized. We've gotten word that they are getting heavy stuff ashore now, tanks and artillery, but it's all twenty miles away and God knows where our ordnance train is right now."

A crewman stuck his head in the door and said, "Sir, signal from flag: execute withdrawal maneuver."

"Right. You heard him, Sam, pull us out of here. Reverse engines, set course one-five-zero."

"Aye sir," said Pickering, "full reverse, course one-five-zero." He worked the telegraph again and *Yellowstone* lurched into motion. Driving backwards was trickier than driving forward, the tall smokestack blocked a direct view to the rear. There was a look out station at the rear with a man with a telephone to the pilothouse to give directions, but it was an awkward arrangement. Fortunately, the ironclads were so large that any collisions would probably be far worse for what they ran into than for the ironclad.

They clanked and lurched and groaned rearward for the better part of a mile, shooting at targets which revealed themselves at intervals, when they received messages almost simultaneously over the wireless and from the lookouts in the observation platform: the ironclad *Laramie* was in trouble.

"She's thrown one of her tracks and can't move," said Harding, looking at the message. "The Martians are closing in on her."

"*Laramie*'s the one all the way over on the right, isn't she?" asked Bridges.

"Yes, damn it. That's where the Martians are thickest, too. We've got squadron orders to close on her and assist." *Yellowstone* was fourth in line counting from the left. Next on their right was *Escalanta*. Beyond her was crippled *Laramie*. In order to best support the infantry, the vehicles had been spaced about a half a mile apart.

The ironclad slowed to a halt and then pivoted on its enormous tracks and then moved forward again, heading almost due south. Peering through the view slit, Bridges saw a frightening concentration of explosions and the blue flashes of Martian artillery in that direction.

"They are trying to get gunfire support from the fleet to help her out," said Harding. "But when we fell back, the ships all retreated down the strait, too. Only the big guns on the battleships can reach that far."

"Well, if all five of us can reach her we ought to be able to set up a defense until... *God's teeth!*" A huge ball of fire erupted in the distance in front of them. It momentarily lit up the entire landscape in a horrid red glow. A few seconds later a deafening roar shook *Yellowstone*.

"Hell," said Harding grimly.

"Must... must have been their magazine."

"Yes."

They continued to move in that direction for another minute or two until a new signal arrived: continue the withdrawal. Harding did not follow the order immediately. Instead he scrambled up the ladder to the observation platform, but quickly returned.

"Just wanted a look to see if there could be any survivors," he explained, shaking his head. "Pickering, get us back on one-five-zero, full reverse."

"Yes, sir."

The delay in turning had taken *Yellowstone* south of *Escalante* and they were now on the right end of the line. Fortunately, the fighting seemed to have died down, they were clear of the town now and the Martians were not pursuing closely. They appeared to have concentrated their attack against poor *Laramie*.

Bridges checked his watch and was stunned to see that it wasn't even midnight yet. It seemed like the battle had been going on for days. He turned to look at Harding. "How far back are we going?"

"Good bit, maybe five more miles so were in range of more guns from the fleet. I think they want to regroup and meet up with the reinforcements coming from the landing site and then we'll hit them again."

"Maybe we should have waited to advance until we had everything landed."

"Maybe. But I think the commanders were hoping that a quick attack would take them by surprise. And the word coming from Constantinople isn't good. They need us there as soon as possible."

Bridges frowned. Not enough time to do it right, but time enough to do it over. His grandfather used to say that a lot. Still, they *had* hurt the Martians with the first attack. Maybe when they went in again it would be easier. But they not only had to defeat the enemy tripods and spiders they still needed to find the big heat rays and...

"Stop! Stop the ship!"

The sudden cry from the man on the telephone to the rear observation post caught them all by surprise, but Harding reacted instantly. "Halt! Full Stop!" he shouted at Pickering. The lieutenant immediately worked the engine room telegraph and the ironclad halted quickly enough to force Bridges to grab something to keep from falling.

"What is it?" demanded Harding of the man on the telephone.

"A group of people right behind us, sir. The lookout says it looks like a field hospital."

"Damnation," muttered Harding. He looked out a view slit, and it did not seem like anyone was shooting at them at the moment. He went out the rear door of the pilothouse and Bridges followed him. They walked along the narrow catwalks that led to the rear. Around the big smokestack, past the secondary turrets and across the large hatches which covered the coal bins. They reached stern and looked down.

Yes, it was a field hospital. A cluster of tents, some of them partially taken down, a large hospital flag still flying, wagons and horses, medical people, and dozens of men on stretchers. The doctors and orderlies were all frozen in place, gawking at the behemoth which had nearly run them over.

"We could go forward a bit and get around them," suggested Bridges. But just then one of the gawkers shouted up at them.

"Hey up there! Can you help us?"

"Who's that?" replied Harding. "Who's speaking?"

"Major John Lennard, Royal Medical Corps. Who are you?"

"Commander Drew Harding, US Navy. What are doing there?"

"Trying to get the hell out! A courier only told us about ten minutes ago that we were retreating. Guess they forgot we were here. Are the Martians coming?"

"Probably. I suggest you get packed up and moving."

"Can you provide us with an escort? Everyone else seems to have buggered off!"

In the flickering light of the flares and star shells which still burst overhead from time to time, Bridges could see the worried expression on Harding's face.

"I can give you ten minutes. Get the wounded loaded up and leave everything else."

"All right, but I've got more wounded than will fit in the wagons we've got. Can you take some?"

Harding swore, but he said, "How many?"

"About twenty. Can you take them?"

"Yes, we can. I'll lower the gangway and send some men to help."

The next few minutes were a frantic blur of activity. While the hospital people loaded their wagons, navy crewmen went down the gangway and awkwardly hauled up men on stretchers. With the crew at action stations, there was space in the bunk rooms for the casualties. At the ten-minute mark Harding blew the ironclad's steam whistle and the immense vehicle and the train of ambulances and wagons lurched into motion. Harding looked peeved. He turned to a yeoman.

"Get a message off to the commodore and tell him about our delay. We'll catch up with the squadron at the fallback position."

"Yes, sir."

They moved in fits and starts for twenty minutes or so. The hospital wagons were having trouble keeping up with the ironclad. There weren't any convenient roads heading in the right direction, so they had to move overland, which caused frequent detours. They tried simply following in the path the ironclad crushed as it moved, but that only worked on really hard ground. On softer ground the machine's tracks pressed into the earth creating a sort of wash-board pattern that the wagons had trouble negotiating.

Reports from the observation platform said that the Martians had regrouped and appeared to be coming on again in a broad front. They called in fire from the fleet, but it was hard to tell if it was accomplishing much.

Then, as they were creeping up a small hill, *Yellowstone* suddenly began slewing around to the left. Harding halted the vehicle and then got on the telephone with the chief engineer down in the engine room. He listened for a moment and then swore bitterly.

"Trouble?" asked Bridges.

"Number three track is out. That bearing we were having trouble with earlier is shot."

"Can it be fixed?"

"Mr. McCullough says he can do it, but it will take a while. Four or five hours he estimates." He paused and looked out the pilothouse window. "But for now, we're stuck here."

* * * * *

Advanced Base 14-5, Cycle 597,845.5

Kandanginar evaluated the situation and was pleased. They had survived the enemy attack and the counterattack had driven them back with significant losses to their ground forces and several of their smaller water vessels had been destroyed as well. They had also managed to destroy one of the prey-creatures' huge war machines. It had been difficult and costly, but it was good to know the things could be destroyed. Losses to the clan had not been insignificant but were acceptable; forty-eight fighting machines destroyed or crippled and nearly three hundred of the small drones and six of the bombardment drones. Most seriously, twenty-two members of the clan had been killed or badly wounded. Machines could be replaced, but people were in short supply.

"The prey creatures continue to retreat, Subcommander," reported Lutnaptinav. "Shall we continue our pursuit?"

Kandanginar considered the question. Experience had shown that the prey-creatures were most vulnerable once they were forced to retreat. Their cohesion would often fall apart and their ability to resist would diminish significantly. Often, they could be slaughtered in large numbers. In this case, however, they had the support of the water vessels and the farther the clan pursued, the more dangerous those vessels would be. Also, the mission here was primarily defensive. They main attack on the narrow water barrier to the east was just getting underway and would require considerable time to complete. Kandanginar's goal was to prevent this force of prey-creatures from interfering. So far it was succeeding in that mission and to take unnecessary losses now might jeopardize the situation if the enemy renewed its attack. Perhaps it would be best to break off the pursuit and return to...

"Subcommander!" A message from Andagmatu one of the battle-group commanders interrupted its train of thought.

"Yes?"

"Subcommander, one of the prey creatures' large machines has come to a halt. It is no longer retreating. It has stopped on a hill about two telequel ahead of our forward-most elements. But the rest of the enemy is continuing to retreat. The machine is becoming isolated. Should we attack it?"

"Could this be a trap of some sort?" asked Lutnaptinav.

"It is possible," conceded Kandanginar. "It will be some time before the artificial satellite can give us information on what forces the enemy is assembling. They could be preparing a new attack and using this machine as a lure—just as we did with our drones in the habitation."

Still, the big machines had proven themselves extremely dangerous and the opportunity to destroy one should not be missed. There were only five of them left and to reduce that to four would improve the odds if the battle was renewed.

"We will keep pressure on the rest of the prey creature force, so they cannot interfere. Andangmatu, take three battlegroups and an appropriate number of drones and destroy the enemy machine."

"At once, Subcommander."

* * * * *

South of the Dardanelles, April 1913

"Come on, come on! Keep moving!"

Every officer and sergeant in the battalion seemed to be saying the same thing. For Harry it had become a kind of automatic refrain. He said it over and over again, despite his parched and dust-filled mouth. His canteen was empty and there was no chance to get it filled.

He wished he knew what time it was, but he had lost his watch during the mad scramble to retreat. It seemed like days since he'd seen the horde of Martian tripods closing in on them. Days since the world had blown up in blinding blue flashes; he still was seeing blue after-images.

Somehow, he'd made it down from the top of the minaret, only moments before one of the explosions had sent it crashing to the ground. The men of the battalion were scattering in all directions, trying to find cover from the unexpected barrage. Dimly, Harry realized that this was the new Martian weapon they had heard about, the one the navy encountered during its last attempt to force its way through the strait. But the reality of it was nothing like he'd expected. There was no whistle of shells like

276

normal artillery; nothing to give any warning. Just dazzling bursts of light followed by savage concussions. Sometimes the explosions were right at ground level or inside a ruined building and then there would be clouds of dust, dirt, and debris thrown up, almost like a regular shell. More often, they seemed to burst just above the ground, like a shrapnel shell with a perfectly cut time fuse. A man caught in the open by one of those would be burned black on the side closest to it—an instant before the shock wave tore him to shreds.

Harry had found cover and hugged the ground for what seemed a very long time, but which was probably only a few minutes. Then the bombardment shifted to another area and the survivors cautiously got up and tried to sort themselves out. After a few moments in a daze, he remembered what he had seen and began shouting a warning about the approaching tripods. By the time he got anyone to listen, the warning was no longer necessary, everyone could see them for themselves.

With luck they'd managed to pull out before they were overrun. The colonel, the captain, and Burford Sampson, had gotten them up and moving and they fled westward, hauling equipment, wounded, and dazed comrades with them. Behind, heat rays were stabbing out, blasting their former location. The fire spread out to their right and left as the enemy attack broadened. Not long afterwards human artillery started to fall; not just on the Martians, but all around. At times the navy's guns and the enemy's new weapon were pounding the same area. God only knew who, if anyone, was under it. A few shells fell on the battalion and Harry was sure they'd lost men because of them. But the friendly barrage had forced the enemy to slow up. They wouldn't have gotten clear without it.

They kept moving, trying to get themselves organized as they went, but in the dark, only fitfully illuminated by star shells, explosions, and flares, it was nearly impossible. They got turned around or stuck in dead end streets which forced them to backtrack dangerously close to the pursuing tripods and spider machines. As they finally broke free of the ruined town, they ran into another unit and got completely jumbled together. He wasn't sure who the others were except they weren't Australian. Both groups retreated together.

Pushing on, Harry suddenly caught his foot on something and fell heavily, knocking the wind out of him. As he struggled to his feet, someone caught his arm and helped him up. In the light of a flare he saw, to his surprise the dark face of Abdo Makur, the native they had rescued from the Martian 'farm' in Egypt. The man had attached himself to C Company and followed along despite all the regulations against it.

"You all right, sir?" he asked.

"Yes, yes," said Harry, automatically brushing himself off, and resuming the march. "You're still with us, eh?"

"Yes, sir. I still wish to help against the devils from the sky."

"You wouldn't happen to have any water, would you?"

"A little, here, sir, take some." He held out a leather water bag and Harry gratefully took a long gulp of warm water. It was wonderful.

"God bless you, man. Thanks."

"I live to serve."

"Don't we all? But some serve better than others. You and Scoggins, eh? Couldn't run the company without you. Have you seen Scoggins lately?"

Abdo's face fell and he shook his head. "A thousand sorrows, sir, but master Scoggins is dead."

"What? How? Are you sure?" Harry was shocked. Scoggins was the sort that you just knew would make it out of any fix. Dead? Didn't seem possible.

"He... he died saving me. When the blue lightning fell on us, I stood there like a fool. He pushed me behind a wall, but before he could join me, there was another flash and he was dead. I am so ashamed, sir." Abdo was crying as he talked.

"Not your fault. That sort of thing happens in war." It was an automatic reply, but there were some things that you didn't expect to happen. A wave of guilt swept over him when he started wondering who was going do the scrounging for the officers now?

The explosion of a salvo of Martian bombs a hundred yards to their right blew those thoughts right out of Harry's mind. They were still in danger here and if they didn't want to all end up like Corporal Ralph Scoggins, they had to find someplace safe to stop and get reorganized.

And they needed to find it soon. The men had been marching or fighting for almost a full day now with scarcely a pause. He had to grab more and more stragglers and get them moving again. If they didn't stop, the battalion was going to be scattered. A little while later, while pushing another man, he bumped into Burford Samson.

"You all right boy?" he asked.

"Don't call me boy. And yeah, I'm just dandy. You?"

"Never better. You hear about Scoggins?"

"Yeah, Abdo told me. But Burf, we can't keep this pace up much longer. Look, I think there's a hill up ahead. Maybe we could rally there and rest for a while."

"Fine idea, except neither of us are in charge to order it. Haven't seen the colonel since this whole rout started. I thought I saw the Captain a while ago."

"Well, let's see if we can find someone and... oh bloody hell!"

"What? Oh, damn."

A dark shape sat atop the hill in front of them. In the gloom it looked like a tripod standing atop a rocky prominence.

"They got ahead of us!" hissed Harry. "We're cut off."

Cries of alarm grew all around them as other caught sight of the thing. But then a star shell burst. It must have been a few miles away, but it still cast enough light to show what the shape really was. A tall observation platform on long leg-like supports, sitting on top of a ship-like hull supported by enormous caterpillar tracks.

"It's one of the Yanks' ironclads!" cried Sampson.

Indeed, it was, and a moment later a searchlight turned on and swept across the mass of men at the base of the hill. Harry thanked God that there was no way to mistake humans for any of the Martian machines. That would have been the final act of a terrible day to be blown to pieces by friends!

Heartened, the men made their way up the hill and converged around the great machine. Someone shouted down from above demanding their identity and Harry was glad to see that Colonel Anderson was still alive and came forward to answer.

"15th New Castle Battalion, ANZACs. We've got men from some other units with us. Who am I speaking to?"

"Commander Drew Harding, US Navy, land ironclad *Yellowstone*," came the reply. "Where you folks going?"

"Not exactly sure, Commander. Just trying to find a place to re-organize. Is this where they are establishing the new line?" Harry looked about and didn't see any other troops, or any semblance of a defense line.

"No, I'm afraid not," called Harding. "We've broken down here and are stuck until we can make repairs. The line's another three miles or so west of here."

"Damn," said Anderson. "My men are completely fagged out. Mind if we stay here and rest a while?"

"Not at all! We'd welcome your help. We were feeling a bit lonely here all by ourselves. If you want to set up a perimeter around the hill, maybe we can hold these bastards off. We've got radio contact with the fleet and they say they can support us with long range fire."

"Sounds delightful commander. We'll get set up. But be ready, those bloody things aren't far off."

"I know, our lookouts can see them from here. Oh, and if you have any wounded, we picked up a hospital unit. They're just behind the hill here."

"Right-o, thank you."

Anderson called his officers to him and assigned portions of the line to each company. The other unit which had joined them was the 2nd Battalion of the South Wales Borderers, but the highest-ranking officer they had left was a captain, who had no problem placing his men under Anderson's command.

Harry managed to round up about thirty men from his platoon, which seemed almost a miracle to him after all that had gone on. C Company was placed on the southeastern portion of the circular defense line. Men dug in if they still had their folding shovels, of just piled up rocks if they didn't. The Lewis gun was set up and they did an inventory of their Mills Bombs and the crossbow bombs for Greene's contraption. Abdo had somehow refilled his water bag and gave Harry enough to half fill his canteen.

One of the men was nearly blind from a Martian bomb but was refusing to go to the hospital. Sergeant Milroy came to Harry for help. "Private... uh, Henderson," he said. "Be a good fellow and come with me. If the doctors patch you up, you can come back to the line with your mates. All right?"

The man grudgingly agreed, and Harry led him around the hill, looking for the hospital. He probably could have gotten someone else to do it, but he wanted to see where the hospital was—just in case he needed it later. It was farther than he expected, but he eventually found it inside the walls of a villa of some sort. There was a cluster of wagons there with some lanterns set up and people moving in and out of the light.

He was stumbling with fatigue and just led Henderson up to the nearest lantern. There was someone there bending over a man on a stretcher. "Excuse me. I've got an injured man here. Can someone give him a look?"

The figure turned and said. "We're a bit busy right now. But if you can wait a moment, I can help you."

Harry stiffened. He knew that voice! It was a woman's voice. The light from the lantern caught her face...

"*Vera!*"

Chapter Nineteen

The Admiralty, London, April 1913

Frederick Lindemann jerked awake when a new round of arguments began in the meeting room at the Admiralty. He sat up in the wing chair set in one corner of the room and rubbed his neck which had become quite stiff. It was another very early day — or very late, since most of the men had been there since the previous evening. There were times when Lindemann wished this critical battle was taking place in North America; the time difference would be more manageable.

But the battle was in the Near East. It was three in the morning there and two hours earlier in London, and if all the talk going on around the room was to be believed it might be the most critical battle yet in the war against the Martians. The army had gone ashore and driven north to attack the enemy's formidable defenses along the Dardanelles. They had met stiffening resistance and the fleet had moved in to assist them. Things had appeared to be going well, when a sudden Martian counterattack had forced the army to fall back, and the fleet had done the same. The question before everyone now was what to do next?

"General Murray says that if he can expect support from the fleet, he's prepared to renew the advance in the morning," said Churchill. "His first corps was badly handled, it's true, but his second corps is coming up, the third is unloading, and the engineers have managed to set up a system to land the heavy equipment at Yenekoy. He still has all the various foreign contingents in reserve. The tanks and heavy guns are moving up now and with them and the Americans' land ironclads he believes he can drive through to destroy the super heat rays along the coast."

"Two of the land ironclads have already been destroyed," said Admiral Pakenham.

"Only one, the other has just broken down; it might be repairable. But there really is no choice. If Murray is willing to resume the offensive, the fleet must support him. We must order de Robeck to make an all-out attack alongside Murray."

"Winston, no!" said Lord Fisher. The First Sea Lord had recovered from his earlier funk and was back in action, but Lindemann could tell that the old man was teetering on the brink of another breakdown. And anything might push him over. "We simply cannot sustain these sorts of losses!"

"Jacky, we only lost four destroyers in the last attempt."

"But we lost far more the first time! Battleships and cruisers and God knows how many good men! No! We can't!"

"Good men, yes, and that's tragic, but mostly old ships. We need to commit our best ships this time. Send in *Queen Elizabeth* and *Colossus* and…"

"No!" cried Fisher, his yellowish face turning red. "Not *Queen Elizabeth*! I won't risk her!"

"But she mounts two of the new heavy coil guns. As Professor Lindemann points out the very flat trajectory of those guns will allow them to fire straight down the tunnels the Martians have put their rays in and destroy them. And her heavy armor will allow her to survive to do so."

"Bah! Lindemann! He's just some ivory-tower egghead! What does he know about naval matters?!"

Lindemann flinched, stung by Fisher's words. A few months ago, when he'd agreed with Fisher on the need for the coil guns, the old man had declared him a genius. How dare he talk like this now?

"Jacky," continued Churchill. "The Ottomans are in a desperate situation; the Martians are closing in on the Bosporus. It's less than a mile wide in most places, their normal heat rays will be able to fire right across it. Without immediate assistance from the fleet they will get across and fortify both shores and we'll never be able to punch through to the Black Sea. We simply must act now."

"Oh, to the Devil with the Ottomans! They should be able to defend their own damn country. We have no business sending our forces so far from home. We're way out on a limb there, Winston! The Martians are just waiting to cut it off and destroy the fleet!"

"It's the Martians who are out on a limb," countered Churchill. "All indications are that they have advanced so far and so fast that they haven't had time to build any of their fortresses close to the Dardanelles. They are being forced to draw supplies from their bases down in Arabia. Why just the other day we got a report from that Major Lawrence, you remember him? He's the one who spotted this Martian offensive in the first place. He was landed with a party of our Deep Desert Group men near Alexandretta and they managed to ambush what appears to be a Martian supply column. Destroyed a number of cargo carriers and sent the rest running back south! The enemy is in a dangerous situation and…"

"*We're* in the dangerous situation!" said Fisher. "We must not risk our ships like this again. Let the army clear out those devils. When it's safe we can send the fleet through."

"That would take far too much time," said Churchill. "The commander of the German squadron insists that we attack. The German troops

283

at Constantinople are in grave danger and he says that he'll go forward alone if need be. How can we stand back and..."

"The Germans!" said Fisher, his face lighting up. "This is all their doing! The Kaiser arranged this whole thing to get us to destroy our fleet. He's sitting there with his own navy in the Baltic, just waiting for his chance to crush us. No! We cannot fall into his trap!"

"Jacky, you know that isn't true," said Churchill in a soothing voice. But Fisher's Oriental eyes grew wider and he stared at him like he'd never seen him before.

"You!" he exclaimed. Then his head swiveled to look right at Lindemann. "And you!" He pointed a finger, and then spun about to point at Prince Battenberg. "And you, too!" He turned back to Churchill. "You're all in this together! You and these two damn... *Germans!* You've betrayed us! The country and the King!"

"Jacky..." Churchill's voice was still soft, but there was growing alarm in his face.

"Yes! Betrayed! Well you won't get away with it! I'll stop you, by God! Yes, I will! I'll put a stop to this... this... *treason!*" Fisher spun on his heel and stomped out of the room.

You could have heard a pin drop for a full minute in the silence that followed. Finally, Churchill shrugged and cleared his throat. "Well! Well, that was... unfortunate. But we still have to deal with this situation. I'm prepared to give de Robeck unequivocal orders to advance into the Narrows in support of the army. Do any of you have any comments?"

"We could take very heavy losses, sir. Lord Fisher is right about that," said Prince Battenberg, the second sea lord.

"Yes, we could. It's regrettable, but sometimes necessary. Where would we be if Wellington had been unwilling to take losses at Waterloo, or Marlborough at Blenheim? And make no mistake, gentlemen, the battle we are now engaged in will be mentioned in the same breath as those other two when men speak of the great triumphs of the British Empire!" Churchill's gaze swept around the room, taking in each man. "Now, if you'll assist me in drafting the order to de Robeck. I want it to be as clear and concise as we can make it."

Throwing off their shock at Fisher's tirade, the men went to work, laying out the objectives of the fleet and what latitude Admiral de Robeck had in carrying them out. There was some debate as to the wording and a few of the admirals grumbled about putting the man in the field in a straitjacket, but Churchill pushed them on, never yielding an inch on any matter he deemed vital. The clock on the wall struck two as they were finishing up.

They were just preparing to send it off to the wireless room when the doors opened and to everyone's surprise there stood a captain of the Royal Marines flanked by two corporals, all resplendent in their scarlet and blue uniforms. *Fisher!* thought Lindemann. *What in God's name has he done?* Everyone in the room froze, except for Churchill; he put his cigar in his mouth, stuck his thumbs in the pockets of his waistcoat and growled, "Can I help you, captain?"

The officer, who looked terribly young, blanched white. He took a step forward and blurted, "Uh, yes, sir. Your pardon, sir, but I've been given orders to escort you to the Prime Minister's residence. He... he wants to see you, sir."

"At this hour?"

"Uh, yes, sir. Right away, sir."

"I see..." Churchill glanced around the room. His eyes settled on Prince Battenberg. "Louis, it seems I've been summoned to answer for my crimes. Would you mind carrying on with what we were doing until I can return?"

Prince Battenberg looked back at him. If Churchill were removed, as seemed likely, and with Fisher irrational, command of the navy would fall, at least temporarily, into his hands. He would have the power to send in de Robeck, or to hold him back. Lindemann held his breath.

After a very long moment, Battenberg stirred. "No need for that, sir," he said as he walked up to the marine officer. The prince was quite tall, and he looked down at the sweating man. "Captain, please inform the Prime Minister, that Prince Battenberg wishes to inform him that the First Lord is currently engaged in matters of the utmost importance to the defense of the Empire and cannot attend him at this time. He will come see him at the earliest possible moment. Do you think you can remember all that, son?"

"I... I think so, sir!"

"Good. Off with you then." The captain saluted and faced about and marched off followed by the two bemused corporals. Battenberg turned to look at Churchill, who was smiling a most peculiar smile.

"Thank you, Louis. Thank you very much."

"You're most welcome, sir. Oh, and might I suggest that we add to the end of de Robeck's orders: *These instructions are to be carried out at all costs?*"

* * * * *

South of the Dardanelles, April 1913

"Vera, what in hel... what in the world are you doing here?" Harry stared at the young woman. In the light of the lantern her face smudged with dirt, her hair spilling out from under her VAD cap, she looked very tired and... simply lovely.

"Harry? Is that really you?" She seemed as dazed to see him as he to see her. "I knew you were out here, but I never thought I'd actually bump into you in all this mess."

"But what are doing on the front lines? They don't send nurses up here! Who's responsible for this?" Whoever it was would get a stern talking to if Harry had any say in the matter!

"Just me. No one sent me, I just... came. They were setting up a field hospital down on the coast where all the troops are landing. Then the wounded started pouring in and they were short-handed, and I volunteered to help out. I... I wanted to help. Then yesterday they were sending a convoy of ambulances to the front to pick up wounded and I just sort of... came along."

"Oh, Vera! That was very foolish!"

"Maybe it was. I don't know. I've been tending the wounded in the rear all this time, years, but never once gotten close to the fighting. Since we were advancing, I didn't think there was any great danger and I... well, I wanted to see the Martians. Their wrecked machines, anyway. I wasn't expecting to get caught in this fix."

"Well, maybe we can get you out. I'll talk to the Colonel and..."

"Out? Out there?" She pointed off into the darkness which surrounded them. It was indeed very dark. A tiny sliver of a moon, just a few days from the new, hung in the eastern sky, but it shed very little light. An occasional flare or star shell still burst, but they were running low on them. "From what I hear, we're surrounded. At least we have some shelter here inside the walls, and soldiers and that huge war machine to protect us. No thank you, Mister Calloway, I think I'd rather take my chances here."

"But..."

"Lieutenant? Lieutenant Calloway, are you there?" Harry flinched as someone shouted his name.

"I'm here."

"Sir, Captain Berwick needs you back right now. The Martians are coming."

"Damn. I have to go, Vera. Promise me that you'll be careful?"

"I will if you will."

There was nothing to say to that. On impulse he reached out and took her hand and squeezed it. He was a little surprised — and pleased — when she squeezed back. Reluctantly he let go and hurried around the hill to his platoon's position.

He got there just in time.

A flare ignited overhead, and the light revealed a horde of tripods and drones on the low ground to their front, maybe a mile away. He couldn't begin to count them, but there was a hell of a lot. Sergeant Milroy led him to a bit of a dugout the men had thrown up for him. There hadn't been time to make any real trenches in the rocky soil and most of the men were terribly exposed; but at least they were on high ground.

They'd barely gotten under cover when the big guns on the land ironclad roared out. The flashes lit up the landscape brighter than the flare for an instant and the concussion slapped him on the back. The biggest gun must have been a ten or twelve-incher; much bigger than the eighteen and twenty-five-pounders he was used to. He looked out to see the shells burst among the advancing Martians. One of the tripods was physically lifted up and flung to the side, landing in a heap.

Moments later he heard shells screaming overhead and they started exploding among the enemy, too. Fire from the fleet; thank God they were still in range of them. But then the Martian artillery began arriving. Those beautiful, but deadly blue flashes started to pelt down on the hill. Each blast created an azure-tinted photograph, a frozen moment in time burned onto the eye and then gone again. Harry scrunched down behind the pile of rocks and logs, feeling very naked. He looked back and saw some of the bombs exploding on or around the land ironclad; what was it called? *Yellowstone?* Odd name for a fighting machine. The explosions didn't seem to have much effect on it that he could see. And he was relieved that the bombs all appeared to be falling on the ironclad or the eastern side of the hill. He cringed at the thought of a bomb exploding in the hospital — where Vera was.

Heat rays stabbed out from the tripods and played over the hillside, searching for victims. One swept across the front of Harry's shelter and the logs puffed briefly into flames and he could feel the heat. But it was long range for the Martian weapon, and it didn't linger long.

The scream of shells grew louder, and he dared to look out again. An almost solid line of explosions created a curtain of fire and smoke across the enemy's line of advance. Some heat rays punched through the curtain, firing blindly, and the enemy bombs continued to rain down, but second after second went by and no alien machines emerged. After a bit the artillery fire slackened and eventually stopped. So did the rain of Martian bombs. The smoke and dust drifted away to the east and another flare revealed that the enemy had pulled back. A half dozen wrecked tripods and perhaps more smashed spider machines were all that were left to see.

The enemy's fire had left a few wrecked and smashed men, too. Those still alive were carried back to the hospital. Harry waited a moment, but when no more bombs fell on them, he dashed over to where Burford Sampson was crouching. "Surely, they haven't given up already, have they?" he asked.

"I doubt it. They haven't given up along the rest of the line." He gestured toward the northwest where there looked to be a lively fight going on. "Probably were just surprised by the strength of our defense. They'll regroup and come again. You get back where you belong, Harry."

"Right. Good luck to you, Burf." He dashed back to his position. Sergeant Milroy looked peeved that he's left cover.

Within minutes it was clear that Sampson was right. Star shells fired farther to the east showed a mass of tripods gathering on the edge of the ruined town. Some artillery started falling there, probably called in by the folks on the *Yellowstone*, but it wasn't intense; not like before, and the Martians seemed to ignore it. Then the mass was in motion and getting closer. The ironclad's guns roared out again and maybe got a tripod or two, it was impossible to tell.

But while the enemy was advancing, they also were angling off to the south. *Trying to flank us? Well, we're in a bloody circle here. No flanks friend.* But if they circled all the way around, Vera and the hospital were back there. Damn, what could he do?

Not a stinking thing, was the answer, but fortunately there were others who could. The artillery followed the enemy's movement and it started coming much more heavily. One thing the humans had learned in this long war was how to use artillery. Even in far off Australia, the techniques had been developed to coordinate the guns so that heavy fire could be called down from multiple batteries in multiple locations against any critical target. And it turned out that the land ironclad wasn't completely immobile. With a squeal and a groan, the huge machine rotated around in place to keep its front end facing the Martians. Its guns fired again, adding to the growing noise.

The Martian bombs started falling again, too, but there didn't seem to be as many of them as before; still far too many though, and the cries of the wounded could be heard between explosions. One fell very close to Harry and he was dazed for a few moments, but otherwise unhurt, saved by the flimsy barricade.

The mass of tripods was off to his right now and they halted about five hundred yards away and opened up with their heat rays, mostly against the ironclad. Parts of its metal skin glowed red in the beams and he saw the flag flying from the mast dissolve in flames. But the Americans were firing back, quickly and accurately and Martian tripods were being blasted apart one after another. The artillery continued to flay them as well.

Suddenly there was firing off to his left and moments later it spread to C Company and his platoon. Tearing his eyes away from the ironclad,

Harry peered out into the darkness and saw movement. *Spider machines!* A mass of the awful things had snuck in while the tripods created a distraction. They were only a few hundred yards away and closing fast. Rifle fire and the Lewis guns chattered away, and the small heat rays began firing back. Harry fumbled out a Mills Bomb he'd scavenged from one of the casualties and unscrewed the cap covering the arming ring.

Several explosions erupted in the middle of the spiders, blowing some of them to bits. The ironclad had guns mounted on all sides and those which couldn't bear on the tripods could fire against the spiders. But it wasn't going to be enough...

They were getting close and the men started heaving bombs. Off to his left the spiders were in among B Company and screaming men added to the bedlam. Harry fired a few shots from his revolver, for all the good it would do. Milroy yanked him back as a heat ray set his barricade ablaze. "Stay down, you young fool!" he snarled. Milroy was right, but what was he going to do? They'd barely been able to handle three or four of these monsters in the town, how would they stop this horde?

Yellowstone was moving again, the squeal of its tracks unmistakable even through the other noise. Looking back, he saw that it was swinging back around in his direction. Was it just trying to shield its overheated armor or...?

A dazzling blue-white lightning sprang from its forward-most turret and leaping above Harry's head, it struck in the mass of spiders in front of him. The bolt spread from spider to spider linking dozens, scores, of them together in a writhing, coruscating net of crackling energy. The spiders withered and popped like bugs in a frying pan. Then the bolt vanished, and an earsplitting thunderclap shook the air.

"God's bloody trousers!" shouted Milroy. "What in hell was that?!"

"Don't... don't know," gasped Harry. "But it was on our side, so I don't care!"

* * * * *

USNLI Yellowstone, *South of the Dardanelles, April 1913*

"Damn, I love that thing!" said Commander Drew Harding.

Major Tom Bridges blinked to clear his vision after the near-blinding discharge of the Americans' Tesla Gun. He'd seen it used several times before during the Memphis campaign, but it was still as impressive as all hell. "Bloody marvelous thing, that's the truth. Your Doctor Tesla is a wonder."

"He's a madman according to Andy Comstock, but I can live with that if he conjures up things like this."

"Amen to that. A shame you can't use it more often."

"Its effective range is only about four hundred yards. And now we have to recharge it."

"That takes what? Ten minutes?"

"Maybe a bit less since we're not using the motors to move. Still it seems to have done the job, the bastards are falling back."

"Same thing happened at Memphis. Took the blighters by surprise."

"Skipper," said the officer of the watch, Lieutenant Pickering, "We've got fires in the forward berthing compartment." Bridges automatically looked forward, and indeed there was some smoke wafting up from the bow of the ironclad.

"Expected that," said Harding nodding. "The forward areas are the extra flotation compartments. Only lightly armored and meant to soak up damage in combat. No real danger since we've got a heavy armored bulkhead aft of..." He paused and his head jerked around. "We didn't put any of those wounded men in there did we?"

"No sir," said Pickering. "Figured this might happen, so they are all aft."

"Good man," said Harding, looking relieved. "But get a repair party sent forward to deal with the fires."

"Yes, sir."

"Any other serious damage?"

"Half the machine guns are out of action and Number Two four-inch mount has its traverse jammed. Probably melted. A few holes in the funnel, and every bit of paint on the forward half of the ship burned away, but other than that we are all right, sir."

"Good. What about ammunition?"

Pickering frowned. "We're down to fifteen rounds for the twelve-incher and the five inch have maybe forty per gun. Plenty left for the four-inch, though."

"If the Number Two four-inch can't be made serviceable shift its ready ammunition over to the other guns," said Harding. He glanced out the rear door of the pilot house. "And get another ensign run up."

"Aye, sir."

"You go through quite a lot of those, I imagine," said Bridges.

"Yeah, they burn up pretty quick, but we keep a good stock. Have to look proper now don't we?"

"Yes indeed," said Bridges. "I've never noticed that the Martians have any flags or identifying marks of any sort, have you?"

"Can't say that I have."

"Strange, even savages use banners of some sort."

"They probably consider us savages. Maybe they are too civilized for such things."

Bridges frowned, not liking the thought of that. "Any word on the status of that bearing?"

"McCullough says another two hours. Which probably means three. He's always overoptimistic."

"So we are still stuck here. Any chance some of the other land iron-clads could come up to help?"

Harding shook his head. "I've exchanged messages with the commodore. He says that the other four are all that's holding the rest of the army together. They're still being pressed pretty heavily. Until the reserves finally get there, he needs to stay with them. But as soon as the reserves do arrive, they will be coming straight to help us."

"Huh," said Bridges peering through the view slit. Another star shell had burst overhead. "Well, then, it's a good thing you have plenty of those flags, Commander, I think you are going to need them."

* * * * *

Advanced Base 14-5, Cycle 597,845.5

"Subcommander, this is Andangmatu reporting. The enemy machine has withstood our attacks and we have suffered very heavy losses. My forces are falling back to regroup. Do you wish me to renew the assault?"

Kandanginar considered the question. Eighteen more fighting machines lost, along with over half their pilots. Fifty more of the small drones destroyed and several of the bombardment drones had been put out of action as well. Ammunition for all of them was running short—the one serious drawback of the new weapon. What had seemed like an opportunity to eliminate a powerful enemy unit was now appearing to be a costly mistake.

But to withdraw now would mean all those losses had been for nothing; totally wasted. "Has any serious damage been done to the enemy machine?"

"Some small fires are burning on it and it is possible some of the smaller weapons have been disabled. Their rate of fire has slowed so they may be running short on ammunition. Except for their strange energy weapon, which presumably is powered by the vehicle's engines."

Yes, the prey-creature energy weapon. Just what was that? Some very incomplete reports had come from the clan so badly defeated on Continent 3, but little real information. The Colonial Conclave had directed that a sample of the weapon be procured if possible. The war machine they had destroyed earlier had carried one, but it had been totally destroyed when the machine exploded. Might it be possible to obtain one here? Would it be worth the cost, even if they did? The clan's losses were climbing in an alarming fashion. Even if the current campaign resulted in victory, would Clan Patralvus be able to afford the cost?

"Subcommander? We are still under fire here. I require direction."

Yes, waiting accomplished nothing. A decision had to be made.

"Renew the attack," said Kandanginar. "I will order our other forces to make aggressive demonstrations to draw off the prey creatures' long-range weapons."

"As you command."

* * * * *

South of the Dardanelles, April 1913

"Any idea what time it is, Sergeant?" asked Harry.

"No, sir, forgot to wind my watch and it stopped around midnight. Got to be getting on towards dawn, I'd think."

"I hope so. This night's gone on forever."

"Yes, sir. Longest of my life. But those blighters are forming to attack again and if they hit us at dawn, the sun will be in our eyes."

"Sergeant, I think that will be the least of our worries."

Milroy snorted. "You're probably right, sir. Well, with the Yank's machine backing us up, we've still got a chance."

Harry nodded. The American's machine was truly amazing. Their astounding lighting gun had definitely saved all their bacon on the first attack. But how much more could it do? In the flickering light of the flares, it looked like a wreck. Scorched and battered, smoke pouring out of the front of it. How much ammunition did it have left after all the firing it was doing? And if its wireless transmitter was lost, how could they bring in supporting artillery?

If the Yanks couldn't stop them, there was little hope the infantry could. They were low on bombs, there had been no time to dig proper trenches or the pit traps they had used so effectively at Sydney. If the Martians got in among them, they'd be overrun in minutes. He remembered the final retreat from Sydney, how all the order and discipline of the troops had dissolved into panic. Men tossing away their weapons, not even trying to fight back, just trying to get away. That could happen here, just as easily. Men burned down as they tried to run. Sliced up by the blade things on the spiders. Or maybe captured alive. The Martians ate their captives, it was said. Pumped them full of some sort of chemicals which dissolved their insides and then the Martians *drank* them. Better a quick death by the heat rays than that! *I'll go down fighting rather than let them get me. But he knew it might not be up to him.* The tripods had metal tentacles they used to seize things. They were much stronger than any man. If one of them grabbed him...*They'll get Vera, too.*

That was the thought that frightened him most. What if they got Vera? The thought of what she might suffer was like an icicle stuck through his heart. Damn it, what horrible twist of fate had put her here? He clenched his fists. No! That was not going to happen! They would hold out... somehow.

"Some light above those hill now, sir," said Milroy. "Dawn's coming."

"Yeah, but so are the Martians, look."

Silhouetted against the brightening sky in the east was a long row of dark shapes, Martian tripods. They were a mile away or so and Harry couldn't really count them accurately, even with his binoculars. Thirty or forty at least. There might have been more, further to the south, but he couldn't be sure. They were just standing there, but Harry suspected that there were swarms of the spider machines down in the shadows of the low ground between the tripods and their positions. The spiders were a lot slower than the tripods and they probably wanted them all to strike at the same time.

Nothing was firing on either side at the moment. *Yellowstone* was probably saving its ammunition for when they got closer. Maybe they were waiting to call in the navy guns for the same reason, although the steady rumble from off to the northwest might indicate that the navy had other problems to deal with.

Minutes passed and the sky brightened into a light blue streak painting the whole eastern horizon. But the tripods didn't move.

"Come on you bastards!" shouted someone off to his left. "What are you waiting for?"

That set off a stream of taunts from the men. 'Come and get us!' 'We're ready for you!' 'Cowards!' and many more, some quite profane. But the enemy did not react, not that they could even hear them from this distance. But then another voice rose up above the others. Not shouting, singing. Harry immediately recognized the tune — and the words.

> *Hark! I see the foe advancing,*
> *Three-legg'd steeds are boldly prancing,*
> *Metal heads in sunbeams glancing,*
> *Glitter o'er the land.*

It was that song they'd heard those Welsh troops singing back on the docks in Alexandria. It had become quite popular, sweeping through the army. Harry suddenly realized that the other unit mixed in with them here was that same battalion. He'd completely forgotten. More voices took up the song and soon it seemed like hundreds were singing. Not all the men singing were Welsh of course, so there had been some subtle changes to the lyrics.

> *Men of Earth, lie ye dreaming?*
> *See ye not their heat rays beaming,*
> *And their monstrous tripods streaming,*
> *Where we make our stand?*

Harry's throat was dry and tight and yet he found himself joining in with the others. An act of defiance not despair.

> *From the rocks rebounding,*
> *Let the war cry sounding*
> *Summon all at Mankind's call,*
> *The haughty foe surrounding,*
>
> *Men of Earth, on to glory!*
> *See, your banners famed in story*
> *Waves these burning words before ye*
> *"Earthmen scorn to yield!"*

The men gave a cheer and then took it up again. As they did, the sun peeked above the rim of the world and its rays indeed glanced and glittered off the enemy's metal war machines.

And then they were moving; heading their way. "Here they come!" shouted someone. Much of the singing died away and men got ready. But there were enough stalwarts to keep it going for a while. Despite, or perhaps because of the intensity of the moment, the tune stuck in Harry's head and one line kept repeating itself:

> *Earthmen scorn to yield!*

As the sun rose higher, the shadows fled from the low ground in front of them and as he had suspected it was full of spider machines scuttling toward them; through the olive groves and gardens that surrounded the small farms in the area. Their big brothers were quickly catching up with them using that bizarre, yet rapid gait of the Martian tripods.

294

Behind him *Yellowstone*'s guns roared out and explosions appeared in the ranks of the enemy. A few seconds later the scream of shells passing overhead told him the navy hadn't completely abandoned them. Geysers of earth and flame erupted among the spider machines, tossing some of them into the air. But they didn't falter, they kept coming. They had been told that they were just remotely controlled machines, there were no pilots like in the tripods. They couldn't be frightened or demoralized; as long as someone gave them orders they would continue to fight.

Three quarters of a mile, half a mile, the enemy closed on them with an awful quickness. A few tripods went down, but not enough, not nearly enough. As Harry had feared, there were more of them coming up from the southeast as well as the main batch he'd seen on the ridge. Forty or fifty of them converging on the hill altogether. How could they stop them?

As Harry stared, motion caught his eye. Looking back to the ridge where the tripods had been waiting, he saw a swarm of tiny specks flying up high into the air. What...? *Bombs!* In a flash he realized that these were the bombs the Martians had been using on them. In the dark it was impossible to see them, but in the bright daylight, the things were big enough and slow enough compared to artillery shells that you could actually see them!

"Take cover!" he shouted. Others saw them too, and the men flattened themselves down as low as they could behind their cover. The blue explosions appeared all over the hill. Concussions hammered at him and he squeezed his eyes shut against the glare. But it was over in an instant and no more appeared to follow. Some of the men had been hit and the wounded screamed for help. But there was no way to get them to the rear; not now. They'd have to stay with their fellows.

At a quarter mile, the tripods caught up with the spiders and that was when the infantry opened fire. Rifles and machine guns sent a hail of bullets across the field at the enemy. There was little hope of doing any harm, but sometimes a lucky shot might do something. And it felt better than waiting helplessly.

Heat rays came back at them, but they all seemed to be aimed at the big American machine. It had been glowing brightly in the clear morning sunshine, the light reflecting strangely off its heat distorted armor. A flag flew bravely from the control tower. But now the glow turned an evil red, and the flag puffed into flames and was gone.

But *Yellowstone* kept fighting. A blue-white star blossomed from its front turret and the lightning leaped out again. It crossed the distance to the enemy in an instant and jumping from tripod to spider to tripod linked a group of them together. The machines twitched and jerked, sparks shooting out of them, and then the bolt was gone and the Martians crashed to the ground. The rest continued on. Three hundred yards, two hundred... nearly here...

They were pulling clear of the area pounded by the naval guns now, too close to shoot at. Maybe a dozen of the tripods in all had been wrecked, but thirty or more were almost on them. They towered overhead, but their rays continued to flay the ironclad instead of the men on the ground, and one of the secondary turrets exploded. The spiders were here, too, crawling in among the infantry, small heat rays firing, blade-things slashing.

But the men were rising to meet them, rifles firing, bombs exploding, grappling with the horrible things, hand to hand. To Harry's left he saw one spider, a man impaled on its blade, being flipped over on its back by his mates. They slapped a bomb on its belly and it blew up, along with its victim.

Earthmen scorn to yield!

But the Aussies and the Welshmen were falling fast, much faster than the Martians. Harry stared out from his cover as a spider came directly toward him. His last bomb was ready in his hand. Sergeant Milroy rose up high enough to fire his rifle at the thing, but as he did so, a heat ray caught him, and he fell.

"Sergeant!" The man rolled on the ground, still alive, but terribly burned. Harry was enraged. Milroy had been his right hand from the moment he'd been given command of the platoon. He'd never have survived this long without him. *Now that he's gone, I won't survive much longer.* The spider was coming on and he grasped the arming ring on his bomb.

Behind him the twelve-inch gun on *Yellowstone* roared again and a moment later there was an explosion. This was followed by a dazzling blue flash. Not one of the Martian bombs, no, sometimes when a tripod was hit, its power storage devices would explode. Harry had seen it happen a few times before—from much farther away.

The explosion that followed made the human and the Martian artillery seem like firecrackers. An all-encompassing roar shook the world, and something snatched the breath out of Harry's lungs. He was slapped flat on the ground like he was a bug. He lay there, dazed, as wreckage came raining down all around; metal arms and legs and other bits of tripod and spider.

Shaking off the fog in his brain, he got to his knees and found himself staring at a spider machine not ten yards away. It had him dead to rights, but it didn't move. Stunned! This time Harry didn't hesitate. He surged to his feet, pulled the arming ring on the bomb, and then slammed the sticky end to the spider right above its eye. He turned and ran, but the bomb went off almost at once and he was thrown to the ground again, a burning pain searing his right shoulder.

He tried to get up, but his legs felt like they were made of water. Then strong hands seized him and hauled him upright. "Come on, boy! We need to get out of here!"

"Burf?" Yes, it was Sampson, and like his biblical namesake, the man was a tower of strength. He pulled him up the hill and he could see that most of the other men were running that way as well. Twisting backwards, he saw the boiling cloud of smoke and dust where the tripod had exploded. The whole Martian force seemed to have halted...

"Where we goin', Burf?"

"Falling back! While these buggers are confused."

They stumbled up the hill and collapsed just to the rear of the ironclad. The *Yellowstone* looked like Harry felt—battered to bits. The whole front end was a raging inferno and smoke poured out of it in a dozen places. But from time to time a gun still fired. It wasn't out of the fight. Not yet.

From his vantage point he was able to look back at the hospital and he gasped in relief when it didn't appear to have suffered any harm. But it won't stay that way long! "We need to get everyone out, Burf."

"Yeah, but I don't think they're gonna let us."

The tripods were moving again, up the hill, spreading out to surround the *Yellowstone*. They ignored the huddled infantry, focusing their attention on the ironclad. Their heat rays were hitting it from all sides now, the armor turning red, yellow, white... The whole vehicle was suddenly engulfed in a cloud of hissing steam. It diffused the heat rays a bit, but it couldn't survive this for long...

A tripod to Harry's right suddenly had a leg sheared away. The machine fell and rolled halfway down the hill before coming to rest. What...? The ironclad hadn't done that. It wasn't artillery, either...

A hole appeared in the head of a second tripod; two holes, one in front, one in back, debris exploding outward from the second hole. The force of the blow knocked it backwards and it collapsed in a heap.

"What in bloody hell...?" said Sampson.

The sound of gunfire came to them from the rear. Harry looked westward, past the hospital which had riveted his attention, to the fields beyond. They were filled with tanks. British tanks, rumbling forward. The older Cromwells which were identical to what they'd had in Australia, and the newer Wellington's which carried the fancy coil guns. There looked to be close to a hundred of them, crossing fields, ramming through low stone walls, stopping briefly to fire, and then coming on again.

Reinforcements. The reinforcements had arrived. They'd been promised they were coming, but no veteran soldier ever believed that sort of thing. But there they were, plain as day. Beyond them Harry could see even more troops on the move. Infantry and cavalry and artillery. In the distance he saw a battery of the Longbows, the self-propelled guns he'd seen back along the Nile. They were suddenly hidden by puffs of smoke and a moment later shells screamed overhead to burst among the spiders at the base of the hill.

The Martians, almost as one, turned away from the stricken *Yellowstone*, to face this unexpected attack. They fired a few heat rays in the tanks' direction, but after three more tripods were wrecked, the remainder turned again and stalked away at top speed to the east. Retreating. Fleeing.

An indescribable feeling of relief filled Harry. They were safe. He couldn't begin to count how many of his comrades had died in this awful day, but those who were still alive were safe. Vera was safe. It was almost too much to take...

"Well... well, that's a hell of a thing, ain't it?" said Sampson.

Harry nodded, his eyes filling with tears.

"Earthmen scorn to yield."

Chapter Twenty

Advanced Base 14-5, Cycle 597,845.6

"Subcommander, this is Gadantinar, I regret to report that Andangmatu has been slain and the attack has failed. Prey creature reinforcements are arriving in great number and I have had no choice but to order a retreat."

Kandanginar processed the information and waved its tendrils in frustration. The situation was deteriorating with alarming swiftness. The initial battle, though unwanted, had gone well enough. The prey creatures had been drawn into the ruined habitation, hurt by the drones, and then forced into a hasty retreat by the counterattack with the fighting machines and bombardment drones. There was every indication that the enemy would be sufficiently damaged and disorganized that they would not be able to launch another attack for some time. By then, the main attack further to the east would have completed its crossing of the water barrier, fortified both shores, and been in position to resist any further attacks while it prepared for the drive north to make contact with the forces coming south from Continent 1.

The situation was now changed and much for the worse. The prey creatures had unloaded additional forces from their water vessels, including many of their armored gun vehicles and heavy projectile throwers and they were joining up with their initial forces. Losses were mounting rapidly among the clan's forces and continued action might well lead to a complete disaster. There were now barely a hundred functional fighting machines and less than four hundred drones. The bombardment drones were nearly out of ammunition and an expected supply convoy with more had been ambushed in the mountains to the south and turned back. The long-term outcome could not be predicted, but the immediate response was clear.

"Kandanginar to all battlegroups: retreat to the prime defensive zone immediately. Recover any downed pilots if practicable. Leave half the drones to cover the retreat."

The acknowledgements came almost immediately. Obviously, the order had been expected. The disengagement went smoothly, catching most of the prey creatures unprepared for an immediate pursuit.

"Subcommander, the prey creature water vessels are advancing again," said Lutnaptinav over the communicator. "Many of the largest ones appear to be joining the attack this time. All the heavy heat rays stand ready."

"Were you able to position any of them to face the landward assault, as I directed?"

"Only, two, and their field of fire is limited. I do not know how effective they will be. And their mounting locations are not as deep or protected as I would like. I am afraid that..."

"You did your best. None can ask more."

"Progenitor, I am young and inexperienced, but my analysis of the situation does not lead to a favorable outcome. If the prey creatures press the attack irrespective of their losses, I do not believe we can win."

"We have our orders: Delay this attack as long as possible."

"Even to our own destruction?"

"Every member of the Race is expendable for the common good."

"Who determines what is the common good?"

"Enough of this! We shall obey our orders!"

"Of course. Do we have any word of how the main attack progresses?"

"Nothing definite. They have reached the vicinity of the water barrier and are preparing to cross."

"How long will that take?"

"There is no way to predict. But we must hold here until they succeed."

"We shall do our best," said Lutnaptinav.

* * * * *

Skutari Airfield, April 1913

Major Erich Serno jumped from the wagon and nearly fell flat on his face. He couldn't remember how long it had been since he last slept. He'd dozed a bit in the wagon, and he knew he was lucky his rank had managed to win him a spot in it, but the jolting, lurching journey had not encouraged sleep. The army had almost completely disintegrated in the retreat from the last defense line to the Bosporus. Only a few units, mostly the German ones, had held together during the retreat, holding back the pursuing Martians so the rest could escape.

He wasn't sure that they really had escaped, the sounds of fighting had been growing louder, getting closer. Off to the north, near the Black Sea coast it seemed like the fighting had already passed them. Columns of black smoke rose into the clear blue sky. Had the Martians reached the Bosporus? The roads had been jammed with troops and refugees trying to escape. For the last few weeks the hordes of civilians fleeing out of Anatolia had been ferried to the west shore as fast as the ships could carry them. There were no bridges and the waters were very deep. Every ship or boat that could be gotten was pressed into service. But there were still thousands more waiting to get across. Serno's wagon had slowly, far too slowly, pressed its way through the throng.

And now he was back at the airfield, the place he'd left on his last mission, the place where he had spent so many hours working to create an Ottoman air force. All that remained of that was a dozen damaged or broken-down aircraft and a handful of men. Where the rest of the ground crews had vanished to he did not know. Scattered? Conscripted as infantry? Deserted? He limped toward the main operations building, hoping to find someone, anyone who could tell him what was going on.

He winced with the pain of walking. He had hurt his right leg in the crash of his Rumpler. He hadn't noticed it at first, but it had been growing hour by hour and now he could barely walk. Hobbling onward he was startled by a cry:

"Major! Major Serno!"

He looked to its source and was surprised and pleased to see Lieutenant Yusef Kenan, the Turkish pilot who had been one of his first students. The man was running toward him, with a huge grin on his face. "Major! We thought you were dead! You didn't come back after the last attack."

He stopped and waited for Kenan to reach him, a smile growing on his own face. "Hello, Yusef, I got hit and I crashed. Good to see you, though, I wasn't sure any of you made it back." Serno's Turkish had improved over the months and Kenan had picked up some German and they were speaking in an odd Turko-German mix.

Kenan's face fell a bit and he shrugged. "Only four of us did. When I reported that you were gone, we got new orders to evacuate the base and send everyone north of the Bosporus. We've been shuttling any aircraft that could still fly out to the new airfield where the zeppelins are based. Most of the ground crews left by boat yesterday. I was just here to make a last look." He gestured at the planes around them and shook his head. "None of this lot will fly without more work than we have time to do. I was just about to head for the boat when I saw you. Thanks to Allah I didn't decide to go back last night!"

"Well, then I guess this is my lucky day—assuming you've got room for me."

Kenan's grin returned. "We'll make room! Come on, we need to hurry." He turned and started away at a brisk walk. Serno couldn't possibly match him and after a few strides, Kenan turned back. "Oh! Are you hurt, Major?"

"Banged up my leg a bit. Not too bad, but I can't walk quickly."

"Here, let me help you." He took Serno's right arm over his shoulder and half carried him along. Another man appeared and also tried to help, chattering in Turkish faster than Serno could follow. By the time they reached the edge of the airfield, all the remaining ground crews had joined them, along with a few armed soldiers, maybe two dozen all told, and they made their way through some of the streets of Skutari toward the Bosporus.

The streets were mostly deserted, although they encountered a few bands of what were obviously looters. They usually fled when they saw the soldiers. "The evacuation boats are all operating a bit farther to the north," explained Kenan. "Hell, of a mess. We have a navy steam launch at our disposal and I had it tie up as far from there as we could manage."

"Good thinking."

As they neared the water, the relative calm was broken by artillery fire from close by. Heavy guns for sure, not field pieces; probably warships from the direction. They went through an alley and emerged on the banks of the Sea of Marmara. The mouth of the Bosporus was about a mile off to the right. In front of them were a half-dozen warships actively firing toward the north. Others could be seen further away. They were all smaller vessels, ancient relics of the Ottoman navy and a few more modern ships of foreign navies, but nothing bigger than a cruiser.

The bow of the launch was drawn up on the muddy bank and a squad of soldiers with fixed bayonets was keeping a small mob of civilians at bay. They were clearly hoping for a lift across the water to the imagined safety of the western shore. The soldiers cleared a path for Serno and the others and he was bodily lifted into the boat. The civilians tried to press forward, begging for help, but the bayonets kept them back. With all the military personnel aboard, there was still quite a bit of space.

"Let the women and children come," said Serno loudly, in Turkish.

Cries of joy came from the people but looks of consternation came from the crew and soldiers. The navy man in command of the launch tried to argue, but he was only a very young ensign and Serno browbeat him into submission and the women and their children were allowed to clamber aboard. At first Serno hoped there would be room for the men, too, but more people started appearing from the town and when it looked as though the vessel might be swamped, the ensign put the launch's engine into full reverse and pulled away from the shore. This produced a great deal of wailing as women reached for their men and children for their fathers and a dozen people ended up in the water either trying to get to the boat or get back to their men. Serno gritted his teeth but there was nothing more that could be done.

The launch backed off a hundred meters and then the ensign put it at full ahead and turned it out into the open water. Constantinople and the Golden Horn was nearly straight ahead, and they steered in that direction, making a detour around the firing warships. Serno tried to see what they were shooting at, but all he could see was clouds of smoke along the shores of the Bosporus.

He looked toward Constantinople. In the morning light the city seemed as it always had, peaceful, imposing, beautiful. The zeppelin base was off to the southwest of the city itself. Ten kilometers at least. "Will the launch take us all the way to the base?" he asked Kenan.

"No, sir, they'll let us off at the docks of the navy yard. We'll have to get the rest of the way on our own. He glanced down at Serno's leg. "But I'll try to find some sort of transport for you, sir, so you don't have to..."

Suddenly some of the people on board gave cries and started pointing back to the northeast. He turned to look, but it was a moment before he saw...

Tripods.

Dark shapes were emerging from the smoke clouds along the eastern shore of the Bosporus. A dozen of them, maybe more. Their heat rays were stabbing out at the ground in front of them and flames shot up. But then more movement caught his eye. A mass of people, fleeing in front of the Martians, appeared along the banks. It was several kilometers away, but he could see that there were thousands of them, like stampeding cattle, heading for the water.

"Allah the Merciful," breathed Kenan.

The mob reached the shores and hesitated for a moment, but the tripods were coming up from behind, heat rays blazing, and the press of the people forced the front ranks into the water. More and more came out of the smoke, crowding into the mob at the water's edge. *Trapped between the devil and the deep blue sea!* Serno clutched the rail of the launch and looked on helplessly.

With the choice between fire and water, the crowd chose the water. The mass surged into the sea, desperate to escape the flames which came nearer and nearer. Between the distance and the continuing roar of the guns it was impossible to hear the screams—except inside his head.

It was too far to really see individual people, they were just dark specks and splashing water. But in his imagination Serno could see the panicked people trying to swim for the opposite shore. The stronger ones staying up, pulling ahead from the weaker ones. Families trying to keep their children's heads above the water, fools hanging on to possessions they couldn't bear to part with, and all eventually slipping beneath the waves. The flames crept closer and closer, the heat rays sweeping from side to side incinerating anyone too slow to find a watery death instead. And this was probably happening along the whole length of the Bosporus as the Martians closed up on it...

As if this was not horror enough, a steamer appeared around a bend in the Bosporus, burning from stem to stern as it tried to escape into the wider waters of the Sea of Marmara. Some smaller boats were following, but the merciless heat rays were faster. Burning people flung themselves from the flaming ships into the water and were swallowed up.

The warships began firing directly at the tripods and one did go down, but it was too late for the doomed people trying to escape. Those that did not burn drowned. A few of the stronger ones made it quite some distance from shore, but no boat dared to try and go in to rescue them.

The launch passed behind the warships and the scene was mercifully obscured by steel hulls and clouds of gun smoke. The people on the launch were weeping and cursing and a few vomited over the rail.

"Damn them! Damn them!" said Kenan, his face wet with tears. "We must stop them! Somehow we must stop them!"

"Yes, we must," said Serno. "Somehow."

"When will the help come? They have promised that help is coming! When will it come?"

Serno looked south and west across the Sea of Marmara. The help was that way. But when would it come?

"I don't know."

* * * * *

USNLI Yellowstone, *Near Kephez, Turkey, April 1913*

"Yes, I know you just got it fixed and I know I'm pushing her too hard, McCullough! And I know she's had the hell beaten out of her. I was here for all of it, remember? But as long as we can move and as long as we have a gun left, we are staying with the advance! Now keep her moving! I know you can do it." Commander Harding put down the telephone and shook his head. "Bloody Scotsmen!" he muttered. "Treat their machines like they were prize stallions or something."

Major Tom Bridges had observed this end of the conversation with no small amusement. Harding was right about Scotsmen, of course, but he did have to sympathize with Lieutenant McCullough; *Yellowstone* was beat to hell and it was a miracle it could still move at all. Honestly, it was a miracle that any of them were still alive after what they'd gone through. Bridges had survived the assault on the Martian fortress near Memphis aboard the ironclad Albuquerque and that had been a near-run thing for sure, but this! What had happened last night still amazed him.

305

Wave after wave of tripods and spider machines had hurled themselves against the land ironclad. They had blasted them down as quickly as they could, but even with help from the infantry and fire support from the fleet it had seemed hopeless. At the end, they had been surrounded, with most of their weapons gone and the armor plates glowing hotter and hotter. They'd released steam as a defensive measure, but he'd been sure it was the end.

But then the reinforcements had arrived, in the nick of time, like the cavalry in some western three-penny novel. Several battalions of tanks, up from the landing beaches, had hit the Martians by surprise and sent them packing. In the light of the new dawn Bridges had counted no less than thirty-five wrecked tripods around them. And that probably didn't include the one which had exploded or any tripod standing too near. Yes, the enemy had paid dearly.

But so had poor *Yellowstone*. The American machine had been battered and scorched very nearly to death. The front part of the ship, the flotation and berthing section, was completely gone, burned and melted until it had collapsed and torn loose. The only weapons left to her were the big twelve-inch gun, one five-incher and one four-incher. The amazing lightning cannon had been wrecked along with all the other guns. And the twelve-inch only had four rounds left. Harding still had some of his flags, but there was nothing to fly them from, all the cables had burned away and the raised observation platform so damaged no one dared go up to rig new ones.

Bridges had expected that the battle was over for them and they would be heading to the rear for repairs. But Drew Harding had other ideas. The Martians had concentrated all their fire against the upper works of the machine, the part where all the weapons were. The huge tracks and the motors which drove them had suffered almost nothing and with the faulty bearing finally repaired the *Yellowstone* could move again and Harding was determined to move forward, not back.

Bridges found that Harding was staring at him. "You think I'm crazy, don't you?"

He snorted. "Not at all, sir. We can still fight, so let's fight. The buggers chased us away from the strait yesterday, can't leave 'em thinking they beat us."

Harding chuckled in turn. "Forgot who I was talking to. You British and your Charge of the Light Brigade and all."

"Well that *was* crazy if I do say so. But I daresay, you Yanks don't like to leave the enemy holding the battlefield any more than we do."

"No, no we don't. In America the bastards still hold nearly a third of the United States, almost all of Canada, and pretty much everything south of Texas. We are *not* going to let them keep it."

"I imagine you'd rather be there than here."

"Yes, but if we can hurt them here, eventually it will help us there. Kill them wherever we can is what I say."

"Yes, certainly. And it looks as though we'll still have the chance to kill some more of them here. Is the wireless working again? Any news about what's happening?"

"We managed to jury-rig an antenna and have some contact, although reception's poor," said Harding. "No specifics on the situation, but we have the same orders as before: push through to the Narrows and clear out the Martian super heat ray positions."

"Well, from the looks of things, that's what everyone is trying to do." He gestured forward, although there was nothing to see since the armored bridge shutters were closed. Closed permanently, it seemed. During the last attack, the enemy heat rays had welded them all shut, and they hadn't been able to get them open again. The door to the bridge had also been sealed and they'd damn near baked to death before men with sledgehammers had been able to free them. The quartz pieces in the view slits had all been fogged and cracked and they'd been forced to smash them out so they could see. The helmsman was being given verbal instructions, since he couldn't see at all.

Harding nodded and then stepped out onto what was left of the bridge wing; Bridges followed. The metal platform on the port side had drooped and buckled, but the starboard one was still useable, although the metal railings were gone and had been replaced with rope.

It was mid-morning now and the army had retaken nearly all the ground it had lost yesterday and was moving into what was left of the town of Kephez. The enemy had fled before them and the advance had been rapid. Too rapid for *Yellowstone* to keep up. What with making temporary repairs, off-loading the wounded soldiers, and saying farewell to the hospital detachment, they had gotten a late start and then Lieutenant McCullough had insisted they keep their speed down to no more than half the maximum, so they were now well behind. From the smoke and explosions, it looked as though the fighting was at least a mile ahead of them, maybe more. Well, even Harding realized they were in no condition to lead the attack. The other four ironclads were far ahead of them.

The slow pace had one benefit: they still had their infantry escort. Those poor blighters had suffered even more than *Yellowstone* which had lost only a handful of casualties among the crew. With no armor to protect them, they had died in droves. There had been two understrength battalions to begin with, but they barely made three companies now. But they burned with the same desire to fight as Commander Harding, so they left their wounded with the hospital and had come along with the ironclad.

The sounds of fighting were getting louder now and from the vantage point atop the ironclad, they could see that the navy was pushing forward into the strait again. Harding turned his binoculars in that direction and whistled. "They're sending in their heavy stuff now," he said. "I can see several dreadnoughts there, they always held them back before. Damn, I think one of them is that German battle cruiser who joined us just before the landings."

"Everyone's getting into the act," said Bridges.

"Damn well about time. That's the only way we'll beat these monsters."

Yellowstone rumbled on, making a path as it went. They passed wrecked tripods and spiders from time to time and the men cheered when they saw one. More often, they passed broken down tanks and jeered at their frustrated crews in a friendly fashion. The British tanks had petrol engines rather than steam since most of the Empire's theaters of war were in arid countries where water was harder to get than fuel. But they still broke down as frequently as the steam tanks and the dash they had made to get up to the front in time to save *Yellowstone* had been more than some of them could take.

Shortly before noon, they began to catch up with the rear of the army. The fighting in the town was fierce and progress was slow. Word came that two of the super heat rays had been knocked out, but both by the navy. The army was still struggling to get close enough to attack them. The navy was paying for its successes, too. A number of ships had been sunk or badly damaged and Admiral de Robeck was urging the army to help. *Yellowstone* still wasn't forward enough to find anyone to fight, but it crushed its way through buildings and the infantry followed in its wake.

A little while later a rating dashed on to the bridge wing. "Signal from the commodore, sir," he gasped. He handed a paper to Harding.

"News?" inquired Bridges.

"Seems like *Cimarron* has found some sort of Martian stronghold. We're the closest support and we've been ordered up to assist." He peered out and then pointed. "That's her over there." The observation towers on the ironclads made them easy to spot. *Cimarron* looked to be about half a mile away. Harding turned to the man at the wheel. "Helm! Twenty degrees starboard! Ahead two-thirds and tell McCullough I don't care if his damn engines can't take it!"

The bridge crew acknowledged and the ironclad increased speed and twisted a bit to the right, vibrating more strongly than before. As they watched, explosion rose up all around the vicinity where their sister ironclad was engaged. Then a blue-white light lit up the clouds of smoke and the distinctive thunderbolt clap of the Tesla cannon rolled across the landscape to reach their ears.

"Looks like they're giving the bastards some hell," said Bridges.

"Yes, well, let's get ready to dish out some of our own," replied Harding. He headed for the armored bridge and he followed. Lieutenant Pickering was on duty and waiting for them.

"All guns manned and ready, sir," he said. "Well, all that we've got left, anyway."

As they closed on *Cimarron*'s position, they saw that she wasn't totally alone. There was some infantry and a few tanks in the vicinity as well. Artillery was falling ahead of them, too. The army had brought up its own guns now and they weren't getting as much support from the navy as before—they had their own troubles, it seemed.

"Almost none of the Martian artillery anymore," observed Bridges. "Wonder if we knocked it all out?"

"Maybe, but as long as it's not shooting, that's all that matters," replied Harding, peering through a view slit. "Helm, a little to your left... yes, that's it, steady up."

They had nearly caught up with *Cimarron* and now got their first sight of the enemy. "Tripod! Three o-clock!" shouted Harding. "D-Turret, engage!" Pickering relayed the order over the telephone. The sole remaining secondary turret rotated right, and the five-inch gun roared out. Bridges squinted through another vision slit and saw the machine stagger backwards as the round hit it. "Again!" ordered Harding. The Martian turned its heat ray on *Yellowstone*, but a moment later another round struck it and it fell. There didn't appear to be any other targets in the immediate vicinity.

They pulled in beside *Cimarron* and Harding exchanged some brief signals with its commander and then the pair started forward, steering around a low hill to their right. Bridges moved over to a portside view slit and looked the other ironclad over. It hadn't been as badly damaged as *Yellowstone*, but it clearly had been heavily engaged. Its forward hull sections were holed in many locations and had burned just like *Yellowstone*'s but had not fallen off yet. It looked like one of the secondary turrets was gone. The forward turret with the Tesla cannon was rotated backwards to protect the projector while the thing recharged.

A pair of tripods appeared in front of them, but both fell back quickly before they could be fired on. "Got them on the run, eh?" said Bridges.

"I hope so," said Harding. "As long as we only have to take them on two or three at a time, we'll be... God!"

Bridges instantly saw what had caused the commander's cry. A heat ray had speared out from the hillside only a few hundred yards away and impaled *Cimarron*. It was far brighter and thicker than any heat ray Bridges had ever seen. *The super rays! That must be one of them!*

The front section of *Cimarron* crumpled up and fell away in flames like a piece of parchment in a bonfire. The beam then struck the armored bulkhead just to the rear. The metal almost instantly turned bright red.

"A Turret!" screamed Harding. "Take that thing out!"

The big twelve-inch gun roared out almost immediately, shaking the vehicle. An explosion blossomed on the hillside, but the deadly ray continued to bore into *Cimarron*. The stricken ironclad's own guns were firing, but with as little effect. "I thought those big ones only faced the sea!" said Bridges.

"Obviously not! We've got to knock it out before..."

Cimarron exploded.

The beam punched through the armor and found the forward magazine. The twelve-inch turret was lifted bodily and tossed high into the air. Flames engulfed the entire forward half of the vessel, and the tall observation platform came crashing down.

The ray swung in their direction.

It swept across one of the caterpillar tracks and then stopped on the forward bulkhead—just like it had on Cimarron.

"A-Turret reloaded!"

"*Fire!*"

* * * * *

Kephez, Turkey, April 1913

Harry and his men caught up with the ironclads just as one of them blew up.

They had been on the go for more than a full day. Marching and fighting and then marching again. They were dead on their feet, but no one wanted to stop. What was left of the 15th New Castle Battalion was out for revenge. Their colonel was dead, their major was badly wounded and over half the men were dead or wounded, too.

No one could actually say what had happened to Colonel Anderson. When they'd pulled themselves together after the desperate fight alongside the Yank land ironclad, he'd just been... gone. Probably burned to ashes by a heat ray, an all too common fate. There was no doubt about Major Stanford. The poor fellow had had an arm lopped off by one of the spiders. As for the rest, well there was no time to make an exact accounting. Harry himself had a nasty shrapnel cut in his shoulder, but it wasn't serious and after having Vera bandage him up, he was ready to go again. Not eager, but ready. Part of him wanted to just stay there with Vera—thank God she hadn't been hurt! - but he was needed.

Captain Berwick was the ranking officer left in the battalion and took command. The four companies were amalgamated into just two. Burford Sampson was commanding C and D Companies. Ian MacDonald had been blinded by one of the Martian bombs, so Harry found himself leading what was left of C as one platoon, and a lieutenant from D Company taking the other. What remained of the Welshmen could only muster enough for a single company, which tagged along with the rest. Harry felt incredibly awkward in charge of a lot of men he barely knew. And he missed Sergeant Milroy terribly. His new platoon sergeant has a man from D Company named Breslin, who he hardly knew either. Abdo was missing, too. He'd felt very alone.

By the time they were reorganized, the *Yellowstone* was ready to move again, and they followed along behind. The rest of the army, including those glorious tanks which had saved them, were far ahead. As they neared the fighting, the *Yellowstone* had increased speed and the footsore infantry could not keep up. They'd fallen behind—until now.

Harry had been staying close to Sampson throughout the advance. Now they crouched together watching one of the super heat rays they'd been told about destroy one of the seemingly invincible ironclads in a matter of seconds and then turn its fury upon the *Yellowstone*.

"We need to do something!" shouted Harry.

"Yeah," agreed Sampson. "Taking those things out was why they sent us here. Get your platoon and follow me!"

Harry waved to Sergeant Breslin, but they had barely started forward when the *Yellowstone*'s big gun fired, and an explosion tore into the hillside and the heat ray blinked off. Everyone stopped and looked around in confusion. There weren't any other live Martians to be seen.

"Well go check it out," said Sampson. "Make sure the thing is really dead."

"Yes, sir." Harry waved his platoon forward and they cautiously approached the smoking hole in the ground where the ray was last seen. Glancing back, he saw that the *Yellowstone*'s front left caterpillar track had been broken and some of the links scattered about. Its front end was shimmering in the heat, the center of it a dull yellow that was fading to red and finally to a blackened gray.

They reached the crater and saw that it was really the entrance to a cave or tunnel. It was partially blocked by fallen dirt and stone, but they could make their way inside. Harry couldn't help but think that this was not the place to be if the ray suddenly started firing again. But it did not and they made their way deeper inside, barely able to see in the gloom. But as their eyes slowly adjusted they could just make some things out with the light that seeped in from the entrance.

About fifty feet back they found a pile of wreckage that must have been the heat ray. It looked pretty thoroughly smashed to Harry. Leaving Breslin and a few others to make sure, he made his way back out into the daylight. *Yellowstone* had let down its gangway and several men in naval uniforms were looking over their ship... tank... whatever it was. He spotted Sampson and Captain Berwick there with them and hurried over.

"Well, I think we've gone as far as we're going to today," said one of the naval officers, a commander, by the gold rings on his coat.

""Fraid I ha' to agree wi' ya sir,' said a lieutenant with a thick Scottish brogue. "Goin' ta' need a real repair yard t'fix up the old girl."

"Which I'm sorry to say you aren't likely to find around here," said an officer who, to Harry's surprise, was in a British major's uniform. Who was he?

The commander sighed. "It could have been worse. A lot worse." He looked over at the second ironclad which was still burning fiercely. Small pops and explosions came from it as its ammunition went up. Just then another naval man came running up. The commander turned to him. "What's the situation with *Cimarron*? Any survivors?"

"A few sir," gasped the man. "Some got out at the stern. But the whole forward section is a total loss. I doubt Commander Rothford or any of the bridge crew made it out. Sorry, sir."

The American commander frowned. "Thank you, Lieutenant."

"Well, sir," said Captain Berwick, "Since my men are in about the same shape as your machine, if you have no objections, I'll set up a perimeter and stand the rest down for a while."

"No objections, Captain. I think we can all do with..."

"Sir! Lieutenant Calloway... oh, er, Captain Berwick!"

The shout made them all turn, and Harry saw that Sergeant Breslin was running toward them.

"What is it Sergeant?" asked Berwick.

"Uh, we did a little explorin' in the tunnel beyond all the wreck. Made a few torches to see by," said Breslin.

"And?"

"It goes on! The tunnel, I mean sir. Goes on as far as we could see. Empty except for a big cable runnin' along it."

"The tunnel might connect with the rest of the Martian base, sir," said the British major. "That cable must lead somewhere."

"What are you suggesting?"

"I had the chance to walk through the Martian base near Memphis. You didn't come with us as I recall."

"No, my arm was bothering me, and I passed up on the chance. So?"

"Well, there were a bunch of engineering chaps who came along. They found something that they said was the power plant for the whole fortress. All the electrical power came from there. They said that all the defense towers and their heat rays were powered by it. Maybe all these super heat rays are being powered in the same way."

"Huh. You think so?"

"Those rays must use a lot more power than one of the tripods. The power has to come from somewhere. If we could wreck it somehow, we might be able to shut them all off."

The commander looked skeptical and Captain Berwick did not seem particularly enthusiastic, either. But just then a loud rumble shook the air and looking northward they saw a huge cloud of black smoke rising up from where the fleet was fighting.

The American commander flinched. "Looks like we're still taking a beating around the Narrows." He turned to Berwick. "Captain, are you game to go in there with your men? I have a half-dozen marines I can lend you but that's about all."

"I... I... my men are exhausted..."

"It's what we came here to do sir," said Sampson.

"We're willing to give it a try," added Harry. "But if we have to blow something up in there, we are nearly out of bombs."

"Is there anything we can give them, Sam?" asked the commander, looking to the lieutenant.

"Dunno, sir," he replied, scratching at his head. "We still got plenty of cordite bags for the twelve and five-inchers, but unless you can pack them in really tight, it's just gonna burn instead of explode. But the four-inch rounds are fixed with brass casings. It you stack up a few dozen of those and set 'em off somehow it ought to make a pretty good bang."

"It'll have to do. Fetch the ammo—and the marines. Oh, and give them every electric lantern we've got. They may need them in there."

"Yes, sir," the man hurried off.

"Major Bridges, this was your idea, are you willing to lead the expedition? You've got more experience with Martian construction than anyone else here."

The major seemed taken by surprise by the suggestion, but after a moment he nodded. "Yes, sir, it will be an honor." He turned to Captain Berwick. "Are you with us, Captain?"

Berwick blew out his breath and his shoulders sagged, but he said: "Yes, sir. Our pleasure." He looked to Sampson. "Burf, get the men ready."

* * * * *

Advanced Base 14-5, Cycle 597,845.5

Kandanginar watched the battle on the video display in the small control center and pondered the consequences of retreat. The prey-creatures were advancing on land and sea and if they continued to accept the losses they were suffering, there seemed little doubt that they would succeed in forcing their way through the water passage.

And they were suffering a great deal. Their land forces had taken many casualties, and the heavy heat rays had sunk or damaged scores of vessels. The approach to the narrow part of the passage was nearly filled with burning wreckage. It was unfortunate that the water was too deep for the wrecks to completely block the passage.

Despite their losses, the prey was coming on. They were now employing their largest vessels and some of these mounted the electromagnetic cannons which had been observed from time to time. Using the same principle as the bombardment drones, they used electro-magnets to accelerate metal projectiles to very high speed. Not only did that give the weapons a long range, the projectiles flew in a very flat trajectory which allowed them to hit the heavy heat rays despite being recessed deep into hill sides. These vessels had, one by one, destroyed the ray positions to the west of the narrows. They could now come all the way to where the passage made a sharp turn, without being fired upon.

Once they reached the turn, however, they could be brought under the fire of twelve heavy heat rays at very close range. The first few vessels to attempt this had been destroyed almost immediately. But more were forming up to try. If they persisted, it was inevitable that some of the heat rays would be destroyed. Fewer rays meant that the vessels would last longer and have a greater chance of destroying even more rays. A simple mathematical progression.

At the same time, the prey land forces were reaching the areas to the rear of the main defense positions. There were fewer than a hundred fighting machines left to oppose them and nearly all the drones had been destroyed. If these ground forces began destroying the heat ray positions from behind, the end could come quickly. When did the logical decision become retreat?

The Colonial Conclave had given it orders to hold the strait as long as possible. But as Lutnaptinav had pointed out, who made the decision about what was possible? If the lives of fifty clan members could buy a full planetary rotation of delay, that could be considered a wise exchange. But was that same fifty worth a half a rotation? Or a quarter? What about a tenth? At what point did the exchange shift from wise to foolish?

Kandanginar reminded itself that it was the one who had proposed this expedition. If it had not done so, it and the other clan members would have remained with the main attack—which would at this moment be facing this same force, deeply entrenched and supported by all of the water vessels at the crossing point to the east. There would be little hope in forcing a crossing against such strength. The offensive would fail—but the responsibility would not be its. If it ordered a retreat now, and the offensive failed, the blame might well be leveled at it. Well, so be it. The Race rarely ever terminated members merely for failure. It only did so if the one who failed was in such a position within the hierarchy of obedience that its continued existence would disrupt the usual chain of authority. Kandanginar was not in such a position. It had never desired a high military command in the first place. If it could return to its scientific pursuits it would be content. *If I retreat and accept the blame, how many lives can I preserve for the clan?*

While it deliberated, the enemy vessels were advancing. One of the larger ones, surrounded by a group of smaller ones, was approaching the turn at high speed, black smoke billowing from the exhaust cylinders on top. These were a slightly different color than the earlier attackers and their design was different, too. They were lower and wider, with fewer vertical projections. A different clan among the prey?

They reached the turn and six rays fired at once at the leading vessel. It was a smaller one and it exploded almost instantly, flames and smoke and debris flying out in all direction. But the others kept coming and soon there was a wild melee of crisscrossing heat rays and salvos of projectiles which ripped at the ray positions. Another vessel exploded and then another, but then one of the heat rays was destroyed. Moments later a second one was lost. Smoke and dust nearly obscured the view and Kandanginar shifted from one vison pick-up to another, trying to see.

The view cleared and the largest prey vessel was being hit by eight rays at once and suddenly blew up in an explosion that made the others seem small. A tower of black smoke, laced with flames, shot skyward and the vessel broke into pieces which quickly sank. Two of the remaining smaller vessels turned and tried to flee. One was destroyed, but the other made it around the bend to safety.

The destruction was satisfying, but three of the heat rays had been lost. When the next group of vessels attacked, there would be fewer to fire at them and more would probably be lost. Had they reached the tipping point?

But wait... what was happening? It shifted to another pickup, one looking down the long approach to the turn. The prey creature vessels were not coming on. The columns had started to circle. They were firing indirectly now. One of their flying machines was overhead and it may have reported the positions of the heavy heat rays and they were trying to destroy them with a long-range bombardment instead of by a direct attack. They might eventually succeed, but it would take a great deal of time, rotations probably. Had it bought the time it needed?

"Subcommander Kandanginar, this is Lutnaptinav, respond please."

"Yes, I am here."

"Subcommander, I regret to report that the prey creature ground forces have destroyed one of the heavy heat rays which was re-positioned to defend the landward approaches to the defense zone. The second one has been bypassed and cannot obstruct their advance. However, the destroyed one did eliminate two of the enemy's large war machines."

"I would consider that a very favorable exchange, Lutnaptinav. That leaves them with only four."

"Yes, but.... Just a moment... Just a moment... "

"What?"

"Progenitor, vision pick-ups have detected prey creatures in the tunnel leading from the destroyed ray site. They are inside the complex."

"Were there no doors sealing the access corridor?"

"There was no time to install any. Indeed, except for the area around your command center, there was no time to install them anywhere. Apologies, Subcommander, we assumed that if any ray projector was destroyed, the access corridor would also be destroyed. I have ordered drones to intercept the intruders, but there are barely any available and it may be some time before they can arrive. There are a few construction machines in the area which might be pressed into service, but I do not know how effective they will be in combat."

A shudder of revulsion passed through Kandanginar at the thought of those horrid things so close by. "If the intruders are inside, what will they have access to?"

Lutnaptinav did not respond instantly, but after a moment it said: "Everything."

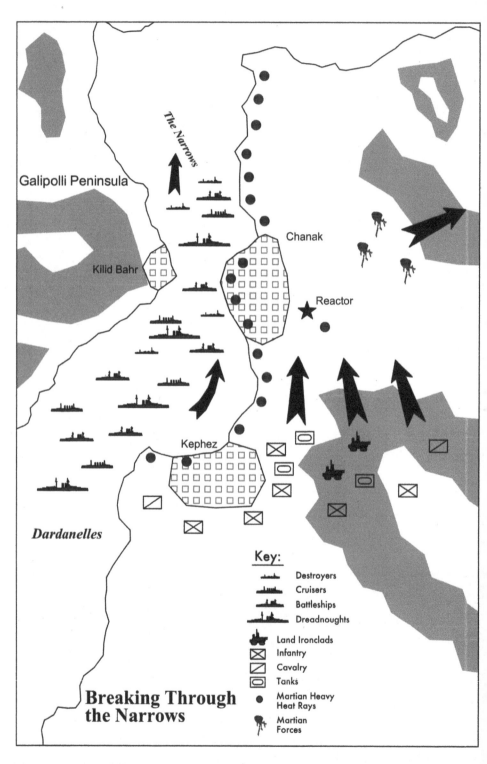

The Narrows

Galipolli Peninsula

Kilid Bahr

Chanak

Reactor

Kephez

Dardanelles

Key:

	Destroyers
	Cruisers
	Battleships
	Dreadnoughts
	Land Ironclads
	Infantry
	Cavalry
	Tanks
	Martian Heavy Heat Rays
	Martian Forces

Breaking Through the Narrows

Chapter Twenty-One

The Admiralty, London, April 1913

"Except for a single light cruiser, the German squadron has been completely destroyed, sir," reported Prince Battenberg. "They just charged right in and were slaughtered, apparently. Admiral Souchon is presumed to have gone down with his flagship. Admiral de Robeck has delayed the advance and is bombarding the enemy ray positions from long range."

Frederick Lindemann watched Churchill take in the information. He frowned, took the gnawed remains of his cigar out of his mouth and frowned more deeply. He tossed the stub away, took out a fresh one, and lit it. "What have we done to the enemy in return?" he growled.

"They estimate that they've destroyed ten or eleven of the heat rays."

"Out of how many?"

"No way to tell for sure, sir. Aerial observation estimates that there could still be as many a dozen left beyond the Narrows."

Churchill said nothing. He clasped his hands behind his back and paced back and forth between the detailed map of the Dardanelles on the table, and the larger scale map of the region on the wall.

"General Murray reports that his troops are closing in on the Martian positions from the landward side," continued Battenberg. "We could wait until we see how quickly he can silence the enemy weapons from his side, sir."

"Wait?" said Churchill spinning to face him. "We've *been* waiting! For weeks!" he strode over to a side table and snatched a paper off it. "Our ambassador in Constantinople reports the Martians have reached the Bosporus. They slaughtered tens of thousands of people who could not escape from them! The Bosporus is less than a mile wide and the tripods are firing right across, destroying anything they can see on the western shore. Once they get across…"

"How will they cross, sir?" asked Admiral Pakenham. "The water is deep and there is a very strong current."

"They'll get across! They aren't stupid, you know. They got across the Mississippi by building rafts. And they took Perim Island by digging a tunnel! I have no doubt they planned this all very carefully. They will be across very soon unless we can get there to stop them. Once they have both shores, they will fortify the passage so strongly we can never get through. And then they can send their forces north to hit the Germans on the Danube in the rear. Disaster! No, we simply cannot afford to wait." He turned to look at Battenberg.

"Louis, send a wireless to de Robeck. Tell him that he's ordered to press his attack. Immediately."

Battenberg nodded. "Right away, sir."

* * * * *

Somewhere near the Dardanelles, April 1913

Major Tom Bridges held the electric lantern up high in one hand, gripped his pistol in the other, and squinted down the dark tunnel. How the bloody hell did I get myself into this? He was a military observer, true. And his job sometimes got him uncomfortably close to combat, also true. But he had not expected to be put in charge of a raiding party descending into the depths of a Martian fortress! He hadn't had command of actual combat troops since he'd been in South Africa fighting Boers. And even then, he'd been in command of artillery, not front line infantry. Shooting at the enemy from miles away was more his style.

But here he was, about three men back from the very front of the advance. A couple of men with rifles were in front and then it was him and the captain of the Australian troops who made up the bulk of the force. He would have preferred to be farther back, but he'd been branded the 'expert' on Martian installations, so he had to be up front to tell then others where to go.

Not that he was likely to be much help. What he had seen so far was nothing like the enemy fortress in Arkansas that he'd toured. That one had been precisely laid out, and neat and clean as a hospital with shiny tile floors and walls, metal doors, and good, if dim, lighting. This was just a rough-cut tunnel through bare rock with no lights at all. Well, not exactly 'rough cut', the tunnel was a near-perfect cylinder, unlike a normal human-dug tunnel. It was about fifteen feet in diameter which would have made the bottom comfortably wide enough for about two men to walk side by side, except there was a metal conduit of some sort lying at the very bottom, which made the footing awkward.

But it was that conduit which was their real guide. It had started where they found the wreckage of the big, super hear ray projector. Bridges had seen the rays carried by the tripods and also the ones the Martians fitted into the defense towers of their fortresses and they were tiny compared to this, which, even wrecked, was about the size of a motor lorry. The conduit ran from the projector back into the tunnel and they had to assume that this is what was supplying the projector with the power it needed to function, and that the power was presumably being generated at the other end of the conduit. In theory, they just had to keep following it to find the generator.

They had been walking about ten minutes, covering perhaps five hundred yards, without finding anything. The tunnel went straight as an arrow and Bridges was uncomfortably aware of what an easy target, they would all be for something at the other end with even a small heat ray. So far, they had not encountered anything, but that couldn't possibly last.

The tunnel was far too small for one of the big tripods, but the spider machines could fit into it easily. If they suddenly encountered them, he didn't know what they would do. *Die, probably.* The party was not well armed, despite being almost two hundred strong. Most of the men had nothing but rifles. They had a couple of Lewis guns, and a few of the Mills Bombs. One of the Australians was carrying some outlandish contraption that looked like a medieval crossbow, but which he claimed could toss a Mills Bomb a hundred yards with fair accuracy. Bridges was skeptical. The small detachment of American Marines had one of the Yanks' stovepipe rocket launchers, which was their best anti-spider weapon, but there was just the one. Near the rear of the party were twenty men, each one carrying a four-inch gun round, which weighed about forty pounds apiece.

They proceeded another hundred yards and then slowed as it looked like there was something up ahead. Bridges paused to let the leading men scout ahead. They advanced about thirty paces and then halted. One of them whispered back: "Another tunnel coming in from the right. Joins up here and... *Oh hell!*" The shout was followed by two rifle shots in close succession. Bridges and everyone behind him crouched down or fell flat.

He expected to see the red glare of a heat ray, hear the screams of the scouts, and then see death scuttling down the corridor for him. Instead there was nothing but the fading echoes of the shots and finally a bit of cursing from the scouts.

"What is it, Haines?" hissed the Australian captain. Berwick was his name.

"Uh, sorry, sir," came back the reply. "There's some sort of machines parked here and we thought... we thought they were the bloody spiders."

"They're not? You sure?"

"Don't look like 'em, sir. Bigger. Long and low. Lots of legs. No weapons that I can see. Not movin' at all. Another machine here, too that's a lot different."

Bridges slowly stood upright, got control of his breathing, and moved forward. As the scout had said, another tunnel joined theirs on the right, and a larger space had been hollowed out where several big machines were standing. One was like the man had said, long and multi-legged, like a giant metal caterpillar. There was a sort of bin on the top. A cargo carrier, perhaps? The other one, a much larger machine, he recognized from the Arkansas fortress. It was like a long cylinder, with short stubby legs, not just on the bottom, but all over it. It had an open maw at what must be the front like a… well, he wasn't sure what it looked like, maybe some disgusting worm he'd seen drawings of in a school textbook. The engineers said it could chew through solid rock, break the rock into gravel inside and spew the rubble out its rear end, probably to be carried off by the other machine.

"That one's a digging machine," he told the men around him. "Probably what cut these tunnels."

"There's another one of those conduits, Major," said Captain Berwick, pointing at the other tunnel. "They join together here, and both head off that way, down the tunnel."

"Well, then that's the way we need to go," said Bridges. "Come on, let's find the power plant before those buggers realize we're down here and do something about it."

They went past the silent, unmoving machines as quickly as they could and headed down the new tunnel. It wasn't in quite the same direction as the first one, but as near as Bridges could figure, it was heading almost due north, toward the Dardanelles. Hopefully it couldn't be much farther to where the power plant was located.

They had gone a few hundred yards when they heard shouts form the tail end of the column. A few shots rang out and Bridges froze. But again, there were no heat rays heard or seen and no terrible screams. "What's going on?" shouted a number of people.

"Those machines!" came back the reply. "They're moving! They're following us!" Indeed, the sound of metal on stone was getting louder.

Bridges looked at Berwick, who was looking back at him. He said: "Keep going, Major, I'll drop back and see what can be done; form a rear guard if necessary. Harry, you come with me, Sampson, you go with the Major."

"Yes, sir," said two of Berwick's lieutenants simultaneously. The young one went with Berwick to the rear, while the older one remained. More shots and yells were coming from the rear now. "We better get moving, sir," said the one named Sampson. "They certainly know we're here now."

"Right, right. All right let's get moving, pick up the pace!"

They hurried down the tunnel, trying to focus on what lay ahead rather than the noises coming from the rear: more shooting and then an echoing bang from a Mills Bomb. Sampson swore. "Damn it, we haven't many of those left."

"Sir! I think I can see light ahead!" exclaimed one of the scouts.

Bridges turned the lantern so it wouldn't interfere with his vision and peered ahead. Yes, there did seem to be some light in the distance; faint and it didn't look like daylight. "All right keep moving and stay on your toes. Could be some of the bastards waiting for us."

They moved forward as quickly as they could, and the faint gleam ahead grew brighter and brighter and resolved itself into a circle of light filling the end of the tunnel which met some larger space. Every moment Bridges expected to see spider machines step into the mouth of the tunnel and begin blasting them, but none did and in another moment, they reached the end of the tunnel...

...and apparently reached their goal.

In a large space the size of a ballroom stood a gleaming metal shape. It was hemispherical, about thirty feet in diameter, with all manner of pipes and cables sprouting from it. Dim lights were attached to the rocky ceiling and there were oddly shaped boxes stacked against the walls and what must be tools scattered about. But no Martians and no spider machines.

Well, almost.

There was a bizarre machine standing on the far side of the chamber. It was about twice the size of the spiders, had six legs instead of three, and sprouted a bewildering array of arms and tentacles. As the men filed into the room, the thing started moving.

"Hey! Look out!" cried a dozen voices.

The machine scuttled towards them with surprising speed, its arms waving menacingly. Several of them had clawed hands and two produced bright blue light, like a welder's arc. Men began firing at it, but the bullets seemed to have little effect. The troops scattered in front of it, but one was too slow, and the thing grabbed him and tore him apart in a shower of blood.

The men spread out and surrounded the machine. One of the Lewis gunners opened fire, holding his weapon on his hip. But the bullets were bouncing off the thing and several soldiers were hit by the ricochets. The American marine with the rocket launcher shoved his way into the room and immediately fired. The rocket hit the machine and blew off one of its legs, but the back-blast of the rocket caught another man right behind the marine and he fell screaming.

"Get a bomb on the damn thing!" cried Lieutenant Sampson.

Several men tried, but the machine had so many arms it was impossible to get close. They were swatted aside before they could attach their bomb. One of the bombs already had its fuse pulled and the smoking thing bounced toward a group of men who had to scramble aside before it exploded. One man went down wounded, even so. The rocket launcher fired again and blew away several of the machine's arms, but it still had plenty left and chased the men around the chamber.

"Let me try!" said one fellow and Bridges saw it was the soldier with the crossbow. He had a helper who held a modified bomb with a long shaft with vanes like an arrow. He pulled the arming ring on the bomb and quickly fit it into the slot on the crossbow. The man aimed and fired...

...and the bomb bounced off the machine.

Lieutenant Sampson swore and leapt forward. He sprinted across the floor and flung himself down, scooping up the bomb and sliding right underneath the machine. He lunged up and jammed the sticky end against its belly. He tried to crawl away, but the bomb exploded before he got five feet.

The blast blew Sampson one direction and the machine the other. He tumbled to a halt, his uniform torn, scorched, and smoking. The Martian machine was flipped over on its back, its arms and legs waving feebly, a hole blown through its metal skin. Another man with a bomb ran up, armed it, and stuffed it in the hole. Everyone ducked and the explosion left the machine an unmoving wreck.

"Jesus, Mary, and Joseph," gasped a man at Bridges' side, a Welshman, not an Aussie.

"You can say that again, son," said Bridges.

Everyone started to relax, but another loud explosion to their rear brought them all back on the alert. They still had a job to do and probably not much time to do it. There was only one other tunnel leaving the chamber and he sent some men down it to scout. The rest began tending the wounded and exploring the space. Bridges looked at the big hemisphere. That had to be the power plant, but how to shut it down?

While he was thinking, there was a commotion from the rear, and he saw the young lieutenant who had gone off with Captain Berwick appear. He seemed breathless. He spotted Bridges and came toward him. "Major, I... *Burf!*" The man had seen Sampson and immediately changed course and fell to his knees beside him. "Burf!"

The men tending Sampson made room for young officer. "He's alive sir, but hurt pretty bad," said one of them. Bridges went over to them.

"What's going on back there, Lieutenant?" There was no immediate response, so Bridges grabbed his shoulder and shook him. "Lieutenant! Report!"

The man looked up at him, his eyes wet, his expression dazed. "Sir...?"

"What's your name, Lieutenant?"

"Harry... uh, Calloway, sir, Lieutenant Calloway."

"Well, Harry, what's going on to the rear? Where's Captain Berwick?"

"Uh, he's hurt sir. Not too bad, but he's down. We... we... wrecked the one machine, the one with all the legs. The other one is trying to get past the wreck, but it's having trouble doing that. Won't be very long before it does though, and I don't think we've got anything that's gonna stop it. The captain sent me to find you and tell you to hurry."

"You didn't just leave him there, did you?"

"No sir! They're bringing all the wounded along, but Berwick sent me on ahead to tell you."

"Good. Good, okay we've got to figure out..."

"Major! Major!"

"What?!" snarled Bridges, turning toward the other tunnel.

"Something coming down the tunnel here, sir! Spiders, I think!"

"Bloody hell!" Bridges looked around; looked for inspiration. They didn't have much to work with. "Drag some of those crates over to the tunnel! Form a barricade! Get the machine guns and the rocket launcher into action. We've got to hold off those damn things. All you men with the artillery shells, bring 'em in here. Move!"

The men moved.

Some of the crates were empty and were easily moved into place. Others needed a dozen men to drag them. The rest of the scouts came running back and jumped over the barriers and then helped to build them up higher. Men readied their weapons and it wasn't long before they had targets. Rifles and machine guns opened up and the Yanks' rocket launcher whooshed. Heat rays came back at them, but the barricade provided good cover.

Bridges, satisfied that they weren't going to be overrun instantly, went back to the main problem: shutting down the power plant. We walked completely around it looking for controls, levers, switches, anything, but finding nothing. There were a few places where it looked like there were access doors, but he couldn't see any way to open them. Halfway around he was joined by Lieutenant Calloway. "Can we just blow it up, sir?" he asked.

"I don't know. The casing looks very sturdy. If we just piled up all the shells against it and set them off I don't know that we'd accomplish anything except blow us all up."

There was a commotion at the barricade and Bridges tensed when he saw a spider trying to climb over. The rocket launcher fired at point blank range and the Martian machine was blown backwards and disappeared. They were running out of time...

"Sir?" said Lieutenant Calloway. "The cables we were following through the tunnels come in here and connect to the power plant there, you see? But look, there are a bunch more of them coming out and they all lead down the other tunnel. Maybe if we just cut the cables, we don't need to destroy the plant itself?"

Bridges stood and stared. He stared some more, and he realized the boy was right. The cabled led away from the machine, under the barricade and down the tunnel. They must be carrying the power to all the other super heat ray positions! Cut them here and they ray projectors would be useless.

"Good thinking, son! You there! Grab those shells and stack them up on top of those cables. Right there! Behind the barricade!"

"You're gonna blow up the barricade, sir?" asked Calloway, looking dubious.

"The barricade and as many of the spiders as we can!" The men were working like maniacs and they soon had all the four-inch shells in a pile a few feet behind the barricade, where the troops were still blasting away at the spiders.

"We need to set them off somehow. Who's got a bomb?" He looked around. All the men looked around. "Anyone? Anyone have a bomb?"

No one replied.

"Bloody hell..." muttered Bridges.

"What about the rocket launcher, sir?" said Calloway. "That might work."

Bridges nodded and dashed over to where the marines were reloading the launcher. "You have rockets left?" he demanded.

"Last one, sir," said the marine.

"Well, bring it here! Everyone! Fall back! Behind the power plant! Take cover!" He dragged the marine with the launcher with him, around the side of the power plant, just far enough so they could still see the pile of shells. The rest of the men were scrambling for cover; the last few men at the barricade turning and running like madmen.

"Aim for those shells!" commanded bridges. "Think you can hit them?"

"Shucks, sir, like hittin' the broad side of a..."

The barn hit him first. A spider appeared on top of the barricade and fired its heat ray point blank. It hit the marine right in the head and the flesh exploding to steam flung him backwards into Bridges, knocking him down. The launcher clattered to the floor.

Bridges tried to get up, tried to grab the launcher, but the dead marine was pinning him down. Calloway sprang past him, scooped up the launcher, aimed and fired.

The chamber exploded.

* * * * *

Advanced Base 14-5, Cycle 597,845.5

Perhaps the battle could be won after all. Kandanginar switched from view to view of the fighting in the narrow part of the water passage. Burning and exploding prey-creature vessels seemed to be everywhere. The heavy heat rays were smashing them as soon as they emerged from the smoke of the ones which had gone before. There were still scores of them undamaged, waiting their turn, but with eight rays still operational, it seemed possible that they could still hold them off, destroying each vessel as it appeared.

Still, the cost had been high. There were only fifty operational fighting machines holding off the prey ground forces and less than a hundred drones. The last of the ammunition for the bombardment drones was gone. And there were over a hundred rescued pilots in their survival pods waiting to be carried out of danger. If the last of the fighting machines were destroyed, they would all be slaughtered. Perhaps the proper course would be to...

The control chamber shuddered slightly, the lights flickered out, the display panels went dead, and then the lights came back on more dimly than before. What had happened?

"Progenitor, this is Lutnaptinav," came a call over the communicator. "The enemy has cut off our power supply."

"The reactor is destroyed?" asked Kandanginar in alarm.

"I do not believe that it has been destroyed, but the main power feeds have been cut. Everything but the emergency systems are inoperable."

"Can they be repaired?"

"Not any time soon. Prey creature forces still hold the reactor room and access to that area has been blocked. It could take a full rotation to restore."

"We do not have that much time."

"No. Progenitor, our course of action seems clear to me."

"Yes, further delay will only increase our casualties to no purpose at all." It switched to the emergency channel.

"All forces attention. This is Kandanginar. Begin the evacuation immediately."

* * * * *

Somewhere near the Dardanelles, April 1913

Harry came back to his senses and realized that he hurt all over. People were shouting, but they all seemed very far away and there was a loud ringing in his ears. What had happened? Oh, right... The Martian power plant... the spider machines... the rocket launcher... Explosion... what was happening now? Where was Burf? *Burf!* He'd been hurt!

He was moving... someone was carrying him. He opened his eyes and saw a jumble of dirt and rock. He was slung over someone's back looking straight down. But there was light, sunlight, real sunlight. He was outside. How?

"Burf...?" he muttered. There was no answer and whoever was carrying him was jostling him very badly. His head felt like it was going to explode.

"*Burf!*" He forced the air out of his lungs and made the loudest sound he could.

"Hang in there, sir," said someone. "We're almost out."

"Burf?"

"We've got Mister Sampson, too, don't you worry."

Reassured, Harry hung there limply. Finally, the ride got gentler and he saw actually grass below him. A moment later hands seized him, and he was set gently down. Someone said: "Keep his head up, he's still bleedin' like a stuck pig."

"Well, get some bandages, damn you," said another voice. He was pulled up a bit and then put in a sitting position, leaning against something; a tree maybe. He appeared to be on a hillside somewhere and in the distance, he could see glittering waters and smoke, lots of smoke. The sun was off to the west, heading toward evening.

But something was wrong with his vision. It was oddly flat, and he couldn't see to his left... His hand came up to his face, but someone grabbed his wrist and pulled it away. "Now you leave that alone, sir. You've got quite a scratch on your head and blood all over you. Don't play with it until we can have a doctor look at you. Ah, here's Jake with some bandages. Now you lie still while I wrap you up." Two men were suddenly kneeling in front of him and he could feel them wrapping cloth around his head, covering the left side of it, along with his...

"Did... have I lost my eye?" he asked.

"Can't really tell, sir. But you just wait for the doctor. Lie still now, I need to tend to some of the other lads." The one man left. The other gave him a drink from his canteen and then left as well. Harry suddenly remembered to ask about Burf, but the men were gone.

There were a lot of other men bustling about, but none of them would pay any attention to him. He could hear the sound of motors, too, and was surprised to see a few tanks rumbling by farther down the hill. What was going on? He was just steeling himself to try and stand up when Major Bridges appeared in front of him. "How are you feeling, Harry?" he said.

"I've felt better, sir."

"Yes, I imagine you have," he said, squatting down. "But that was a hell of a job you did down there. We'd all be dead but for you and I'll be sure to mention that in my report."

"What happened? All I remember is firing the rocket launcher. I wasn't even sure how it worked, but the trigger was right where it ought to be and..."

"The rocket hit the piled ammunition and it all went up together. Blew the cables apart as we'd hoped, but the blast brought the roof down, too. Buried all the spiders and gave us a way out."

"Lucky..."

"Damn right. But look." Bridges moved to his side and pointed. "When we cut the power, the Martian heat rays were all shut off, too. The fleet's getting through, look."

Sure, enough in the distance he could see the long line of ships passing through the narrows. Dozens and dozens of them. There seemed to be an awful lot of burning ships, too, but the bulk of the fleet was getting through.

"How's Burf? Lieutenant Sampson?"

"He's hurt worse than you, but it looks like he'll make it. We're trying to get some proper medical people here to tend both of you and all of our injured, but things are a bit of a mess right now. The Martians are all on the run and we're trying to keep up with them."

"So, what happens now?"

"Well, the fleet gets to Constantinople as fast as it can. As for all of us? I think we've earned the rest of the day off!"

Chapter Twenty-Two

The Bosporus, April 1913

Major Erich Serno completed his climb, leveled off, and turned northeast toward the Bosporus. The sun was just rising above the distant mountains and the Sea of Marmara to his right was shrouded in mist. The obsolete Fokker A.1 was very nearly at the maximum altitude it could fly, just barely high enough to be safe from the Martian heat rays. The mere fact that he'd been reduced to flying this piece of junk proved just how desperate the situation was. The Ottoman Air Force had been virtually obliterated, and the only mission left for its commander was to fly an unarmed observation aircraft to watch what might be the death throes of the empire itself.

He was surprised to be back in a plane so soon. It had only been yesterday that Lieutenant Kenan had spirited him away from the massacre on the eastern shore and delivered him to General von Sanders' headquarters, which had also been relocated to the western shore. Von Sanders had been happy to see him but was buried with work. He was trying to build some sort of defense which would keep the Martians on the east side of the Bosporus, and it was obvious that he doubted he'd be able to do it. He'd told Serno to get some rest but be back in the air at dawn to take a look at what the Martians were doing.

So here he was in an old two-seater at 2,500 meters flying toward the flame-wrapped Bosporus. He'd been lucky to find anything at all that could still fly. The two zeppelins had been withdrawn days ago and sent north to the Danube front which the high command had deemed more important. All that had been left were some older planes used as trainers. The few Rumplers which had escaped from Skutari were so battered they needed major repairs before they could fly again. Lieutenant Kenan was flying with him as the observer.

Serno shifted in his seat and winced. His leg was still very painful from the crash, but there was no way he could use it as an excuse to get him out of this duty. Every single person was needed for this fight. They were soon over the Bosporus and that was not a good thing. When he'd first arrived, the battle front had been almost a thousand kilometers to the south. Now he could take off from the field outside Constantinople and be in sight of it within minutes. The Ottoman Empire had shrunk to a strip of land less than a hundred kilometers wide and a few hundred long.

The land below was wrapped in fog and smoke. Smoke from artillery fire against the eastern shore and smoke from burning houses on the western. The Martians had closed up to the Bosporus along its entire length, massacring anyone who hadn't been able to escape. Now they were spraying the western shore with their rays, setting everything within range afire. It was clear that once they had driven away – or burned away – the defenses, they would cross. No one was quite sure how they would do it. The water was fairly deep and had strong, tricky currents. It had been observed all over the world that the Martians were very reluctant to try to wade their machines across deep water when they encountered it. But they had built rafts in America and used a tunneling machine down under the Red Sea. They must have some plan for a crossing here or why else would they have come?

And once across, there would be little left to stop them. The Ottoman Army was in shambles. The division of German troops which had come down was in little better shape, although the Austro-Hungarian one, which had not been sent forward was in fair condition. A German division and another Austrian one had arrived by train last night, but they would not be enough and everyone knew it. Once they were disposed of, the Martian host, still at least six hundred strong, could march north through Bulgaria and fall upon the troops defending the Danube line from the rear. After that... who knew? From there, the combined force, fifteen hundred tripods or more, could go anywhere they pleased. Vienna, Berlin... home. They had to stop them somehow, but the only hope for that was the mythical allied fleet. People had been talking about it for weeks, months, but no fleet had materialized. That morning more rumors were rampant around the airfield. The fleet had broken through the Dardanelles. No, it had been stopped again. Not stopped, wiped out. The whole German squadron and Admiral Souchon were gone. They were coming. They would never arrive. Serno hardly listened to them anymore. All he could do was the job assigned to him.

They flew across the southern end of the Bosporus and Serno looked down on the Martian positions. There were tripods everywhere, most close to the water's edge. They were firing across to the western side, but Serno wasn't sure what at. Most of the buildings there, suburbs of the great city to the southwest, were already burned to the ground, but he supposed there could still be troops huddled in the ruins. Sporadic artillery fire fell among the Martians. Most of the German artillery had been successfully pulled back to the western side and the new arriving divisions would be bringing more, but it wouldn't be enough. Not to guard the whole thirty-kilometer length of the waterway.

A few ships, barely visible through the mist, were cruising around on the Sea of Marmara, firing from time to time, but he'd heard they were low on ammunition, and wouldn't be much help. He turned the Fokker to the north and cruised along the line. He didn't see many of the telltale blue flashes of the Martian artillery. Perhaps they were low on ammunition, too. Or maybe they were saving it for their big push.

At about the midway point to the Black Sea he spotted something below that made him circle to look closer. Some sort of activity was raising a cloud of dust. Not smoke, dust. Lieutenant Kenan, sitting behind him, tapped him on the shoulder and pointed down, and offered him his binoculars. Serno took them and painfully using his knees to hold the control stick steady peered down as the plane circled.

Through the binoculars he could see that a large mound of earth had been piled up. As he watched some sort of machine appeared from a hole in the ground and dumped more dirt on the pile. "They're tunneling!" cried Serno. "Just like they did down on the Red Sea!" Kenan nodded and took back the binoculars. "Make a note of the location, maybe we can put some artillery fire on them." Kenan nodded again and scratched at his pad.

A moment later, the Martians started firing at them.

"Hell! Hang on!"

Serno pushed the throttle to the maximum and made a sharper turn and headed south, twisting this way and that. Things got uncomfortably warm, but they were beyond the effective range of the normal heat rays. How long until they started mounting their bigger rays to shoot at aircraft? The Fokker was vibrating alarmingly, but they didn't catch fire and after a minute the rays winked out.

"Too close!" shouted Kenan.

Serno nodded. "Let's go home and report this."

He throttled back to a speed the old Fokker liked better and headed south, still watching the ground, counting tripods. He realized that they probably should have continued north to the Black Sea to make sure there weren't any other digging sites. Oh, well, they could report this and then go up later for another look.

They were nearing the southern exit of the Bosporus when the ground below them seemed to erupt in smoke and flame. A loud rumble shook the air and the plane jerked and shuddered. Amidst the rumbles he could hear the shriek of big shells. What was going on? Had the newly arrived troops brought along a few battalions of big guns? But no, there were dozens of explosions every moment; not even the artillery of a whole corps could produce what he was seeing!

Just then another plane came out of nowhere and flashed past him not a hundred meters away. Who was that? Had someone back at the airfield gotten another plane operational? But no, that wasn't any German plane! It was a seaplane with large floats beneath it and as it banked slightly, he could see the red, white, and blue rondels that the British used. British? Here? As the plane drew away, he thought he saw the pilot wave.

"Major! Major, look!" shouted Kenan. He saw that the Turk was pointing straight ahead. He looked forward and beheld the most magnificent sight he'd ever seen.

The fog was dissolving on the Sea of Marmara and the sea was filled with ships.

Dozens, scores, a hundred or more ships dotted the water, where there had been only a handful an hour earlier. Dreadnoughts and battleships and cruisers and swarms of torpedo boat destroyers, they seemed to fill the sea from edge to edge. And they were firing, firing their big guns at the Martians. Tearing his eyes away and looking down, he could see tripods being blown to bits by this incredible barrage. The ships were well out of range of their heat rays so all they could do was mill around in confusion, like sheep.

"Allah be praised!" cried Kenan, his voice barely audible above the wind and the explosions.

"Yes, thank God, thank God," whispered Serno, looking back to the beautiful ships. The fear and the strain of the last few weeks melted away and he found his flying goggles fogging up as tears spilled out of his eyes. Too much, it was all too much.

An especially loud whistle brought him back to reality. He was getting dangerously close to the path of all of those shells. It wouldn't do to get hit by one. Not now, not after all he'd been through. He banked the plane to the east and headed for a safer bit of air. He curved around until he was behind most of the firing ships. He glanced to the west and saw at least a hundred more vessels approaching. Most were bulky transports rather than warships. They brought an army, too? He stared at them for a moment and then just circled and watched the grandest show on earth.

The bombardment went on for quite a while and then he saw that some of the ships were heading into the Bosporus. Much of the shelling was shifting farther north. They were driving the Martians away! They were retreating in the face of this armada. They hadn't had time to install any of their super heat rays and their tripods could not slug it out with the warships face to face. Retreating, running away, stopped.

His hands were shaking, but he continued to stare at the spectacle. He would never forget this sight if he lived to be a hundred. Never.

It was only when his engine sputtered and died that he realized he'd been looking too long. *Out of petrol! Damn!*

He'd been losing latitude, too, without realizing it. He cursed himself for a fool and quickly realized that even though the Fokker was a fair glider, he could never make it back to the airfield. In fact, he doubted he could even make it back to land. Go down in the sea? Well, there were certainly plenty of ships there to rescue him!

Serno headed for the rear of the fleet, away from any of the firing ships and looked for one he could land next to. There were dozens to choose from, but his eye suddenly spotted a German naval ensign flying from one of them. *Yes!* He came in low over the ship and shouted down to the men on deck. He couldn't hope that they'd hear what he was saying, but they couldn't miss the fact that his engine wasn't running.

He turned and came back and pulling back sharply on the stick he did a controlled stall and pancaked into the water barely a hundred meters from the side of the ship. He and Kenan scrambled out and clung to the wreckage while the ship, a light cruiser from the looks of her, lowered a boat.

As the boat rowed up to them, he saw the name *Breslau* painted on it. A young ensign was near the front and he shouted: "Hello! Who are you?"

He shouted back in German and saw the man's eyebrows go up in surprise. "I'm Major Erich Serno, Imperial German Air Service, on loan to the Ottoman Empire. And friend, am I ever glad to see you!"

* * * * *

Admiralty House, London, May 1913

"And here's to the man of the hour! First Lord of the Admiralty, Winston Spencer Churchill!" David Lloyd George held up his glass and everyone in the room cheered and held up their glasses as well. The celebration had been going on for over an hour and showed no sign of ending soon.

Frederick Lindemann joined the toast with all the others and looked at the pink and beaming face of the man he now thought of as a friend. Churchill was obviously extremely pleased with this adulation, but there was no doubt he had earned it. He truly was the man of the hour. Only a few days earlier it looked as though his career was at an end. His grand design was floundering with very heavy losses. With his former friends, like Lord Fisher, and his long-time political enemies sharpening their knives, there appeared to be little hope for the man.

But then everything changed. Admiral de Robeck and General Murray had rallied their forces and smashed their way through the Dardanelles and made it to Constantinople in time to turn back the Martian advance. There were still some people grumbling over the casualties, and it was true that they had been shockingly high, but the victory they had bought was undeniable.

"There will be no putting up with the man for weeks, after this," said Clementine Churchill, who had come up next to him. She had spoken tartly, as she often did about her husband, but Lindemann could see the gleam in her eye. She was just as pleased as Winston.

"He looks tired," said Lindemann. "Can you persuade him to get some rest? He's been going non-stop for weeks."

"God knows I try," said Clementine, sighing. "But when he sinks his teeth into something, he just will not let go."

"He's like a bulldog."

"That observation has been made before, Freddy," said Clementine, chuckling. Her expression sobered. "But at least with Fisher gone and Louis Battenberg in his place, things might be a little less stressful for him."

Lindemann nodded. Yes, Jacky Fisher was gone. Officially he had retired 'for reasons of health', and Lindemann supposed that was technically true. In fact, the old hero had been bundled off to a sanitarium in Switzerland and it was unlikely he would return. "He and the prince seem to get along very well."

"Yes, Louis is a dear. He may not have Fisher's genius, but he has a lot more common sense—something that's sadly lacking in the government if I dare to say so."

Lindemann didn't dare say so, so he said instead: "With this victory, he surely deserves some time off. Perhaps you could take him down to your place by the seashore for a few days. Where is it, Kent?"

"Pear Tree Cottage? It's in Norfolk, and it's only rented, but yes, he does like it there. Perhaps I'll suggest it to him. Thank you for your concern."

"Least I can do. Not that I have any other real function around here."

"Now don't think that way," said Clementine, turning her sharp eyes on him. "Winston always makes his own decisions, but he depends on the people around him to help him formulate those decisions. You have been a tremendous support to him in these difficult times."

"Nice of you to say so,"

"It's the truth! Now don't you start moping or I'll fix you up with some nice young lady to cheer you up!"

Lindemann blinked, not sure what to make of that particular threat, but at that moment Churchill strolled over to them, glass in one hand, cigar in the other. "Well, there you are," he said. "What are you two talking about?"

"You, mostly," answered Clementine. "Freddy thinks you work too hard. And so do I."

Winston gave one of his trademark *harrumphs* and then said: "No harder than anyone else. No harder than those poor, splendid buggers who did the fighting."

"But even they get a chance to rest once the fighting's over, dear. Can't you take a few days off? Come down to Pear Tree Cottage. The children would love to see you."

Churchill took a draw on his cigar and shook his head. "It's a fine idea and I'd love it. But it can't happen for a few weeks at the soonest." He gestured at the crowd of people. "This celebration is a bit premature. There's still a huge amount of work to be done."

"And there always will be," said Clementine. "You can use that excuse from now until doomsday if you want to, dear."

"But surely the situation is vastly improved from a week ago," said Lindemann. "The Martians are falling back into Syria and the threat to Constantinople is over for now. The threat to the rear of the German defense line on the Danube has been eliminated, too. And aren't the Germans sending more ships to the Black Sea to help shore up their defenses?"

"They are," nodded Churchill. "A battle squadron just passed through the Skagerrak yesterday. It will be in the Channel in a few days. And I've given them permission to refuel at Gibraltar" He chuckled. "Jacky would go into a fit if he knew."

"The Kaiser seems to be joining the international coalition."

"For now. With Willie, you just never know what he's thinking. But yes, that was perhaps the biggest result of the recent victory; countries are finally starting to cooperate. At the Dardanelles we had forces from Britain, France, Germany, Italy, the United States, Turkey, Greece, Portugal, Belgium, and the Netherlands. Probably a few more I'm forgetting. Almost from the start of the war, the nations have talked about cooperating, but this is the first time they've actually done it in any significant way. We just need to make sure it doesn't stop with this."

"How do we do that, sir?"

Another puff, a sip from his glass. "Not sure, really. Now that this crisis is passed, Kitchener is demanding that we resume the drive on Khartoum. I still need to retake Perim Island and reopen the passage through the Red Sea. Both of those are important objectives, but neither is really going to inspire the other countries to help. That's been the problem all along: every country has its own interests and objectives. Only when something comes along that directly threatens all of us—like the recent incident— will everyone work together. For example, considered dispassionately, the fighting along the Danube is probably more important than the drive on Khartoum. But can you see K of K diverting his army to Bulgaria?"

"No, I suppose not," said Lindemann. "So, what are you going to do?"

"Well, I can only influence our grand strategy, not order it. I'm not the prime minister."

"Yet," said Clementine, arching an eyebrow.

Another *harrumph*. "Now don't start saying that in public, Clemmie! Last thing I need is for Asquith to think I'm after his job."

"He can't help but be thinking it, dear, everyone else is, I assure you."

"Sheath your claws, Dear Cat."

"Yes, Pig."

Lindemann failed to keep a straight face when the Churchills started using their pet names for each other. They really were very close. Not at all like so many marriages among the upper class. "Clearly there's a lot to do," he said. "What's first on your list?"

Churchill's good humor faded. "Well, despite the victory, there will still have to be an accounting for the losses. There's no getting around the fact that in the recent battles we lost more ships and more men than in any other battle the Royal Navy has ever fought. People are going to want to know why."

"That's hardly fair,' said Clementine. "It's a war. People and ships are lost in wars."

"True, and in a war like this any loss is acceptable if it leads to victory. People need to understand that. Still, the inevitable hearings and reports might lead us to some better methods and tactics which will make future battles easier. You scientists will have a hand in that, of course," he said, turning to Lindemann. "These new super heat rays and their artillery weapon, for instance. You need to find an answer to them, Professor. And then an answer for the next problem and the next, and for problems we haven't even foreseen yet."

"Uh, we'll try…"

"I know you will, and it occurs to me that I have a job for you right now."

"Sir?"

"The Americans' land ironclads performed brilliantly in the battle. Made a decisive contribution from what I've heard. And we don't have any! We've started work on them, but they aren't even off the drawing board yet. We need them, we need them quickly, and we need then to be as effective as we can possibly make them. I'd like you to be my eyes and ears on this project. Get with the engineers, see what they are doing and if you have ideas for doing it better or faster, I want to hear about it. Think you can do that for me, Professor?"

Lindemann's eyes widened. "Yes, sir, I'd be honored," he said, and he meant it. This was more than just being Churchill's advisor and supplying information and an occasional opinion in meetings. He would have real responsibilities and inevitably a certain amount of real authority. He would help guide the direction the project went. It was what he'd been hoping for when he began his friendship with Churchill. "Truly honored, sir."

"Good, good. Get started on it right away, Professor."

Clementine nudged him—hard. This produced a final *harrumph*. "Well, after the celebrations over, I mean. Enjoy it. God knows when we'll have another."

* * * * *

The Dardanelles, May 1913

"You're leaving, Major?"

Tom Bridges nodded to Commander Harding. "Yes, back to London to report on all this. I'll need the whole voyage—and then some—just to write my report. And what about you? I suppose you'll still be a while making your repairs." He gestured to where the land ironclad *Yellowstone* was sitting by the shore of the Dardanelles. The battered machine had been repaired enough to move down here, but it could not take to the water again without some major repairs. A barge with a crane was drawn up alongside and the work was under way, but there was a lot left to do.

"Yes," said Harding, frowning. "Probably a month or more to get her seaworthy and even then, we'll need the services of a shipyard to get us ready for another fight like that last one."

"Will you be sailing all the way back to America for that?"

"I don't know. There's some word of us staying around until you Brits start getting your own land ironclads ready. God knows how long that will take. But if we do stay, I imagine they'll tow us down to Alexandria, or somewhere else with proper facilities. How about you? Know where you'll be going next?"

Bridges shook his head. "No one's told me anything. Maybe I'll be sent off to see what the Germans are doing on the Danube. Or the Japanese in China. I'm just praying I don't get sent to St. Petersburg; too damn cold up there!"

"And dangerous, I imagine. The Russians are having a really hard time of it, I hear."

"Well, I can't imagine anything more dangerous than my little jaunt with you and those Aussies. That was very definitely not part of my plans!"

Harding laughed. "But it was a good thing you were here. That was a hell of a job you did down there. I hope you get proper recognition for it."

Bridges shrugged. "We'll see. But as you know I hardly did it alone. Without you and your machine we never would have found our way in. And without the Aussies and Welshmen and your marines we couldn't have gotten the job done. It will all be in my report. Maybe someone will notice."

A ship's whistle caught their attention and they looked out as another convoy moved into the Dardanelles. There was a huge amount of traffic these days. A dozen European countries were pouring men, guns, and supplies into the region. Either to shore up the Ottoman's defenses, or to join the line on the Danube, or reinforce the Russians who were still holding out in Crimea. Suddenly everyone wanted to get involved.

Activity closer to them caught his eye. Another body had washed up on the shore and a party of British soldiers was driving away some locals who were trying to strip it. There were still huge numbers of refugees in the area, trying to survive, and this sort of thing was all too common.

Turning back to Harding he held out his hand. "Well, I have to be off. It was a privilege working with you, Commander. Best wishes for the future."

Harding took his hand and shook firmly. "You too, Major. I hope we run into each other again."

"Who knows? It's a small world."

* * * * *

Skutari Airfield, May 1913

Lieutenant Colonel Erich Serno limped across the runway toward what was left of the headquarters building. There wasn't much to see. The Martians had been through here and they had pretty much burned everything they saw. The distinctive triangular-shaped footprints of their tripod machines pocked the runway and Serno had to watch where he stepped to keep from falling into one.

"Looks like we've got quite a job ahead of us, Colonel," said Lieutenant Wulzinger.

"Yes, starting almost from scratch, it seems like. Well, at least this time we'll have a better idea of what we're doing."

"Do you think the new Turkish government will give us the cooperation we need?"

Serno shrugged. In the wake of the disaster there had been a coup and the old rulers had been... disposed of. The Sultan, Mehmed V, was still officially in charge, but he was even more a puppet now than he had been before. There was a new triumvirate ruling the empire, Enver Pasha, Talaat Pasha, and Djemal Pasha, a group of military and political leaders who had been prominent in the so-called 'Young Turk' movement. Enver Pasha was the new minister of defense and from what Serno had heard, he might actually be halfway competent. At least the new bunch realized just how much they depended on German aid.

"I guess we'll see."

"I imagine you'd rather be up on the Danube front, though, wouldn't you, sir?"

Serno paused. Would he? Trying to build something here for the Turks could be incredibly frustrating. It would be so much simpler if he was back with a German unit. No language problems, better equipment and supplies, people who would actually follow orders.

On the other hand, he'd probably still be a captain. If he was even still alive. Casualties among the fliers on the Danube Front had been terrible from what he was hearing. Maybe he was better off here.

"We live to serve, Lieutenant," he said. "Come on, let's get to work."

*　*　*　*　*

Holdfast 14-1, Cycle 597,845.6

Kandanginar steered its travel chair into the chamber used by Commander Jakruvnar, senior member of Clan Patralvus on the target world. The corridors of the holdfast leading here had seemed unusually empty, more evidence of the severe losses the clan had suffered in the recent disastrous campaign.

"Greetings, Commander," it said.

"Greetings, Kandanginar, we have much to discuss."

"You were recently in council with the Colonial Conclave, yes? Do they have new instructions for us?"

Jakruvnar waved its tendrils in frustration. "Kandanginar, I have never witnessed such a contentious meeting. The recent setbacks seem to have robbed many of us of any sense of common purpose or direction. Each group is more inclined to work for itself rather than the common good. The forces from Continent 2, which came through the tunnel to join us in the offensive north are now demanding to return to their own territories. They say the prey-creatures there are advancing against them and they must return to defend their holdfasts. When the Conclave refused to give them permission, they threatened to go anyway. Some then suggested that we prevent them from using the tunnel. The Continent 2 people then said they would fight their way through if necessary. Then suggestions arose that we destroy the tunnel to prevent them! Madness!"

"This most disturbing," said Kandanginar. "Should we prepare defenses around the tunnel entrance?"

"I don't know. Things calmed down after a while and it is unclear what they will do. But that was only one of the conflicts. Some of the Continent 1 forces now engaged to the north of us, the other prong of the great offensive, are also demanding to return to their territories. The battle there is not going well, and they are questioning the wisdom of these far-reaching attacks, so far from supporting holdfasts. They suggest that we should revert to our proven methods of making short advances. Building new holdfasts and when we are secure, repeating the process."

"There is some wisdom in that, Commander. It is a proven method."

"Although even that can fail, as was proved on Continent 3 last cycle."

"True. So, was anything decided?"

"No," said Jakruvnar. "The existing orders remain in effect: establish contact between the continents. But no one had any suggestions on how to bring that about beyond continuing what we are doing."

"It will be some time before we can resume the offensive," said Kandanginar. "They do realize that, don't they? Our losses were very heavy, and we need time to rebuild our strength. The enemy has reinforced their defenses and trying to supply an offensive through the mountainous terrain will only grow more difficult now that the prey-creatures have learned they can ambush our convoys. And what about the construction of the launching guns to deliver resources to the Homeworld? Are we still expected to contribute to that... effort."

"We are."

"We might be able to accomplish one thing or the other, I cannot see how we can do both."

"Be that as it may, we have no choice but to try. And, despite these setbacks, we do grow stronger. The new heat rays, the bombardment drones, both have proven very effective. Perhaps they will turn events in our favor."

"Perhaps, but we need to develop a machine which will make the heavy heat rays mobile. Only having them in fixed positions limits their usefulness. And the prey-creatures have proven themselves to be unusually adaptable. We should expect new devices and techniques from them. And they have such a huge advantage in numbers over us, I cannot foresee a quick victory."

"But we can increase our numbers faster than them," said Jakruvnar. "Our scientists have observed that although the prey-creatures can reproduce nearly as quickly as we do, their offspring require an almost unbelievable amount of time to mature enough to be useful. Our buds can become productive in only a quarter-cycle."

"That is so, but approximately a third of our buds must be used as replacement bodies for ourselves due to the contagions on this world, rather than as new members of the race." Kandanginar pointed to the bud sack on its side. "My next bud will have to be used for that. It appears that I became infected during the journey to the north. Drugs will keep me alive until the new bud is ready for me to transfer my consciousness to it."

"That is good," said Jakruvnar "we could not afford to lose one of your talent. And with each transference our new bodies are more resistant to infection."

"Slightly more resistant," corrected Kandanginar. "The danger still remains. There have been a number of instances where people ignored the signs of infection in their desire to add a new member of the Race and could not create a new body for themselves in time to avoid death. But it is true that the new buds created here are even more resistant."

"The buds, "said Jakruvnar, twitching its tendrils in frustration. "Utterly necessary, but they create new problems."

"Their lack of automatic obedience? Yes, that is most troubling."

"Very troubling." Jakruvnar hesitated for a moment and then went on. "This is not widely known, but on Continent 3 several clan leaders were killed in battle and this created a block of buds, nearly forty of them, created here which had no direct progenitor to control them. They actually attempted a revolt against higher authority. They all had to be destroyed. This is such a danger that the one new order to come from the Conclave is that we draw up plans to keep key individuals out of dangerous situation so that no interruption in the chain of authority can occur."

"That could be awkward, but I can see the necessity." Kandanginar's thoughts went back to the earlier conversation with Lutnaptinav about the 'network' of communication between the buds created here, the *Threeborn*. He suspected that they were fully aware of this revolt by now. "It seems as though this world creates one unanticipated problem after another. Where will it end? More to the point: what shall we be forced to become to survive here?"

"I do not know, Kandanginar. All we can do is carry out our duty."

"So it seems."

* * * * *

Lemnos Island, May 1913

"I'm so sorry, Harry," said Vera Brittain. She took the mirror away from him and set it on the table beside his bed.

"Oh, it could be worse, I suppose," he said automatically, trying to put a smile on his face. But it wasn't easy. The first look at himself with the bandage off was a bit shocking. The explosion in the Martian power plant room had sent a fragment of metal slicing down his forehead and cheek, which tore away his left eye. There was nothing that could be done, and he was now half blind. The doctors had done a good job sewing him up though, and the scar would be faint after a while. But the eye…

"Think how dashing I'll look with a black eye-patch," he said as cheerfully as he could. "It will make me look older and more experienced, too. Sometimes I get so tired of being the 'kid' in the company. Now they'll all pay attention."

"You're planning to go back to your company?" asked Vera.

He shrugged. "Where else have I got to go? And I'm nearly all healed up. I can still do my job with one eye."

"And do it damned well, too, Harry," said another voice. "Don't ever doubt that you're a good officer."

He turned to look at Burford Sampson, lying on his stomach on the next bed in the hospital on Lemnos. His injuries had been worse than Harry's, but he was expected to recover, and he had no doubt that Sampson would also be returning to the ranks.

"Yes," said Vera. "Mr. Sampson has told me about what you did during the battle. You should receive a decoration."

"And how would he know what I did during the fight?" asked Harry. "He was already wounded by the time I… did what I did."

"I have my sources of information," said Sampson. "And anyway, I wasn't talking about that. Or not only about that. "We've served together for over four years, y'know. You *are* good officer, Harry. Wouldn't surprise me if you were made a company commander once they put the battalion back together."

"*If* they put the battalion back together," said Harry gloomily. "There wasn't much left. They might break it up and use the survivors to rebuild a different battalion."

Burf didn't have an answer to that. It was entirely possible and they both knew it. The flow of replacements from 'home' was erratic and if there weren't enough new men to rebuild the 15th New Castle Battalion—and all those other savaged battalions in the ANZACs—it might well cease to exist. Harry didn't like that thought at all. The 15th was the only home he had left.

"I think the doctor is going to release you in a few days, Harry," said Vera. "I... I'm going to miss..."

"Brittain! Enough lollygagging! Back to work!" One of the older nurses, who in some fashion Harry didn't understand not only outranked, but seriously resented the volunteer nurses, had come up and was standing there with folded arms and a scowl on her face.

"Yes, ma'am," said Vera getting to her feet. She started to turn away, but then hesitated and pulled a folded sheet of paper out of her pocket. She held it out to him. "I wrote this last night. It's... it's for you, Harry."

He reached out and took it, his fingers ever so slightly touching hers. "Thank you. Thank you, Vera."

She went back to her duties. Harry's eyes followed her for a few moments and then he opened the paper and looked at it.

"What are you smiling about?" growled Sampson.

Epilogue

Excerpt from "The First Interplanetary War, Volume 1", by Winston Spencer Churchill, 1929. Reprinted with permission.

The victory at the Dardanelles, though no doubt important, is often exaggerated in the public mind. To many it was the 'turning of the tide' or the 'beginning of the end'. It was neither. Ever since their first landing, the tide had been flowing entirely in favor of the Martians, overwhelming cities and whole continents. The Dardanelles, and a few other gallant stands, may have interrupted that flow, slowed it for a time, but it would take more time and more sacrifice before the flow truly turned the other way.

Still, there is no denying that the unprecedented international cooperation seen at the Dardanelles, was of the utmost importance. Without it, no final victory would have been possible.

But that victory was years in the future. We had weathered one storm, but a much greater storm was still gathering.

The End

Look for more books from Winged Hussar Publishing, LLC – E-books, paperbacks and Limited Edition hardcovers. The best in history, science fiction and fantasy at:

https://www. wingedhussarpublishing.com
or follow us on Facebook at:
Winged Hussar Publishing LLC
Or on twitter at:
WingHusPubLLC
For information and upcoming publications